SILENT SCREAM

"I absolutely loved it!... This one is one of the best crime thrillers I've read in a long time, and that includes mainstream authors such as James Patterson! I would seriously put this book in the same league." —*Fiona's Book Reviews*

"Wow. That's all I need to say.... One of the best books I've read so far this year.... Gripping.... Hooks you in from chapter one.... You won't want to put it down.... Fantastic." —*Little Northern Soul*

"I found myself biting my nails numerous times.... To say that this book is brilliant is an understatement." —*Relax and Read Reviews*

"Marsons for me is the QUEEN of this genre. She knows how to add the human touch to each story.... Bloody FABULOUS." —*Postcard Reviews*

"The uber-sharp Kim Stone has to be one of the best detectives out there." —Bookpreneur

"D.I. Kim Stone is the most fascinating character to arrive on the scene since Val McDermid gave us Tony Hill." —Mark Edwards, author of *Follow You Home*

"I have not been so impressed by a debut novel in a long time, and I'm actually now itching for more.... D.I. Kim Stone is like the British Jane Rizzoli. She's so ballsy and doesn't understand the meaning of the word *no*." —Leah Loves

EVIL
GAMES

Also by Angela Marsons

Silent Scream

EVIL
GAMES

Angela
MARSONS

GC

GRAND CENTRAL
PUBLISHING

NEW YORK   BOSTON

Copyright © 2015 by Angela Marsons

Cover design and photos of woman, sky, and road by Henry Steadman
Photo of cottage by Helen Hotson/Shutterstock
Cover copyright © 2021 by Hachette Book Group, Inc.

Grand Central Publishing
Hachette Book Group
1290 Avenue of the Americas, New York, NY 10104
grandcentralpublishing.com
twitter.com/grandcentralpub

Originally published in 2015 by Bookouture in the United Kingdom
First US edition: April 2021

Grand Central Publishing is a division of Hachette Book Group, Inc. The Grand Central Publishing name and logo is a trademark of Hachette Book Group, Inc.

The publisher is not responsible for websites (or their content) that are not owned by the publisher.

The Hachette Speakers Bureau provides a wide range of authors for speaking events. To find out more, go to www.hachettespeakersbureau.com or call (866) 376-6591.

Library of Congress Control Number: 2020946454

ISBN: 978-1-5387-0402-8 (trade paperback)

Printed in the United States of America

LSC-C

Printing 1, 2021

DEDICATION

This book is dedicated to my nan, Winifred Walford. My best friend and with whom no time would ever have been enough.

ONE

Black Country–March 2015

Three minutes to go.

Dawn raids didn't come bigger than this. The case had taken months to build. And now Kim Stone and her team were ready. The social workers were positioned across the road and would be given a signal to enter. Two little girls would not be sleeping here tonight.

Two minutes to go.

She keyed the radio. "Everyone in position?"

"Awaiting your command, Guv," replied Hawkins. His team, parked two streets away, was poised to secure the rear of the property.

"Good to go, Guv," said Hammond from the car behind. He had possession of the "big key" that would gain a fast and deafening entrance.

One minute to go.

Kim's hand rested above the door handle. Her muscles tensed, an adrenaline rush borne of impending danger; her body making the choice between fight or flight. As if flight had ever been an option.

She turned to look at Bryant, her partner, who had the most important thing: the warrant.

"Bryant, you ready?"

He nodded.

Kim watched the second hand hit twelve. "Go, go, go," she called over the radio.

Eight pairs of boots thundered on the pavement and converged at the front door. Kim got there first. She stood aside as Hammond swung the enforcer at the door. The cheap wooden frame collapsed against three tonnes of kinetic energy.

As per the briefing, Bryant and a constable ran straight up the stairs towards the master bedroom to serve the warrant.

"Brown, Griff, take the lounge and kitchen. Strip the place bare if you need to. Dawson, Rudge, Hammond, you're with me."

Immediately the house was filled with the sound of cupboard doors being swung open and drawers crashing shut.

Floorboards above her creaked and a woman wailed hysterically. Kim ignored it and gave the signal for the two social workers to enter the property.

She stood before the cellar door. A padlock secured the handle.

"Hammond, bolt cutters," she called.

The officer materialised beside her and expertly snapped the metal.

Dawson stepped ahead of her, feeling along the wall for a switch.

A funnel of light from the hallway lit the stone steps. Dawson carried on down and powered up his torch, lighting the walkway beneath her feet. The smell of stale smoke and damp permeated the air.

Hammond headed over to the corner which held a spotlamp. He switched it on. The beam was aimed at the square gym mat that dominated the middle of the room. A tripod stood just beyond.

In the opposite corner was a wardrobe. Kim opened it to find a number of outfits including a school uniform and bathing costumes. On the floor of the wardrobe were toys: a rubber ring, beach ball, dolls.

Kim fought back the nausea.

"Rudge, take photos," she instructed.

Hammond knocked on each of the walls, checking for any secret spaces.

In the furthest corner, in an alcove, sat a desk with a computer. Above it were three shelves. The top one was filled with magazines. The thin spines offered no clue to their content but Kim knew what they were. The middle shelf held a selection of digital cameras, mini discs and cleaning equipment. On the lowest shelf, she counted seventeen DVDs.

Dawson took the first one labelled *Daisy Goes Swimming* and put it into the disc drive. The high-powered machine quickly sprang into life.

Daisy, the eight-year-old, appeared on the screen in a yellow bathing costume. The rubber ring encircled her tiny waist. Her thin arms hugged her upper body but did nothing to stop the trembling.

Emotion gripped Kim's throat. She wanted to tear her eyes away, but couldn't. She pretended to herself that she could prevent what was about to happen—but of course she couldn't, because it already had.

"Wh— what now, Daddy?" Daisy's tremulous voice asked.

All activity stopped. The cellar stood still. Not a sound came from four hardened officers paralysed by the little girl's voice.

"We're just going to play a little game, sweetheart," Daddy said, coming into camera view.

Kim swallowed and broke the spell. "Turn it off, Dawson," she whispered. They all knew what happened next.

"Bastard," Dawson said. His fingers shook as he replaced the disc.

Hammond stared into the corner and Rudge slowly cleaned his camera lens.

Kim pulled herself together. "Guys, we are gonna make this piece of shit pay for what he's done. I promise you that."

Dawson took out the paperwork to itemise every piece of evidence. He had a long night ahead.

Kim heard a commotion upstairs. A female screamed hysterically.

"Guv, can you come up here?" Griff called.

Kim took one last look around. "Rip the place apart, guys."

She met the officer at the top of the cellar steps. "What?"

"Wife is demanding some answers."

Kim strode to the front door, where a woman in her mid-forties stood clutching a dressing gown to her gaunt frame. Social workers placed her two shivering daughters into a Fiat Panda.

Sensing Kim behind her, Wendy Dunn turned. Her eyes were red against a colourless face. "Where are they taking my children?"

Kim controlled the urge to knock her out. "Away from your sick, perverted husband."

The wife clutched the garment at her throat. Her head shook from side to side. "I didn't know, I swear I didn't know. I want my children. I didn't know."

Kim tipped her head. "Really? The wife tends to disbelieve it until she's shown proof. You haven't seen any proof yet, have you, Mrs. Dunn?"

Her eyes darted everywhere but back at Kim. "I swear to you, I didn't know."

Kim leaned forward, the image of Daisy fresh in her mind. "You're a lying bitch. You knew. You're their mother and you allowed them to be damaged forever. I hope you never know a moment's peace for the rest of your miserable damn life."

Bryant appeared beside her. "Guv..."

Kim dragged her gaze away from the trembling woman and turned round.

She looked over Bryant's shoulder, straight into the eyes of the man responsible for ensuring that two young girls would never view the world as they should. Everything else in the house faded away and for a few seconds it was just the two of them.

She stared hard, noting the flaccid, excess skin that hung from his jaws like melting wax. His breathing was fast and laboured, his forty-stone body exhausted by any type of movement.

"You can't... fucking... come in here... and just do what... the hell you want."

She walked towards him. Her entire being recoiled at closing the space between them. "I've got a warrant that says I can."

He shook his head. "Get out of... my house... before I call my... solicitor."

She removed the handcuffs from her back pocket. "Leonard Dunn, I am arresting you on suspicion of assault of a child under thirteen by penetration, sexual assault of a child under thirteen, and causing a child under thirteen to engage in sexual activity."

Her eyes bored into his. She saw only panic.

She opened the handcuffs as Bryant grabbed Dunn's forearms in preparation.

"You do not have to say anything. But it may harm your defence if you do not mention when questioned something which you later rely on in court. Anything you do say may be given in evidence."

She closed the handcuffs, taking care not to touch the hairy, white flesh. She threw his arms away from her and looked at her partner.

"Bryant, get this foul, sick bastard out of my sight before I do something that we'll both regret."

TWO

Kim smelled the aftershave before the wearer came into view.

"Piss off, Bryant, I'm not home."

His six-foot frame bent under the half-raised garage shutter door.

She muted her iPod, silencing the silvery notes of Vivaldi's *Winter Concerto*.

Snatching up a stray rag, she wiped her hands, and using every inch of her five-foot-nine height, she faced him squarely. Her right hand instinctively ran through her short shock of black hair. Bryant knew that was her pre-battle habit. She placed the errant hand on her hip.

"What do you want?"

He carefully stepped around the explosion of motorcycle parts that littered the garage floor.

"Jesus, what does this want to be when it grows up?"

Kim followed his gaze around the space. To him it looked like a small corner of a scrapyard. To her it was forgotten treasure. It had taken almost a year to track down every part to build this motorbike and she couldn't wait.

"It's a 1954 BSA Goldstar."

His right eyebrow lifted. "I'm gonna take your word on that one."

She met his gaze and waited. This wasn't the reason for his visit and they both knew it.

"You weren't there last night," he said, retrieving the exhaust manifold from the floor.

"Well deduced, Sherlock. You should consider becoming a detective."

He smiled and then sobered. "It was a celebration, Guv."

She narrowed her gaze. Here, in her home, she was not Detective Inspector and he was not Detective Sergeant. She was Kim and he was Bryant, her work partner and the closest thing to a friend she had.

"Yeah, whatever. Where were you?" His voice softened. It wasn't the accusation she'd been expecting.

She took the exhaust from him and placed it onto the work-bench. "It wasn't a celebration for me."

"But we got him, Kim."

And now he was talking to her as a friend.

"Yes, but we didn't get her."

She reached for the pliers. Some idiot had secured the manifold to the housing with a screw a quarter-inch too big.

"Not enough evidence to charge her. She claims she knew nothing about it and CPS can't find otherwise."

"Then they should get their heads out from their arses and look harder."

She clipped the pliers around the end of the bolt and began to turn gently.

"We did our best, Kim."

"It's not enough, Bryant. That woman is their mother. She gave birth to those two little girls and then allowed them to be used in the worst possible way by their own father. Those kids will never lead a normal life."

"Because of him, Kim."

Her eyes bored into his. "He's a sick bastard. What's her excuse?"

He shrugged. "She insists she didn't know, that there were no signs."

Kim looked away. "There are always signs."

She turned the pliers gently, trying to tease the bolt free without causing any damage to the manifold.

"We can't shake her. She's sticking to it."

"You're telling me she never wondered why the door to the cellar was locked, or that there wasn't one time, just one, that she came home early and felt something wasn't quite right?"

"We can't prove it, though. We all did our best."

"Well it wasn't good enough, Bryant. Not even close. She was their mother. She should have protected them."

She applied extra force and turned the pliers anti-clockwise.

The fixing collapsed into the manifold.

She threw the pliers against the wall. "Damn, it took almost four months to track down that bloody exhaust."

Bryant shook his head. "Not the first set of nuts you've broken, is it, Kim?"

Despite her anger, a smile tugged at her lips.

"And I'm sure it won't be the last." She shook her head. "Pass me those pliers back, will you?"

"A please would be nice. Didn't your parents teach you any manners, young lady?"

Kim said nothing. She'd learned plenty from all seven sets of foster parents and not much of it had been good.

"The team appreciated the tab you left behind the bar, though."

She nodded and sighed. Her team deserved the celebration. They had worked hard to build the case. Leonard Dunn would not see the outside world for a very long time.

"If you're staying, make yourself useful and pour the coffee…please."

He shook his head, walking through the door that led into the kitchen. "Is there a pot on?"

Kim didn't bother answering. If she was home there was a pot on.

As he fussed around the kitchen, Kim was again struck by the fact that there was no animosity from him that she had risen through the ranks at a much faster pace than he had. At forty-six, Bryant had no problem with taking instruction from a woman who was twelve years his junior.

Bryant handed her a mug and leaned back against the bench. "I see you've been cooking again."

"Did you try one?"

He guffawed. "Nah, it's okay. I wanna live, and I don't eat anything I can't put a name to. They look like Afghan landmines."

"They're biscuits."

He shook his head. "Why do you put yourself through it?"

"Because I'm crap at it."

"Oh yeah, of course. Got distracted again, did you? Saw a bit of chrome that needed polishing or a screw that needed..."

"Have you really got nothing better to do on a Saturday morning than this?"

He shook his head. "Nope, the ladies in my life are having their nails done. So, no, I really don't have anything better to do than bug the hell out of you."

"Okay then, but can I ask you a personal question?"

"Look, I'm happily married and you're my boss, so the answer is no."

Kim groaned. "Good to know. But more importantly, why can't you find the backbone to tell your missus you don't want to smell like the dressing room of a boy band?"

He shook his head and looked to the ground. "I can't. I haven't spoken to her for three weeks."

Kim turned, alarmed. "Why not?"

He lifted his head and grinned. "'Cos I don't like to interrupt."

Kim shook her head and checked her watch. "Okay, finish your coffee and naff off."

He drained his mug. "Loving your subtlety, Kim," he said, heading towards the garage door. He turned. His expression asked her if she was okay.

She grunted in response.

As his car pulled away, Kim sighed deeply. She had to let the case go. The fact that Wendy Dunn had allowed her children to be sexually abused made her jaws ache. The knowledge that those two little girls would be returned to their mother sickened her. That they would again be in the care of the one person who was supposed to protect them would haunt her.

Kim threw the used rag onto the bench and lowered the roller shutter door. She had family to visit.

THREE

Kim placed the white roses in front of the gravestone that bore her twin brother's name. The tip of the tallest petal fell just below the dates that marked the duration of his life. Six short years.

The flower shop had been aglow with buckets of daffodils, the flower synonymous with Mother's Day. Kim hated daffodils, hated Mother's Day, but above all, she hated her mother. What flower did one buy for an evil, murdering bitch?

She stood upright and gazed down at the freshly mown grass. It was hard not to visualise the frail, emaciated body that had been ripped from her arms twenty-eight years earlier.

She ached to recall a memory of his sweet, trusting face, full of innocent joy and laughter; of childhood. But she could not.

No matter how many years passed, the rage never left her. That his short life had been filled with such sadness, such fear, haunted her every day.

Kim unclenched her right fist and stroked the cold marble as though she was smoothing his short black hair, so like her own. She desperately wanted to tell him she was sorry. Sorry that she couldn't protect him and so sorry that she couldn't keep him alive.

"Mikey, I love you and miss you every day." She kissed her fingers and transferred the kiss to the stone. "Sleep tight, my little angel."

With one last look she turned and headed away.

The Kawasaki Ninja waited for her outside the cemetery gates. Some days the motorbike was 600cc of pure power that transported her from place to place. Today it would be her salvation.

She put on her helmet and pulled away from the curb. Today she needed to escape.

She rode the bike through Old Hill and Cradley Heath, Black Country towns that had once thrived with Saturday shoppers hopping from the stores to the market and then the cafe for a weekly catch-up. But now the brand names had moved to out-of-town retail parks, taking the shoppers and the lively buzz with them.

Unemployment in the Black Country was the third highest in the country and had never recovered from the decline of the coal and steel industry which had boomed in Victorian times. The foundries and steelworks had been demolished to make way for trading estates and flats.

But today Kim didn't want to tour the Black Country. She wanted to ride the bike, hard.

She headed out of Stourbridge towards Stourton and an eighteen-mile stretch of road that wound its way to the picturesque town of Bridgnorth. She had no interest in the riverside shops or cafes. What she wanted was the ride.

At the black and white sign she accelerated the bike. The anticipated shot of adrenaline ripped through her veins as the engine came to life beneath her. She leaned into the machine, her breasts against the fuel tank.

Once unleashed, the power of the bike challenged every muscle in her body. She could feel its impatience and agitation in wanting to explode. And at times she was tempted to let it.

Come on, get me, she thought as her right knee kissed the ground on a sudden, sharp turn. I'm waiting, you bastards, I'm waiting.

Just now and again she liked to taunt the demons. She liked to goad the fates that had been denied when she hadn't died beside her brother.

And one of these days they would get her. It was just a matter of when.

FOUR

Doctor Alexandra Thorne circled the consultation room for the third time, as was her custom prior to a meeting with an important client. To Alex's knowledge, her first patient of the day had achieved nothing remarkable in the twenty-four years of her existence. Ruth Willis had not saved anyone's life. She had not discovered a miracle drug, or even been a particularly productive member of society. No, the significance of Ruth's existence was for Alex's benefit only. A fact of which the subject herself was blissfully unaware.

Alex continued her inspection with a critical eye and lowered herself into the chair reserved for her patients, and for good reason. It was crafted of brain-tanned Italian leather which gently caressed her back and offered reassuring comfort and warmth.

The chair was angled away from the distraction of the sash window, instead offering the patient a view of the certificates adorning the wall behind the reproduction Regency writing table.

On top of the desk sat a photograph turned slightly so the patient could see a handsome, athletic man with two young boys, all smiling for the camera. A reassuring photograph of a beautiful family.

Most important for this particular session was the eyeline view of the letter opener with its carved wooden handle and thin long blade that graced the front of her desk.

The sound of the doorbell sent a shiver of anticipation through her body. Perfect, Ruth was right on time.

Alex paused briefly to check her own appearance from toe to head. Three-inch heels added to her natural height of five foot six. Her long, slim legs were encased in navy, tailored trousers with a wide leather belt. A simple silk shirt enhanced the illusion of understated elegance. Her dark auburn hair curled at the ends in a sleek, tidy bob. She reached for the spectacles in the drawer and fixed them on the bridge of her nose to complete the ensemble. The prop was unnecessary for her vision but imperative for her image.

"Good morning, Ruth," Alex said, opening the door.

Ruth entered, personifying the dreary day outside. Her face was lifeless, shoulders drooped and depressed.

"How have you been?"

"Not too good," Ruth answered, taking her seat.

Alex stood at the coffee maker. "Have you seen him again?"

Ruth shook her head, but Alex could tell she was lying.

"Did you go back?"

Ruth looked away guiltily, unaware that she'd done exactly what Alex had wanted her to do.

Ruth had been nineteen and a promising student of Law when she'd been brutally raped, beaten, and left for dead two hundred yards from her home.

The fingerprints from the leather rucksack that had been torn from her back had revealed the rapist to be thirty-eight-year-old Allan Harris, whose details had been in the system for petty theft in his late twenties.

Ruth had faced an arduous trial that had seen the perpetrator sent to prison for twelve years.

The girl had done her best to put her life together but the event completely changed her personality. She became withdrawn, left university, and lost touch with her friends. The subsequent counselling had been ineffective in returning her to any semblance of a normal life. Her existence consisted of going through the motions. And even that frail façade had been destroyed three months earlier when she'd passed a pub on the Thorns Road and seen her attacker leaving with a dog by his side.

A couple of phone calls had confirmed that Allan Harris had been released on good behaviour after serving less than half his sentence. This news had driven the girl to a suicide attempt and the resulting court order had brought her to Alex.

During their last session, Ruth had admitted to spending every night outside the pub, in the shadows, just to see him.

"If you recall, I did advise against going back when we last met." This was not a total lie. Alex *had* advised her not to go back, but not as strongly as she could have done.

"I know, but I had to see."

"But what, Ruth?" Alex forced tenderness into her tone. "What were you hoping to see?"

Ruth gripped the arm of the chair. "I want to know why he did what he did. I want to see in his face if he's sorry, if he's got any guilt for destroying my life. For destroying me."

Alex nodded sympathetically but she had to move this along. There was much to achieve in a short time.

"Do you remember what we talked about last session?"

Ruth's pinched face became anxious. She nodded.

"I know how hard this will be for you but it is integral to the healing process. Do you trust me?"

Ruth nodded without hesitation.

Alex smiled. "Good, I'll be here with you. Take me through it from the beginning. Tell me what happened that night."

Ruth took several deep breaths and fixed her eyes above the desk in the corner. Perfect.

"It was Friday the seventeenth of February. I'd been to two lectures and had a mountain of study to get through. A few friends were going for drinks in Stourbridge to celebrate something, as students do.

"We went to a small pub in the town centre. When we left I made my excuses and started home 'cos I didn't want a hangover.

"I missed my bus by about five minutes. I tried to get a taxi but it was peak clubbing time on a Friday night. It was a twenty-minute wait and I was only going a mile and a half to Lye so I started walking."

Ruth paused and took a sip of coffee with a trembling hand. Alex wondered how many times in the years since she wished she'd just waited for the taxi.

Alex nodded for her to continue.

"I left the taxi rank in the bus station and put my iPod on. It was freezing so I walked quickly and got to Lye High Street in about fifteen minutes I went into the Spar and grabbed a sandwich because I hadn't eaten since lunch time."

Ruth's breathing quickened and her gaze was unblinking as she recalled what happened next.

"I kept walking while trying to open the damn plastic container. I never heard a thing, nothing. At first I thought a car had run into the back of me and then I realised that I was being dragged backwards by my backpack. By the time I understood what was going on there was a huge hand covering my mouth. He was behind me so I couldn't hit him. I kept thrashing but I couldn't reach him.

"I felt like I'd been dragged miles but it was only about fifty yards into the darkness of the graveyard at the top of the High Street."

Alex noted that Ruth's voice had become distant, clinical, as though reciting an event that had happened to someone else.

"He stuffed a rag into my mouth and threw me to the ground. My head hit the side of a gravestone and blood ran down my cheek. At the time, he was reaching underneath me to unzip my jeans and all I could think about was the blood. There was so much of it. My jeans had been pulled down to my ankles. He put his foot onto my calf and put his weight on it. I tried to ignore the pain and push myself up. He kicked the right side of my head and then I heard his zip being pulled down and the rustle of his trousers."

Ruth took a deep breath. "It was only then that I realised he was going to rape me. I tried to scream but the rag in my mouth muffled the sound.

"He ripped off my backpack and then used his knee to spread my legs apart. He lowered himself onto me and thrust himself into my back passage. The pain was so horrendous I couldn't breathe and the screams couldn't get past the rag in my mouth. I lost consciousness a couple of times and each time I came back I prayed for death."

Tears had started to roll down Ruth's cheeks.

"Go on."

"It seemed to go on for hours and then he was spent. He stood quickly, zipped himself up, and bent down. He whispered into my ear, 'Hope that was good for you, darlin'.' He kicked me again in the head and was gone. I blacked out and only came to as I was being lifted into the ambulance."

Alex reached across and squeezed Ruth's hand. It was ice cold and trembling. Alex hadn't been listening too closely. This needed to be moved on.

"How long were you in hospital?"

"Almost two weeks. The head injuries healed first; apparently head wounds bleed a lot. It was the other thing."

Ruth was uncomfortable speaking about the other injury, but Alex needed Ruth to feel the pain and humiliation of it all.

"How many stitches again?"

Ruth winced. "Eleven."

Alex watched Ruth's jaw grow firm as she recalled the horror in her own private hell.

"Ruth, I can't even begin to understand what you've been through and I'm sorry for causing you to have to relive it but it's necessary for your long-term healing."

Ruth nodded and fixed her with a look of total trust.

"So, in your own words, what did this monster take from you?"

Ruth thought for a moment. "Light."

"Go on."

"Nothing is light anymore. I have this idea that before that night I viewed everything with light. The world was light, even a dull, thundery day was light, but now it seems that my vision has a filter, making everything darker.

"Summer days are not as bright, jokes are not as funny, no motives are without agenda. My view of the world and everyone in it, even people I love, is changed for good."

"What prompted the suicide attempt?"

Ruth uncrossed and re-crossed her legs. "When I saw him I was in shock, initially. I couldn't believe that he was out so soon, that justice had failed me so miserably, but it was more than that," she said, as though finally realising something she hadn't explored before. "It was the realisation that I will never be free of the rage that's inside me. Pure hatred runs in my veins—and it's exhausting. I realised that he would always have that hold over me, and that there's nothing I can do about it. It will only end when one of us dies."

"But why should that be you and not him?"

Ruth pondered. "Because there's only one of those options I can control."

Alex stared at her for a few seconds and then closed her notepad and placed it on the table. "Maybe not," she said thoughtfully, as though an idea had just occurred to her, when really it was what she'd been heading towards for their entire time together. "Would you be prepared to indulge me in an experiment?"

Ruth looked hesitant.

"Do you trust me?"

"Of course."

"I'd like to try something that I think might help. I think we can give you some light back."

"Really?" Ruth asked, pathetically, hoping for a damn miracle.

"Absolutely." Alex sat forward, her elbows on her knees. "Before we start, I need you to understand that this is a visualisation and symbolic exercise."

Ruth nodded.

"Okay then, just stare forward and we'll take a journey together. Put yourself outside the pub where he drinks, but you're not a victim. You feel strong, confident, righteous. You are not dreading him leaving the pub, you are anticipating it. You have been waiting for this opportunity. You are not skulking in the shadows and you are not frightened."

Ruth's back straightened and her jaw inched forward slightly.

"He exits the pub and you walk a few metres behind. You are not threatening, you are a lone female behind a grown man and you are not afraid. Your hand is wrapped around a knife in your coat pocket. You are confident and in control."

Alex saw Ruth's eyes drop to the letter opener, where they stayed. Perfect.

"At the end of the road he turns into the alley. You wait for the perfect moment when there is no one else around and you speed up. You get within a couple of feet and you say, 'Excuse me.' He turns with a surprised expression and you ask if he has the right time."

Ruth's breathing had quickened at the thought of coming face to face with her attacker, even in the role play, but she swallowed hard and nodded.

"As he lifts his wrist to check his watch you drive the knife into his stomach as hard as you can. Again you feel his flesh against yours but this time it is on your terms. He looks down in shock as you step backwards. He stares into your face and recognition dawns. Finally, he knows who you are. He recalls briefly that night as he falls to the ground. Blood stains his shirt and pools all around him. You step further away and watch the blood leaving his body and as it flows it takes with it any hold he has over you. You watch the blood puddle and you know that his control over you is gone. You reach down and take the knife. You take back your own control, your own destiny, your *light*."

Ruth's face was slack. Alex was tempted to offer her a cigarette.

She allowed a couple of minutes to pass before speaking.

"Are you okay?"

Ruth nodded and tore her gaze away from the letter opener.

"Do you feel any better?"

"Surprisingly, yes."

"It's a symbolic exercise that gives you a visual representation of taking back control of your own life."

"It felt good, almost like I feel cleansed," Ruth admitted with a wry smile. "Thank you."

Alex patted Ruth's hand. "I think that's enough for today. Same time next week?"

Ruth nodded, thanked her again, and left.

Alex closed the door behind her and laughed out loud.

FIVE

Kim strode into the station, her mind whirring from the phone call. There was a suspicion nagging at her stomach but she hoped she was wrong. Surely no one would be that stupid.

With more than 11,000 employees, West Midlands Police rated as the second largest in the country, second only to the Metropolitan Police in London. The force was responsible for Birmingham, Coventry, Wolverhampton, and the Black Country.

Divided into ten Local Policing Units, Halesowen came under the Dudley LPU and was one of four police stations under the supervision of Chief Superintendent Young.

Halesowen wasn't the largest station in the pack but Kim preferred it to any of the others.

"What the hell happened?" she asked the Custody Sergeant. He coloured instantly.

"It's Dunn. He's had a little ummm...accident."

Her suspicion had been correct—clearly someone *was* that stupid.

"How bad an accident?"

"Broken nose."

"Jesus, Frank, please tell me you're testing the theory that I can't take a joke?"

"Certainly not, Marm."

She swore under her breath. "Who?"

"Two constables. Whiley and Jenks."

She knew them both. They lived at opposite ends of the police force age range. Whiley had been a police officer for thirty-two years and Jenks for just three.

"Where are they?"

"Locker room, M—"

"Call me Marm once more, Frank, and I swear…"

Kim left the words unsaid as she keyed herself into the station and turned left. Two PCSOs walked towards her. On seeing her expression, they parted like the Red Sea to let her through.

She stormed into the male locker room without knocking and followed the maze-like direction of the cabinets until she found her targets.

Whiley stood against an open locker, hands in his pockets. Jenks sat on the bench, clutching his head.

"What the hell were you two thinking?" Kim cried.

Jenks looked up at Whiley before he looked at her. Whiley shrugged and looked away. The kid was on his own.

"I'm sorry…I just couldn't…I have a daughter…I just…"

Kim turned her full attention on Jenks. "So has half the damn team that worked night and day to catch the bastard." She took a step closer and leaned down, bringing her face closer to his. "Do you have any clue what you've done, what you've jeopardized?" she spat.

Again he glanced at Whiley, who looked pained but did not meet Jenks's gaze.

"It happened so quickly. I don't…oh God…"

"Well, I hope it was bloody well worth it 'cos when his clever barrister gets him off due to police brutality it's the only punishment he's ever gonna get."

Jenks's hands cupped a shaking head.

"He just fell…" Whiley said, without conviction.

"How many times?"

He closed the locker and looked away.

A vision of Leonard Dunn came to her. Him waving goodbye with a smile as he walked away from the courtroom. Free to abuse again.

Kim considered the hours of work her team had sunk into the case. None of them had needed to be told to disregard the rota. Even Dawson had been first to his desk on occasion.

As a group they worked on a variety of cases ranging from assault to sexual crimes to murder and every case became personal to one of them. But these two little girls had become personal to them all.

Dawson was father to a baby girl that had somehow wheedled herself into his limited affections. Bryant had a daughter in her late teens, and Kim herself...well, seven foster homes didn't leave anyone without scars.

The case had never left them for a minute, in or out of work. Off-duty, the mind wandered to the fact that the girls were still trapped in that house with their so-called father, that every minute spent away from the office was a minute prolonged for two innocent lives. That had been more than enough incentive for the long hours.

Kim thought of the young teacher who had summoned the courage to report her suspicions to the authorities. She had risked her professional reputation and the derision of everyone around her but she'd been brave enough to do it anyway.

The possibility that it had all been for nothing was a wrecking ball to her stomach.

Kim looked from one constable to the other. Neither looked back.

"Don't either of you have anything to say for yourselves?"

Even to her own ears she sounded like a headmistress chastising a pair of schoolboys for putting a frog in her desk drawer.

Kim opened her mouth to say more, but even she couldn't continue to shout in the face of such abject despair.

She gave them one last glowering look before turning on her heel and leaving the room.

"Marm, marm...hang on a minute."

She turned to see Whiley rushing towards her. Each one of his short grey hairs and inch to his waist had been accrued throughout his career in the police force.

She stopped and folded her arms.

"I...I just wanted to explain." He nodded back towards the locker room. "He just couldn't help himself, I tried to stop him but he was too quick. See, we went there once...a while back. It was a domestic disturbance and he's beating himself up 'cos we saw 'em, you see. The little girls...huddled up on the sofa. I tried to explain that there's no way we could've known...stopped it..."

Kim understood the frustration. But damn it, they'd had him.

"What'll happen to Jenks now? He's a good officer."

"Good officers don't beat up suspects, Whiley."

Although she'd been tempted herself once or twice.

There was a part of her that wished every courtroom was fitted with a trapdoor that opened and released child abusers to a special place in hell.

Whiley dug his hands deeper into his pockets.

"See...and I've got one week to retirement and..."

Aah, now she got it. What he really wanted to know was how the whole episode was going to affect him.

Kim thought about Dawson's face when they had entered the cellar in Leonard Dunn's house and the first DVD had paralysed them all. She pictured Bryant ringing his missus to cancel a trip to the theatre because he couldn't leave his desk. She was reminded of Stacey's frequent sniffing and trips to the bathroom. As the newest member of her team, the bright, young detective constable had been determined not to show the depth of her feelings to the rest of the team.

And now the case might not even get to bloody court.

She offered Whiley a shake of the head. "You know something, Constable; I really couldn't care less."

SIX

Satisfied after her session with Ruth, Alex stood before the framed certificates that her patients found so reassuring. The MBBS from the UCL Medical School, the MRCPsych, ST-4, and Certificate of Completion of Specialist Training represented the most arduous years of her education, not because of the hard work—her IQ of 131 had breezed her through that—it had been the tedium of the study and the sheer effort of not exposing the stupidity of her peers and professors.

By far the easiest qualification she'd achieved was the PhD in Psychiatry. The only certificate on her wall that her clients really understood.

Alex felt no pride in her paper achievements. There had been no doubt in her mind that she would reach her goals. Her qualifications were displayed for one reason only: trust.

Following her education, Alex had embarked on the second part of her master plan. She had spent two years building a history; writing papers and case studies within the stymied boundaries of the mental health profession that would earn respect. The opinion of her peers couldn't have been less important to her—the only motivation had been to construct a reputation that would be unquestionable in later years. For when she was ready to begin her real work. For now.

During those years she'd been forced to whore out her expertise to the court system, providing psychological assessments on the great unwashed embroiled within the judicial process. A distasteful necessity, but one that had brought her into contact with Tim, a teenage victim of a broken home. He'd been an angry, mean-spirited individual, but a skilful pyromaniac. Her assessment had held the power to commit him to a lengthy sentence in an adult prison or a short-term stay in a psychiatric unit.

Always resourceful in using the skills available to her, Alex had forged a partnership with Tim that had benefitted them both. He spent four months in Forrest Hills Psychiatric Unit, after which he started a fire that had produced two fatalities and an inheritance to set up the private practice she still enjoyed now. Where she could pick and choose the subjects she wished to see. Thanks, Mummy and Daddy.

Tim's eventual suicide ensured that he had tied up his own loose ends quite fortuitously on her part.

Nothing in those years had been wasted. Every patient had served a purpose in building a better perspective of people driven by emotions; their strengths, their motivations, and most importantly, their weaknesses.

At times she had been tormented by her desire to commence the research, but the timeliness had been governed by two crucial factors.

The first was the construction of safety nets. The impeccable reputation she'd built would throw doubt on any later accusation of misconduct levelled at her.

Additionally, she'd waited patiently for suitable candidates to present themselves. Her experiment required individuals easily guided and with a subconscious desire to commit unforgivable acts. The sanity of the subject needed to be intact but with the potential to be unhinged if she so chose that extra layer of insurance.

Alex had known that Ruth Willis would be perfect for the study from their very first meeting. Alex had felt the desperation within the woman to take back control of her life. Poor little Ruth wasn't even aware herself just how much she needed that closure. But Alex knew—and that was all that mattered. Months of patience had led to this moment. The finale.

She had chosen a subject whose allegations would, should anything go wrong, be dismissed. She had taken the time to ensure that she would not fail. There had been other prospects along the way, individuals courted for the privilege of being chosen, but ultimately Ruth had been the one.

Her other patients were irrelevant, a means to an end. They had the pleasure of underwriting her enviable lifestyle whilst she conducted her real work.

Alex had spent many hours nodding, soothing, and reassuring her patients whilst mentally preparing her shopping list or developing the next part of her plan, all at a cost of £300 per hour.

The payment for the BMW Z4 was funded by the wife of a Chief Constable suffering from stress-induced kleptomania. Alex enjoyed the car, therefore it was unlikely that that particular patient would be recovering any time soon.

The £2,000 per month rent for the three-storey Victorian property in Hagley was paid for by the owner of a chain of estate agents whose son was experiencing paranoid persecution complex and came to see her three times per week. A few well-chosen words, dropped casually into conversation and yet subconsciously reinforcing his beliefs, dictated that his recovery would also be slow.

She stood before the portrait that took pride of place above the fireplace. She liked to look into the depths of his cold, unfeeling eyes and wonder if he would have understood her.

It was a rich oil painting that she had commissioned from a grainy black and white photograph of the only ancestor Alex could trace in whom she had any pride.

Uncle Jack, as she liked to call him, had been a "Higgler," better known as a hangman in the 1870s. Unlike the town of Bolton, which had the Billingtons, and Huddersfield, which had the Pierrepoints, the Black Country had no family dynasty that performed the gruesome task and Uncle Jack had stumbled upon the trade by accident.

Jailed for not supporting his family, Uncle Jack had been incarcerated in Stafford Prison during a visit from William Calcraft, the longest-serving executioner, with a record of around 450 hangings of men and women to his name.

On this particular day, Calcraft arrived to perform a double hanging and so needed a volunteer. Uncle Jack was the only inmate to offer. Calcraft favoured a short drop which produced a slow, agonising death, requiring the assistant to swing on the legs of the convicted to speed up death.

Uncle Jack had found his forte and thereafter travelled the country as an executioner.

Standing before his portrait always gave Alex a sense of belonging, an affinity with a member of her distant family.

She smiled up into his harsh, emotionless face. "Oh, if only things were as simple as in your day, Uncle Jack."

Alex seated herself at the desk in the corner. Finally, her magnum opus was underway. Her journey to find the answers to questions that had puzzled her for years had begun.

She let out a long, satisfied breath and reached into the top drawer for the Clairefontaine paper and the Mont Blanc pen.

It was time for her own form of recreation.

Dearest Sarah, she began.

SEVEN

Ruth Willis stood in the shadows of the shop doorway, her eyes trained on the park. The cold seeped from the ground up through her feet and into her legs like a metal stake. The odour of urine surrounded her. The plastic bin to her right overflowed with rubbish. Crisp packets and fag ends had spilled onto the tarmac.

The visualisation exercise was crystal clear in her mind. Alex was beside her.

"You are not skulking in the shadows and you are not frightened."

She had no fear; only nervous anticipation last experienced right before her A-level results. Back when she was a real person.

"You are not dreading him leaving the pub, you are anticipating it."

Had *he* felt this way on the night he'd taken her light? Had *he* shivered with excitement as he'd watched her walk out of the supermarket? Had *he* felt the sense of righteousness that coursed through her body right now?

A figure exited the lower park gate and stood at the crossing. The light from the street lamp illuminated a man and his dog. There was a lull in the passing traffic but the dog walker waited for the crossing to beep before traversing the dual carriageway. Following the rules.

"You are not a victim. You feel strong, confident, righteous."

As the figure levelled with her, he paused. Ruth stilled. Ten feet away he leaned down and placed the handle of the dog lead beneath his left foot as he retied the lace on his right shoe. So close. The dog glanced in her direction. Could he see her? She didn't know.

"You are confident and in control."

For the briefest of seconds she was tempted to rush forward, to drive the kitchen knife into his arched back and watch him fall face first to the ground, but she resisted. The visualisation had climaxed in the alley. She must stick to her plan. Only then would she be free. Only then would she retrieve her light.

"You are a lone female behind a grown man and you are not afraid."

She exited the shadows and fell into step a few paces behind him. Her trainers made little sound against two cars racing along the stretch of road.

In the alleyway, the sound of her footsteps was exposed. His body tensed, sensing a presence behind him, but he didn't turn. He slowed slightly, as though hoping the pedestrian would pass by. She would not.

"Your hand is wrapped around a knife in your coat pocket."

Halfway into the alley, at the exact spot she'd visualised, her heartbeat quickened with her step.

"Excuse me," she said, surprised by the calmness of her tone as she repeated the words Alex had given her.

His body relaxed at the sound of a female voice and he turned with a smile on his face. Big mistake.

"Do you have the right time?" she asked.

Her expression remained open when confronted with his face. He had raped her from behind and his facial features meant nothing to her. It was the sound that transported her back. His breathing was laboured from walking the dog. It was a sound she remembered well in her ear as he had split her insides open.

He used his right hand to uncover the watch beneath the elasticated cuff of his jacket.

"I make it half past..."

The knife plunged into his abdomen with ease, traversing its journey through flesh, muscle, and throbbing organs. The blade turned north and met bone as she thrust upwards. She turned the knife slowly, mincing anything in its path, like a kitchen blender. Her hand rested briefly against his stomach and could travel no further.

"Feel his flesh against yours but this time on your terms."

A sense of achievement washed over her as she withdrew the blade from his stomach. The thrust and turn needed to overcome resistance had been satisfying.

"You watch the blood puddle and you know that his control over you is gone."

His legs wobbled as his right hand clutched the wound. Blood ran over his splayed fingers. He clutched harder. He looked down, bewildered, and then into her eyes and back down as though unable to comprehend the unrelated incidents: her presence and a knife wound.

"You take back your own control, your destiny, your light."

He blinked rapidly and for a second his vision cleared and he stilled.

Every sense she had charged into life: a truck thundered past at the end of the alley. The sound lit her ears on fire. Her stomach heaved as a thick metallic smell filled her nostrils. The dog whimpered but did not run.

"You take back your own control, your destiny, your light."

Ruth drew back the knife and plunged it in again. The second penetration was not as deep but the momentum forced him backwards. A sickening thud sounded as the back of his skull met the concrete.

"You take back your own control, your destiny, your light."

Something hadn't gone quite right. She'd missed a crucial detail. In the visualisation her body was suffused with peace, calm.

She towered over his writhing body and thrust the knife into his flesh again. He groaned, so she stabbed him again.

She kicked at his left leg. "Get up, get up, get up," she screamed but the leg lay inert like the rest of him.

"You take back your own control, your destiny, your light."

"Get the fuck up." She aimed a kick to his ribs. Blood spurted from his open mouth. His eyes rolled back in his head as he squirmed like a demented mammal. The dog ran around his head, seemingly unsure what to do.

The tears rolled over her cheeks and fell. "Give it to me, you fucker. Just give it back to me," she ordered.

The body went still and the alley silenced.

Ruth drew herself back to her full height.

As the blood pooled like a paint spill beneath the lifeless body, Ruth waited.

Where was her relief?

Where was her salvation?

Where the hell was her light?

The dog barked.

Ruth Willis turned and ran for her life.

EIGHT

It started with a body, Kim thought, getting out of the Golf GTI.

"Nearly got him there, Guv," Bryant said of the uniformed officer who had jumped out of the way to avoid the bonnet of her car.

"I was miles away from him."

She ducked under the barrier tape and headed for the bunch of fluorescent jackets milling around the white tent. The Thorns Road, a dual carriageway, formed part of the main link from Lye to Dudley town.

One side of the road was primarily made up of a park and houses. The other side was dominated by a gym, a school, and The Thorns pub.

The mid-March day temperature had almost broken double figures but the darkness had sent the mercury plummeting all the way back to February.

While Bryant confirmed their credentials, Kim ignored everyone and headed for the body. A dark gulley ran along the side of an end terrace that stretched up towards Amblecote, one of the finer parts of Brierley Hill.

To the left of the pathway was a plot of land overgrown with weeds, grass, and dog shit, currently being trampled by crime scene officers or car body shop workers.

She entered the white privacy tent and groaned.

Keats, her favourite pathologist, was bent over the body.

"Aah, Detective Inspector Stone. It's been too long," he said, without looking at her.

"I saw you last week, Keats. Post mortem of a female suicide."

He looked up and then shook his head. "No, I must have blocked it out. People do that with traumatic events, you see. It's a self-preservation mechanism. In fact, what's your name again?"

"Bryant, please tell Keats he's not funny."

"Can't lie to the man's face, Guv."

Kim shook her head as a smirk passed between them.

Keats was a diminutive figure with a smooth head and a pointy beard. Some months earlier his wife of thirty years had died unexpectedly, leaving the man far more bereft than he would ever admit.

Occasionally she would allow him a little fun at her expense. Just now and again.

She turned to where a Border collie cross sat patiently beside its prostrate master.

"Why's the dog still here?"

"Witness, Guv," Bryant said smartly.

"Bryant, I'm not in the mood for…"

"Blood spatter on the fur," Keats added.

Kim looked closer and saw a few spots on its front leg.

She blocked out the peripheral activity and focussed on the most important part of the crime scene: the body. She saw a white male, early- to mid-forties, overweight, wearing Tesco jeans and a white T-shirt that had been washed so many times it was the colour of cigarette ash. A stain of crimson coloured the front of the garment, which was littered with slash marks. A pool of blood had seeped from beneath. Looking at the ground, he had fallen backwards.

His jacket was a new, medium-quality leather bomber that clearly didn't stretch across his stomach. Fastening the two sides of the zipper was nothing more than a pipe dream. A Christmas present from someone who loved him and was blind to his increasing girth, probably his mother. The garment had offered no protection against the penetration of a sharp object.

His hair was peppered with grey and too long. His face was clean-shaven and still bore a look of surprise.

"Murder weapon?"

"Nothing yet," Keats said, turning away.

Kim leaned down and made eye contact with the forensic photographer. He nodded, indicating that he'd taken the shots he needed of the body. He turned his attention to the dog.

She carefully lifted up the sodden T-shirt. One stab wound would have been responsible for most of the blood.

"I'm guessing the top one is the fatal wound," Keats added. "And before you ask I'd say kitchen knife, five to six inches."

"It won't be far away," she said to no one in particular.

"How do you figure? It could be anywhere. He could have taken it with him."

Kim shook her head. "The attack may have been planned: late night, dark alley, but there was frenzy involved. There was emotion in this attack. The first injury did the job but there are three 'stay dead' wounds."

She continued to stare down at the corpse, feeling the fury that had accompanied the attack as though it had been captured in the air around her.

She lifted her head. "The killer was blinded by rage while committing the act, but once it's finished that adrenaline recedes, and then what?"

Bryant followed her logic. "You see what you've done and what's still in your hand and you want to discard the connection as quickly as possible."

"Stabbing is very personal, Bryant. It requires a closeness that is almost intimate."

"Or it could be a mugging gone wrong. There isn't any wallet on him."

Kim ignored his last comment and lowered herself to the ground to the left of the body. She lay on her side and placed her feet right next to the victim's. The cold gravel path bit straight through her clothes.

Keats looked on, shaking his head. "Oh Bryant, every day must be a challenge."

"Keats, you really have no idea."

Kim ignored them both. She pulled back her arm and then lunged it forward in a stabbing motion. The trajectory put the wound at the centre of the breast bone. She tried to match a swipe from her arm to the wound but the momentum wasn't there.

She shuffled along the floor and did it again. Once more the trajectory was off by an inch or more.

She shuffled just a touch lower, closed her eyes, and blocked out the curious gazes around her. She didn't care what they thought.

She thought of Daisy Dunn standing in the middle of that seedy basement. She pictured that frightened, shivering child dressed in an outfit of her father's choosing. This time she swung her arm with anger. With the rage of someone who was ready to kill. She opened her eyes and leaned over. Her index finger was right on the wound.

She looked down and their feet were no longer level. She had dropped by a good four to five inches to achieve a comfortable, natural stabbing position that matched the trajectory of the wound.

She pushed herself to her feet and dusted off her jeans.

She subtracted the difference from her own height. "Murderer will be no taller than five three or five four."

Keats smiled and stroked his beard. "You know, Bryant, if Carlsberg made detectives..."

"Is there anything else I should know?" Kim said, moving towards the exit flap of the tent.

"Not until I get him home for a proper look," Keats said.

Kim took a moment to survey the scene. Crime scene officers were searching the area for evidence, constables were going door to door, statements were being taken, and the ambulance was awaiting the release of the body. Her presence was no longer required. She had everything she needed. It was now up to her to pull it all together and establish what had taken place.

Without speaking, she exited the tent and walked past the two officers guarding the end of the alley.

She was ten feet away when she heard the mutterings between them. She stopped short, causing Bryant to almost crash into the back of her. She turned and headed back.

"What was that, Jarvis?"

She stood before the DS and thrust her hands into her trouser pockets. He had the grace to colour.

"Would you like to repeat what you just said? I don't think Bryant heard you."

The tall, reedy officer shook his head. "I didn't..."

Kim turned to Bryant. "DS Jarvis here just called me a 'cold bitch.'"

"Oh, shit..."

She continued to talk to Bryant. "I mean, I'm not saying his assessment is completely wrong but I would like him to explain it." She turned back to Jarvis, who had moved back a step. "So, please, go on."

"I wasn't talking about…"

"Jarvis, I would have far more respect for you if you could find your backbone for long enough to actually qualify your statement."

He said nothing.

"What would you have me do, eh? Am I required to burst into tears for the loss of his life? Would you like me to grieve for his passing? Say a prayer? Lament his fine qualities? Or should I just put the clues together and find whoever did this?"

Her eyes held ground with his. He looked away.

"I'm sorry, Marm. I shouldn't have…"

Kim didn't hear the rest of his apology, as she had already walked away.

By the time she reached the cordon, Bryant was just behind her. She ducked under the tape and then hesitated. She turned to one of the constables.

"Can someone make sure that dog is taken care of?"

Bryant guffawed. "Jeez, Guv, just when I think I know you."

"What?"

"There are constables being abused 'cos of diversion signs, first-time officers who've never seen a crime scene, a DS with his nuts chewed off, and you're bothered about the welfare of the bloody dog."

"The dog didn't figure this into his career plans. The rest should've done."

Bryant got into the car and checked his seat belt, twice.

"Cheer up, it might not be a simple mugging gone wrong."

She pulled away from the scene without speaking.

"I can see it in your face. You look like someone stole your Barbie doll and boiled it."

"I never had a Barbie doll, and if I had I would've dismembered it myself."

"You know what I mean."

Kim did know what he meant and he was the only detective that could say it and remain unscathed.

Bryant took a pack of sweets from his jacket pocket. He offered her one and she refused.

"You really should try and cut down on those things," she said, as the aroma of menthol filled her car.

Bryant had become addicted to the extra strong cough lozenges after kicking a forty-a-day smoking habit.

"You know they help me think."

"In that case, have a couple."

Unlike Bryant, she already knew for certain this case was no mugging, so other questions needed to be answered: who, when, how, and why.

The "How" was straightforward enough, a blade that she guessed to be somewhere between five and seven inches. The closest "When" would be confirmed at the post mortem. That left the "Who" and the "Why."

Although establishing the "Why" was of paramount importance to the investigation of a crime, for Kim it had never been the most essential part of the puzzle. It was the only element that could not be corroborated by scientific means. It was her job to establish the 'Why," but the last thing she needed was to understand it.

She recalled one of her earlier cases as a detective sergeant, when a child had been knocked down on a zebra crossing by a woman whose blood contained three times the legal alcohol limit. The seven-year-old boy died slowly of horrific internal injuries caused by the bull bars on the front of the woman's jeep. It transpired that the woman had been diagnosed with ovarian cancer and had spent the afternoon in the pub.

This information had no effect on Kim whatsoever, because the facts remained the same. The woman had still chosen to drink; she had still chosen to get behind the wheel of a car; and the seven-year-old boy was still dead.

Understanding the "Why" of an action brought with it an expectation of empathy, understanding, or forgiveness, however brutal the act.

And, as her past would bear out, Kim was not the forgiving kind.

NINE

At 1:30 a.m. Kim headed through the communal office that housed the police constables, PCSOs, and a couple of civilian staff.

"Good, you're here."

The other two detectives that completed her team were already seated. There had been little time to recover since closing the Dunn case. But that's how her team rolled.

The room held four desks in two sets of two facing each other. Each desk mirrored its partner, with a computer screen and mismatched file trays.

Three of the desks accommodated permanent occupants but the fourth sat empty since they had been downsized two years earlier. It was where Kim normally perched herself, rather than her office.

The space with her name on the door was commonly referred to as The Bowl. It was nothing more than an area in the top right-hand corner of the room that was partitioned off by plasterboard and glass.

"Morning, Guv," Detective Constable Wood called brightly. Although half-English and half-Nigerian, Stacey's desk held a sign stating, "The only way is Dudley." She wore her hair short and natural. Her complexion and gentle features suited the style.

On the other hand, DS Dawson looked as though he'd left a hot date. Dawson had been born wearing a suit. And just as some men were unable to look smart even in Armani, Dawson was the opposite. His numerous suits were not expensive but he managed to make them look good. His shoes and tie normally dictated his activity. Kim glanced to the ground as he headed to the percolator. Oh yes, he'd been on the pull all right. Just a few months after being accepted back into the loving embrace of his fiancée and young child.

But it wasn't her business, so she left it alone.

"Stace, you get the board."

Stacey jumped up and reached for the black marker pen.

"No identity yet. Wallet wasn't on him so we'll go with what we know: white male, mid-forties, low income, four stab wounds, first one fatal." Kim paused for a moment, giving Stacey a chance to catch up.

"So, we need to get a timeline. Did he go to the pub and his wallet was taken afterwards or did he simply take his dog for a walk?"

Kim turned her attention to Dawson. "Kev, talk to the uniforms, check with the bus service and taxi ranks. It's a busy road; someone might have seen something. Get the witness statements for yesterday. Bryant, check for any missing persons reports."

Kim looked around the room. Everyone was moving.

"And I'll go and brief the boss."

She took the stairs two at a time and entered without knocking.

DCI Woodward's five foot eleven stature could be gauged even from a sitting position. His torso sat straight and proud and Kim was yet to spot a crease in his crisp, white shirts. His Caribbean heritage had gifted him with skin that belied his fifty-three years. He had begun his career as a constable on the streets of Wolverhampton and had persevered through the ranks during decades when the Police Force was not as politically correct as it liked to think it was.

His unwavering passion and pride were reflected in the book-case displaying his Matchbox car collection. The police vehicles took centre stage.

He picked up the stress ball from the edge of his desk and started kneading it with his right hand.

"What do we have so far?"

"Very little, Sir. We just started outlining the investigation."

"The press have already been on the phone. You need to give them something."

Kim rolled her eyes. "Sir..."

He squeezed the ball harder. "Forget it, Stone. Eight a.m. tomorrow. Give them a statement: body of a male, etc."

He knew she hated talking to the press but he periodically insisted. Her career progression plan for herself differed from his plan for her. Rising any further in the ranks took her further away from actual police work. Any further escalation on the food chain and her day would be filled with codes of practice, policies, arse-covering, and godforsaken press conferences.

She opened her mouth to argue, but a slight shake of his head discouraged that course of action. She knew which battles to fight.

"Anything else, Sir?"

Woody put the stress ball back and took off his glasses. "Keep me updated."

"Of course," she said, closing the door behind her. Didn't she always?

She entered the squad room to a mixture of expressions.

"We have good news and bad news," Bryant said, meeting her gaze.

"Hit me with it."

"We have a positive identification on the victim ... and you're not going to like it one little bit."

TEN

Alex was startled from sleep by the sound of The Beatles singing "I'm a Loser" from her mobile phone. It was her private joke to signal that she had an incoming call from Hardwick House. It wasn't as amusing at almost three in the morning.

She glared at the phone for a couple of seconds, trying to gain her composure, eventually silencing John Lennon.

"Hello..."

"Alex, it's David. Can you come over...?" His voice disappeared into the distance but she heard him shout for someone to get Shane back into the common room. "Look, we've had an incident between Shane and Malcolm. Can you get here?"

Alex's interest picked up. "What type of...?"

"Eric, get Shane in there and close the damn door."

He sounded fraught and Alex could hear a lot of shouting in the background.

"I'll explain when you get here."

"On my way."

She dressed quickly but thoughtfully in fitted jeans that hugged her hips and caressed her bottom. On top she put a cashmere jumper that revealed just a hint of cleavage when she leaned forward—invaluable when visiting a house full of men.

A light dusting of blusher and a quick pout of lipstick and the "just out of bed" look had been carefully constructed. She grabbed a notepad from the kitchen drawer on her way out.

As the three-litre injection engine cut through the silence of the leafy road, Alex considered her options with Hardwick House. The partnership had become one-sided and the benefits of the liaison were becoming less attractive to her.

She'd been careful when choosing the facility on which to bestow the gift of her expertise. After researching the local good causes, Hardwick House had been the only bunch of do-gooders she could stomach.

She had wanted to see if there were any candidates for her research but when she found no particularly good subjects she had grown bored and just used them to perfect her manipulation techniques. Now, even that was growing tiresome, Alex thought as she pulled onto the drive and killed the engine. She sensed a gradual withdrawal somewhere in her future.

The door was opened by David, the only remotely interesting person in the building. At thirty-seven, his black hair was showing just a hint of grey that added depth to his features. He carried himself with the ease of someone who had no idea how attractive they were to the opposite sex. For him, Alex would break her "married men only" rule.

She knew little about him outside of Hardwick House other than he'd sustained serious damage to a knee in a sporting accident. She'd never asked because she didn't care.

She also knew he worked tirelessly for the men within his remit, getting work placements, benefits, basic education. For David, they were souls to be saved. For Alex, they were target practice.

"What happened?"

David closed the door behind her and Alex was again reminded that, despite the renovations, the former nursing home still held the aura of God's waiting room.

The door to the common room was closed and guarded by Barry, a subject she had considered for her project when choosing potential candidates four months earlier. Unfortunately his progress had been slow. They'd had many conversations about his hurt at his wife's betrayal with his own brother but he'd been missing that last incentive to galvanise him into action. His hatred had not been deep enough, raw enough, to affect his long-term conscience. And ultimately that's what she was interested in.

Yet another disappointment.

She caught his quick appraisal of her and held his gaze for just a second to show that she'd noticed. He looked away.

"Shane is in there," David said urgently. "Malcolm is in the kitchen. We're having to keep them apart at the moment. To cut a long story short, Shane didn't make it up to bed. He fell asleep in the den in front of the television. Malcolm could hear the TV and came in to turn it off. He gently shook Shane awake to get him to go to bed."

David paused, running his hand through his hair. Alex already knew where this was going.

"Basically, Shane woke up then beat seven shades out of Malcolm. He's in the kitchen; nothing broken, but he's a bit of a mess. He's shouting for the police and Shane is shouting for you."

Alex felt rather than heard the presence of her "bodyguard," Dougie, behind her. She reached into her bag and pulled out a writing book with a psychedelic design on the front cover. Dougie was severely autistic and rarely spoke, but he had a fascination for notebooks. To make herself look good she brought him a new one every time she came. He took it and held it close to his chest and took a step backwards.

He was six foot tall and gangly. His family had disowned him at twelve, yet somehow he'd survived on the streets until David caught him taking leftovers from the bins. He spent his days walking mile after mile along the Dudley canal routes. Dougie wasn't an official resident of the foundation because he'd never been in prison, but David had stated that his room was for life.

Alex found him repulsive but she hid it well and tolerated him following her around like a lovesick puppy. One never knew when such adoration would be useful.

"Let me see Shane first. I need to get him to calm down."

David opened the door to the den. Two residents flanked Shane, who was leaning forward, rocking on his knees.

"Thanks, guys," Alex said, dismissing the minders.

Dougie stood in the open doorway with his back to her. The rules stated no female could be in a closed room with any of the occupants. He would ensure that no one entered.

She took the seat opposite. "Hey, Shane."

He didn't look up but his bruised hands clenched each other tightly.

Alex knew Shane's story well because she'd considered him for part of her study. He was a tall, skinny lad who looked younger than his twenty-three years. From the age of five he had been sexually abused by his uncle. When he was thirteen, and a foot taller than his abuser, he had beaten him to death with his bare hands.

Physical examinations had proven Shane's accusations of abuse to be truthful but he had been imprisoned for eight and a half years anyway. He had been released to find that his parents had moved away and left no forwarding address.

Alex debated how to handle him. What she really wanted to do was shake Shane and tell him he'd fucked up big time but she couldn't let her annoyance with him show. She drew on her store of manufactured compassion.

"Shane, come on, it's me, Alex. What happened?"

She was careful not to touch him. Shane recoiled from physical contact of any kind. He remained silent.

"You can talk to me. I'm your friend."

Shane shook his head and Alex wanted to hit him. Being dragged out of bed to deal with a bunch of fucking misfits was bad enough, but mute misfits was trying her limited patience just a little too much.

"Shane, if you won't talk to me, the police…"

"Nightmare," he whispered. Alex leaned forward.

"You were having a nightmare and Malcolm woke you and you thought he was your uncle?"

Shane looked at her for the first time. His face was pale and tears streamed down his cheeks. Oh, how manly, she mused.

"So, when you woke, you thought he'd come back to rape you some more?"

She saw him wince at the word. Payback for getting her out of bed.

He nodded.

"Was the light on?"

"Yes."

As she had suspected.

"So, after the first punch you would have known it wasn't your uncle. You would have seen it was Malcolm. Why did you carry on hitting him?"

She knew the answer and it was now in her best interest to ensure the police were not called. Shane was so stupid he would blurt it all out—her conversations with him, his confusion. Even the smallest finger of suspicion pointing her way would be unthinkable.

He shrugged. "I dunno. I was thinking about stuff you said about his nieces."

Alex recalled their chat two weeks earlier when she'd tried to explain to him that not every middle-aged male was like his uncle.

She had chosen her words carefully and she recalled them word for word. "Take Malcolm over there, he's a perfectly nice man. There is no proof that he's ever interfered with his nieces. And if he had, I'm sure the authorities would know."

Her words had been designed to elicit this exact reaction, but when it hadn't happened within a couple of days, she'd written Shane off as a candidate as he wasn't predictable enough.

Although a part of Alex was secretly delighted that he'd finally done what she'd wanted, it didn't change anything; she was pissed off it had taken this long. She didn't have time for this.

"But if you recall, Shane. I deliberately said that Malcolm had *not* done anything to those little girls, to demonstrate that he was nothing like your uncle and that nice men do exist."

The tears stopped and his face creased in confusion. "But you said..." Shane couldn't remember exactly what she'd said. "I kept picturing those little girls and what he'd done to them and you said the authorities would know." He raised tortured eyes to hers. "But they never knew with me."

Alex looked away. His neediness was distasteful.

"But then you stopped talking to me." He sounded lost and alone. He was right, she had spent more time with Malcolm to try and prompt a violent outburst from Shane, which it had, but much too late to be of any use to her.

"Do you know why I stopped talking to you, Shane?" she asked, gently.

He shook his head.

"It's because you are a waste of my time. You are so damaged that you will never lead a remotely normal life. There is no hope for you. The nightmares will never go away and every balding middle-aged male will be your uncle. You will never be free of him or what he did to you. No one will ever love you because you are contaminated and the torment you go through will be with you forever."

Every last ounce of colour drained from his face. She leaned in closer. "And if you bother me in any way from this point on, I will speak to the parole board and instruct them that you are a danger to others and you will be returned to prison." She stood, towering above the gibbering wreck. God, she hated disappointment. "And we all know there are plenty of middle-aged men in there, don't we, Shane?"

His head dropped and his shoulders trembled. She took his silence as complete understanding. They were done. Permanently.

She brushed past Dougie and headed to the kitchen. Most of the occupants had gone back to bed now the excitement was over. Only David and Malcolm remained, with Dougie hovering somewhere behind her.

Alex couldn't help but be impressed at the job Shane had done on the plump, harmless victim sitting at the table. Now all she had to worry about was damage limitation. It didn't suit her for the police to be involved. This was her playpen.

"Oh, Malcolm…" she said, sitting beside him. "You poor thing." She reached up and tenderly touched the swollen flesh of his face, already starting to bruise. His lip bulged with a cut to the right hand side. Alex could only imagine what he would look like in the morning.

"He's a damn lunatic. Needs to be locked up."

Alex glanced at David and understood his position. A crime had been committed, but David knew that Shane could not survive being returned to prison. Alex nodded and David left the kitchen to check on Shane.

"Look, Malcolm. You're perfectly justified in calling the police. You've been terribly assaulted. It's difficult for you to fully understand some of the other residents."

She leaned forward slightly and Malcolm's gaze wandered to her intended target. Malcolm had never harmed a soul in his life. Painfully shy and socially inept, he had fallen prey to an online scam with a "Thai woman" who had fallen in love with him in the romantic setting of a tropical fish chat room. Many sick relatives and a bunch of money transfers later, Malcolm was broke and began embezzling from the steel company for which he was an accountant.

He had served only two years, and although he hadn't had much before, he was now starting from scratch. At fifty-one years old, he had no wife, no children, no home, and no profession.

Alex coated her voice in saccharin and leaned forward another two inches.

"You have to remember, Malcolm. You're not like these people. You are an educated, professional man with a lot to offer. You've been hurt terribly but you are not permanently damaged. These pathetic creatures deserve your pity. They will never have an ounce of your intelligence."

Alex re-crossed her legs and brushed his knee with hers.

"But he should be held accountable…" he said weakly and Alex knew she had it in the bag.

"And he will. I think you need to take the action that is right for you. Do what will make you feel better, but it's only fair that you understand that Shane will be returned to prison and he will never come out again. I don't want you to have that on your conscience if you are acting in the heat of the moment. Once you make that call you won't be able to take it back."

Alex took a deep breath so her breasts rose and fell. The core of decency he now fought was the very reason she had ruled him out as a research subject.

"I have a suggestion if you'd like to hear it?"

Malcolm nodded but continued to look down her top. It no longer suited her to have Shane around. She didn't want to see his pathetic little face again.

"Well, I think it would be impossible for you both to continue living here. You shouldn't have to be frightened of any repeat attacks. My opinion is that you leave the police out of it, as long as Shane leaves the house."

Malcolm finally raised his face to hers. God, he was a mess. "But where will he . . . ?"

"That's not really your concern after what he's done to you, is it?"

"Well . . . not really . . ."

"So, shall I tell David your decision?"

Malcolm nodded. Too easy.

Alex leaned across and patted him lightly on the knee. The old fool blushed slightly. This poor guy had never had an orgasm with any other living, breathing being within one hundred yards of the event.

"I think that's the right decision, Malcolm. Now you go to bed and I'll talk to David for you."

Alex sighed deeply as Malcolm left and David re-entered.

"How did it go?"

Alex blew out air. "Well, it took a lot of persuasion but he's not calling the police."

David's face crumpled with relief. "Thank God. Shane is so sorry for what he's done. He knows it was wrong and we both know that returning to prison would kill him. He really isn't a bad kid."

"However, Malcolm's one condition for not calling the police is that Shane has to leave."

David swore under his breath.

"I know it's difficult and I tried to change his mind but he wouldn't budge. I suppose you can see his point. He would be terrified."

David shook his head. "I just don't know what got into him."

Alex shrugged. "That's the problem. There's no way to ensure it won't happen again. You can't guarantee Malcolm's safety if Shane stays."

David dropped his head into his hands.

Alex reached over and touched his bare arm. "There's nothing more you can do, David."

It was maddening that the only fault she could see in this man was his ability to empathise with the hopeless charges within his care. Just a touch of ruthlessness or a devious mind and he'd have been her perfect match.

He moved his arm beyond her reach.

"Jesus, David, I tried my best, you know," she snapped, smarting from the rejection. He didn't know that she had manipulated the situation to keep the authorities away. For all she cared Shane could be thrown back in prison and abused every day of his life. Whatever her motives she had saved this situation and still this man rebuffed her.

"I know, Alex, and I really appreciate it. I just need to figure out what I can do to help Shane."

She stood up and brushed past him as she reached into the cupboard for two cups.

"How's Barry getting on, I thought he'd have been gone by now?" she asked for the sake of conversation. One last coffee and it was goodbye. David's indifference to her advances was the final straw. She had better ways to spend her time.

David shook his head. "Poor guy suffered a major setback. Heard from a friend of a friend that his ex-wife and brother got married last week. Barry's daughter was a bridesmaid. He had a major meltdown and smashed up some stuff. He's not ready to go yet."

Alex felt the smile begin low in her stomach. Luckily she had turned away by the time it reached her face. She might have just been offered a reason to stay.

"Oh dear, that's such a shame. I'll make the coffee and you can tell me all about it."

ELEVEN

Kim seated herself at the spare detective's desk. "Hope you all got a bit of sleep, because there won't be any more until we make some headway on this case."

Personally, she'd had very little herself. She had eventually drifted off, only to be woken two hours later after dreaming of little Daisy Dunn. She had often fallen asleep thinking about a case, and even more often a suspect had been the first thing she'd thought of in a morning. But the vision of Daisy had unsettled her; she'd watched her being led away, but Daisy was pulling back, refusing to go, staring back at her.

Kim shook the vision away. The case was over and it was on with the next. She had done her part and now she just had to hope it made it to court, despite the stupidity of Jenks and Whiley.

She tuned back just in time to catch a grumble from the other side of the room. It originated from Dawson's corner.

Her eyes challenged him. He looked away.

Kim didn't operate to a rota and their rostered working hours were viewed in an advisory capacity only. If a witness needed to be interviewed she didn't care if it was five minutes before the end of shift. The job got done.

"Anybody who expects dead bodies to turn up at their convenience should download a transfer form immediately. Anyone?"

Not even Bryant responded. He had a gift for knowing when not to open his mouth.

"Okay, refresh; our victim is Allan Harris, a forty-five-year-old male who did time for rape. Got out about eighteen months ago and appears to have been clean ever since. He lives on benefits with his elderly mother and hasn't worked a day since his release."

"It was a brutal rape, Guv," Bryant offered.

"I know that." She'd read the reports and didn't need a history lesson. The horrific injuries sustained by his victim had sickened her. Would she shed tears for his loss as a human being? No chance. Would she allow her personal feelings to affect the way she handled the case? Same response. "Look folks, he served his time, minimal as it was, and hasn't blipped on the radar since. Allan Harris isn't Gandhi and we don't get to pick our victim. Got it?"

"Yes, Guv."

"Dawson, go talk to taxi drivers, bus drivers, dog walkers, and the owner of the pub. See if there was anyone who was particularly vocal about their dislike for Harris. And take Stacey with you, she could do with some air."

Stacey was truly gifted in I.T. and had always supported the team from behind a computer screen. It was time to expose her to a little more of the outside world. The fact that Stacey looked just a little bit anxious proved to Kim she was making the right call.

Wood and Dawson rose and headed towards the door.

Dawson hung back. "Umm...Guv, just wanted to apologise for my crack about sleep."

"If I thought you meant it you'd already be on your way home."

He nodded his understanding and headed out. Dawson was a good detective, but Kim expected more than good. She pushed them hard, believing it made them better officers. Police work didn't come with a clock card, and any of her team who wanted nothing more than a job could piss off to McDonald's and flip burgers all day.

Bryant waited until they were out of earshot. "Don't we make a good team? Your cool intelligence, my warm demeanour. Your dispassionate analysis, my ability to play nice. Your brains, my beauty."

Kim grunted. "Come on, gorgeous, our press awaits."

Kim hadn't called a press conference. She hadn't needed to. They'd been arriving since four in the morning.

She took a deep breath and nodded before pushing open the double doors.

Reporters and photographers stood in huddles. She recognised a few of the locals from the *Express and Star* and the free papers. A Central News reporter and a BBC *Midlands Today* cameraman were sharing something on their mobile phones. A *Sky News* correspondent was busy texting.

"Okay, gather round," Kim shouted. A bouquet of microphones appeared before her face and tape recorders were activated and thrust forward. God, she hated this.

She nodded at the expectant faces. "I'll just hand you over to DS Bryant, who will give you the details so far."

Kim stood to the side. If Bryant was bewildered by her sudden deference he hid it well and immediately offered his sympathies to the family.

Yeah, bet Woody's stress ball's seeing some action now, Kim thought.

"... Midlands Police Force will do everything within its power to bring this perpetrator to justice. Thank you for your time."

Kim headed towards the car and Bryant followed.

"Thanks for that, Guv," he grumbled, throwing a *Classic Bike* magazine onto the back seat.

"Handled like a true professional, Bryant."

"You know Woody is gonna kill you for..."

"Got the address?"

"Back to the island at the bottom of Thorns Road but take a left onto Caledonia."

"Thanks, TomTom."

"Just for info, Guv. I know you didn't bother going home last night."

Kim said nothing.

"About the only thing that does live in your office is a change of clothes and some toiletries."

"Gold star, Sherlock."

"Added to the fact that your mileage is the same as when we parked up last night."

"What the hell are you, a walking tachograph?"

"No, I'm a detective. I notice things."

"Well, focus your efforts on this case and leave me the hell alone."

He was right, of course, which narked her all the more.

"I think you need a reason to go home at night."

"Bryant..." she warned. It was true that he could push her further than anyone else could. But not that far.

She continued the drive in silence, right up until a laboured sigh escaped from her partner's lips.

"What is it, Bryant?"

He sighed. "I'm not sure how we're gonna convey any sincere sympathy to Harris's mother when we get there."

Kim frowned. "Why do you say that?"

Bryant continued to stare out of the window. "Well, isn't it obvious?"

"Not to me."

"With what he did to that girl..."

Bryant stopped speaking as she hit the brakes and turned left onto a pub car park.

"What are you doing?"

"Okay, get it out now."

He looked away. "I didn't say anything in front of the others but my daughter is a similar age as that girl was when he raped her."

"I get that but we don't have the luxury of investigating murders of the righteous alone."

He looked at her. "But how can we offer the same level of passion for that piece of shit?"

Kim did not like the direction of this conversation. "Because it's your job, Bryant. You did not sign any agreement stating that you would only protect the rights of the people you feel are worthy. It's the law itself we uphold and that law applies to everyone."

His eyes searched hers. "But can you really, knowing what you know, commit yourself without prejudice?"

She didn't flinch. "Yes, I can. And I fully expect the same from you."

He bit the skin on one of his knuckles.

The air was charged between them. There were few times she'd had to pull Bryant into line and it wasn't an easy thing for her to do. But their friendship could stand it. She hoped.

She stared ahead, her voice low. "Bryant, I expect nothing less than total professionalism when we go into that house. If you can't give me that then I would suggest you remain in the car."

She knew that was harsh but she would not tolerate any display of his personal feelings about the victim.

He didn't hesitate. "Of course."

The fact that she would take the necessary action if he defied her instruction was known to both of them. Friendship or not.

She put the car into gear and pulled away.

Sensibly he remained silent until they reached the island at the bottom of Thorns Road. On both sides were family dwellings that she guessed to be two bedrooms, each with a driveway just long enough to hold a family-sized car.

Bryant told her to stop in front of number twenty-three.

The house sat approximately fifty feet from the end of the alley where Harris was murdered.

Bryant slammed the car door. "Jesus, another fifteen seconds and he'd have been home."

The front garden was in the process of being slabbed. Mounds of grass had been crudely dug out, leaving a tufty, pock-marked surface. A box porch jutted from the front of the property, which was straight if Kim tilted her head slightly to the left. Every window was suffocated by net curtains and a small glass pane upstairs had a crack in the lower left-hand corner.

Bryant used his knuckle to rap three short taps to the door. It was opened by a female family liaison officer dressed in sweatshirt and jeans.

"She's quite frail, hasn't stopped crying yet."

Kim squeezed past her and entered the lounge. Stairs led out of the room to the upper level. Brown and orange swirls covered every surface except the beige velour corner suite that dominated the room.

The dog that had sat beside the body sauntered towards her wagging its tail. His collar of white fur still held dried brown spatters of his owner's blood.

She ignored the animal and continued to the rear of the small house. She found the elderly female sitting in a comfortable rocker in the dining kitchen that stretched the width of the small house.

Kim introduced herself as Bryant materialised beside her. He took the lady's hand.

"Mrs. Harris, my name is DS Bryant and firstly I'd like to offer our condolences for your loss." He held onto the gnarled bones for a few seconds then placed the hand gently back in her lap.

Kim offered him a slight nod as they sat on the two wicker chairs. His professionalism hid the feelings he'd revealed to her in the car. She could ask no more of him.

The liaison officer made tea and the dog placed itself next to Kim, leaning against her right leg. She moved her leg away and focused her attention on Mrs. Harris. Her hair was completely grey and tufty in places. Kim was reminded of the front garden.

Mrs. Harris's face was pleasant but marred by the ravages of hard work and anguish. Her whole body was so consumed by arthritis it appeared that each bone had been fractured and reset incorrectly. Her right hand picked at the tissue in her left hand, producing hundreds of tiny white flakes that had formed a puddle in her lap.

The old lady fixed red-rimmed eyes on Bryant. When she spoke, her words were thick with a Black Country accent. "He wor a bad lad, Detective Inspector. Prison 'elped him."

In her mind, Kim's quick translation told her that Mrs. Harris meant he wasn't bad and that prison helped him.

Kim nudged the dog away. "Mrs. Harris, we're more interested in what happened to your son than his past."

Mrs. Harris fixed Kim with a stare. Her eyes were raw but dry. "What he did was 'orrible and disgustin' and I'll never get the back on it. He pled guilty to all the charges and never tried any fancy defence with big words. He took the punishment o' the court whether yo' agree with it or not. He came out a changed man, real sorry for wor he'd done to that poor girl. If he could have took it back he wou'da done." Her eyes filled and she shook her head. The impassioned defence of her son was over, leaving the cold reality that he was still dead.

She continued but her voice was shaky. "My lad wor never gonna be able to work again; his sentence was for life."

Kim kept her face neutral and spoke honestly. "Mrs. Harris, we fully intend to investigate the murder of your son. His history has no bearing on how we do that."

Mrs. Harris met her gaze and held it for a few seconds. "I believe yer."

Bryant took over. "Can you tell us exactly what happened last night?"

The woman dabbed at her cheeks with the decimated tissue. "He 'elped me to bed about ten o'clock. He switched on the radio. I goo to sleep to the late night talking programmes. He whistled for Barney and then took him out. They always went for a long walk at night. Barney don't like other dogs much.

"Sometimes he'd stop at The Thorns and 'ave 'alf a pint before gooin over to the park. He just sat outside on his own with Barney. He'd buy a bag of scratchings and share 'em with the dog."

"What time did he normally get back?"

"Usually 'alf eleven. I could never ger off to sleep properly 'til he was back in the house. Oh my, my, my, I cor believe he's gone. Who'd do this?" she asked Bryant.

"I'm afraid we don't know yet. Was he having any problems with anyone you know of?"

"The neighbours wunt talk to either of us once I ler 'im move back in." Again, Kim realised this meant that the neighbours wouldn't talk to her once she let him back in. "I think folks shouted stuff to 'im if he went out in the day. One night he come back with a black eye but he wunt talk about it. There were a couple of nasty letters and some threatening phone calls and a couple of months ago we 'ad a brick thrown at the window."

Kim felt sorry for the old woman left behind. Despite what her son had done, his mother had taken him in and tried to protect him.

"Did you keep the letters or get the phone numbers?"

Mrs. Harris shook her head. "No, chick, Allan threw 'em away and we changed our phone number."

"Did you call the police when the brick got thrown?"

"You pair might be tekkin his murder serious but I doe think a brick through the window of a convicted rapist woulda brought much of a response."

Kim didn't answer; she knew Mrs. Harris was probably correct. There were no clues to be found in the threats and abuse he'd suffered, so Kim moved on.

"Did he always take his wallet with him, you know, to pop into the pub?"

"No, he never went to the pub on Friday or Saturday; too many folks. His wallet is on the table in the other room."

"Did he ever carry a knife, say for his own protection?" Bryant asked.

Mrs. Harris frowned. "He dint tell me if he did."

They were prevented from asking any further questions by a knock at the door. The constable who had been observing went to answer it. Kim idly wondered how the frail woman was going to manage once this resource was removed. Eventually the case would be solved and the liaison officer would be reassigned.

"That'll be the Blue Cross," Mrs. Harris said sadly.

As she spoke the words, the dog again rested against Kim's leg. She did nothing as she realised that short of a good kick the bloody thing wasn't going anywhere.

"Blue Cross?" Bryant asked.

"The rescue centre that Barney come from. They've come to tek him back. I cor look after him. It ay fair."

Fresh tears welled in her eyes. "My lad loved that dog, liked to think he'd given him a second chance."

A male and female, both bearing the logo of the rescue centre, entered the room.

"His dog lead is hanging over there. His bed is in the lounge and tek that brown teddy bear. It's his best toy."

The dog's body trembled as it backed up against Kim's legs. A feeling of sadness washed over her. The dog hadn't judged his master on past crimes; he'd been a loyal, faithful friend and now his life here was over.

The male gathered the dog's belongings as the woman retrieved the lead.

Mrs. Harris leaned forward and patted the dog one last time. "I'm sorry, Barney, but I cor look after yer, mate."

The woman attached the lead and began walking the dog out of the house. He turned at the front door, fixing Kim with a sorrowful, questioning stare.

She watched as the dog was led away from everything he knew. He was being returned to the display shelf, back on parade for another chance at a good home. A feeling she knew all too well.

Kim stood, abruptly. "Come on, Bryant, I think we have all we need."

TWELVE

Alex headed towards Cradley Heath, impressed with her ability to adapt. In her field of research there were bound to be disappointments along the way. Shane had let her down but she'd turned that little situation to her own advantage without any detection.

There were always casualties of research but as yet Alex had not encountered any collateral damage that was not worth the end result. Disappointments were an occupational hazard but she was nothing if not resourceful.

Like now. After the events of the previous night it would only be right to pop back to Hardwick House to make sure everyone was okay, and if Barry happened to be around, then it could be a very good day after all.

She needed the distraction from thinking about Ruth. She had to accept that she would not get any data until their next scheduled appointment. The story was all over the news but the police would never put it together in that time, especially if Ruth had listened to her properly and removed the knife.

The day was bright but breezy. The trees moved as the last traces of winter were blown away.

As she drove through Cradley Heath she stopped at the Tesco superstore and picked up a selection of cheap cakes and pastries. It didn't cost a lot, but again perception was everything.

She pulled onto the drive of Hardwick House and noticed a couple of extra cars. The weekend brought visitors to the occupants.

"Refreshments," she said, entering the kitchen. David turned and Alex could see he was on the phone but not speaking. He ended the call and shook his head.

"Everything okay?"

"What are you doing back here so soon?"

"Oh well, I'll just take my goodies and go, shall I?" she asked coyly.

"Sorry, I didn't mean it like that."

"I just wanted to check that Malcolm and Shane were both okay." Sometimes, she surprised herself with how convincing she could be. She couldn't have cared less about the two losers, but Barry was a different story entirely.

"Malcolm looks like he went ten rounds with Tyson and then got run over by an ice road trucker, but he's fine in himself. Feels like the bigger man for not contacting the police. His sister is in The Den with him. She's given me an earful for allowing this to happen but she's mildly appeased by the fact that Shane's not here anymore."

"Already?" Alex was surprised but also pleased.

David held his arms open. "He left during the night. I went to wake him early to talk to him and his room had been cleared. I've left him a couple of messages but he's now switched off his phone."

"Oh David, I'm so sorry. I know how much you liked him."

"Poor kid's got no one. Never had a break in his life. I really thought we could help him."

"He's a grown man. He has to make his own decisions. It's possible that he just couldn't face Malcolm and thought this was the best way. At least you don't have to ask him to leave."

"Hello, Dougie," she said, without turning. "Don't you ever get bored of following me around?"

He shook his head and shuffled from one foot to the other. She opened her mouth to say something and then closed it again. There wasn't even any sport in being mean to Dougie. She liked her adversaries to have possession of at least one brain cell.

Alex took the plates through to The Den.

Ray, the oldest resident, was sitting on one of the sofas enduring another uncomfortable silence that frequently occurred between him and a daughter that he barely knew.

Ray was the epitome of what Jeremy Hardwick had in mind when opening the House When Ray left the free world in 1986, a computer hard drive had filled an entire room. A mobile phone came with a battery the size of a suitcase and the founder of Facebook was two years old.

She approached the two of them with a plate. She wished she didn't have to waste her time with such trivialities but appearances were important. They both took a cake and thanked her, eager for the distraction.

Malcolm sat in the far corner, looking sheepish and intimidated by his austere younger sister. Malcolm would have made a domineering woman a very good husband. He accepted his place well. Alex offered him a secret smile and then lowered her eyes.

She started to look around the room when a voice sounded behind her.

"Err... excuse me, you're the doctor, aren't you?"

Alex was surprised to find Malcolm's officious sister glaring up at her. She was an unfortunate-looking woman with buck teeth and small squinty eyes.

"My name is Alexandra Thorne and I..."

"So, you're the woman who talked my brother out of calling the police?"

The hands were resting on the hips and the pock-marked jaw had thrust forward. Alex stopped herself from laughing. The height difference between them made Alex want to reach down and pat the woman on the head. If only she didn't have to waste her time with such inconsequential people.

"Would you like to explain to me why you would do such a thing?"

"I don't feel I need to explain anything to…"

"Just look at the state of him." She gestured towards Malcolm, who looked mortified and yet remained seated.

"How could you let that bastard do this to him and get away with it?"

"It was Malcolm's decision not to call the police."

The woman harrumphed in a manner way beyond her years. "Yeah, I'll bet it was." She looked Alex up and down. "You with your Vicky Beckham jeans and high heels; he'd sacrifice his own nieces if you asked him to."

On cue, two girls zoomed past, catching Alex's left thigh and she briefly considered putting that theory to the test.

People were beginning to look their way. And Alex's boredom threshold had been reached.

Alex lowered her voice. "I did not persuade your brother to do anything. He is a fully grown man with a mind of his own."

"Aha, thought so. I know your game."

Alex seriously doubted that but she smiled tolerantly anyway. "And, what would that be?"

"You're after him. That's what this is about."

Oh yes, of course that was it, Alex thought, almost laughing in the woman's face.

"You're trying to get him all dependent on you so you can trap him into marriage." A drop of spittle from the woman's mouth landed on her cheek. A step too far.

She gently guided the woman into a corner and placed a smile on her face for the benefit of onlookers. She spoke quietly.

"Okay, you stupid, ignorant bitch, I encouraged Malcolm to leave the police out of it and you should be fucking grateful that I did. Shane was making all kinds of accusations about Malcolm molesting your two little demons over there.

"Any attending officer would have been obliged to investigate such claims, which would have resulted in painful, humiliating physical examinations for your little darlings—not to mention the distinct possibility of them being removed from your care."

Alex was gratified that the woman's mouth had dropped open far enough to dry any remaining droplets of spittle.

Alex continued to smile. "So, I suggest you keep your vicious little mouth shut and continue visiting with your brother and stay away from what doesn't concern you."

A very slight nod was the response.

Alex turned away and took a deep breath. Now, back to the real reason for her visit.

THIRTEEN

Alex spied Barry sitting in the furthest corner, reading a magazine, alone.

She stood before him, the plate offered and her game face back on. "Apple turnover?"

"Is that an offer or some kind of request?"

"Take your pick." Alex took a seat beside him. "How are you doing?"

He shrugged in response and returned his gaze to the magazine. His head was freshly shaved and his body more toned and muscular than she remembered. Barry had been a semi-professional boxer before going to prison, a fact that hadn't helped him at trial.

Alex stretched her legs before her and crossed them at the ankles. She chuckled tolerantly as the irritating little girls ran to the table, grabbed a cake, and ran off again. Had she been on her own she would have raised a leg and sent them tumbling to the ground but she stopped herself.

"Aren't they adorable?"

Barry didn't look at them. "Are you still here?"

"Yep. You appear to be the only person here without a visitor so you get the consolation prize of me."

"Woohoo."

"Now, now, contain your excitement. I can tell that you're thrilled on the inside and you're just choosing not to show it."

Honestly, these boys were so sensitive. First Shane had reacted badly to her rejection and now Barry was giving her the cold shoulder for the same thing. No matter. She'd get him back.

"Yeah, that'll be it."

She tipped her head. 'Not in the mood to talk to me today?"

Barry laughed out loud. "That's rich. You haven't spoken to me for months."

Alex worked the angle. "I know, Barry, and I'm sorry. But the thing is there are people that needed my help far more than you. You seem to be through the worst of it now."

He grunted and Alex stopped herself from smiling. She knew full well he wasn't even close to being through the worst of it. Her plan depended on that fact.

She nudged him sideways. "Come on, I thought we were friends. Why so pissed off?"

"I'm sure David has already filled you in."

"No," she lied. "I'm not here in an official capacity so he doesn't divulge histories to me. That's up to the individual." What she really wanted was for Barry to tell her himself so she could gauge where his vulnerabilities were. David had given her the facts but she wanted the emotional triggers. She had already deduced that Barry couldn't look at the two little girls. They reminded him that his own daughter was being cared for by another man. His own brother.

He stared at the cakes.

She pushed. "Okay, no more one-sided conversations. Ask me anything and I'll tell you."

He turned towards her with interest. "Married, kids?"

"Separated and a daughter," she said, looking over at the girls. She lowered her gaze. It was a good work of fiction that would

bring them closer. She needed that affinity of being separated
from a child.

He caught her subtlety. "Where's the kid?"

"With her father. It's his weekend." She looked away.

"Look, I'm sorry…"

She waved away his apologies. "It's okay. Breaking up a family
is always painful but we're trying to work it out."

Fantastic, she thought. Now he felt guilty that he'd caused her
pain and he'd be more likely to open up.

She already knew his story inside out. Barry had been an
amateur boxer with a young wife. Under pressure from his wife
to quit the sport, he started driving a delivery van. Some time
later his wife became pregnant, but eight months in, the baby's
heart had stopped beating. His wife went through labour to give
birth to a dead child.

Barry had tried to be strong but had returned to boxing to
alleviate the rage. Every fight saw him more damaged, but he
couldn't stop. During the time Barry should have been comforting
his wife, his brother had been doing it instead.

When he caught them, Barry had beaten his brother so badly
he was paralysed from the waist down. Seven months later, Lisa
gave birth to Barry's child. A daughter.

"What did your husband do?" Barry asked, quietly.

She looked him square in the eyes. "Hazard a wild one."

"Affair?"

She nodded.

He shook his head. "Anyone you know?"

Alex considered inventing a best friend to fit into her fictional
scenario but she felt that was stretching credibility a little too far.
"No, some girl he met at a coffee shop. She's a barista, whatever
that is. Apparently, she's less challenging."

"Bet that makes you feel good."

"Tremendous." She smiled at him. "Hey, who's the shrink here? I'm half expecting you to present me with a bill before I leave."

"Yeah, a cool coupla hundred quid for me," he quipped.

"Anyway, enough about me. How are you doing?" she asked, eager to resume her experiment.

"Not good, they're married now," he said, miserably.

"Oh, Barry. I'm so sorry. I had no idea."

He waved away her apology. "Not your fault."

Alex sat in silence beside him for just a minute, allowing his mind to linger on what he'd said.

But now it was time to begin.

"Does she love him?" she asked, softly.

That question pained him, as she'd intended. And a flash of confusion registered in his eyes.

"I don't know. I mean ... I assume so. She married him."

"Do you think Lisa married him due to a sense of responsibility?"

"Does it matter?"

"It would to me if I was still in love with her," Alex said, gently.

He shook his head. "She'd never take me back."

Alex paused for a few seconds. "Hmm ... did you and your brother fight as children?"

Barry smiled. "That's the first shrink thing you've said."

"I apologise. I'm just interested in whether this was purely accidental."

He frowned. "What do you mean?"

"Aah, hang on, you told me I couldn't be a shrink. Make your mind up."

"Go on."

"Well, sometimes siblings compete throughout their childhood, normally for the affection or validation of a parent. If a child feels their brother or sister is more intelligent, attractive, or favoured, they try to compete and emulate the more successful sibling. Normally this naturally dies out as siblings take different directions outside of the childhood home, but occasionally envy continues into adulthood."

Alex could see he was giving this serious thought. Of course he was. Every person with a sibling could remember fights over toys, clothes, and CDs. It was perfectly normal.

She shrugged as though she couldn't care less either way. "It just sounds as though you're taking full responsibility for the whole situation yet you don't know if part of it was by design. So, I ask again. Does she love him?"

"I still don't understand how that matters. She could never forgive me."

"It doesn't matter at all if you've given up."

"But what can I..."

"You've said you would have forgiven her anything to be a family. How do you know that she wouldn't do the same? At the moment, your brother has stolen your life. He's taken your wife and is father to your daughter and you don't even know if she's in love with him."

One hundred and eighty. Now just one last jab.

"You shouldn't envy him. I mean, what's his quality of life? He is unable to leave that chair. It might have been kinder if he hadn't survived." She paused for a few seconds. "It would probably have been kinder to your wife."

Barry was staring at her intently. Fresh hope hovered behind his eyes.

Alex shrugged and sighed. "Perhaps she regrets it all and wants you back; a strong, able-bodied man that she loves and is the true father to her child, but can't extricate herself from the obligation of taking care of your brother."

Barry looked confused and restless. "I dunno..."

"You know," she said, bending her legs and leaning slightly into him. "I told my husband I would never forgive him, but if he turned up tomorrow genuinely sorry for what he'd done, I'd have to consider giving him another chance. I love him, miss him, and he's the father of my child. Basically, I'd want my family back."

Barry was silent for a few minutes. He stood. "I think I'll go for a walk. I just need to clear my head a bit."

Alex nodded and smiled. She reached for one of the pastries. This experiment was a bit like playing with a spinning top. You wound it as tightly as you could and put it down with no idea of the direction in which it would go.

FOURTEEN

Kim threw down the last report. "Absolutely bloody nothing, taxi drivers, bus drivers, residents. A man gets knifed to death and no one saw or heard a damn thing."

"There's that one report," Bryant said, searching through his own pile.

"Of course, an eighteen-year-old lad, totally wasted, thought he saw someone sitting on the wall just before eleven fifteen, right by the bus stop."

"Yeah but the last bus went past at..."

"Not really a smoking gun, is it? Someone sitting on a wall at a bus stop."

Bryant sighed. "Maybe the knockers did it."

"Huh?"

Bryant took both their mugs and stood at the coffee maker. "The miners had fairies they called 'knockers.' If they got upset they'd hide the tools, steal the candles, jump out from behind pillars of coal, and generally cause a nuisance. No one ever saw them but there was no doubt in the mines that they existed."

"Very helpful. So, now we're looking for bloody Tinkerbell..."

"Carrying a five-inch kitchen knife, judging by the wound," Dawson added.

"The preliminary examination supposes the fatal stab wound was the first and that the knife pierced the lining of the lung."

A phone rang. Kim ignored it. Bryant picked it up.

"So, the killer either stabbed upwards because they knew what they were doing or because there was a substantial height difference. The other wounds were rage or frustration."

"Guv..."

She turned to Bryant. "What?"

"Potential murder weapon's on its way in."

"Where was it found?" she asked, her mind already piecing together the fragments of information they had.

"Spare land on the Dudley Road where a local guy keeps some horses."

"On the road that heads towards..."

"Lye," he answered.

"And the home of Ruth Willis."

FIFTEEN

Kim waited until she and Bryant were alone in the car before asking the question that was on her mind.

"He's at it again, isn't he?"

If Kim had thought her partner would need her to spell it out she would have done.

Bryant sighed. "You caught the tie the other night?"

"And the shoes," she confirmed. "Not to mention the attitude."

There was an added cockiness to Dawson when he was fooling his fiancée but he wasn't fooling any of them.

Bryant pulled up at a set of lights that she would have challenged.

"You'd think after the last time…"

He didn't need to say any more. Just a couple of months after giving birth to their daughter, Dawson's fiancée had found out that he'd cheated while she was pregnant. She had thrown him out and the team's lives had been made miserable while he'd attempted to win her back. But, eventually, he had.

Bryant shrugged. "I dunno. The bloke doesn't know a good thing when he's got it."

And lost it and won it back again, Kim thought, but said nothing. What Dawson did in his private life was his own business but his attitude on her time was not.

The terraced house two streets away from the site of the rape was unremarkable. It stood in a line of twelve, identically reflected across the narrow road. There were no front gardens and a stone plaque in the middle of the row dated the buildings back to 1910.

"Guv, seriously, is this a good idea?"

Kim understood his reservations. It wasn't normal practice but her gut was like a washing machine on spin cycle. She'd felt it before and it would churn away until it was satisfied.

"For God's sake, I'm not going to walk right in there and arrest her. I just want to talk to her."

He didn't appear mollified. They waited in silence for a response to their knock; finally the door was opened by a petite woman wearing a navy blue tracksuit. The expression of guilt almost overwhelmed her and Kim immediately knew. This was Ruth, the rape victim, and as their eyes met, Kim also knew that she was looking at Ruth, the murderer.

"Detective Inspector Stone, Detective Sergeant Bryant. May we come in?"

The woman hesitated momentarily and then stood aside. Kim noted that there was no request for identification or explanation.

Kim followed Ruth Willis into the front living room. The walls were a timeline of Ruth's childhood, a mixture of professional posed pictures before a sky blue backdrop and other family favourites that had been enlarged and framed. No other children were present in the photographs.

Sky News played on the television. Kim indicated to Bryant that she wished to take the lead. His return expression read "go lightly." She had no intention of doing otherwise. Unlike Bryant, she knew their search was over.

"What's this about, Officer?" Ruth asked, reaching for the remote control and changing the channel.

Kim waited to make eye contact with her. "We're here to inform you that a man was murdered two nights ago, not far away, on Thorns Road."

Ruth tried to hold her gaze and failed. Her eyes darted between the two of them but didn't settle. "I heard something on the news."

"The male has been identified as Allan Harris."

"Oh, I see."

Kim noted that she tried to remain expressionless, unsure of the appropriate response. Every reaction fed the growl in Kim's stomach.

"The male was stabbed four times. The fatal wound entered . . ."

"Okay, I get the picture, but what does that have to do with me?"

The effort of trying to sound normal made the woman's voice tremble more.

"That's what we're here to find out, Miss Willis."

Kim was careful to keep her expression benign. Slowly, slowly, catchee monkey.

Kim sat, Ruth followed. Her hands rested in her lap, clasped together.

"We know what he did to you, Ruth. He raped and beat you to within an inch of your life. I'm not going to pretend to know what that attack did to you. I can't even imagine the horror, the fear, the rage."

Ruth said nothing but the colour began to drain from her face. The woman was using every ounce of strength she had to mask her true emotions but her body had not read the same memo.

"When did you find out he'd been released?"

"A few months ago."

"How did you find out?"

Ruth shrugged. "I don't recall."

"You live within a couple of miles of his home. Did you see him?"

"Honestly, I don't remember."

"How did you feel about his release?"

Kim watched as Ruth's right hand instinctively caressed the scarred tissue on her left wrist, a permanent reminder of her suicide attempt.

Ruth looked towards the window. "I really didn't give it much thought. It's not like there was anything I could do about it."

Kim pushed. "Do you think it was a fair punishment?"

Ruth's eyes flared with emotion and Kim could see that there was much that this woman had to say on the subject but didn't.

"How do you feel knowing he's finally got what he deserved?"

Ruth's jaws were clamped together, not trusting herself to speak. Kim could feel Bryant's discomfort but these were not lazy questions. She'd formulated them in the car and the responses should have been emotional.

From an innocent person the reaction to such probing would have been immediate and uncensored. *The bastard should have been locked up for life*, or *I'm glad he's fucking dead*. There should be fire in Ruth's eyes and animation, not a silent acceptance and refusal to speak because she couldn't work out the correct response.

"I'm not sure how this is relevant to the murder."

The woman's voice was starting to break and the tension fed her wringing hands.

"I'm sorry, Miss Willis, but I have to ask where you were on Friday night between the hours of nine p.m. and midnight?"

"I was here, watching television."

Kim was aware that the pitch of the woman's voice had risen. The words had been rehearsed too many times in her mind.

"Is there anyone that can verify that you didn't leave the house?"

"I...umm popped to the chip shop at around nine thirty."

So, Kim realised, perhaps a neighbour had seen her either leave or return to the house, so she had to invent a short trip somewhere.

Kim nodded. "If we speak to the owner he'll verify he served you sometime after nine thirty?"

Ruth looked panicky. "Well…I don't know. It was busy. He might not recall."

Kim smiled reassuringly. "Oh, I'm sure he would. It's your local chippy. You must have been there many times over the years. After all, you've lived here all your life."

"Well, yes, but the owner wasn't working and I don't know the others very well."

Kim followed Ruth to the corner into which she'd backed herself.

"Oh, that's fine. If you just give me the description of the assistant that served you I can make sure we speak to the right person."

Kim watched the fight drain out of her. She'd offered an alibi that would not be corroborated and any about-turn now would be highly suspicious. Innocent people didn't need to invent alibis.

Kim stood and Ruth looked up at her. Her complexion was grey, her eyes frightened, her body collapsed like a wind-battered tent.

Kim spoke softly. "We have the murder weapon, Ruth. It was right where you threw it."

Ruth buried her head in her hands. Sobs wracked her body. Kim turned to Bryant and their eyes met. There was no triumph or pleasure that passed between them.

Kim sat beside Ruth on the sofa. "Ruth, what Allan Harris did to you was horrific but I think you should know that he was sorry. We all hope that prison will rehabilitate offenders but we don't always believe it. On this occasion it did. Allan Harris was genuinely remorseful for what he'd done."

Bryant stepped forward. "Ruth Willis, I'm arresting you…"

"I wasn't frightened," Ruth said quietly as Kim moved to stand. She sat back down.

"Miss Willis, I have to warn you…"

"I was nervous but I wasn't frightened," she repeated.

"Miss Willis, anything you say will be..." Bryant started to say.

"Leave it," Kim said, shaking her head. "This is for her, not us."

"I watched him exit the park. I was standing at the crossing. I felt powerful, righteous. I stood in the shop doorway, in the shadows. He bent down to tie his shoe lace. The dog looked right at me. He didn't bark."

She raised her head, her face wet with tears. "Why didn't he bark?"

Kim shook her head.

"I was tempted to drive the knife into his back right then but it wouldn't have been right. I wanted my light."

Kim looked at Bryant, who shrugged.

"I was confident and in control. I followed him and asked him the time."

"Ruth, we need..."

"I plunged the knife into his stomach. His flesh was against mine, but this time it was on my terms. His legs wobbled as his right hand clutched the wound. Blood ran over his fingers. He looked down and then back at me. And I waited."

"Waited?" Kim asked.

"I withdrew the knife and stabbed him again. And I waited."

Kim wanted to ask what she'd been waiting for but dared not break the spell.

"And again, and again. I heard his skull land on the concrete. His eyes began to close so I kicked him, but he wouldn't give it back to me."

"Give what back to you, Ruth?" Kim asked, gently.

"I wanted to do it again. Something had gone wrong. He still had it. I shouted at him to give it me back but he wouldn't move."

"What did he have that belonged to you, Ruth?"

Ruth looked at her as though it were perfectly obvious. "My light. I didn't get my light."

Instantly her body folded and the sobs were being ripped from her throat.

Kim once again looked towards Bryant, who shrugged in response. She sat silently for a full minute before nodding her head towards her colleague.

He took a step towards the woman who had just confessed to murder. "Ruth Willis, I'm arresting you for the murder of Allan Harris. You do not have to say anything but anything you do say…"

Kim left the house before Bryant had finished. She didn't feel triumphant or victorious, only satisfied that she'd caught the person who had committed a crime and that her job here was done.

A victim plus a perpetrator equalled case closed.

SIXTEEN

It was just after midnight when Kim entered the garage. The quiet family street had closed down ready for the week ahead, truly her favourite part of the day.

She switched on her iPod and chose Chopin's *Nocturnes*. The solo piano pieces would ease her through the early morning hours until her body demanded sleep.

Woody hadn't helped her state of mind either. After she'd sent the others home Woody had stopped by her desk bearing gifts: a sandwich and coffee.

"What am I not going to like, Sir?" she'd asked.

"CPS wants to tread carefully with this one. They're not keen on a murder charge yet. They want some background. They don't want some clever defence trying for a diminished responsibility plea."

"But..."

"It needs to be tight."

"I'll get Wood and Dawson on it tomorrow morning."

Woody shook his head. "No, I want you tidying this one up, Stone."

"Oh come on, Sir."

"There's no debate. Just get it done."

Kim let out a huge sigh, putting every ounce of dismay she could muster into that one exhalation. It changed nothing but she felt it got her point across.

Woody smiled. "Now, for goodness' sake, go home and . . . do whatever it is you do when you're not here."

So she had.

As she lowered herself to the ground beside the motorcycle parts, she growled in disgust.

She hated mopping up. The case was over. She'd caught the bad guy, or girl in this instance, within forty-eight hours. A full confession had been recorded and now the CPS wanted their arses wiped as well.

She crossed her legs and began to assess the pieces around her. Every part of the bike was here and would fit together to produce a classic, beautiful British machine. Now all she had to do was figure out how.

An hour later, every part of the puzzle was still in the same place. There was something in her stomach that refused to play dead.

A sudden thought occurred to her. She stood and reached for her boots.

Maybe her insomnia wasn't being caused by this case, after all.

SEVENTEEN

Kim dismounted the Ninja and unlatched the waist-high gate. The stubby drive and snatch of lawn appeared to be contagious throughout the street. Many residents of the small clutch of council properties on the Dudley border with Netherton had taken advantage of the right-to-buy scheme and secured themselves a spacious property for a fraction of the cost. The Dunn family had been one such household.

This time there was no rush of activity, thundering of boots, or loud access to the property with the enforcer. Just her and a set of keys.

She wandered through the house more slowly than the first time. The urgency had been spent. The house had been prodded, probed, and stripped of anything that might help the case. There was a sense of abandonment in the air. As though the occupants had been painted out of the picture. Reading books and toys were stored in various corners. A cereal box and bowls stood ready in the kitchen. In addition to the abuse, normal life had taken place in this house. At times they'd just been two little girls.

Eventually she reached the wooden door at the top of the stairs. Kim was struck by the fact they all described the space as a cellar. It was not. Kim had seen poky cellars in a few of her foster homes around the Midlands. The houses had been called back-to-backs and came in rows of twenty. Homes built by factory and mine owners during the industrial revolution that would house as many as six families. The cellars were tiny spaces, barely the width of a person, situated down a couple of stone steps and created for the storage of coal.

But not this one. This house had been especially remodelled to create this space buried down in the ground.

Many men hungered for a man cave; a place to call their own. A garden shed, a spare room to build models, play computer games, but Leonard Dunn had wanted a space to abuse his children. That he had spent many hours adding a basement especially for that pleasure added a sickness to his depravity that Kim could barely stomach.

The physical space was now almost empty, inoffensive since the removal of the evidence. But Kim still saw it as it was on the morning of the raid. The gym mat, the lamp, the digital camera. But more than that, the foul acts that had taken place were embedded in the fabric of the room and would never disappear.

The far corner now held only the desk. The computer and discs were at the station. The area could have belonged to an architect, an accountant, anyone wishing for a little privacy to think, concentrate, or create.

She crossed the room to the wardrobe, now emptied of the costumes used for Dunn's sickening games.

The lamp had been pushed to the far wall during the evidence collection. But she needed no reminder of where it had stood. It had been positioned behind the camera, casting a spotlight on the gym mat.

Kim's mind automatically flashed back to the vision of Daisy standing in the centre of that mat, her small voice trembling as she asked her daddy what she should do next.

She shook her head to remove the picture from her mind. She often wished there were things that could be unseen and unheard, but there was no simple erase button on the side of her head.

Kim headed for the stairs, still unsure why she had been drawn back to this room.

She took a deep breath. "I wish I could have stopped it sooner, Daisy," she said, as her hand cast a shadow over the light switch.

Her fingers stopped dead and trembled.

Her head turned and looked at the lamp. Something wasn't making sense.

Kim took a step back and concentrated hard as the suspicion that had gnawed finally bit.

"Hell, no," she said, launching herself up the stairs.

EIGHTEEN

Kim travelled through her workplace, matching the momentum of the bike that now cooled outside.

The viewing suite was located on the third floor of the station.

There was no simple entry to this part of the building. She buzzed the access button and allowed her fingers to rest against the wall, looking up into the camera that was now searching the features of her face.

Her finger lifted to buzz again but the familiar click sounded. She pulled the door open and entered the airlock. The first door closed behind her, allowing her to keycode herself into the suite.

Four sets of two desks filled the windowless space. One noticeable difference between this and the other offices in the building was the lack of paper.

This was the room that held the people that pored over every second of CCTV evidence seized, and on a case like the Dunn investigation, Kim would not have done that job for every motorbike in Japan.

"Hey Eddie, working late?" she asked, approaching the only occupied desk.

He straightened and stretched a torso that had spent far too many hours hunched at the keyboard. Kim was sure she heard something crack.

"You too, Marm?"

Kim had seen Eddie at work on numerous occasions. And everything about him was average: height, weight, complexion, and photo on his desk. He was not a man that stood out.

But once his left hand commanded the keyboard and his right steered the mouse there was a meeting, a connection that was a pleasure to watch.

"Ed, I need you to look at some of the footage from the Dunn..."

Kim was interrupted by the sound of the buzzer.

"It's like New Street Station in here tonight," Eddie said, turning to the camera.

"It's Bryant," Kim said.

Eddie glanced sideways. "What—you psychic now as well?"

"Err...no, I called him on the phone."

Eddie groaned as he pressed the access button.

Bryant was already removing his jacket. "Look, Guv, I know you can't stand to be without me, but..."

"Don't flatter yourself. You just live nearest."

"Fair enough," he said, dropping the jacket onto one of the desks.

Eddie pushed himself away from the desk and turned his chair. He took a moment to flex the fingers on his right hand. "Well, lovely as it is to have a bit of company on the night shift, there's no beer and pizza so I'm guessing this ain't a party."

Kim turned to Bryant. "See how quick he worked that out. You could learn..."

"Cheers, Guv, now would you mind telling me why my cheese and pickle supper is back in the fridge?"

"Eddie, can you show me the footage marked *Daisy Goes Swimming*?"

Eddie pulled himself back into the desk and within seconds the screen had filled with folders marked with names, dates, and reference numbers.

Kim was instantly saddened by just how many folders there were.

He clicked quicker than she could keep up but suddenly the screen filled with the eight-year-old girl trembling.

"Mute the sound," Kim said quickly.

Bryant looked around the office, at anything but the screen.

Her eyes travelled away from the little girl as the camera zoomed out and displayed more of the room. The video was exactly as she'd remembered it.

Her stomach churned in response.

"Eddie, show me the photos we took on the dawn raid."

A couple of seconds later a directory appeared. He clicked on the first photo and began to scroll through.

"Stop," she said, on photograph number nine.

The photo was taken at the same angle as the video camera.

"Can you put them side by side?"

Eddie filled the screen with two separate images: the photograph and a freeze-frame of the video.

"What lighting did we use that morning, Bryant?"

He still hadn't looked at the screen.

"The spotlamp, 'cos Dawson couldn't find the light switch."

She nodded. "So it was the exact same conditions. No natural light, no movement of the lamp?"

"Suppose so."

"Okay, look at this," she said, motioning him closer. "See that black mass creeping up the wardrobe?"

He nodded.

"Where is it on the photo?"

He looked closer and glanced from one to the other.

Bryant stood back and looked at her.

"Guv, are you saying what I think you're saying?"

She took a deep breath before speaking.

"Yes. Bryant, there was someone else in the room."

NINETEEN

"Am yer serious, boss?" Stacey asked, quietly.

Kim nodded her head. "Checked the footage last night. Definitely the shadow of a figure." She nodded backwards towards Bryant. "Me and Columbo went back to the property to recreate it with the lamp placement and a video camera. It's definitely a person."

Dawson pushed a folder roughly across his desk.

"Mature, Kev," Kim snapped.

He coloured and looked away. "Sorry, Guv."

She turned back to Stacey, who was still glaring at Dawson.

"Find out everything about Leonard Dunn's neighbours, family members, everybody he's ever worked with, spoken to, or brushed past on the bus. I want to know if any of them are on The List." It was what they all called the register of sex offenders.

The initial clue to the abuse had come to them from a perceptive and attentive school teacher. But the focus of the investigation had been on Leonard alone. And when they'd got him, they'd thought the case was closed. Damn it, they were hunting for another sicko who had been involved.

"Kev, I want you to interview everyone again, especially the neighbours. If this person was a regular visitor, then someone must have seen them. Okay?"

"What about Wendy Dunn?" Bryant asked.

She shook her head. Not yet but that time would come.

"Got any suspicions, boss?" Stacey asked.

She certainly did, but she wasn't going to share them yet.

Kim looked to Bryant. "Come on, partner. We're clearing up."

TWENTY

Alex hit the refresh button on each of the online news outlets she'd put into her favourites. What she should have been doing right now was meeting Ruth and collecting the data that was vital to her experiment; but the stupid bitch had got herself caught within forty-eight hours.

Alex had known that the incompetent police would eventually stumble over Ruth as a suspect, but she'd miscalculated. Either a police officer with a smattering of intelligence had landed the case or Ruth had left her name and address at the crime scene with a sign saying, "It was me."

What she had expected was a few days, time enough to extract the information she required. Jesus, had she needed to draw the imbecile a picture? She'd been given the motivation, method, and opportunity in the visualisation. Alex had hoped that Ruth's one contribution to the process would have been a modicum of self-preservation.

Alex hit refresh again. No change. She turned her attention to her usual morning checks. She signed into Facebook and typed in the name, "Sarah Lewis." Twenty minutes later, after logging in and out of every social networking site on her list, she sighed. Sarah was still in virtual hiding, but no matter.

Having Sarah back in the cross hairs made Alex's life complete. Oh, to have seen the reaction on her face would have been priceless. She wondered if the poky little cottage in the middle of Hicksville was on the market yet. She clicked into Rightmove .com and added it to her favourites. It wouldn't be long.

She thanked God for this age of electronic access that prevented total anonymity. People could always be found, if one knew where to look. Dark corners didn't exist in cyberspace.

The doorbell sounded, prompting Alex to check her watch. She'd booked no other patients. Ruth would have been her only appointment of the day.

She opened the door to a male and female standing before her. The male smiled. Alex didn't smile back. Damn it, this was exactly what she'd hoped to avoid.

"Doctor Thorne, my name is DS Bryant and this is DI Stone. May we come in?"

Alex's hand tightened on the doorknob as she checked his identification card. She looked from one to the other. "What's this about?"

"We won't take much of your time. We'd just like a word about one of your patients."

"Of course, come this way."

Alex led them into her consultation room. Once inside, she appraised them both quickly. The male she guessed to be mid- to late-forties, who clearly liked to keep fit but was fighting the inevitable paunch of middle age. His chestnut hair was greying at the temples but the haircut was efficient and professional. His face was open and friendly.

The woman's expression was moody and dark. Her hair was a short shock, the colour just this side of black. It was the eyes that almost took Alex's breath away. A dark intensity brooded within the unsmiling face and tight demeanour. From a distance it was only just possible to see the separation between the irises and the pupils.

She forced herself to look away and focus on the male, whose body language was like an open book.

"So, Detective Bryant how can I help you?"

"We believe that Ruth Willis is one of your patients?"

Alex had regained her composure at the surprise visit and with it, her control.

"I ask again, what is this about?" she responded, without offering confirmation or denial.

"Your patient is in police custody at the moment. She is under arrest for murder. Her parents have given us your name."

Alex's hand flew to her open mouth. It was a mannerism that she had practised in the mirror many times. It had taken a while to strike the balance between soap opera overkill and first year drama school, but as with every expression in her repertoire it had been observed, practised, honed, and perfected.

One of her earliest lessons had been the funeral of her paternal grandmother. She was five years old and stood between her parents on a grey October afternoon.

Alex had been transfixed at the raw emotion of the mourners. The old woman had smelled awful and had horrible, ugly spots all over her skin. Alex was pleased the old goat was gone.

Beside the grave, she had watched the mourners' expressions. The downcast eyes, the stoic withholding of emotion, the biting of the lips, and, most infuriatingly, the tears.

Alex stared and stared down at the coffin without blinking, fixing her gaze on the stem of a lily atop the casket. Sure enough, her eyes started to water. She recognised that the mourners with the most tears had trembling shoulders. She added that in and managed the two together.

She felt her father's hand squeeze her shoulder and although she didn't like the physical contact she had been pleased with what she'd learned and had used her new skills at every opportunity.

Now, Alex's database told her the correct response for her current situation was shock.

She gripped the edge of the desk for support. "No, I'm sorry. You must be mistaken."

"I'm afraid not. Miss Willis has admitted to the crime."

Of course she had, stupid bitch. "But...who...where?"

She noted that the male glanced at the female. A slight nod was the response, barely noticeable. The female's expression, Alex observed, had not changed once. She would be a formidable poker player.

"She stabbed a man named Allan Harris."

He said no more, knowing that she would immediately recognise the name.

Alex shook her head and lowered her gaze to the floor. "I'm sorry, but this is quite a lot to take in."

"Of course, Doctor. Please take a moment."

Alex did take a minute, to organise her thoughts. How could she turn this meeting to her advantage? To start with, she needed more information. She looked at DS Bryant imploringly, doubt etching her features. "Are you able to tell me what happened?"

Bryant hesitated but didn't look to his superior before nodding. As she'd hoped, they had come to her for information and sought her co-operation.

"Miss Willis waited for the victim, either in or close to a dark alley, and then stabbed him with a kitchen knife. The first wound was most likely fatal."

There was more than one wound. Alex closed her eyes for a second, selecting a lighter shade of disbelief. "Oh my goodness, I still can't believe it."

Things hadn't gone exactly according to plan, but all she needed to measure her success was a face-to-face meeting with Ruth. She pushed her hair behind one ear with slightly trembling fingers. "I thought we had made such progress." She looked from one to the other. "Can I see her? She must be desperate."

"That won't be possible, Doctor," the female said definitely.

Damn, Alex thought. That would have solved all her problems. Given enough time she could probably have worked on DS Bryant, but DI Stone, clearly, was the boss. Alex would bet the BMW outside that the intense detective inspector had been responsible for the speedy apprehension of her subject.

"If we could just ask you a couple of questions?"

Alex returned her attention to the male. "Please feel free to ask any questions you like, however I will only answer the ones that I feel are ethically permissible."

She softened her words with just a hint of a smile, meant solely for him.

The detective took out his notebook. "Can you tell us how long Miss Willis has been a patient of yours?"

"Ruth has been coming to me for about three months."

The detective's forehead wrinkled. "Oh, that's quite some time after the rape. What made her seek help at that point?"

"Court order after a suicide attempt. Quite common for victims of rape."

"Was she using any prescription medication?"

Alex shook her head. She preferred her subjects clean. "No, she had been dosed by her GP for years on different antidepressants, which, at times, numbed the feelings, but they never worked for long and we removed her from that dependency together. I find other methods to be more effective in the treatment for victims of rape."

"Like what?"

"Cognitive Restructuring."

"And how did she react to that treatment?"

Alex shook her head. "I'm not going to give you specifics about my patient. That information is confidential, but I can tell you about the psychology of a rape victim, understood?"

DS Bryant nodded his acceptance. The female detective had lowered herself into the patient's chair and crossed her long legs. She appeared either totally relaxed or bored to death.

"You obviously know the details of this case, so you understand just how horrific this attack was. A rape victim can suffer many after-effects, primarily self-blame. A rape victim might think they deserved the attack either because their behaviour invited it or because there is something in their personality that attracted it. They may feel that they should have done something differently. A victim of rape will often blame themselves.

"Self-blame brings with it shame about the incident. Shame is more destructive than people can possibly imagine. Rape victims sometimes isolate themselves from their previous life, friends, family members, but most destructively, shame breeds anger and aggression."

Alex paused to give either of her visitors an opportunity to ask her any questions.

"Shame has a special link to anger. When victims are shamed and angry they are motivated to seek revenge."

"Had Ruth accepted that it wasn't her fault?"

"Ruth was prepared to consider that it wasn't totally her fault."

Alex enjoyed speaking about a subject of which she was knowledgeable, but she was aware of DI Stone's attention travelling around the room; appraising the certificates, looking at the photograph that was just within her view.

"Can you tell me what the treatment might entail?"

"Cognitive Restructuring involves four steps. The first step is to identify problematic cognitions, known as automatic thoughts, which are dysfunctional or negative views of one's self, the world, or the future. Next is identifying the cognitive distortions in the automatic thoughts. What follows is a rational disputation of the automatic thoughts and finally developing a rational rebuttal to the automatic thoughts."

"Phew, sounds complicated."

Alex smiled, selecting charm as her weapon of choice. "Not really, I just threw in some big words to impress you. Simply put, it's a method of retraining the response of the mind to destructive thoughts."

There was no reaction from the woman but DS Bryant coloured slightly. "Was it helpful to her?"

It would have been if I'd actually used the technique, Alex thought. It would have helped her come to terms with the attack and move on with her life, but for Alex that would have been self-defeating.

"I thought she was responding well to it."

Alex's attention was drawn to the female detective who was checking something on her mobile phone. The woman did not have the decency to listen while she was being generous with her expertise.

"Is there anything in that method of treatment that could have had any impact on Ruth doing what she did?"

Alex shook her head. "The treatment focuses on the thoughts of the victim and trying to change those patterns rather than on the attack itself."

"Did she say anything to give you any indication of her intentions?"

Alex decided she'd given enough free information. If they wanted any more they could go and study for ten years or pay for her knowledge. "I'm afraid I can't share any of the details of what was discussed in our sessions."

"But this is a murder enquiry."

"And you have a confession, therefore I'm not obstructing your investigation into the crime."

Bryant smiled at her, acknowledging the point.

She smiled back. "And, one last thing. If I contacted you every time one of my patients explored a fantasy, people would begin to talk."

Bryant cleared his throat. Yes, now she was having fun. Men were so much easier to manipulate; such simple, vain creatures.

Alex lowered her voice to little more than a whisper, as though there was only the two of them in the room. So far, this had been a one-way relationship and Alex now wanted payment for her services. "Can you just tell me how the poor girl is doing?"

Bryant hesitated. "Not too well, I'm afraid. It seems that the victim was sorry for what he'd done."

Alex steeled herself for what was to come.

"Oh no, that must be terrible for her."

Bryant nodded. "She's wracked by guilt. It seems she'd never considered that possibility. In her mind he was still the monster that raped her, not a man who was remorseful and sorry for what he did, and now she's taken his life."

Rage burned through Alex's veins. If she'd been alone, ornaments would have flown and furniture would have travelled. The fucking stupid woman felt guilty for killing the bastard. She actually felt remorse for snuffing the life of a fucking monster who had brutally raped and beaten her and left her for dead.

Alex hid her anger behind a benign smile. Ruth had let her down badly. She'd had high hopes for that subject and she'd ended up being pathetically feeble-minded. Alex wanted her here right now so she could gladly wring her neck.

"Doctor, we'd like to know a bit more about Ruth's state of mind at the time of the attack."

So here it was, the reason for the visit and for the delay on a criminal charge. The detectives were carrying out background checks in case the defence tried to plead insanity. They didn't want a murder charge that wouldn't stick.

"That's really difficult to state. I wasn't with her on the night in question so..."

"But would you be prepared to testify in the defence of Ruth Willis that she was not of sound mind when carrying out the attack?"

"It would be foolish to assume that because she was seeing a psychiatrist she is insane"

"That didn't quite answer the question, Doctor."

Of course not, but she was building the tension and showing them that this was a difficult situation for her. Still, the female officer had not looked her way.

"That was the intention. You have to understand that I have known Ruth some time and have built up a rapport during our sessions. She trusts me."

"But we have to understand her a little better before moving forward."

Alex understood that her next statement could change the course of Ruth's life. If her expert opinion was that Ruth was suffering diminished responsibility or some type of temporary psychosis, there was a good chance that the CPS would consider charging Ruth with manslaughter to ensure a conviction.

Whatever she said next could make the difference between a life sentence and five to eight years.

"No, I cannot in all good conscience testify that Ruth Willis is insane."

Boy, she hated it when people disappointed her.

She had their attention now. Both of them. Bryant in particular became more animated.

"Doctor, would you actually be willing to testify for the prosecution?"

Alex remained silent for a couple of minutes, appearing to torture herself between loyalty to her patient and good, honest civic duty.

She let out a long breath. "Only if absolutely necessary."

There you go, Ruth. Payback's a bitch.

Bryant shot a look at his superior before extending his hand. "Thank you for your time, Doctor Thorne. You've been a tremendous help."

Alex nodded silently, still dealing with the internal struggle.

Bryant headed towards the door and the detective inspector followed. She stopped at the doorway and turned. The female detective spoke for only the second time. Her voice was low, smooth and confident.

"Just one last thing, Doctor Thorne. I'm a little surprised that with your training, your years in practice and the length of time spent with your client, you couldn't see this coming."

Alex met the woman's unflinching gaze and saw a coldness there that sent a frisson of excitement along her spine. Their eyes locked for a few seconds before the detective shrugged and headed out of the room.

Alex stared at the closed door. Although the anger still ran red hot through her veins it was tempered with intrigue. One thing she never shied away from was a challenge.

As a plan began to form in her head, Alex smiled. When one door closed, another one opened.

TWENTY-ONE

Shane Price stood back as the door opened. A man and woman left and got into a Golf.

Despite his rage, Shane's heart quickened slightly as he caught a brief glimpse of her closing the door. His anger paused as he contemplated her perfection.

Emotion erupted within him. He hated her, he loved her, he needed her.

It wasn't a sexual desire within him. He felt no sexual desire for anyone. His ability for that had been destroyed years ago.

What he craved was her perfection, her purity. She was so clean. He knew from their time together that her hair smelled of coconut and that she used a jasmine-scented body wash. Her nails were free of polish but manicured and tidy. Her clothes were fresh and crisp.

His own clothes were the ones he'd been wearing when he'd left Hardwick House in the middle of the night. The light blue jeans were stiff with dirt. The knees caked in grime from "working" behind the derelict bingo hall in Cradley Heath. Each time he'd accepted only a fiver as payment; just enough to eat.

It wasn't the dirt on the outside that bothered him. It was the filth on the inside. Every cell of his body was soiled with his past. Shane often visualised removing each body part one at a time and washing it in hot soapy water. If he scrubbed hard enough he could put them all back, shiny and new.

But Alex had taken that hope away from him. He would never be free of the memories of his uncle's organ throbbing inside him. Or the sickness he felt when he recalled the soft caresses to his hair and the intimate murmurs of encouragement that had accompanied the acts. The whispered endearments had been worse than the rapes.

Shane felt the bile rise in his throat as the memories engulfed him. He lunged into a side street and bent over. His hard-earned McDonald's hit the pavement.

The rage returned so forcefully he almost folded to the ground. Until his last meeting with Alex there had always been that tiny sliver of hope that he could be cleansed. That somehow, someone would eventually find a way to remove the grime.

But in that final conversation she had taken that dream away from him. She had taken everything, and now she had to pay.

Shane wiped the spittle from his mouth on the sleeve of his jacket. He already knew how he'd get in. A small bathroom window was slightly open at all times.

Shane knew he would get through the small gap. As a child he had excelled at fitting himself into small spaces. To hide.

The next time she left the house he would gain access to her home, her safe place, and then he would wait.

TWENTY-TWO

"Oh, come on, Bryant. Why would she agree to testify against her own patient?" Kim asked, back in the squad room.

Bryant shrugged as he opened his lunchbox. He appraised the contents although they had never once changed: an apple, a ham and cheese sandwich, and an Actimel drink.

"Conscience."

Kim remained silent. Bryant, she guessed, had been taken in by the cool, attractive woman and the flirtatious smile, and even Kim had to concede that there was a certain allure to her persona, but a couple of things were not sitting well with her. They had visited the psychiatrist to get information and that's what they'd got, but Kim couldn't help the uneasy feeling that they'd come away with more than they'd asked for.

Kim also felt that her natural instinct for detecting emotion had been switched off the second they walked in the door. Perversely, despite her own emotional detachment she was perceptive to the emotions of other people and yet with Alex she had felt nothing.

"Jeez, Guv, what's your problem? She's answered our questions and agreed to testify. Happy Birthday to us."

"And you're not the least bit swayed by her looks and flirting?"

"Not at all." Bryant held a sandwich in one hand and a pen in the other. "Granted, she's a very attractive woman, a bit on the skinny side for me, but last I heard being gorgeous was not against the law. I mean, ultimately she knows what she's talking about. Those certificates didn't come out of Photoshop."

"I'm not saying she's a fraud…"

Bryant threw down his pen. "Then what are you saying, Guv? The doctor told us everything we wanted to hear. We know that Ruth Willis is not insane and CPS are going to be our best friends forever. This case could be tried in the River Severn and come out dry. It's watertight so I just don't see the problem."

Kim rubbed her chin. Everything he said was true, but it didn't stop the nibbling in her belly.

"And that crack on the way out, what was that about?" Bryant asked.

"Just an observation."

"She's a doctor, not God. How could she know what Ruth was going to do?"

Kim could feel Bryant's frustration as reflected in the state of his appearance. His jacket had been discarded, the tie knot loosened and the top button of his shirt undone.

Kim carried on. "She's a psychiatrist. She specialises in the workings of the mind. Don't you think she should have known it was a possibility?"

Bryant finished his first sandwich and wiped his mouth.

"No, I don't. We were asked to gather information for the charge. You were convinced it should be murder and everything we've done confirms that you were right, yet you still see darkness in everything, an ulterior motive if someone tries to help. The whole world is not calculating and evil, Guv." He let out a long sigh. "And on that note, I'm going to the canteen to get something to drink."

By the time he came back, things would be fine between them. They always were.

In the meantime she'd just satisfy herself with a Google search. She entered the doctor's full name into the search bar, which turned up twelve reports. She started at the top.

Ten minutes later she'd visited the website for Alexandra Thorne's practice, read about the articles she'd published, learned of her charity work, and been redirected to a couple of sites where she volunteered online counselling advice.

As Bryant re-entered the room with coffee, she realised he was right. Her search had turned up nothing. It was time to let it go.

For now.

TWENTY-THREE

Kim dismounted the bike and tried to leave Woody's words in the fabric of the helmet but they still rang in her ears. Under no circumstances was she to approach or talk to the Dunn girls. If her memory served her correctly, she had not agreed. Well, not explicitly. Therefore, realistically, no contract existed.

She hadn't even told Bryant where she was going. They'd had enough spats for one day.

Fordham House was a new facility built on the west side of Victoria Park in Tipton. Listed in the Doomsday Book as Tibintone, the area had been one of the most heavily industrialised towns in the Black Country. It had once been known as the "Venice of the Midlands" for its abundance of canals. But, like many other local towns, the nineteen-eighties had seen the closure of many factories, and housing estates had been built in their place.

The entrance to Fordham House was an extended porch formed of glass and brick with a simple gold sign etched in black to name the property. Kim knew it catered for victims of sexual abuse pending an outcome of their future. The children here were either transferred into a long-term care home or returned to a parent or family member. It was transitional accommodation and the duration of each stay varied from a few days to a few months. Social Services would decide when or if the girls would be returned to their mother.

On entering the building Kim was instantly struck by the difference to other care facilities. The glass of the front porch welcomed all available light from outside.

Children's paintings were pinned to the noticeboard but had overflowed to the bare walls.

More glass at waist height displayed an office behind reception. A woman was bent over the lower drawer of a filing cabinet.

Kim pushed the red attention button that was the nose in a smiley face.

The woman jumped backwards from the cabinet and turned towards her.

Kim held her warrant card up to the glass.

She guessed the woman to be early thirties. Her hair may have started the shift in a tidy bun but appeared to have had a rough day. Her slim frame was clad in light blue jeans, a green T-shirt, and a cardigan that was falling off her left shoulder.

After checking the warrant card, the female stepped out of the office. A couple of door buzzes later, the woman stood before her.

"May I help you?"

"Detective Inspector Kim Stone. I'd like to speak to the Dunn girls."

"I'm Elaine, and I'm sorry but that's not possible."

The tone was not unpleasant but it was firm.

Kim had to remember that Bryant was not beside her with his endless supply of manners. She tried to think how he might handle this situation.

"I understand this may be a little unorthodox but I could really do with just a quick word...please."

Elaine shook her head. "I'm sorry but I can't allow you to..."

"Is there someone else I can speak to?" Kim asked, cutting her off. Damn it, she had tried.

Elaine glanced into the office to where a man now sat.

She put two fingers of her right hand to her lips. He nodded in response to the smoking gesture.

"Come with me," Elaine said, heading towards the exit doors. Kim followed until they were around the side of the building and out of view.

Elaine took a pack of cigarettes and a lighter from the cardigan pocket. She put one to her mouth and lit it.

Kim leaned back against the wall. "Look, I know this is highly irregular but there's been a development in the case. I really need to speak to them... or even one of them."

"They are both very vulnerable. You're not trained..."

"Oh, come on, Elaine, help me out here. Don't force me to go through a process that will end with some snot-nosed, jobsworth psychologist telling me I can't speak to them."

Elaine smiled. "There's no process needed. *I* am that snot-nosed, jobsworth psychologist and I'm telling you right now that you can't speak to them."

Shit, Kim thought, that had worked well.

Kim decided to go with the only tactic she knew. Honesty.

"Okay, here it is. I don't think that Leonard Dunn was acting alone. I think there was someone else in that room during at least one of the films."

Elaine closed her eyes. "Ohhh... shit..."

"I want them, Elaine. I want to get whoever it is that, at least, spectated or, at worst, participated."

Elaine took another draw on the cigarette.

"Neither of the girls are volunteering a great deal of information as yet. I'm getting the occasional yes and no answer but the questions have to be properly phrased to get any response at all."

Yeah, Kim knew. Abusers found the victim's most vulnerable point and used it as a threat to maintain silence. The physical removal of the abuser did not remove the fear. Any threats that he had made would stay with them for a very long time.

Answering yes or no was not as bad as a full description. In a young, naive mind it was a way of avoiding the danger that came from telling the truth.

"So, can I speak to them?"

Elaine took one last draw on the smoke and shook her head emphatically.

"Unless you just got four years of training during my fag break the answer is still no."

"Jesus, didn't you hear..."

"I heard everything you said and I want anyone involved arrested as much as you do."

Kim took a look at her face and believed her. Her own job was bad enough but Elaine's was a whole new level. She was paid to tease and elicit information from damaged young minds. If she did her job well she was rewarded with the most horrific stories one could imagine. Some kind of prize that was.

For once Kim fought her natural instinct and kept quiet.

"I will talk to the girls and you may be present, but if you interact in any way, I'll end it. Clear?"

It wasn't ideal. Kim wanted to ask her own questions in her own way, but she got the feeling it was this or nothing.

"Okay, clear."

"Right, is there anything in particular that you want me to ask?"

Kim nodded and spoke without hesitation.

"Yes, I want to know if the other person in that room was their mother."

TWENTY-FOUR

Kim was pleased to see that the girls had been kept together. She suspected it would only be a matter of days until they were reunited with their mother. With Wendy Dunn having been cleared of any involvement, the decision to reunite the family would be imminent.

Although small, the room held two single beds separated by a bedside table. A small wardrobe and dressing table completed the furnishings. Kim found the room far less stark than the ones she had stayed in as a child. One simple word had driven every decision on furnishing and decoration: functional.

These white walls were decorated with a painting of red and green ivy that travelled around the room. The bedding and pillows were a mismatch of Disney characters.

The girls sat on the floor between the two beds, both dressed in onesies. Daisy was a Dalmatian and Louisa an owl. The air was permeated with the smell of soap and shampoo from their freshly washed hair.

Suddenly, Kim's heart ached. For a split second before she'd noticed them, Daisy's expression had been open-mouthed and joyful as she entertained her sister with a teddy bear in shorts.

But now the face was closed and Kim understood it. However horrendous Daisy's life had been, it had been familiar. And although fearful, she had known the people around her. There had been constants: her mother, her friends, her possessions. And now all of that had been replaced with strangers and constant questions continually returning her to the memories.

Kim hated that she was responsible for inflicting further pain.

"Hi girls, what are you playing?" Elaine asked, sitting on the floor.

Kim noted that she sat close to the girls but not too close. She made sure that there was less space between the two girls than between them and her, placing her firmly on the outside of their circle, without threat.

Kim stood in the doorway as Daisy's eyes gazed upon her.

"This lady is a friend of mine. Just pretend she's not here. She's not going to ask you any questions or do anything that makes you feel uncomfortable, okay?"

Daisy looked away, unconvinced, and Kim didn't blame her.

"Daisy, I just want to ask a couple of questions if that's okay."

Daisy glanced at her sister, who looked at everyone in the room.

"Sweetheart, I want you to think back to when you were downstairs."

Kim noticed the psychologist didn't name the room specifically or use any words that would force the child's memory. Daisy had the freedom to travel there herself.

The child blinked furiously but she offered no response. The teddy bear remained gripped in her hand.

"Sweetie, was there anyone else in the room?"

Daisy glanced at her sister but offered no response.

"Sweetie, did your mommy ever come down to the basement?"

Again the glance at her sister.

Shit, Kim realised, that had been the threat. The bastard had told her that if she ever told the truth something bad would happen to her sister. And she was still fearful of that now. An older sister protecting her sibling. Kim got it. She had been the older sister, only by a few minutes, but she would have protected Mikey with her life.

Kim felt the hope draining away. No wonder she wouldn't speak, and Kim would push it no further. She stepped forward to tap Elaine on the shoulder. It was over. She would not cause this girl any more pain.

As her hand hovered over Elaine's shoulder, Daisy turned and glared at her and Kim stopped dead.

Her eyes were beseeching, her mouth tense. Daisy was trying to tell her something.

She appraised the girl from head to toe and the simplicity of the truth stared her in the face.

Kim smiled at the girl and nodded her head. She got it.

Her words were gentle when she spoke. "Elaine, ask her again."

Elaine turned to look at her.

"Please."

Elaine turned back towards Daisy, who now stared straight ahead.

"Daisy, was your mummy ever in the basement?"

The teddy bear's head moved from side to side.

"Daisy, was there a man in the room with you and your dad?"

The teddy bear's head moved backwards and forwards.

"Daisy, was it a man that you knew?"

Kim held her breath.

The teddy bear said yes.

TWENTY-FIVE

Alex started the BMW as she saw the black Golf pull out of the side street that led onto the Wordsley Road. Her furtive observations had uncovered that the female detective was unmarried and without children. The fact that the woman was psychologically damaged she'd assessed during their first meeting, and although that information in itself was enough to pique her interest, she needed more.

The detective inspector was providing a welcome distraction while she waited for news on Barry. And she knew for sure it would come.

She allowed two cars to move out in front to put some distance between the two of them.

She had discovered all she needed to know about the detective's professional life. Kimberly Stone excelled at her job and had been promoted quickly. She had an inordinately high success rate with solving cases and despite her lack of social skills, was quite well respected.

What Alex needed was another clue and knowing the subject would not come to her voluntarily, yet, she was forced to be a little more creative. The only way to further this research was to follow the woman on a Saturday afternoon to establish what she did when she wasn't being a high-achieving detective inspector and that journey had currently landed her outside a florist in Old Hill.

Alex was intrigued when Kim exited the shop with a bouquet of lilies and carnations. The detective didn't strike her as the flower-giving type.

Alex eased into gear and remained a few cars behind as she followed the Golf over a couple of islands towards the outskirts of Rowley Regis.

The only two places of substance were a small hospital and the Powke Lane Cemetery. An accidental meeting was far easier to engineer in the latter.

As though bending to Alex's will, the Golf entered the cemetery at the entrance directly off the island. Alex took the earlier exit and headed up towards the hospital to put a little distance between herself and the detective.

She passed around the hospital car park and exited. As she drove slowly back down the road that ran alongside the cemetery, she located where the Golf was parked.

She stopped outside the gates and headed in, immediately spotting the figure clad in black walking up the hill. Alex appraised the area and chose a row of headstones that stood between where the detective was headed and where the Golf was parked. Perfect. The woman would have to pass Alex to return to her car.

She picked a gravestone and stood before it. The black marble was unfettered by flowers or ornaments, a good indication that she wouldn't be inconvenienced by actual grieving relatives.

She couldn't help the intrigue she felt for Kimberly Stone. There was a remoteness in those dark, vampiric eyes. Alex was often able to get a snapshot of a personality in a few seconds. She studied the minute details of non-verbal communication, which was lucky as the woman had barely spoken during their first meeting. She hadn't been able to deduce much, but someone so reserved had experienced trauma and pain, and that made the woman interesting.

Alex knew she would have to be at her most manipulative against the calculated intelligence she sensed in the detective but she also knew she'd win eventually. She always did.

The figure started moving, so Alex put her plan into action. Leaning down, she placed a small pebble inside her right shoe. She timed her exit from the row of gravestones and started limping up the hill, meeting the detective halfway. Alex took a gamble and kept her head down.

"Doctor Thorne?"

Alex raised her head and hesitated briefly, pretending to try to place the woman who had interrupted her deep thoughts.

"Detective Inspector, of course," she said, offering her hand.

The other woman shook her outstretched hand for the briefest of seconds.

"How is Ruth doing? Can I ask that?"

The detective burrowed her hands deep into the pockets of her jeans and Alex had the impression that the physical contact was being wiped away on the inner lining.

"She's been charged with murder, no bail."

Alex smiled sadly. "Yes, I heard that on the news. I meant, how is she?"

"Scared."

Alex realised this was going to be difficult. The woman was more closed than she'd expected. "You know, I've thought about what you said as you were leaving my office."

"And?"

No apology, no backtracking. No attempt to explain the harsh words or pretence that they had been misconstrued. She liked this woman's style.

Alex moved from one foot to the other, pained. She looked around and saw a bench ten feet away. "Could we sit for a moment?" she asked, hobbling towards it. "I twisted my ankle yesterday."

The detective followed and sat at the other end of the bench. Her body language screamed "get on with it," as Alex had suspected. People stayed longer if you got them sitting down. The reason every venue imaginable made room for a coffee shop.

"I went over some of my notes, searching for any clue I might have missed during our sessions. I looked for any indication of her intention, but there was nothing. Except..."

Alex hesitated, and for the first time she saw a flicker of interest. "Except, maybe I should have realised that she wasn't responding as quickly as she should have. She was making little effort to move forward, and although it's not a form of treatment that can be worked to a particular timescale, looking back, I think perhaps she was fighting the process a little."

"Oh."

Bloody hell, this woman was hard work. Alex tipped her head. "You think I failed, don't you?"

The detective said nothing.

"May I explain my position or is this matter completely closed to you?"

The woman shrugged and continued to look forward. The fact that the detective was not yet back in her car told Alex there was some residual curiosity. The woman was still sitting here for a reason.

"The mental health community doesn't view damaged psyches the way other people do. Take yourself; you think that someone like Ruth can enter therapy and be completely restored to normality in a specific, scheduled timescale: a rape victim takes four months, a bipolar sufferer ten months, a victim of sexual abuse two years. It's not a shopping list."

Alex looked for a reaction to the triggers she'd mentioned but saw none. Her trauma lay elsewhere.

"As a psychiatrist, I accept that people are broken. Psychologically, some of us are injured for a short period of time following a loss." She looked over at the gravestone of good old Arthur, and swallowed bravely. "And we find a way back, never to normality, but we mend as best we can."

"Who's over there?" the detective asked, without finesse or apology for the directness of the question.

Alex sighed deeply. "You saw the photos on my desk. My family, killed three years ago in a car crash." Alex's voice broke on the last few words. She could sense the woman's discomfort. She raised her head and stared forward. "Grief does strange things to you." Alex thought she saw a reaction and pressed on. Any response just whetted her appetite for more and she had plenty of heat-seeking missiles in her pocket. "I don't think one ever truly comes to terms with a loss."

The woman offered no encouragement but Alex persevered anyway.

"I lost a sister very young."

Aah, a noticeable bristle. Now they were getting somewhere. "We were very close almost best friends. There was only two years between us."

The lack of response or encouragement to carry on was infuriating. Alex decided she needed to give them something in common.

"After she drowned, my sleeping patterns changed drastically. I've never slept for more than three to four hours a night. I've been tested, examined, prodded, and monitored. For my trouble, I got a nice name for my condition but no cure."

Truthfully, Alex slept for seven hours solidly every night but the hours parked outside this woman's house indicated that the detective did not.

"I'm sorry. I shouldn't be talking like this. I'm sure you want to get back to your family."

The woman beside her shrugged. Still she hadn't engaged verbally and yet she remained on the bench.

Alex laughed ruefully and toyed nervously with the belt on her jacket. "Even psychiatrists sometimes need someone to talk to. Loss changes us all. I've learned to fill the long hours of the day productively. I write up notes, research, use the Internet, but sometimes it feels like the night will never end."

A slight nod. Every reaction, however small, told Alex something.

She noticed a small change in the demeanour of her companion. The body had turned slightly in on itself, like a sandwich left uncovered. It could have been an effort to protect herself against the biting wind, but Alex knew otherwise.

She decided on a no-lose gamble.

"May I ask who...?"

"Nice chatting, Doc. See you later."

Alex watched as the detective strode back to her car, got into the Golf, and sped out of the grounds.

She smiled as she removed the stone from her shoe and headed up the hill. The woman's actions in beating a hasty retreat were as significant as a lengthy conversation. Alex had learned plenty and was beginning to get the measure of her opponent.

Detective Inspector Kim Stone was socially inept. She lacked the manners that if not naturally present could easily be learned, if required. She was driven and intelligent. It was possible she had been sexually abused but she had definitely experienced tragedy and loss. She didn't enjoy physical contact and didn't care who knew it.

Alex reached the gravestone she'd been aiming for. She read the simple inscription and made no effort to hide her pleasure.

Solving any puzzle involved methodical, logical stages. First came the eagerness to get started, followed by an understanding of the enormity of the challenge ahead. Next comes the focused concentration required to make headway, the commitment to achieving the end goal.

Finally, the most exciting part: the point at which the next piece you fit will be instrumental in the completion of the entire puzzle.

Alex reread the information engraved gold on red and knew she'd found a key piece of the puzzle.

TWENTY-SIX

The doorbell sounded and Kim didn't have to ask who was at the door as she undid the chain.

"The Missus made too much lasagne." He shrugged. "She insisted."

Kim smiled. "The Missus" sent round a home-cooked meal every other week and was as charitable in nature as her husband.

Kim remembered some months earlier when Bryant had rescued a Staffordshire bull terrier and her pups from a flat on the notorious Hollytree estate. The puppies had been saved from a life of dog fighting and the mother from constant litters until her ultimate fate as bait in the dog ring.

The Bryant family had reared the pups and found them homes with family and friends, keeping the mother for themselves.

"So, what do you really want?" she asked, reaching for a second mug.

"Well, I've been thinking..."

She smacked her brow. "Bryant, I've told you about dangerous activity."

He narrowed his gaze. "Kim, did you just make a funny?"

She shrugged.

"I think you need to let the Ruth Willis case go. You seem obsessed with Doctor Thorne and it's not going to do you any good."

"Oh really, well guess who I bumped into today?" Kim was careful not to say where. For some reason the conversation she'd had earlier with the doctor had replayed itself in her head over and over but she was unsure why.

"Surprise me."

"Doctor Thorne. She asked how Ruth was."

Bryant shrugged. "As you would expect, I suppose."

"Hmmm…"

"What?"

"I don't know."

"What don't you know?"

"She had quite a lot to say."

"About Ruth?"

"Not really, more about herself."

"What sort of things?"

"That her family died, she doesn't sleep much, she has few friends…"

"Are you two best mates now?"

"There's just something…strange."

Bryant sniggered. "Rich, coming from you."

"Okay, forget it."

"I'm sorry, go on, strange how?"

Kim was trying to work that one out herself. Maybe if she used Bryant as a sounding board it would make sense to her and then she could forget it.

"The things she said, the way she said them. Statements about herself that seemed like she was trying to get something from me. Do you know what I mean?"

"No."

"Why would she tell me so much about herself?"

"Perhaps you caught her at a weak moment and she felt drawn to you."

Kim could concede that was possible. The conversation had taken place in the cemetery.

"Yeah, but I got the impression that the chat was for my benefit rather than hers."

"Did she ask you any questions, pry into your life?"

"Not directly, but..."

"Is it possible that she was feeling vulnerable or that she was simply trying to engage you in a conversation?"

"I suppose, but..."

"Look, Kim, people meet and chat. They talk about themselves and then you talk about yourself. It's called making an acquaintance. Truthfully, dogs have it easier. They simply sniff each other's..."

"Enough." Okay, she knew she wasn't good at making friends but she just knew when something didn't feel right.

"I'm serious. You might not know this but it's normally how people get to know each other. They converse. In some rare cases I've heard it said that they can eventually become friends."

Kim dismissed this. "There's something else."

"Of course there is."

"There's something about her that's not quite... real."

"How so?"

Kim searched her memory for an example. "Did you ever see that program, *Faking It*?"

"Where people were given a crash course in something like brain surgery and had to try and fool experts at the end of the show?"

Kim nodded. "It's like that. It's as though Alex is acting through the emotions. They're registering on her face but nowhere else. She takes them out one at a time and the pause in between is just blank. It's weird."

"Kim, I say this with respect as you are my boss and I'm the closest thing to a friend you've got..." Bryant paused, seeking permission to continue.

Her lack of response was her answer.

"...but I'm not too sure that you're the best judge of anyone's demonstration of emotional response."

Kim wasn't hurt by his words. Truth didn't upset her and she had to concede he had a point.

"Why is the conversation still bothering you?"

Kim thought for a moment. "I honestly don't know."

"Just let it go. You're never going to see her again so it has no impact on your life."

Bryant's reassurances hadn't worked. A niggle remained that she hadn't yet seen the last of Alexandra Thorne.

TWENTY-SEVEN

It was almost nine when Alex closed the front door behind her. The house was in total darkness.

She headed through the hallway into the kitchen. After leaving the cemetery she had nipped to Marks & Spencer and picked up a '96 Chateau Lascombes. She'd earned it.

Alex placed the bottle onto the marble worktop and paused. Something was not quite right. Immediately, she was hit by the smell. She looked around. An unpleasant odour filled the room. She took another sniff but couldn't identify any particular element. It was foul and it was all around her.

"Goodness, what died in here?" she muttered to herself, as she opened the six foot door to the combined fridge freezer.

The bottom tray held a half bag of mixed salad that she'd opened earlier in the day. There was no milk as she rarely used it and everything else was in sealed containers.

She swung the heavy door closed. Her heart jumped into her mouth as her eyes met with those of the figure stood right in front of her.

Stunned, she stepped backwards.

"Shane...wh— what the..."

Shane grabbed her upper arm to prevent her moving away from him. "Hello, Doctor. Have you missed me?"

Alex tried to slow her erratic breathing and get her bearings. Shane was here, in her house. How the fuck had that happened? Shane no longer even entered her thoughts.

His grip on her arm was firm, his eyes calm and controlled.

He towered above her by a good ten inches. He moved closer and the stench filled her nostrils. Nausea rolled around her stomach. It was a mixture of body odour, damp, and stale food.

She gagged but kept her lunch the right side of her throat.

She tried to pull free of his hand but it was strong and determined. "Shane, what the hell are you doing here?"

Alex wondered if the tremor in her voice was as clear to Shane as it was to her. She didn't know him well enough to gauge the full extent of his capabilities. But she had manipulated him once, could she do it again?

"I've come to punish you, Alex."

Alex swallowed. His expression was cold. He didn't look like the vulnerable little boy anymore. He looked like a man. A real one.

She said nothing. She had no clue what was running through his head. She needed to think of a strategy. If she could just reach her mobile phone…

As the thought occurred to her, Shane reached behind for her handbag with his free hand. He upturned it so the contents spilled onto the dining table, then took her phone and placed it in his pocket.

Shane used his grip to push her back against the kitchen counter. He loosed her arm and placed each hand to the side of her, trapping her in that position.

She considered her options. She could try and raise her knee and thrust it between his legs in the hope he would fall to the ground. That would give her enough time to get to the door, unlock the bolts and chain, and get out. Fantastic if it worked but not if she couldn't get enough force behind the action. She'd seen what he'd done to Malcolm and he'd killed his abusive uncle with his own bare hands.

She decided on a different approach.

She swallowed her fear and smiled at him flirtatiously. "I have missed you, Shane."

His head moved slowly back, his mouth forming a look of mild distaste.

Bad idea. She backtracked quickly and tried to look earnest. "I really have."

Shane shook his head. "You're a liar and a bitch. Before I met you I had a chance at a life. David gave me a roof over my head and those guys understood me. They were friends. And now I've lost them. I've lost everything because of you."

She tried to keep her breathing even. She opened her mouth.

"Don't speak," he instructed. "Everything that comes out of your mouth is fucking bullshit. You made me believe I could be normal. You convinced me that I could feel clean and whole and you knew all along that I couldn't."

Lines too deep for a twenty-three-year-old furrowed his brow. "And you used me to hurt Malcolm. I don't know why you did that but I hurt him real bad because of you. I think you damage people, Alex, and then walk away untouched, but not this time."

Alex's heart missed a beat. She couldn't even begin to imagine what he was going to do to her. In a physical fight he held all the cards, but the psychological playing field was a different battle altogether.

"I really trusted you, you know. I thought you were my friend and now I've lost everything because of you."

She tried not to flinch as his right hand reached up and touched her cheek. "So, clean, so beautiful, so perfect."

Shane's coarse skin against her own almost choked her but she kept her expression benign. There was a wistfulness in his face that she recognised from many of her patients. There was still something he wanted, craved.

She needed to reach out to the little boy. Her safety depended on it.

She took a gamble and lightly touched his left hand. His jaw tensed but he didn't remove his hand.

And, finally she had her strategy. She lowered her voice to a whisper. "I'm so glad you found me, Shane."

His eyes bored into hers.

She ploughed on, forcing the fear from her voice. "I've been looking so hard for you. I went back to the house early the next morning to see if you were okay and David told me you'd gone. I wanted to say sorry for being mean to you. I was just angry at what you'd done to Malcolm." She shook her head. "I thought we had a connection. I thought I could help you."

The brief shadow of indecision slowed her rapidly beating heart and she pushed on. "All those hours we spent together I thought we'd been making progress. I thought you believed in me, but when I saw the state of Malcolm it was as though our time together had meant nothing."

He shook his head slowly but his right hand fell to the side, away from her face.

"Come on, Shane. You felt it too. We had a friendship. I shouldn't have said what I said." She looked down and shook her head. "It was cruel and it wasn't even true."

"What wasn't true?"

"That I couldn't help you."

Total confusion now contorted his face. "But you said…"

"I know what I said, Shane. But I was wrong to say that. It was only because I was angry at you. Of course I can help you. That's why I walked the streets the following night looking for you."

"But…"

The balance had tipped. She moved out of his space and then turned, holding out her hand. She was back in control and this would end her way.

"Come with me and I'll start helping you now."

He stayed where he was.

The danger had passed. Enough confusion had been caused to distract his rage. The little boy had resurfaced.

Alex coaxed him forward and led him to the consultation room. "I'll put on the desk lamp, it's more comforting."

She reached to the side of her desk and switched it on. Another button sat to the right of it. She pushed it twice.

The room was bathed in a low, intimate glow. She led Shane to the patient's chair. He sat.

A few minutes; that's all it would take. Help was less than a mile away. She needed closure to this particular subject and the plan was now crystal in her mind.

She removed her jacket and placed it on the table between them. "Do you want me to start helping you, Shane?" she asked, gently.

He said nothing but simply stared at her.

"If you let me, I can make it all go away. We can start now and then in a little while I'll call David and you can go back to Hardwick House. Is that what you want?"

He looked doubtful. "Can I?"

She nodded emphatically. "Of course you can. You chose to leave. Your room is still there for you."

He looked at her disbelievingly. "You'd do that?"

She smiled reassuringly. "Shane, I would do anything to help you. You are my friend."

His face collapsed and his head dropped into his hands. "Oh, God, Alex. I'm so sorry for what I've done. I thought I hated you. I thought you hated me. I thought I was so dirty that you couldn't even stand to be near me."

"Don't be so silly," she said, as though he was five years old. "Now close your eyes and focus only on my voice."

He sat back in the chair and closed his eyes.

She rolled up the right sleeve of her blouse. Without taking her eyes from his firmly closed lids, she began pinching the skin on her forearm with her left hand.

"First of all, just relax and clear your mind. I'm going to help take some of the pain away."

His face relaxed and his jaws slackened. Alex smiled as she rolled up the sleeve on her left arm. She continued talking to Shane in a calm, soothing voice as she dug a fingernail into the skin as hard as she could. She traced a line to her wrist. It was a diagonal line with the skin broken in places. Already it looked worse than it actually was.

"You have to let your hatred go, Shane. I can help you put the past behind you. I can help to make you feel clean again."

And she could if she chose to, but as she looked at her watch, she saw that she really didn't have the time.

"What are you doing to your arms, Alex?"

Damn, she'd taken her eyes off him for one second to glance at her watch.

He looked from her face to her reddened, scratched arms. Realisation began to dawn in his eyes.

A knock sounded at the door. Alex had been prepared for that. The personal attack alarm beside her desk had been pressed once before and it had worked perfectly. Shane jumped to his feet and headed towards the door that led into the hallway.

"It's okay, Shane. Just ignore it, they'll go away."

She knew full well that they wouldn't.

Shane looked panicked. His gaze glued to her right arm.

Alex stood and positioned herself away from the door. "It's okay, they'll..."

The sound of her front door crashing in cut off her words.

Shane looked towards her, stunned and frightened. She ripped at her blouse, revealing her breasts. She shook her head to mess up her hair and pinched a red mark onto her cheek.

Two male police officers entered the room swiftly and took in the scene.

"He...he...tried to rape me," she cried before her legs gave way. She fell against the wall. The taller officer reached out to steady her.

Shane's gaze was darting between all three of them, no clue what had occurred. He really was pathetic. So easily fooled into believing she had any interest in helping him. He would never possess the skills to beat her.

"I didn't...I swear...I didn't..."

The tall officer was inspecting the damage to her arms. "Cuff him," he said, guiding her to a seat. Shane's eyes were fixed on her, his expression a picture of confusion.

Alex offered him a triumphant smile.

The realisation that he was headed straight back to prison registered on his face. He bucked against the handcuffs.

"No, please, I can't...you don't understand...please...I can't go back..."

Any type of violence from Shane after the crime he'd committed would unquestionably revoke his parole and she needed to know that this particular subject would never bother her again.

"Tell them, Alex," he cried as the tears coursed over his cheeks. "Tell them I didn't hurt you. Please, tell them I can't go back."

Alex rubbed at her forearms and looked away.

"Goodbye, Shane," she whispered as the tall police officer led Shane to the car.

TWENTY-EIGHT

As Kim shut the car door, she still wasn't sure why she'd come to this place. All she knew was that a face filled with uncertainty kept swimming before her eyes.

She walked through the double doors and stopped at a reception desk. A young girl with a shock of pink hair greeted her with a smile.

"May I help?"

Kim was unsure how to respond. "I'll just take a look."

The girl nodded and pointed to another set of double doors. Kim headed through and her senses were assaulted. The smell was a mixture of disinfectant, dog food, and faeces. A cacophony of barking erupted at the sound of a bell when she'd pushed the doors open.

The first cubicle held two Staffordshire bull terrier puppies; small, compact, and solid. Kim didn't stop. She passed a variety of sizes and breeds as she looked into each pen. The only other visitors were a young couple leaning down and cooing at a Jack Russell doing his best to impress. She carried on walking right down to the last cubicle: Siberia.

The dog lay in his basket. He raised his eyes but stayed where he was. Kim swore she saw a hint of recognition.

"Oh, that's Barney," said a voice behind her. She turned to find a portly middle-aged woman with tightly curled greying hair. The name badge told her she was being addressed by Pam. Underneath it said, "Volunteer."

Kim made no reply and realised that Barney didn't even have a name tag on his kennel.

"Poor thing," the woman sighed. "He doesn't even bother to get up and greet anyone. It's like he's given up."

Situated in Siberia, without a name tag, Kim couldn't help but wonder who had given up on whom. The woman carried on talking.

"We were lucky to get him rehomed last time; it's all but impossible now. He's a bit difficult."

"Why?" asked Kim, speaking for the first time.

"He doesn't like crowds." Check.

"He doesn't like kids." Check.

"But he likes lots of love and fuss." Well, two out of three wasn't bad.

"Poor thing. He was treated badly as a puppy, and 'cos he doesn't play well with kids or other dogs he's been brought back countless times. A few of his owners tried to make him better. One employed a dog whisperer to try and help him."

Kim raised one eyebrow. A bloody doggie shrink?

"Nothing worked. In eight years he's had as many homes. He's a bit weird, but people just try and make him better and then end up disappointed. No one just accepts him for..."

"I'll take him," Kim said, surprising herself as much as the chatterbox beside her.

Barney's head had lifted, as though echoing the portly woman's next statement.

"Are you sure?"

Kim nodded. "What now?"

"Err... if you follow me we'll go to reception and do the paperwork. I'm sure we can forego the home visit on this occasion."

Kim followed the way she'd come. She guessed they were eager for the kennel. Barney was the only dog with a pen to himself.

Two forms and a debit card payment later, Barney was sitting in the back of her car with, she would swear, a bemused expression on his face. She still had no idea why she'd gone to see him, let alone brought him home with her. Kim only knew that watching him being led away to uncertainty had stayed with her and the more she'd heard the volunteer speak about his social ineptness, the more the words had resonated within her. The offer of a new home had been out of her mouth before she could take it back.

The staff had been so surprised they'd loaded her car with his bed, toys, raw hide chews, and two weeks' supply of dog food. Kim thought they were so eager to be rid of him she could have pushed for a lifetime supply and they would have agreed.

"Okay, boy, we're here," she said, as she parked outside her house. He remained seated until she opened the car door and gripped his lead. She led him inside and removed the clip from his collar. Once the door was closed he covered every inch of the available floor space with his nose, his tail wagging.

Kim stood against the door. "Oh, Jesus, what have I done?"

The panic set in immediately. Her home had been invaded by another living creature. The enormity of her actions dawned on her. She was barely capable of taking care of her own basic needs, never mind anything else. She ate when she was hungry, she slept when her body dictated, and she very rarely sought exercise voluntarily.

She fought the instinct to bundle him back into the car and return him. She knew how that felt. She took a deep breath and moved forward, taking control.

"Okay, boy." Barney stopped what he was doing at the sound of her voice. "If this is gonna work we need some rules. Erm...I'm not sure what they are right now but the first one is absolutely no sofa, get it? There's laminate flooring, a rug, and your own bed. The sofa's mine."

Strangely, Kim felt better now that was understood. She walked around him to go into the kitchen. Barney continued his exploration but less fervently.

Coffee made, Kim sat and watched him wander around her space, his tail wagging contentedly. She took a moment to wonder what he was thinking. Was he really so easily transplanted or was he wary? Did he suspect that he was on nothing more than a holiday from the dog's home and that his return would be guaranteed?

Barney approached and sat beside the coffee table, looking at her. He turned his head and appraised her mug and then returned his gaze to her. She did nothing and he repeated the motion.

"Are you kidding me, dog?"

His tail swished the floor as she spoke.

She leaned forward and dipped her little finger into the cooling drink. His rough tongue lapped at the liquid and then he waited. Kim smiled; only she could get a dog that liked coffee as much as she did.

She poured a little of the liquid into his water bowl and cooled it with milk. His tongue slapped the bowl until it was bone dry. He raised his head, showing a creamy moustache.

Kim laughed. "No more. Dogs and coffee don't mix."

She took the rest of her drink back to the sofa. Barney seemed to get the message and lay close to her feet, almost touching.

She lay her head on the back of the sofa and closed her eyes. She had to make this work. As uncomfortable as it was having another living being sharing her space, *something* had driven her forward to the dog shelter. The idea of discarding him again made her feel sick.

Kim felt a movement on the sofa. She opened her eyes and found him sitting beside her. Still not touching.

"Barney, I told you..."

In a single move that channelled the speed and deftness of a ferret, he was in the crook of her arm.

Okay, it was time to show the dog how this relationship was going to work. There would be food, water, a couple of toys, a bone or two, late night walks, but certainly not this.

As she opened her mouth, he nudged closer, rested his head on her right breast and looked deep into her eyes. His own gaze full of questions.

Her hand found its way to the top of Barney's head, her fingers moving backwards and forwards in the smooth fur.

He sighed and closed his eyes and so did Kim. Yeah, she'd certainly shown him who was boss.

The rhythmic motion of stroking his soft fur lulled her into a state of relaxation.

Gradually the sensation of a small, warm body nestled against her evoked a memory so powerful, of another time, many years ago, of another small body beside her seeking protection and reassurance.

For the first time in twenty-eight years the tears escaped and rolled silently over her cheeks.

TWENTY-NINE

"Jesus, Kev, put it away," Stacey said, turning left out of the car park. "It's like your palm cor let it go."

Kev ignored her and continued to mess with his phone. "Fuck off, Stace."

A slow smile spread across his face before he expertly used two hands to text.

Stacey had offered her services as designated driver to the Dunn house. No way was she trusting Kev to drive in his permanently distracted state.

"If I had a dick, I'd name it Dawson," she observed.

"Stace, I don't know what you think you know, but whatever you think you know ain't your damn business anyway, got it?"

Stacey shrugged. She didn't get offended when he told her to butt out. In fact, she rarely got offended at all. She had an opinion and she wasn't afraid to use it.

"I know you'm heading for trouble, Sonny Jim."

"Since when did my private life become available for public consumption?"

"Since you hassled us all for advice the last time she caught ya."

Although his phone was on silent, she heard the soft vibration of a reply.

"I'm gonna keep talking until yer phone goes back in yer pocket."

"Is this your version of 'I've got a song that'll get on your nerves'?"

"Yeah, I like to call it, 'I've got an opinion that'll get in yer brain.'"

He sent another text message.

"You are so gonna get caught. It's a good job she don't work in our office."

"What are you talking about, Stace?" he asked, his fingers pausing above the keys.

"We all know you're putting it about, Kev. You're a cocky bastard at the best of times but normally you're a bit likeable to boot. But not right now. I don't really like yer at all. And you're getting on the Guv's last nerve."

Reluctantly, he put the phone away.

"Aah, network gone down, Kev?"

He stared ahead.

Stacey shook her head. Whether he realised it or not, he was more bothered about the boss finding out than his missus.

"Remind me again why we're going to the Dunn house," she asked.

"Scene of crime have finished the second sweep and the boss wants us to sign it off."

Stacey knew that the techs had been back searching for forensic evidence since it had been discovered there was a potential second person in the room while Dunn had been abusing his child.

"Now, I know it's your first time with forensics but you're not gonna embarrass me are you? I mean, it's not like a computer game. These are real people, yeah?"

"Oh, Kev, I think I preferred you messing with your phone," she said. Her addiction to the game World of Warcraft was a constant source of amusement to him.

"Park just here on the left," he said, undoing his seatbelt.

"I'm a detective, Kev. The big white van kinda gave it away."

"Smart-arse," he said, getting out of the car.

She locked the doors and followed him into the property. Her heart rate had increased just a little. He didn't know how accurate he was.

Since joining the team of detectives eighteen months earlier, Stacey's place had been in the office. The boss and Bryant tended to pair up. Dawson was often sent out on his own and she made friends with the computer.

For a short period she had resented it, but had eventually come to love the technological digging and searching for facts that would support the rest of her team.

And now the boss had thrown her a curveball and pushed her out of the safety zone. So, in some ways Dawson was right. She wasn't quite sure how to act and as much as it pained her she would have to follow his lead. For now.

There was no activity in the living area as they strode through the house. She took the steps down into the basement. Three white suits remained.

"All done, Trish?" Dawson asked the one in the middle.

Stacey would never have guessed the figure was a woman. She pulled the white hood back to reveal a shaved head and a tattoo of a rose behind the left ear.

"Trish, Stacey, Stacey, Trish," Dawson offered as an introduction. Trish offered her a brief smile. Stacey nodded in response.

Dawson faced the technician. "So, what did you find?"

Trish moved to the left. "The shadow in the footage was here," she said, standing by the wardrobe. "The camera was set up here, and the spotlamp was here."

Stacey followed the woman as she used herself as a prop around the room.

"So, given the mathematics and common sense, our subject would have been standing right there. Just where you are now, Stacey."

"Oh, shit," she cried, as though standing on hot coals.

Trish smiled in her direction. "It's okay, he's not there now."

Stacey felt the colour rush to her cheeks. She was thankful that her skin didn't show it.

"Pass me the light, Mo," Trish said to another tech.

The infrared lamp was placed in her outstretched hand like a scalpel in a theatre.

Mo immediately headed for the light switch and the room was plunged into total darkness. The blue light was aimed at the ground. Stacey knew the forensic light source was most successful at picking up body fluids: semen, vaginal fluids, and saliva, which were all naturally fluorescent. From her basic knowledge it could also locate latent fingerprints, hairs, fibres, and shoe prints.

Trish stepped forward and highlighted the area. A small puddle, invisible to the naked eye, was now obvious upon the concrete.

"Aww...shit," Kev said with disgust. The marking needed no further explanation.

Stacey stepped back and stumbled as the reality of her surroundings bore down on her. Yes, she'd seen photos. Yes, she'd seen footage. But she'd always been one step removed. Right now she was standing in a room where an eight-year-old girl had been stripped of her childhood forever. Daisy Dunn had stood in the middle of this space, terrified and alone, shivering, confused.

Stacey felt the tears prick her eyes. As the light came on she took two paces back and lowered herself onto the step.

A figure appeared above her. "First time?" Trish asked, quietly.

Stacey nodded, not trusting herself to speak.

"It's tough. But don't ever lose that connection. It's what helps you do your job."

"Thanks," Stacey said, swallowing the tears.

Trish touched her gently on the shoulder. "And anyway, I have a little present."

She took a small packet from the evidence tray on the desk. Bagged, taped, and neatly labelled.

"I have a single pubic hair."

THIRTY

"You know, Guv, you were pretty good up there," Bryant said, as they pulled away from Dudley County Court.

Kim shrugged off the compliment. Unlike some police officers, she never dreaded the inevitable court days. She'd never lied on the stand or even stretched the truth and so had nothing to fear.

The defence barrister had been Justin Higgs-Clayton, an officious terrier who had paid for his four-bed, three-bath, double-garage property by defending high-paying serious fraud cases.

She'd been handed the complaint almost twelve months earlier and had made a case against his client that would stick. The man in question had been registering false business credit cards to the AIDS charity for which he worked and had amassed a cool two hundred thousand.

This particular barrister knew when a case was strong and switched his focus to police procedure in an attempt to find a loophole that might get the case thrown out on a technicality.

"Did you have the PACE book in your back pocket?" Bryant asked her now.

The Police and Criminal Evidence Act of 1984 laid down every regulation and Code of Conduct for the Police Force.

"No, but I think he did."

"What's your bet?"

"It'll be guilty." Kim knew when she had done everything she possibly could to ensure that the lawbreaker went to jail.

Her puzzle was complete on the fraud case. The Dunn case, she wasn't so sure about.

"Pull in here," she said as they passed the Brewers Wharf Pub on the edge of the Waterfront complex. It was a collection of bars, restaurants, and offices built on the canal. The site had previously been the famous Round Oak Steelworks, employing 3,000 people at its peak and 1,200 at the time of its closure in 1982.

"What, you want a pint, Guv?"

"I'll have a coffee. Your shout."

Bryant groaned and parked the car. The pub was caught in the mid-afternoon lull between the lunchtime crowd and the after-work crew.

Kim took a seat by the window overlooking a black and white wrought-iron bridge that straddled the canal.

Bryant placed two coffees on the table. "You know, Guv. It just struck me that after all this time I've never once seen you take even a sip of alcohol."

"That's because I don't drink, Bryant."

He leaned forward, intrigued. "Not even an occasional glass of wine?"

She shook her head.

"A tipple at Christmas?"

She cut her eyes. He knew she hated Christmas.

"Okay, scrub that. So you've never tasted alcohol?"

"I didn't say that."

"So, you just didn't like the taste?"

"No, that's not it either. Now, just leave it."

He pulled his chair closer. "Oh no, I couldn't possibly. As soon as you want me to leave something it tells me there's something to leave."

Fantastic, she'd fallen into that one pretty well. "Actually, it was the second one. I didn't like the taste."

Bryant rubbed at his chin. "No, don't believe you."

"Leave it, Bryant." Sometimes he just wouldn't let go. Only he could push her like this.

"It could be that you refuse to make a fool out of yourself because your inhibitions would be shot to hell. You could be an alcoholic." He paused. "Are you an alcoholic?"

"No, I'm not."

"Then why don't you ever take one little drink?"

Kim turned to face him and forced him to look into her eyes. "Because if I started, I might never stop."

Shit, she hadn't meant to say that.

She turned back to the window. On the night that Mikey's headstone had been fitted she'd treated herself to a large bottle of vodka and a small bottle of Coke.

The resulting hangover brought with it the memory of alcohol-induced oblivion. For a few hours the pain and loss had been dissolved and her mind had been free of guilt and hate. Kim dared not visit that happy place again, for fear she might never come back.

"Chicken baguettes?" a male asked questioningly, holding two plates aloft.

Bryant nodded and thanked him.

"Bryant," she growled.

"You don't do breakfast and we've been in court for six hours so I know you haven't eaten."

"You really do have to stop mothering me."

"Well, start taking care of yourself and I won't have to. Now, what's on your mind?"

Kim watched as he took a bite of the crusty end of the baguette and followed suit, amazed at how their friendship worked. It was like an elastic band, at times stretched to its limit, taut with intensity, and then twang, right back into place.

"There's something still bugging me about the Ruth Willis case."

"No shit. Is this personal, Guv?"

"How so?"

"It was obvious that you didn't have a lot of time for Alex Thorne. You took an instant dislike to her, so is this just self-perpetuating your negative view of her?"

Kim had asked herself the same question, but Bryant was mistaken on one point. She didn't dislike the doctor. There hadn't been any emotional reaction at all.

"My gut is telling me something."

"Normally I have the greatest respect for your gut, but I think on this occasion it might be picking up white noise."

Kim opened her mouth to speak, but decided against it. She took another bite of the baguette as Bryant rested his back on the plate.

"Guv, I'm just dying to ask, is that a bloody dog hair on your jacket or what?"

The earlier conversation was closed. Kim knew that if she wanted to delve any deeper into what was troubling her about Doctor Thorne, she would be doing so on her own.

THIRTY-ONE

"Okay, kiddies, update on the Dunn case. Dawson?"

"Semen sample and pubic hair has gone for analysis. Still waiting on the results."

Kim nodded. Useful, but not until they had a suspect.

"So far I've spoken to most of his colleagues. Can't seem to pin down Leonard's manager, though. Last place of employment was a branch of a car spares chain in Kidderminster. I've been twice now and the bloke's never there."

Kim turned to Bryant. "Note it down."

Dawson continued. "Spoken to all of his family, and most of Wendy's. Nothing but disgust for Leonard Dunn. Her brother is fiercely protective and wouldn't allow me in the house. But he did make his feelings clear from the doorstep."

Kim turned to Bryant. He noted it down.

"Focus on the neighbours, Kev. I want to know everything about visitors to the house. Find the resident curtain twitcher and have yourself a cup of tea."

"Stace?" Kim asked.

"No new messages on Facebook since the arrest. Another nineteen folks have unfriended him and blocked his account. I'll go through the ones he's got left, to see if there's anything of use."

From the corner of her eye, Kim saw Dawson take his phone from his pocket and turn away from her.

Bryant coughed loudly and Stacey kicked the wood where the desks met between them.

Kim held up her hand to silence them both, crossed her arms across her chest... and waited.

The room had been silent for almost a full minute when Dawson turned back towards his colleagues.

"Are you with us, Dawson?" she asked.

With six unimpressed eyes gazing upon him, he coloured instantly.

"Sorry, Guv, it's the father-in-law. He's..."

"Kev, shut up. Don't embarrass yourself any further. Our next conversation will be very different. I will not warn you again. Clear?"

He nodded and stared ahead.

"Good, okay, everybody get to it."

Dawson was the first out of the door.

Kim remained seated where she was but tossed Bryant the keys to her car.

He looked at her and then Stacey.

"Ah. *Bryant, get yourself out of the room,*" he acknowledged to himself.

Kim smiled as he breezed past her.

"Stace, don't look so worried," Kim said with a smile, when just the two of them were left. "You've done nothing wrong."

And that was the truth. The DC very rarely did anything wrong.

"I need you to do something for me. Just to put my mind at rest. Can you do a little digging on the doctor?"

"Thorne, yer mean?"

Kim nodded. It wasn't an official request.

"Looking for anything in particular?"

Kim thought for a moment. "Yeah, I want to know how her little sister died."

THIRTY-TWO

Kim brought the Golf to a standstill in front of the car spares warehouse. Bryant visibly relaxed and checked himself for injury.

"Jeez, Guv, I hate it when your driving speed tries to keep pace with your brain."

"A little whiplash never hurt anyone," she said, getting out of the car before he could respond.

The entrance to the premises was a heavy, glass push-door that led into a small reception. The area was clean and tidy with a desk that rose to her midriff. A two-seater leather sofa sat to the right of the desk.

"Ugh...smell that," Bryant said.

It was a smell Kim recognised. Oil mixed with grease and a top note of lubricant. To her, it was delicious.

A man stepped through the doorway carrying a front brake assembly, then placed it on top of the reception desk.

Kim guessed him to be early forties, with a receding hairline that was trying to hide behind a short, spiky style that was better suited to a teenaged son. He wore a light blue shirt that was clean despite the environment. A badge marked "Brett—Manager" indicated they had found the elusive employee.

"May I help you?" he said, looking from one to the other. His customer-service-training smile was just a second later than the words, indicating he was working from a checklist in his mind. Greet. Smile.

Bryant showed his warrant card and introduced them both.

No longer needed, the smile disappeared. "Someone's already been here a couple of times and spoke to the lads. I don't know what I can tell you."

"Perhaps you could just tell us a bit about Leonard Dunn."

Asking the man an open question gave them the opportunity to assess him as he spoke freely.

"He came to us through a government scheme. We got paid to take him on. Started him in the stores but he was making too many mistakes."

"Were you required to keep him for a set period?" Kim asked.

There had been many back-to-work schemes initiated by the government to reduce unemployment figures. And they all did. For a while.

Brett smiled in her direction. "Yes, twelve months minimum, but it just wasn't working out."

"What did you do about it?" Bryant asked.

"Obviously, spoke to him. There wasn't any improvement, so we put him in a van."

"And?"

"I got two complaints about his attitude and one about his body odour."

Kim hid her smile. "What next?"

"I offered the government their money back."

"You tried for a refund?" Bryant asked.

Kim didn't normally like people being referred to as possessions but in the case of Leonard Dunn she was happy to make the exception.

"Any strange habits?" Bryant asked.

He shook his head. "He was overweight and could have showered a bit more but not particularly remarkable."

And not an obvious child abuser, Kim thought, knowing that there was no such thing.

If only they could be picked out by skull size, or by the distance between the eyes—once thought to be an indicator of criminality. All she'd need was a tape measure and a notepad and they'd all be behind bars.

"Did he have any friends here?" Kim asked.

"No, and I lost a few for putting him forward."

"For what?" Kim asked.

"The employment scheme," he said, irritably.

Bryant frowned on her behalf. "I thought the government put him forward."

"It was me that suggested it . . . after meeting him at a bloody book club."

Bryant cast a glance her way. She offered no response.

"Okay, Brett, thanks for your time."

Kim nodded in his direction and led the way back out the door.

Once back in the car, Kim's fingers tapped on the steering wheel.

"Well, that was a complete waste of time," Bryant grumbled.

"You think?"

"He gave us nothing."

"I disagree, Bryant," Kim said thoughtfully. "I think we might want to have a closer look at this book club."

THIRTY-THREE

Barry watched as his wife, daughter, and brother left the front garden and entered *his* house through a door frame constructed by *him* beneath a canopy *he* had designed.

He had only meant to look, catch a glimpse of Lisa and Amelia, to get a sign, a clue of their suffering, before making any kind of decision. But, standing here now, he knew that he could not go back. Who the hell did Adam think he was? It was his family, and his brother had no right trying to take them from him. Everything he loved was in that house and he was not prepared to let it go without a fight. He owed Lisa that much. Alex had been right.

Barry knocked on the door, mildly irritated that he was forced to seek permission to enter his own property, but that was about to change.

The door swung open and the face he had dreamt about for four years greeted him in horror.

For just a second, neither spoke.

"Barry, what are you doing here? You know…"

"I've come home, Lisa," he said, brushing past her.

He strode into the living room, leaving Lisa no choice but to close the door and follow him.

In Barry's mind the house had remained the same and the only difference was Adam in his place, but he now saw that was not the case. The room had less furniture than before. The corner sofa that had taken three years to pay for was gone. A three-seater and a two-seater lined the walls. In front of the TV, in prime position, *his* position, was a big empty space, ready for a wheelchair.

Barry briefly acknowledged that Lisa had needed to make short-term changes to accommodate Adam, but it wasn't permanent. It could be put back to how it had been before. Soon, he would have a job and would be able to refurnish the house.

The brick fire surround and gas fire had been replaced by an inbuilt electric screen, flush with the wall, displaying a fake flame.

Again, nothing that was irreversible.

"Who is it, darling?" Adam called from the kitchen.

As he entered the room, Barry was vaguely aware of the lowered work surfaces and kitchen units but his eyes rested immediately on the tangled mop of blonde curls of his daughter. He caught his breath. She was even more beautiful than he remembered.

A dash of fear passed through Adam's eyes but he placed a protective arm in front of Amelia.

Oh, that hurt. He was her father and she didn't need protecting from him.

A cold front moved into his brother's eyes. "What the hell are you doing here?"

"I'm here to see my family, of course," Barry answered, simply. He had no need to be hostile to his brother. Barry was about to take his life back and then Adam would be out in the cold. Adam deserved *his* sympathy.

"Amelia, go to your room."

She looked at the bowls and cake mix ready for use on the lowered counter. "But Daddy..."

Uncle, Barry thought but said nothing. It didn't matter. She would soon know who her father was.

"Amelia, please," Adam asked, gently.

She nodded and headed for the door.

Barry ruffled her soft hair as she passed by. She moved away from his touch. He understood that and didn't blame his child. She didn't know him. But she would.

"You're not supposed to be here. You know that."

His wife stood with her arms crossed in front of her.

He moved towards her. "Lisa, we have to talk."

She stepped back. "About what?"

"Us."

Barry heard the motorised wheelchair as Adam came in from the kitchen. That single sound confirmed that Alex had been right in encouraging him to come. Lisa could not possibly be happy.

He had built this prison for her and now he had to set her free.

"Barry, there is no us."

"Sweetheart, we can try again…"

"Don't call me that," Lisa snapped.

"It's time for you to go," Adam offered.

Barry turned to his brother. "This has nothing to do with you. It's between the two of us."

Adam reached for the phone to the right of the sofa. Barry turned and grabbed it, ripping the lead from the wall.

"Barry, for fuck's sake…"

"Is it too much to ask for a bit of privacy with my own wife?"

"She's not your…"

"We divorced, Barry, remember?" Lisa said, softly.

Barry turned back to her, phone still in hand. "And I understand that you had to do that, Lisa. I know what I did was wrong. I've paid the price for it."

Lisa looked sad, regretful. "Not in a million years have you paid the price for what you did to us."

"But we can be 'us' again. Just give me a chance to show…"

Lisa nodded towards Adam. "No, I meant *us*."

Barry moved towards her and gripped her upper arm. "You can't be imprisoned with him forever to compensate for what I did. You can't stay with the man out of guilt."

She winced and then shook off his touch. "Is that what you think?"

"Look at him," Barry spat. "He's a fucking cripple and I won't let you give up your life when you know we should be together."

"You fucking bastard," Adam raged.

"Stay out of it, you thieving wanker."

Lisa stepped out of his reach. The familiar smell of her was overwhelming. She only ever wore Eternity.

His wife stood beside his brother. Her voice was kind, sympathetic. "Barry, it's time to move on. There is no us anymore. You need to make another life for yourself."

The words were gentle, patient, in a tone usually reserved for persuading children to eat their vegetables.

He met her earnest gaze.

Suddenly, he turned and saw what he'd missed on entry. Photographs. Above the fireplace was a family photo. The angle had been cleverly positioned to disguise the wheelchair but the tuxedo and bouquet jumped out with the clarity of a 3D movie. As did Lisa's smile. He knew that smile.

He looked again.

Lisa stood beside Adam with her hand on his shoulder. There was no pain, no regret, no bowed head, no apology. Just fact.

Adam's hand found Lisa's and squeezed. A show of togetherness, unity. Lisa's other hand, the one with the gold band, rested on her stomach, protectively.

At that moment, Barry's world ended. All the hope Alex had given him died in his soul. His body felt like a shell, devoid of bone, muscle, or organs. There was nothing.

Alex had been wrong.

He looked at the two of them, side by side. His brother, who had everything that had once belonged to him: his house, his wife, his daughter. His crippled brother had taken his entire life away from him. Erased him. Barry could imagine them lying in bed at night, laughing at the feelings he still had for his ex-wife.

The familiar red mist cloaked his mind and he welcomed it back like an old friend. He had perfected techniques over the years to keep it away, or at best to control it. Right now, he embraced it.

Everything outside of these four walls dissolved into a vacuum. Right here, right now, was all there was. The holocaust had arrived and there was nothing else left.

Barry moved towards them slowly, offered his hand to Adam.

Barry saw the tension leave the upper body of his brother. Adam knew it was over. Barry knew it too. Adam raised his hand to accept the handshake.

With one fluid movement born out of having a ruthless trainer in the boxing ring, Barry's right hand pulled Adam from the chair and loosed him onto the ground. A well-placed kick to the temple rendered him unconscious.

"You fucking bastard," Barry spat.

Lisa managed one quick gasp before Barry's left hand grabbed her throat, silencing her. 'And you are a deceitful bitch."

He pushed her against the wall and gazed into her eyes. Like a drowning man, their whole life together played out in his mind.

Her eyes showed fear and hatred. Good.

His wife's terror fed the rage that filled every cell of his body. Every nerve ending in his fingers demanded satisfaction. They must both suffer what he had been made to endure.

His hands encircled flesh that he had caressed, kissed, bitten.

He spat in her face. "You cheating, disgusting whore. You did this to me."

He squeezed the soft skin, compressing the airway that gave her and her unborn baby life.

Her arms flailed as her lungs screamed out for air. Desperate.

He squeezed harder, his eyes burning into hers.

"B...arry..."

The sound of his name on her breath aimed straight for his heart. It was a sigh he remembered, but not like this.

The tears sprang to his eyes, blurring her already distorted features. His left hand released her throat as his right fist thundered against her temple.

"Fuck you, bitch..."

Damn it, he still loved her.

She coughed and spluttered, her hand clasped to her neck. "Ame— "

Even then Barry would have forgiven her anything; accepted her mistakes, until he saw her direction of travel.

Her nails dug into the carpet pile as she struggled to reach the inert form of her crippled, unconscious husband.

"You'll never see our child again," he said, kicking the back of her head.

Barry closed the lounge door behind him and shouted up the stairs. "It's okay, Amelia. You can come down now. Come on, come down to Daddy."

THIRTY-FOUR

The flat was situated on a snatch of land on the periphery of the Merry Hill shopping complex. The third-storey property was blessed with views of the entrance to the Food Court to the west and the busy Pedmore Road dual carriageway to the east.

Kim couldn't help her curiosity at the marketing strategy.

"Better than some blocks we've been in, eh?" Bryant said.

Anything without daubed obscenities and the smell of urine was a step up from most blocks of flats they visited.

Bryant knocked on the door and waited.

Kim heard the clatter of something hitting a wall and a curse.

A chain was pulled across and the door was opened by a man she barely recognised.

Chris Jenks was dressed in sludge-coloured tracksuit bottoms. A university T-shirt was stained to the right of the logo. His growing stubble was dark and dense.

His face registered surprise at their presence.

Bryant leaned forward. "May we..."

"Of course... of course..." Jenks said, stepping back and opening the door wide.

Kim stepped into a narrow hallway where two people couldn't pass without touching. The absence of a window was not helped by the dim light of an energy saving bulb. Two closed doors isolated the small space entirely.

Kim stepped carefully around the toys that appeared to be out of proportion with the size of the property. She headed towards a brightly lit room at the end of the tunnel which she guessed was the lounge.

"Please...sit down..." Jenks said, moving two colouring books and a box of felt pens.

Kim took the seat that had been cleared. Bryant took the other end of the sofa but shifted uncomfortably before removing a remote control from somewhere beneath him.

Jenks took the remote and remained standing.

"Can I get you anything...coffee...tea...?"

Kim shook her head.

"Is this about the hearing?" he asked, wringing his hands.

"No, there's something else," Bryant said.

They would have no involvement with the disciplinary hearing. Both Jenks and Whiley had been suspended pending a formal investigation and that was being handled by their superiors.

"You visited the home of Leonard Dunn for a domestic abuse complaint?" Bryant asked.

Jenks sat in the single chair but remained on the edge. He nodded, still holding the remote control.

"Yeah, just a couple of months ago. Why?"

Kim was happy to let Bryant lead. She glanced around the room.

It was a home that had been taken by surprise by the arrival of children. The pebble detail fire was now obscured by a mesh guard. Floor vases that probably used to adorn the fire display now looked cumbersome on a recessed bookshelf. A collection of books and music discs were now interspersed with Calpol bottles, a nappy bag pack, and two rattles.

"There was someone else involved in the abuse of the Dunn girls."

Jenks's mouth fell open as he looked from Bryant to her and back again.

Bryant continued. "We don't know the extent of the involvement yet, but we do know that another person was present during the filming of the abuse."

Jenks ran a hand through his hair and rubbed at his forehead. "Shit."

"We need to know if there's anything you picked up that night, anything at all that might help us find out who was there."

Jenks's eyes fell to the floor and he started to shake his head. "There's nothing. I mean, it was just routine . . . it was . . ."

"Tell us about the incident," Kim suggested.

He nodded. "We got the call about seven thirty-ish, complaint from a neighbour concerned about the noise. When we got there we could hear Dunn shouting from the gate. We knocked . . ."

"What was he shouting about?" Kim asked.

Jenks thought. "Couldn't make it out from the gate but I think it was something about a school teacher."

Kim nodded and motioned for him to continue. It must have been the teacher's first attempt at speaking to the parents about Daisy's behaviour. From Kim's recollection the woman had tried on three separate occasions before making the call. The resulting investigation had been carried out with the assistance of Social Services but had still taken almost two months until an arrest could be made.

"Dunn let us in. You could see he was still raging. Mrs. Dunn was on the phone at the time."

"Do you know who she was speaking to?"

Jenks nodded. "Robin something. Her brother, I think. Whiley shuffled Dunn through to the kitchen and I went into the lounge with Mrs. Dunn. I got her to hang up the phone and talk to me."

"What did she say?"

"Just that her husband was upset at the actions of an overzeal-ous teacher. She didn't elaborate further."

Textbook response so far. The officers had separated the parties to defuse the situation.

"Once we got there it all calmed down very quickly. I asked Mrs. Dunn if there'd been any violence and she insisted not. I asked if she wanted to make any complaint against her husband and she refused. She maintained it was just an argument that had got out of hand."

Kim recalled the witness statement of the teacher. Kim knew this must have been the first time she'd tried to speak to the Dunns. She'd had little opportunity to voice her concerns about the child before being asked to leave the house by Leonard Dunn, who must have been incensed by the woman bringing the girls home.

Jenks continued. "Whiley was having the same conversation in the other room with Leonard Dunn. We were there no more than fifteen minutes. Everything was quiet when we left."

"Were the girls there?"

For the first time Jenks looked pained as he nodded. "They were sat together on the sofa. Daisy had her arm around the little one."

She heard Bryant's phone vibrate in his pocket. He placed a hand over it. Her own signalled the receipt of a message. Damn it, her team knew where she was.

Bryant's sounded again. She tipped her head to the hallway.

Bryant left the room.

"So, is there anything else...?"

"You know, Marm. There's a picture in my head that I just can't shift," he said. His eyes were still fixed on a teddy bear in the middle of the room. "When I think back now, that girl just stared at me. Daisy. It was intense...like she was trying to tell me something. And I don't even know if I'm right or if I just imagined it because of what I know now."

For a second Kim was tempted to tell him he was right. She had been on the business end of that stare.

But Jenks was fighting for his job, his career, and his method of providing support for a young family. Paid suspension was no holiday. He had struck a suspect and there would be consequences. Kicking the shit out of him when he was down would not change anything. He already knew that he should have read the situation better and Kim could not advise him otherwise.

She heard Bryant curse from the hallway. He appeared in her peripheral vision and motioned for her to join him.

She nodded at Jenks and stood.

"What?"

"We gotta go."

"What the...?"

"Incident at the multi storey car park in Brierley Hill."

Kim took out her phone. What the hell was dispatch thinking, calling her and Bryant?

Bryant put a hand on hers. "Entire force is caught up on the demonstration in Dudley."

Recently, there had been many outbreaks of violence between the English Defence League and Islamic residents of Dudley, over plans to build a new mosque.

"Pretty bad. It's all over social media. Both sides calling supporters to join the riot. Seven injured so far."

Kim growled.

Bryant raised an eyebrow. "No offence, Guv, but ours is a potential suicide. Do you really think they'd send you if they had a choice?"

She turned to Jenks, who was now standing behind her.

"Okay, Jenks, we're gonna have to leave it there for now. If you do think..."

"I couldn't have stopped it, could I, Marm? I mean there's nothing I could have done, is there?"

Kim fired up the engine and overtook anything that got in her way, flashing her lights and hitting the horn. They made it to the edge of Brierley Hill in record time.

THIRTY-FIVE

"I'll drive," she said, rushing past him.

"On this occasion I was actually going to suggest it."

Kim fired up the engine and tore out of the station car park in a squad car. She overtook anything that got in her way, flashing her lights and hitting the horn, making it to the edge of Brierley Hill in record time.

"Get out the fucking way," she screamed at a black Range Rover whose female occupant was speaking into a mobile phone.

"I know you'd love to book her, Guv, but first things first, eh?"

Kim manoeuvred around the vehicle and parked at the cordon, currently manned by two uniformed police officers. A quick assessment told Kim they were the only presence on site.

The four-storey structure was no more than six months old and was part of a regeneration of the town in an effort to lure customers away from the free parking at the nearby shopping complex. Vehicle access was from the front but the cordon was set at the top of a service road that ran the length of the car park to the right.

Kim fought through the swelling crowd and ran along the darkened service road, stopping about halfway.

She looked up into the darkness, and thanks to one street light, could easily make out the figure who had stepped over the metal fencing on the top level of the car park and was hanging onto the barrier from the wrong side.

Bryant caught up with her. "Four PCSO's just turned up. Two are manning the entrance and two doing a second sweep to make sure the car park is evacuated. Eyewitness says he's been in this position for about twelve minutes now."

"Accurate?"

Bryant nodded. "Yeah, she's recording it on her mobile phone."

Of course she was. "Has he asked anyone for anything?"

Bryant shook his head but was prevented from speaking when a casually dressed male started shouting to them from the cordon. Great, just what they needed.

"Go see what that nutter wants."

Bryant ran over to the cordon as she considered any strategy that would just keep the man in place until a negotiator arrived. There were officers trained specifically to be able to talk potential jumpers down with the least amount of fuss. Kim knew if she opened her mouth he'd lose the will to live and drop immediately. She barely knew how to talk to people who weren't on the brink of suicide, so this was a no-go.

"Guv, this is David Hardwick, of Hardwick House. He knows this guy."

The male was two inches taller than her and appeared pensive and out of breath. "Long version or short?"

"Well, he's been up there for about fifteen minutes now, so I'd go for short."

Bryant touched her arm. "I'll go and give a quick briefing," he said, nodding towards the cordon. Two squad cars and an ambulance had just caught up with them.

"His name is Barry Grant. He called me about an hour ago to say that he wouldn't be coming back and to divide his stuff up. He said he didn't deserve to live after what he'd done."

"What's he done?"

The male shrugged. "I don't know, but one of the guys at the house recalled him mentioning this place as an ideal suicide point, so I headed down here to see if I could find him. I kept trying to call but his phone is switched off."

Kim looked up. "No point trying again, he can't really answer. What's his story?"

"He was released from prison a few months ago. He was jailed for GBH on his brother for having an affair with his wife. He put the guy in a wheelchair."

"Charming."

"He's an ex-boxer so he knows how to cause pain. He did his time without getting into any scrapes and seemed genuinely sorry for what he'd done. That's why we accepted him at Hardwick House."

Kim wasn't sure what Hardwick House was but she recognised the name from somewhere.

"Had he said anything about wanting to die?"

"Nothing. He'd been adapting well to life outside of prison. We were looking to get him back into a driving job and he seemed to have accepted that his previous life was over."

"So, what changed?"

David shook his head, bewildered.

Kim turned and saw Bryant heading towards her with another person.

"You have got to be bloody kidding me?" Kim said as her eyes fell on the familiar shape of Doctor Thorne.

The woman nodded towards her. "Detective Inspector."

"Doctor Thorne," Kim acknowledged.

Bryant shrugged and stood beside Kim as David started filling in the doctor.

"She says this guy called her. Apparently she does pro bono work for this shelter or halfway house or something."

"Really?" Kim asked, surprised.

Bryant nodded and shrugged.

Kim stepped away. Bryant followed. "Where are we?"

"Umm...negotiator is dealing with a situation the other side of Birmingham. Alcoholic with a knife won't let his wife out the house." Bryant looked at his watch. "Even if he left now, with the traffic, we're looking at forty minutes at least."

Yep, getting through the city centre at five thirty was not going to be easy. "Damn. Anything else?"

"Press is arriving. They're all busy interviewing witnesses, who are only too happy to share the story so far. The area is as sterile as it can be and there's a cleaning company on the way in case we need to clear him up."

Bryant did not say this callously. It was a fact of life that the man might fall or purposely drop at some point.

A quick assessment confirmed that the press and onlookers would get a great shot from the end of the road. And there would be an air of disappointment if it never occurred.

She glanced at the sea of eager faces at the cordon. She had briefly considered letting them stay where they were and if they were fortunate enough to witness the impact of his bones breaking like breadsticks they would have the pleasure of reliving it in their dreams for months. Only procedure stopped her from making that call.

"Bryant, we need a second cordon. Get those folks moved back around the corner."

Bryant took a few steps away from her, then bellowed the instruction to the growing swell of fluorescent jackets.

"Let me go and talk to him," Alex said, speaking to her for the first time.

"Have you been prescribing yourself stupid pills?"

Kim was sure Bryant could have offered a more professional response but she didn't have the time.

Alex looked around and smiled. "I couldn't help but overhear—you seem to be running out of options. I know Barry. He'll listen to me."

Kim ignored the doctor and turned away.

Bryant returned to her side. "We just need something to break his fall."

Kim nodded and then had an idea. She'd read a report recently of police officers hiring a bouncy castle and inflating it at the projected point of impact. Because he was on a ledge that ran the entire length of the car park he would only need to shuffle two feet along and miss the thing completely.

"Send some officers into the shops. Round up as many of those garden gazebos as they can find." She looked up at the height. "If we get enough we can line them up along the edge. It's not a high-rise building, so if he drops they might just reduce the impact."

"The difference between dead and not."

"Exactly."

Bryant issued the instruction over the radio to the officers at the cordon.

"Freud over there has offered to go and speak to him. She knows him and his background."

Bryant looked around. "Don't see that we've really got all that much choice, Guv. The clock's ticking."

Kim did not find the prospect appealing, but she was running out of viable options.

"Thorne isn't even registered with us, Bryant. Can you imagine what…"

"Right now I'm picturing you telling an inquest that you turned her away."

Just now and again, Bryant was just what she needed.

Kim turned around. "Doctor, you're going up and I'm coming with you."

"Detective Inspector, it would be better if…"

"Not a hope in hell, now come on."

Kim climbed over the railing and sped towards the column in the centre of the car park that held the lifts and stairs, Alex running alongside her. The power to the lifts had been switched off to prevent anyone accessing at the lower levels and getting to the top level. The PCSO stepped out of her way.

She headed for the stairs and took them two at a time. The doctor matched her easily.

"What's your strategy?" Kim asked.

"I don't have one yet. I don't even know what's prompted this, so I'll just have to see. Just don't speak. Whatever I say, don't speak."

Kim gritted her teeth. She didn't appreciate being told what to do at the best of times and accepting it from this woman was completely intolerable.

As they exited the lobby onto the open-air top level of the car park, Kim was hit by an icy wind that carried just a hint of sleet. She allowed the doctor to overtake her and head to where she could see the upper body of Barry Grant. He stood facing outwards from the car park, his feet on a ledge five inches wide with his arms behind him, holding on to the louvre-designed metal. Kim realised that it was only the muscles in his boxing arms keeping him in place.

"Hi Barry, how're you doing?" Alex asked, resting her arms on the fencing over which he'd climbed.

"Don't touch me."

Alex held her hands up. "I promise. But, look, if you'd wanted some time alone with me that badly, you only had to say and I could have arranged something."

Kim was surprised at the calm, sing-song quality of the doctor's voice. There was no tremor, no hint that this man's life could possibly be hanging, literally, within her control.

Kim took a moment to assess the physicality of the situation. The barrier over which he'd climbed reached up to his shoulder blades. Even if Kim tried to reach for him she wouldn't be able to gather enough strength to haul him back over something that was nearly as tall as she was. The best she could do was grab him and hope that she could hold on, but gravity would not be on her side.

"So, shall we talk about our day so far? I'd go first but it looks like yours has been more of a bitch than mine."

Still, Barry said nothing but continued to stare forward.

"Come on, Barry, don't tell me I've run up those stairs for nothing. At least tell me all about it before you jump. If the last vision I'm going to have of you is in pieces down there I'd like to at least know what's happened."

No response.

"I mean, look at me. Tatty old clothes, no make-up. I've never left the house for a man in this state before. Take a look."

Barry did as she said and Kim noted that the doctor had established eye contact, removing his gaze from the hard ground below. Clever.

"So, what's happened since we last spoke?"

He didn't answer but he didn't look away.

"Come on. Even in this situation I promise no shrink talk."

Barry smiled weakly and Kim guessed that was a private joke.

"I went to the house," he said, quietly, and Kim allowed herself to take a breath. At least he was speaking.

"Did you see them?"

Barry nodded and returned his gaze to the ground. "It's over."

"What did you see?"

"I saw her. She was tidying the front garden, just pulling out weeds and stuff. She looked so good. And then Amelia came out all wrapped up. She's such a beautiful child, so lovely. I watched from across the road for a while and there they were, my family. It was as though they were just waiting for me. I remembered what you said about…"

"You didn't do anything silly, did you, Barry?"

From the sketchy details she'd got from David, Kim was managing to keep up with the cast of characters, so she was guessing he'd gone to the house to try and win his family back. But nobody had mentioned a bloody child.

"I couldn't allow it to carry on, Alex. I've destroyed my family. Jesus, how could I have…"

Kim could hear the emotion in his voice as the rest of his words were carried away from her on the wind. Alex seemed to grip the railing harder. Kim sure hoped the doctor knew what she was doing. He looked far more precarious now than when they'd first arrived.

Kim heard movement behind her, knew without turning that it was uniformed officers arriving to offer back-up. Alex must have sensed it, as she turned and gave a slight shake of her head. Kim held out her hand to the approaching officers to tell them to stay crouched behind her.

The male was still on the ledge; so far it was okay.

Alex glanced in her direction. Kim tapped her lips, hoping that Alex would get that she needed to keep him talking.

"Barry, there's no need to feel guilty. Trying to take back your life is understandable."

Barry shook his head. "No, you don't understand. You don't know what I've done. They're gone."

The finality in his tone struck a chord of fear into Kim's bones. She quietly edged out of earshot and into the staircase lobby. She took out her mobile phone.

Bryant answered on the second ring. "Bryant, have you heard on the radio about any other incident going on close by?"

"Yeah, officers deployed from the riot to a house fire in Sedgley. One dead, one almost."

"Only two occupants?"

"Yeah, why?"

"I'm pretty sure that's going to be a murder and this is our guy. Check on the details and call me back. I'm guessing there should be a third."

Kim placed herself back into the eyeline of Alex. The doctor turned her head slightly to the side so that Barry still had her attention but she had Kim in her peripheral view.

Kim made the only sign she felt Alex would understand: a finger across the throat to indicate death was involved. If the doctor understood, she made no sign, but turned her head fully back to Barry.

The phone in Kim's pocket began to vibrate. She stepped back into the lobby.

"Definitely two, Guv,' Bryant confirmed.

"Then where the hell is the child?"

THIRTY-SIX

"What child?" Bryant asked.

"I'm in the top level lobby, come up."

Kim could hear his keys and loose change jangling as he made light work of the stairs.

"What's this about a kid?"

"Our guy out there went to see his ex-wife who is now married to his disabled brother to try and get her back. Didn't work out that way—but there is also a daughter that is biologically his."

"Jesus…"

"Get on to that David guy to see if he knows what type of car Barry's driving and the age of the kid. I'm gonna do a quick sweep of this level to see if there's anything obvious."

"You mean like a little girl sitting in a car on her own?"

Kim knew it was a long shot but she couldn't stand and do nothing. "Hey, I'm the damn pessimist in this relationship."

Kim exited the lobby and turned right, searching the area furthest away from the incident first. From her position she couldn't see a car matching the description in the area nearest to Barry. She had no wish to disturb the equilibrium between the doctor and the man on the ledge, but if she needed to get closer to search for a missing child, he could bloody jump.

She covered the entire right side in less than three minutes and reached the lobby. DI Evans stood beside Bryant, who was talking on the phone.

"Want me to conduct the search or take over here?" Evans asked. They were equal rank but she was here first. It was her scene.

"You take over here. I'll search."

He pointed to the two officers crouched on the other side of the glass. "I'll try and get Pinky and Perky closer under the cover of the wind. Two might have a chance of pulling him back over the railing. Think this doc is intelligent enough to understand some hand signals?"

"Oh yes, she's clever all right."

Bryant ended the call. "We're looking for a dark-coloured old Montego. Booted. Kid is four years old. Also, Guv, lady with the mobile phone almost had an accident as he was coming onto the car park. She says there was no kid in the car."

"Shit." Either the child was somewhere else or she was in the boot of the car, with a limited supply of oxygen. "Okay, pass the information down. They can take levels one and two, we'll take level three."

"David had Barry's sister, Lynda, on record as next of kin. She's here."

"Leave her where she is for now. We have nothing for her."

Kim headed down the stairs to the level beneath. Bryant caught up with her after relaying the information downstairs.

"I'll take right, you take left," she instructed.

Kim raced along the aisles, passing hatchback after hatchback. The eerie silence heightened her senses. The child was here somewhere. She knew it. In what state, she had no idea.

As she travelled along the rows she spotted a booted, dark-coloured vehicle in the corner. Her pace quickened. As she got closer she saw it was a Mondeo. But a new one. Shit, she thought she'd found it. There were few cars left on this level.

The car park doors burst open opened and four officers emerged. Two headed towards her and two went the other way.

"Other levels are only half full, Guv. Nothing," Bryant said, appearing beside her.

Damn it, she had to be here somewhere.

"Start at the lobby and check again," she instructed.

"Marm, over here," Hammond shouted.

Kim sprinted to the far right corner of the car park, in the shadows of the ascent ramp.

He stood beside a navy Montego on an X plate. Bingo.

"Hammond, give me options?" The officer could get into anything.

He took a lock-picking case from his pocket but ignored it and produced a mini hammer from the other. "Accuracy or speed?"

She nodded towards the hammer. "Stand back, everybody."

Two taps and the window smashed, raining crystal shards onto the driver's seat. Hammond reached inside and opened the door. Within seconds he had ripped off the steering column cover and hotwired the vehicle into life.

He glanced back at her. Kim nodded, and he pressed the button.

The boot lid swung open.

Kim looked into the eyes of a terrified little girl. Her tiny body trembled with fear, curled amongst the debris of a filthy car boot.

Kim let out a long breath. Frightened but alive. She'd take that.

Bryant moved forward. The child let out a whimper. The terror in her eyes moved up a gear.

"Back off, Bryant. I'll do it."

Kim stood over the boot, shielding the child's view of anything else around. "Hi sweetheart. My name's Kim, what's yours?"

The child was looking around her, eyes darting, trying to find something safe or familiar on which to anchor herself. Her cheeks were streaked with tear trails.

Kim turned to the two officers and Bryant. She motioned for them to move away. She dropped to her haunches so that her face was level with the girl's.

Kim smiled and softened her voice to a whisper. "Just look at me, sweetie. Everything is all right now. Nobody here is going to hurt you, okay?"

Kim kept eye contact with the child. Some terror left her eyes.

Reaching in, Kim removed a diesel-soaked rag from the child's hair. The girl didn't flinch but her eyes followed every movement.

"Sweetheart, Aunty Lynda is on her way up to get you. Now, you need to tell me if you're hurt." There were no visible signs of trauma but she had to be sure before she even thought about moving her.

There was a slight shake of the head; barely discernible from the trembling, but still communication.

"Good girl. Can you move all your fingers and toes? Can you wiggle them for me?"

Kim looked into the boot and saw all her extremities moving.

She resumed eye contact. The terror was fading. "Can you tell me your name, sweetie?"

"Amelia," she breathed.

"Well, Amelia, you are doing a great job. How old are you?"

"Four and a half."

At Amelia's age, the half was crucial.

"I thought you were at least six. Now, is it okay if I take you out of the car?" The sight of her lying there amongst oily tools and dirty sponges was offensive to Kim.

Amelia nodded slowly.

Kim reached in and gently placed her hands under the child's armpits and pulled the small body up and into her own. Amelia instinctively grasped her hands around the back of Kim's head, her legs encircled around her waist. Her head buried itself in Kim's neck.

"It's all right, Amelia. Everything is going to be okay," she soothed into the girl's hair. And she hoped she was right.

The girl's tears were wet against her neck. She wondered how much the child had heard.

Kim heard the lobby door unlock. Two police officers, the male from the halfway house and a blonde female, rushed towards her.

"Amelia, I have to go now."

Amelia held on with the muscles of a boa constrictor.

"It's all right, sweetie, Aunty Lynda is here."

Kim used all her might to extract the sticky four-year-old from her torso and into the waiting arms of the relative.

Kim stroked the blonde hair once.

"Detective Inspector, thank..."

Kim was already running across the car park. The entire search and rescue had taken less than eleven minutes but it felt like hours.

She took the stairs two at a time. DI Evans was crouched where she had been.

"Kid okay?" he whispered.

She nodded. "Lower level sorted?"

"Looks like a fucking garden party. There's about ten feet at one end not covered. My least useful officers are stood there. They should break his fall."

"What's the doc holding?"

"Business end of a safety harness. Nugent slid it up the doc's leg while she was talking. Reckon she knows what to do with it and is either waiting for an opportunity to slap it on him or there's nothing she can clip it to."

"What's attached to the other end?"

"Nugent's belt." Evans shrugged. "Either he'll stop the guy from falling or he'll go over with him."

"Correct procedure?" Kim questioned.

"Fucking gazebos?"

"Point taken."

Sometimes you just had to work with what you'd got. If you got it wrong you faced a disciplinary hearing, and if you got it right you were a hero.

Kim checked her watch. By her reckoning he'd been on the ledge for forty-five minutes. "He can't last much longer."

"I'll get back downstairs and serve tea and scones."

He backed away and Kim took his position. The increase in wind speed meant that she could only make out parts of the conversation between them.

"What good...jumping...Amelia?"

Kim could no longer hear Barry's response.

"Once...explain...judge...understand."

That would be a cold day in hell, Kim thought.

"You...Amelia...life...together." Suddenly there was a lull in the wind. The silence was broken by the clasp slipping from Alex's hand and landing on the ground.

Barry flinched, almost losing his grip on the railing. He tried to turn and look over the railing. "What was that? Who's there?"

"It's nothing, Barry," Alex soothed calmly. "I just dropped my mobile phone."

As Alex spoke she motioned for the two officers to retreat back to where Kim was crouched, holding her breath.

They looked to her for confirmation. She nodded. The sound had spooked Barry and he looked as though he could drop any second.

The two officers returned to their original position behind Kim.

Barry was still trying to negotiate his footing to turn on the ledge. Alex motioned for them to move back further.

Barry had now fully turned and faced Alex across the railing. If they hadn't moved he would have easily seen the three of them crouched ten feet away.

Kim seriously hoped the doctor knew what she was doing. Her skills were about to be tested and for now, she was on her own.

THIRTY-SEVEN

And now they stood face to face. Alex's second disappointment was up close and personal. Hardwick House really had turned into a pain in the ass. No sooner was Shane tucked up nicely in Featherstone, she now had another damn loser trying to get her attention.

Alex was aware that on three separate occasions she could have talked Barry back over the fence but she wasn't finished yet. She wanted answers.

Kim's position behind the wall was hidden from Barry, but Alex could still make eye contact with the detective if she needed to. Ultimately the woman was out of earshot and that's what she wanted. She didn't need any interference.

"They've found Amelia," she said.

Barry appeared confused. "But why has it taken so long? I told you straight away where she was."

Oh yes, he had, hadn't he? It must have slipped her mind. Of course he'd told her immediately but Alex had quite enjoyed watching them all chase their tails trying to find the little girl. She'd had information that Detective Inspector Stone had needed and had chosen not to share. Alex had never shared all that well.

"Well, they have her now." She couldn't really have cared less. "Is she okay?"

"Barry, I think you need to concentrate on yourself first. We'll talk about Amelia in a minute."

"I want to see her."

And there sailed by another opportunity to get him back over the ledge safely. She waved it goodbye.

This was the first opportunity she'd had to question a case study after the act. Ruth's pathetic confession had robbed her of that opportunity already. She'd exercised caution when Kim had been close by. It was important to her to gain the detective's respect. But now they were speaking privately, the collection of data was her top priority.

"How did you feel, Barry?"

He visibly paled. For Alex, the events that had unfolded were beyond her wildest dreams; the fact that her manipulations had been strong enough to incite such a high level of violence was an A plus for her. The perfect result would have been if the kid got it as well, and Barry hadn't caused this high-profile suicide drama, but she'd work with what she had.

"I don't remember doing it." He shook his head. "I knew what I'd done but I couldn't remember actually doing it. I remember dragging Amelia out of the house. She was crying so I panicked and put her in the boot of the car. Then I went back and set fire to the house. I just wanted to destroy all trace of what had happened. Jesus, I don't know what I was thinking."

His eyes met hers and in them she saw a ridiculous shadow of hope. "They are dead, aren't they?"

"Oh yes, Barry. They're dead." The detective inspector's sign hadn't confirmed who was dead but someone was. Alex preferred he have nothing to live for.

"So, what drove you to consider suicide? Was it just the fear of being caught and punished?"

Please say yes, she prayed. The fear of being caught was a concern only for the consequences of his actions. How it would affect him. Actual remorse was a different thing entirely.

He thought for a moment and she fought to hide her expectation. She felt like shaking the answer from his mouth. All she needed was one positive result.

He nodded and Alex almost reached over and kissed him. Barry had done it. He had proven her point. He had carried out a heinous crime and done so without guilt. The failures, the disappointments, had all been worth it.

Barry continued talking.

"At first, yeah. I was still panicking about what I'd done and couldn't bear the thought of ending up back inside. But once I got up here the memories started coming back to me. I could see Lisa's face, full of fear and hate, gasping for air."

A tear escaped from his left eye and travelled down his cheek. Others followed and within seconds he was crying like a big baby.

Repulsion coursed through her. For just one moment he had been her triumph. He had been the result she'd been searching for. Briefly he had proven her right but now the guilt was written into every feature on his face.

"Oh Barry, that's such a shame."

"I don't know how I could have done that to her. I love her. And Adam's my brother. How could I just leave them there to die? What kind of man am I to do this to people I love? Amelia will grow up without a mother because of me."

Alex hadn't quite meant that. Her disappointment was at his failure to perform but she let it go, along with her hopes of a positive result.

For the second time her research had been destroyed by her fucking nemesis: guilt.

Oh lord, how she abhorred disappointment.

"No, she won't, Barry."

"What?"

"Amelia won't grow up without a mother."

That ridiculous hope again widened his eyes. "You mean Lisa isn't..."

Alex shook her head. "I mean Amelia won't grow up at all. She died in the boot of the car. You killed your daughter too, Barry. They're all gone."

The words she spoke were soft and final.

A look of total despair shaped his features.

He looked into her eyes, searching for the truth. A slight nod gave him the answer and she allowed the coldness in her eyes to reflect the gravity of his actions.

He let go of the railing and fell to the ground.

"Barry, no," she cried, reaching for him. It was an empty gesture. She was glad he'd let go.

Kim ran towards her. "What the fuck happened?" she screamed looking over the railing.

Alex moved away from the edge of the car park and the sight below. She formed her expression into a state of shock.

Kim grabbed her arm roughly and turned her so they were face to face. Kim's body shook with rage. "Tell me, what the hell just happened?"

"Oh my God...oh my...I can't believe...oh Jesus..."

"What was he saying? Why did he jump?"

Alex wrung her trembling hands. "I don't know, I don't know what happened. I think he realised what he'd done and he couldn't live with it."

Alex could see the detective wasn't quite buying it.

"But he knew what he'd done. I heard him tell you what he'd done almost an hour ago. Why did he jump now?"

Alex summoned a few tears. "I don't know."

Kim opened her mouth but the sound of her mobile ringing stopped her.

"Yeah, Bryant?"

She listened for a couple of seconds and then looked over the railing. "You've got to be kidding. They worked?"

She listened to his response and then switched the phone off and put it back in her jacket pocket.

"Canopy broke his fall. He's not dead. Yet."

"Thank God," Alex breathed, while her mind screamed, Fuck. Fuck. Fuck.

Kim grabbed her by the arm. "You're coming with me. We both have questions to answer."

Alex allowed herself to be guided by the detective. Just this once.

THIRTY-EIGHT

Police constable Whiley's home was a three-bed semi-detached house built in the Fifties. A tidy porch jutted out from the property with a colourless dried flower arrangement as decoration.

The day had been dry and the front garden bore the sight and smell of the first grass cut of the year.

Kim suspected Mrs. Whiley was putting her husband's free time to good use. Training for his forthcoming retirement.

"Good to get out though, eh?" Bryant said, knocking on the door.

Kim nodded her agreement. The incident with Barry had produced a small forest of paperwork which had kept them busy for most of the day.

The door was opened by a woman dressed in navy cotton trousers and a sweatshirt. A few damp blades of grass clung to the hem of her slacks. Maybe she hadn't been training her husband after all.

Her face was round and pleasant, framed by a greying hazel bob that fell an inch below her ears.

"May I help you?"

"Detective Sergeant Bryant. Detective Inspector Stone. May we speak to your husband?"

Her expression altered slightly.

"He's on holiday."

Bryant didn't miss a beat.

"It's just a couple of questions to do with a case…"

"Barbara…let them in," Whiley's voice called from the end of the hallway.

Kim entered and headed towards Whiley's position at the back of the house. A second sitting room was positioned next to the galley kitchen. The room was small but uncluttered, a single chair facing the window with a matching two-seater separating the room from the kitchen.

She and Bryant both sat at the same time. It was a snug fit.

"You haven't told her you're on suspension?" Bryant asked as soon as Whiley closed the adjoining door.

Whiley shook his head and sat on the single seat. "No point. I don't want to worry her."

He removed his reading glasses and placed them on a small table to the left of his chair.

"Barbara's worked as a cleaner for forty-two years. She's counting the days until I retire. The mortgage is paid and my pension, together with a bit we've put aside, should see us okay."

"How long can you keep this story going?" Bryant asked.

"Dunno. I'm hoping the force will realise soon that it had nothing to do with me. It's not like I could have stopped him."

Kim marvelled at his calm demeanour. Whiley was far more concerned about the repercussions from his wife than the outcome of the disciplinary hearing.

Bryant sat forward as the door opened.

Barbara stepped inside. "Tea…coffee…?"

Bryant shook his head.

"White coffee, no sugar, please," Kim said. Whiley would want his wife occupied while this conversation took place.

She felt for this officer. He'd offered his whole working life to the police force and his retirement was in jeopardy because of the actions of someone else.

Barbara left the adjoining door open. Whiley stood to close it. A shadow passed the doorway.

"Ha, young lady, you're not going out like that," Whiley said, looking the figure up and down.

Kim craned her neck to see a girl about eighteen years of age coming down the stairs. Her skirt was tight and black and barely the width of a tea towel. Black stockings, a leather jacket and one earlobe enlarged by a central ring completed the look.

Kim had seen worse and from the murderous look of disgust the girl offered her father, so had she.

The girl said nothing to Whiley, mumbled something to her mother, and left through the front door.

Whiley sighed before closing the door and sitting in the single seat.

Kim marvelled at the knowledge that out there on the streets of the Black Country Whiley commanded respect and obedience. As an officer of the law, he was a figure of immediate authority. In his own home he lied to his wife and had no control over his daughter.

"So, we need to know more about the night you visited the Dunn house," Kim said, moving the conversation along.

He wrinkled his nose. "Nothing to tell, really. Just a routine domestic."

Kim waited for more. Nothing came.

"There was someone else involved and we need…"

"What do you mean by someone else?" Whiley asked, sitting forward.

"In the basement. When Dunn abused Daisy."

He let out a whistle. "Jeesus."

Bryant slid forward on the sofa. "If you could just talk us through the night two months ago when you visited the Dunn household. We've already spoken to Jenks. He told us they'd been arguing about some teacher. Can you tell us any more?"

Whiley looked up to the ceiling as Barbara entered with a mug of coffee for Kim. She nodded her thanks before Barbara exited the room and closed the door.

"We got the call at tea time or thereabouts. Jenks was driving. He knew where it was and got us there within a few minutes. I know Dunn was still shouting when we arrived."

"Did you take him into the kitchen?"

"Yeah, normal practice," he said, defensively.

"Of course," Bryant said. "Did he say anything while you were in there?"

"Just raging about this teacher who'd tried to say something wasn't right with Daisy. I could empathise with the bloke. We were told our Laura had learning difficulties and it was a load of rubbish. Some of these teachers get a bit too involved in people's business. So, I just calmed him down, told him I agreed with him."

"Jenks said Mrs. Dunn was on the phone when you arrived?" Bryant asked.

"Yeah, don't know who she was talking to. Jenks dealt with her and the kids until I brought Dunn back into the room."

"Jenks mentioned a look from Daisy. He said he thought she was trying to tell him something. Did you notice anything?"

Whiley rolled his eyes. "He's imagining it. I was the one who sent them off to bed and I didn't see any look." He smiled, indulgently. "He's a kid, thinks he sees things everywhere. The girls were a bit nervous 'cos of the shouting but nothing out of the ordinary."

Kim stood. They were learning nothing.

Bryant followed suit. "Well, if anything else comes to mind…"

"You know, I've just remembered something. The reason Dunn was so agitated. It was 'cos the teacher had come to the house. Yeah, that was it. He was angry 'cos the teacher had brought the girls home."

Once outside, Kim turned to Bryant.

"Dawson interviewed the teacher during the investigation, right?"

"Of course."

"Well, I think she's worth another shot," Kim said, feeling her spirits lift.

They had learned something, after all.

Kim already knew that Wendy was not the person in the basement but if the teacher had managed to voice her concerns on that first visit, had the woman covered for her husband? And if so, did she know the identity of the person who was in the room?

It was a question that needed to be answered.

THIRTY-NINE

Kim parked the car and sat for a moment, bracing herself against the wind that rocked her vehicle from side to side.

From her first day of training, Kim had firmly believed that people should pay for crimes they committed. During her career, any unsolved case was like an open wound in her skin. She didn't believe in extenuating circumstances. It was black and white; you pay for what you do.

She knew that Bryant thought she was crazy for suspecting Doctor Thorne of any involvement in the murder of Allan Harris, and in part she had to agree with him, but the events with Barry Grant would not compute in her mind.

For herself there would be no enquiry, as it was felt she had taken all "reasonably practicable steps to ensure a positive outcome." Basically, the idea of erecting garden gazebos had saved both her ass and Barry's. Finding Amelia hadn't hurt her case either.

The doctor had scored brownie points for having skilfully kept Barry on the ledge long enough for the gazebos to be snapped into place.

Objectively Kim could understand that. But she'd been up there as well and towards the end of the conversation between Barry and the doctor, he had been talkative, animated. That didn't seem to be the demeanour of a person about to end their own life. She'd been to other jumpers and every minute mattered. She'd never seen one who had bothered to hang around for almost an hour and still jump.

She turned to the dog in the rear seat. "Okay, Barney, this is it. Bark once if you see anyone coming."

She got out of the car, climbed over the metal gate, and entered the cemetery. As she walked up the hill any illumination from the street lights faded. She kept to the path until she reached the bench on which she'd sat with Alex a week earlier. They had walked up a few steps, so Kim started her search there. She took the torch from her pocket and moved along the rows of gravestones, saddened by the lives cut short.

She travelled to the very bottom of the hill and back up again, more slowly, making sure. When she arrived back at the row that was level with the bench, she knew there was no grave marker that was less than ten years old and certainly no resting place of a male and two boys.

She blew a kiss to the top of the hill towards the grave of her brother.

FORTY

The appeal of the Cotswolds was lost on Alex. Labelled an "area of outstanding beauty," she had substituted the last word to boredom after passing through one sleepy village after another. Her journey had ended at Bourton-on-the-Water. Alex remembered reading that the area was rich in fossils. And most of them appeared to still live here, she thought, as she glanced around the village hub.

Stone buildings lined each side of the street, all individually owned shops that had probably been trading for two hundred years. Her brief appraisal confirmed there was no chain store in sight, not even a Costa or Starbucks. For Alex, that said it all. How the hell did these people survive?

If nothing else, the fifty-mile journey had been successful in cleansing her of the disappointment of Barry Grant. Initially, her expectations had been exceeded at the news he'd tried to murder his beloved wife and his brother.

For a few moments, standing on the top of that car park in the biting wind, Alex had felt he could be the one. A true sociopath could never find a sense of moral responsibility; could never defy their innate nature and feel guilt. But her experiment required only one success. One person to defy their true nature and, momentarily, Barry had been her triumph.

And then he'd opened his mouth again.

His pathetic bellyaching about "red mist" and the overwhelming guilt he felt had tempted her to push him forward herself. Luckily, Alex's lie about his daughter had been enough to provoke the desired action.

She had been surprised that he'd lived through the fall, but only just. He was hooked up to life support, being kept alive by machines. And, although he wasn't dead, he wasn't far off. The physicians were not hopeful for any kind of recovery. Good enough.

Her disappointment in Barry was tempered with her excitement about Kim. The detective was a tantalising project into which she was compelled to delve deeper. It was her interest in Kim which had brought her to this godforsaken backwater.

Alex headed over to the designated meeting place, an establishment that offered an entire day's sustenance: breakfast, brunch, lunch, afternoon tea, coffee, and she would imagine, for them, the exotic new inventions of cappuccinos and paninis.

She entered through a waist-high gate and noted that the only table occupied outside was by a portly male, completely bald but for a skirt of hair that travelled the back of his head from ear to ear. He wore glasses on the tip of his nose and appeared transfixed by the Kindle he was holding. In his left hand was a cigarette, explaining his residency outside.

Alex felt he was a safe bet and approached the table. "Henry Reed?"

The male looked up and smiled. He stood and offered his hand. "Doctor Thorne?"

She smiled in response.

He sat back down. "I hope you don't mind if we talk out here. I am hopelessly addicted to the drug nicotine, which now makes me a social outcast."

Alex did mind. Although the winds were tempered with the odd ray of sunshine, it was still bitterly cold. However, she wanted something from this man so she'd play along.

"Of course. May I get you another drink?"

"A latte, thank you."

Alex headed inside and ordered two lattes. She paid, and was told the drinks would be brought out. She took a seat as her companion placed his reading device on the table.

"Dickens as an ebook, who would have thought it?"

Alex smiled, not caring one way or another.

"So, Doctor Thorne, how exactly can I be of assistance to you?"

Alex had decided flattery would work well in this situation. "I've been researching a particular subject and I came across your book, mentioned as a great insight into the field. Every review I read claimed that your book had broken ground at the time."

Only part of this was true. There were no reviews she could find. Alex had researched the name Michael Stone and learned a great deal from newspaper articles. A small piece on Wikipedia had stated that a young reporter had self-published a book depicting the events, but she had been unable to locate a copy anywhere. In the absence of the book, Alex had decided to approach the author. Press clippings were one thing but, twenty-eight years ago, the man before her had interviewed people close to the case whilst events were still fresh.

He appeared pleased with her words, and shrugged. "In my opinion, it was a story that needed to be told, although the reading public differed and the book sold a total of seven hundred copies."

Alex nodded as the waitress placed tall glass mugs on the wrought-iron table.

"So, how can I help you, Doctor?"

"Alex, please," she said, with a smile. She wanted to glean as much information from this man as she could. "I have a patient—

obviously I can't go into detail, but she has been subjected to a similar type of trauma recorded in your book and although it was written over twenty years ago, I think you may be able to help me."

"Of course, if there's anything at all I can do."

Alex noted that his ruddy cheeks had reddened more. Good, he was flattered.

"Where would you like me to start?"

"Wherever you're comfortable." Alex would steer him if he veered off the course she'd plotted.

"I was twenty-three at the time, working for the *Express and Star* local office in Dudley. On Sunday second of June I was writing about the tombola winner at a school fete in Netherton and the following day I was covering the most horrific case of child neglect the Black Country had ever seen. Two days later the story had been knocked off the news cycle by a factory fire in Pensnett that had claimed the lives of three firefighters "

"But you didn't move on so quickly?"

He shook his head. "I was young enough to be full of journalistic ideals. I thought there were many questions that needed to be answered. I wanted to know how it had been allowed to happen: who or what had been at fault. So, when I could, I would talk to neighbours, friends, and any social workers that would speak to me. I gathered statements from psychiatrists and put the whole story together.

"The trial wasn't sensational and got little press attention, after which no one seemed particularly interested. There was no public outcry for an inquiry and that suited the authorities just fine. I realised that all the material I'd collated could fill a book. No publisher was interested and so I self-published the story."

Alex felt she'd been indulgent enough. "Could you tell me about the case?"

He finished his drink and began to speak again.

"Patricia Stone was a troubled child. Her father was of Romany descent and took a Gorja wife. By the time Patty was five her father had abandoned the family and returned to the Gypsy fold. At the age of seventeen Patty was committed to an asylum near Bromsgrove due to randomly hitting people in the street. She was committed by her mother, who simply left her there, relieved to have one less mouth to feed. When the doctors finally got round to her, she was diagnosed with schizophrenia. It took five years to stabilise her condition, finding the most effective cocktail of drugs. By this time, Patty was twenty-two.

"Shortly after her diagnosis, an unfortunate event occurred under the Thatcher regime. The Care in the Community initiative that had been floating around for about twenty years gathered speed. Many institutions were closed and some very sick people were discarded into a community that was ill-prepared to accept them."

Alex didn't speak. She was grateful to the regime. It ensured a never-ending supply of unbalanced minds; however, places such as the outdated asylums had proved their usefulness in providing captive subjects for research purposes.

As Arthur bemoaned the government strategy, she recalled an experiment carried out in such surroundings in 1950s America. Doctor Ewan Cameron had received CIA funds to research the theory of "depatterning." His aim had been to erase the minds and memories of individuals, reducing them to the level of an infant and then rebuilding their personality in a manner of his choosing. His methods had included drug-induced comas and high-voltage electric shocks. As many as 360 per person.

In addition, he had implemented "psychic driving" which entailed strapping the subject into a blacked-out helmet, for sensory deprivation, and playing a recorded message though the inbuilt speakers for sixteen hours per day, for up to one hundred days.

Although all of the subjects were permanently damaged by the research, Alex felt that such institutions had provided an invaluable service over the years.

Alex tuned back in to her companion, who was still wittering on.

"...that the benefit did not outweigh the cost. Some patients went on to live 'relatively' normal lives, whilst others went on to murder, rape, and commit acts of cruelty." He nodded towards her. "However that is a discussion for another time. Patty was released into the community, judged to be no danger to herself or anyone else. She was placed in a council flat in a high-rise building in Colley Gate and simply disappeared from the system.

"Every patient was *supposed to be* monitored, but case workers had no chance of evaluating everyone, and so the quieter, less troublesome patients fell through the cracks.

"Within a year, Patty was pregnant. No one ever knew who the father was. Patty was known as a bit of an oddball, 'the local loon,' if you like. There was a neighbour that took an interest in Patty and made sure nobody gave her too much trouble. She was the closest thing to a friend that Patty had, her only visitor when she gave birth to twins.

"She had a boy and a girl—named Michael and Kimberly. Because of her history she was placed under supervision. She left the hospital and the next few years are sketchy, but it is noted that the children were placed on and off the 'at risk' register quite a few times. A lack of physical contact between mother and children was noted as was the boy's slow developmental rate, both physically and mentally.

"They fell off the radar for a couple of years until it was discovered that they hadn't started school. The authorities got involved again and the children started school two terms behind everyone else. The girl soon caught up, and although withdrawn, was intelligent. The boy was kept in remedial class.

"Reports were made about the children: their weight, cleanliness, refusal to interact. The girl was questioned but wouldn't speak. She would just stand and hold her brother's hand."

"You have amazing recall of the events," Alex noted. The facts were almost thirty years old.

He acknowledged her comment with a sad smile. "I lived and breathed this case while I was researching the book. The story of those two children has never left me."

"Was nothing done by the authorities?" Alex asked.

"The girl wouldn't speak. I interviewed a Miss Welch, one of the school teachers who had taught Kimberly. She recalled one lesson when the sleeve of the child's dress had risen up, revealing a red welt around her wrist. The child looked into the teacher's eyes for a few seconds, as though trying to send a message, before quietly pulling the sleeve back down.

"At break time Miss Welch sought Kimberly out and tried to ask her about the injury but, as usual, the child said nothing."

"Did the girl have no friends?" Alex asked, with interest.

"Apparently not. Each break time she would find her brother and hold his hand. They would sit or stand together somewhere in the playground. Children can be exceptionally cruel and they were bullied mercilessly for many reasons: they were scruffy, they smelled, he was underdeveloped and much smaller than the other kids, and their clothes were atrociously ill-fitting. Fodder aplenty for primary school."

He looked at Alex with real feeling in his eyes.

Oh God save me from nice, caring people, Alex thought.

"And do you know, that girl never retaliated once. She simply held her brother's hand tighter and walked away, just blanking them out."

So this was why DI Stone's barriers had been formed long ago. Alex's interest was growing. She watched Arthur take a deep breath, eager for him to continue.

"Spring half-term of 1987 came and went. The children didn't return to school. Efforts were made to contact Patty, to no avail. A social worker who cared little for protocol persuaded a neighbour to help her break down the door."

He lowered his head but continued. "I managed to interview that particular neighbour: a six-foot Nigerian drug-dealer who cried as he told me what they found. In the bedroom behind another locked door were the two children, chained to the radiator pipe. Michael was chained directly to the pipe and Kimberly was chained to him. It was a very warm week and the radiator had been left running. On the floor was an empty packet of cream crackers and a bone-dry Coke bottle.

"The boy was dead and the girl was barely conscious. She had laid beside his lifeless body for two whole days. She was six years old."

Alex placed a look of horror on her face, when what she really felt was excitement.

"Did you follow the case after that?"

"I tried to, but the people I really wanted to talk to weren't saying very much by this time. The council conducted an internal investigation which was no more than a finger-pointing exercise, producing no real conclusions. Don't forget, news was not what it is today. People bought their newspaper, read it, threw it in the bin, and forgot about it. There was no public outcry for answers and this suited social services very well indeed. Compare that with the Victoria Climbié case which prompted a public inquiry and was the catalyst for major changes in the child protection policies for the whole country."

"What happened to Kimberly Stone after the trial?"

"My understanding is that she went from foster home to foster home. As you can imagine, the poor child would have been significantly damaged and it would have taken a very special family to know how to help her. I have no idea where she is now but I still think about her and just hope that she's found some measure of happiness."

Well, Alex did know where she was and doubted very much that any true measure of happiness had befallen her. She recalled a passage from Milton's *Paradise Lost*: "The mind is its own place, and in itself can make a heaven of hell, a hell of heaven." Alex wondered what Kim's mind had made of itself.

Sensing there was nothing more to gain here but emotional lamentation, Alex reached down for her handbag. She stood and offered her hand.

"Thank you very much for your time, it has been incredibly helpful."

Henry leaned down and extracted a book. "Here you are, my dear, I still have a few left. You're welcome to a copy if it will help with your case."

Alex again thanked him and took leave of his company. The man had no idea that the spring in her step was due to the detail of his recollections. He had offered her an armoury of ammunition and she couldn't wait to get started on the biggest challenge of them all.

FORTY-ONE

"You alright there, Guv?" Bryant asked, pulling up at the school gates.

Even through the sealed unit of the car the sound of the school playground could be heard. It was a universal symphony conducted around the world. Loud, excited chatter from groups that moved and changed like the tide. Playing, screaming, chasing in the last few minutes of freedom before the start of the day.

Already ties were being loosened, backpacks abandoned in the corner to be grabbed on the way in.

She knew this playground well. She looked to the oak tree that still dominated the top right corner. She half expected to see herself there, playing tag with Mikey around the tree. Just the two of them.

On cue, the bell rang and startled her. The doorway acted like a vacuum as it sucked all the little bodies inside.

"Jeez, you look like you've seen a ghost," Bryant said.

She didn't need to see the ghost. It lived inside her every minute. What she hadn't needed was the familiarity of the surroundings. It was why she'd sent Dawson to interview the teacher in the first place. It was also why they'd asked Miss Browning to meet them at the gate. Just so they didn't disrupt the children.

"Guv, are you..."

"Looks like that's our girl," Kim said, opening the car door. And as she walked towards the figure, Kim realised that the description of her as a girl was frighteningly accurate.

The figure wore a navy A-line skirt that fell just below her knees. Shapely legs were encased in black tights all the way down to court shoes. Her upper half was encased in a North Face jacket zipped up to the neck. The blonde hair was pulled back into a ponytail and little make up graced her face. Despite her understated appearance, nothing could hide the raw beauty of her features.

"Miss Browning?" Kim asked.

The woman smiled and the expression lifted her whole face. "Don't worry, I'm older than I look."

Kim laughed. She'd be thankful for that drawback in later life.

Kim introduced herself and Bryant, who stood beside her, his hands dug into his jacket pockets.

In doing so, she'd made it clear to her partner that she intended to lead this one. Better that than succumb to the memories reaching out for her.

"I know that Detective Sergeant Dawson spoke to you some time ago when we began our initial investigation into the abuse at the Dunn household."

She nodded.

"Can you tell me what alerted your suspicions in the first place?"

"Wiggling in her seat. At first I thought Daisy was just restless but it seemed to be happening a lot. Especially when both hands were above the desk."

Kim frowned. "I don't get the significance…"

"Itching, Detective Inspector. One of the physical symptoms of abuse, along with pain, bleeding, swelling etc. Without realising it, Daisy was trying to rub her private parts against the chair to relieve the itching."

Well spotted, Kim thought.

"So, I started watching her more closely for behavioural changes. There was a drop in school engagement and achievement. She interacted with her peers less and her school marks dropped from an A minus average to C plus."

"Any other signs?"

Miss Browning nodded. "Another common indicator of abuse is regression to a more childlike state. Three days running I saw her sucking her thumb."

Kim couldn't help being impressed by this woman's vigilance.

"Did you try and talk to her?"

"Oh yes, many times, but she'd withdrawn so far into herself I could barely get a word out of her."

"Did she ever mention anyone else? Even before the withdrawal."

Dawson wouldn't have asked this previously. They had only ever been focussed on Dunn.

The teacher quickly drew a line between the dots.

"There was someone else involved in the abuse?"

Kim nodded.

Miss Browning closed her eyes and shook her head, absorbing the information.

"Every time I tried to talk to her she was uncommunicative. On demand, she could erect this wall and I couldn't get past it. One time I just touched her lightly on the shoulder and she jumped right out of her skin. One time I tried to speak to her sister but Daisy wouldn't let me anywhere near her. The woman shook her head some more. "Those poor little girls."

Kim got to the question she really wanted an answer to.

"When you took the girls home did you manage to voice your concerns to either of the parents?"

"Not even a sentence. As soon as Mr. Dunn opened the door and saw me he bundled the girls in and shut the door in my face.

"Mrs. Dunn?"

She shrugged. "I don't even know if she was home."

So, that theory was destroyed. From what they'd learned, Kim suspected that Wendy Dunn had been upset at his ignorant treatment of the teacher.

Kim had a sudden thought.

"Why did you take the girls home that day? It's not exactly normal practice, is it?"

The woman smiled. "No, but I wanted to speak to the parents. The message I sent about my concern appeared never to have reached them."

"Who did you give the message to?"

"Mrs. Dunn's brother, Robin."

"Her brother picked Daisy up from school?"

"Oh, yes, he collected both girls all the time."

Kim glanced at Bryant who raised his eyebrows in response. That was something they hadn't known and was a very enlightening detail indeed.

FORTY-TWO

Kim unclipped the collar. Barney went to his water dish and slurped twice.

It was well after midnight and they had just returned from their long walk. Kim varied the exercise; some nights they walked the streets, other times she took him to the park and let him off the lead.

The nightly solitude soothed her. She had learned early on that Barney didn't much like games. She'd thrown a tennis ball for him and he'd looked at her as if to say, "well, what was the point of that?" She'd retrieved the ball herself and tried a couple more times. It had turned into a great form of exercise for her, not so much for the dog. Eventually she had worked out that Barney was a follower. If she walked, he walked. If she ran, he ran.

This evening they had walked for almost an hour and half. She felt he must be hungry by now.

"Come on boy, try one, just one?"

She held out one of the mini quiches she'd baked earlier. The dog backed away and jumped onto the sofa, resting his head on the cushion.

"Go on, try just a little bit."

He burrowed his head down into the sofa.

She sighed. "You know, Barney, you're about the only male in my life who doesn't do what I say. And for that I respect you."

The quiches landed in the bin with a thud.

"Alright, have one of these."

All fear forgotten, he jumped down and took the crunchy apple from her hand.

It was disturbing just how easily he had fit in to her lifestyle. Probably more disconcerting was the amount of time she spent talking to him.

That first night had taken her to a place she rarely visited. The feel of his small, warm body nestled against her had brought back emotions that engulfed her; the guilt at not having died along with her brother, the anger at her inability to prevent his death, and the rage at her mother for having done that to them.

Momentarily she had been transported back to that flat and the memory of her brother's last breath, but she had pulled herself back from the edge. The past was a place she could visit only briefly to remember Mikey's open, trusting face. She tried to recall only his smile or the feel of his small hand in hers but inevitably her mind pushed the fast forward button to those last few days.

She had never talked about it and she never would. Kim's whole world depended on it.

She took a coffee into the garage and sat amongst the scattered debris of her new project. The flutes of Beethoven's *Second Symphony* sounded in the background.

She'd given herself the deadline of tonight to make a decision on whether to pursue the doctor any further.

Kim had the notion that their meeting at the cemetery had been engineered, but for what purpose? And how would she have known that Kim would be there? Unless she'd been followed.

Jesus, she reprimanded herself. If this continued much longer she'd be framing Alexandra Thorne for the Kennedy assassination.

She smiled to herself as her phone vibrated along the worktop. It was almost one in the morning.

The phone had lit up with a text from Stacey. She read the words with interest.

If you're up ring me

Kim was immediately concerned. Stacey would never contact her at this time if it wasn't urgent.

She immediately hit the dial button. Stacey answered on the second ring.

"You okay, Stace?"

"Fine, boss. Listen, this doctor thing yer asked me to look at. I've been doing it from home. Yer know, just in case…"

"Cheers, Stace." At the station there were I.T. watchdogs everywhere.

"The doctor's sister, Sarah. I found a birth certificate but no death certificate."

"But she exists?"

Kim was mildly surprised at the fact.

"Oh yeah, she exists all right, she's alive and well and living in Wales."

Kim steadied herself against the workbench. "You sure?"

"Oh yeah, married with one child. A daughter. Moves around more than a bloody army wife. Took some bloody tracking."

"Stace, you're an angel. I appreciate it." Kim checked her watch. "Now get some sleep."

"Will do, boss," Stacey said, before ending the call.

Kim stood for a few moments, turning the phone around in her hand.

Being beautiful and clever was not breaking any law and Kim realised that she would need to think carefully about her next move. Her own façade had been carefully and diligently constructed, course by course, over many years, but she'd never met anyone like Alexandra Thorne.

The phone dropped from her grip.

Ultimately it came down to a single question. Was she prepared to enter this arena and risk her own fragile psyche to uncover the total truth?

On balance, was there even really a choice?

FORTY-THREE

Kim switched off the engine and removed her helmet. The house was unremarkable in its row of terraced properties. The only thing that distinguished it was the "For Sale" sign that protruded from the wall halfway up the property.

More remarkable was where it was placed. Llangollen was located along the A5, just over halfway between the Black Country and Snowdonia. The small town nestled at the foot of Llantysilio Mountain. From where she now stood there were stunning views of the Dee Valley, the Clwydian mountain range, and the Berwyns in the distance.

Kim enjoyed the view for a whole thirty seconds before she turned and knocked on the door.

Her eye was drawn to the left as two fingers appeared to separate the venetian blind.

The door opened part way. "Yes?"

"Sarah Lewis?" Kim asked, trying to peer around the two-inch opening.

"You are?"

Jesus, she was talking to a front door. "Detective Inspector Kim…"

The door was pulled open and Kim almost stepped back with surprise. Before her was a woman that bore a striking similarity to Alexandra Thorne. It wasn't a vague family resemblance. Kim would have picked her out in a line-up.

Kim held up her hands to still the panic that had tensed her mouth. "There's nothing wrong. I'm not local, I'm from the Midlands, an area called..."

"How did you find me?" she asked.

"Umm...does it matter?"

The woman's shoulders dropped slightly. "Not anymore. How can I help you?"

"It's about your sister."

"Of course it is," she said, without emotion.

Kim looked around. "May I come in?"

"Do you need to?"

"I think so," Kim answered honestly.

Sarah Lewis stepped back and allowed her in. She waited for the woman to close the door and then followed her. The house had once been a two up, two down cottage but as Kim followed she saw that a full kitchen had been added, extending the property into the sizeable back garden.

"Sit down, if you must," Sarah said, leaning against the work surface.

A glass dining table looked out onto a space that held a slide, a swing set, and a patio area with a barbecue. A couple of doll parts had been tossed in the grass. Those discarded limbs gave Kim the comparison her mind had been seeking.

Sarah was about two inches shorter and a few pounds heavier than her sister. And as curt as she was now, real emotion registered on those striking features. If they were toys, Alex would be the doll made of plastic perfection with a box for protection. Sarah would be the teddy bear in the spotted dungarees getting the love and the cuddles.

Kim felt her fascination grow. She couldn't help wondering just how long it had been evident that the sisters were polar opposites.

"I suppose it's too much to hope that she's dead?"

Kim was prevented from responding as a little girl gambolled into the room. Dark curly hair poked out from beneath a woollen hat and tiger earmuffs. A hand-knitted scarf was draped haphazardly around her neck and mittens dangled from the sleeves of her coat.

The girl stopped dead and looked to her mother. Kim was surprised to see a look of panic in the eyes of the child.

Sarah's features softened at the sight of her daughter. Everything else was forgotten.

"Good girl," Sarah said, double wrapping the scarf around the child's neck. "You're wrapped up lovely."

Sarah took the girl's face in her hands and smothered it with kisses.

"How about me, am I wrapped up lovely?"

A man appeared behind the child. Kim saw the woollen hat and polka dot ear muffs before he saw her.

When he did he frowned and looked to Sarah.

Sarah gave a slight shake of the head and bundled them towards the door. "Have a nice walk and don't forget the beef oggies."

Kim had no idea what an oggie was but she could hear a whispered exchange at the front door.

Sarah's face was once again set but Kim had caught a snapshot of this family picture. The surprise in the eyes of the child. The concern that shaped the mouth of the husband.

They had stood in the middle of the lounge for no longer than ten seconds and Kim could tell they were a unit, a team, and that they were happy.

But there was an element of fear at the core of this family.

"So . . . is she dead?" Sarah returned to her original question.

Kim shook her head.

"Then how can I help?"

"I need to learn more about her."

"What does that have to do with me?" Sarah asked, biting her lip.

"You're her sister. Surely you know her better than anyone?"

Sarah smiled. "I have not seen my sister since she emptied her room and went to university. None of us did. My dearest wish is to never see her again."

"You have no contact at all?"

Sarah dropped her arms but her hands immediately found a place in the front pockets of her jeans.

"We're not close."

"But surely you..."

"Look, I don't know why you're here but I really can't help you. I think you should..."

"What are you all frightened of?" Kim asked, not moving an inch.

"Excuse me..."

She hadn't meant the question to sound so direct, but now it was out she had to stick with it.

"Your daughter is not used to visitors, is she?"

Sarah couldn't quite meet her gaze.

"We're just private, that's all. Now, if you don't mind..."

Kim pushed the chair out and looked around. She assessed the collection of photographs. The three of them stood on the bridge she'd rode across where it straddled the river Dee. The child in a horse-drawn barge. The child and her father on the steam railway that ran alongside the river.

Kim decided on a different approach. "Yeah, can't wait to leave. Bloody horrible place to..."

"It's a beautiful..."

"So, why are you moving, Mrs. Lewis?"

Sarah's hands balled into fists in her pockets.

"It's Nick's job, he's a..."

Kim waited for a response but it was clear that Sarah had realised her blunder. She hadn't thought quickly enough of a profession so was left sounding like a woman who didn't know what her husband did for a living.

"Mrs. Lewis...Sarah, one of my team commented that army wives don't move around as much as you. What are you running from?"

Sarah moved towards the front door but her step was far from steady.

"I'd really like you to leave now. I have no information that can help you."

Kim followed her through the lounge.

"I don't believe you. You're terrified and your whole family is fearful of something. Your first question was to ask me if she was dead. I saw your anxiety when I confirmed she was not. Why won't you tell me...?"

"Please, just leave."

The woman's hand trembled on the door.

"Sarah, what are you afraid of?"

"Just go."

"Why won't you just talk to..."

"Because if I speak to you about her, she'll know."

Silence fell between them.

Kim realised this was not the same Sarah who had opened the door. That woman had been hostile, then hopeful to anxious, but conversation regarding her sister had reduced her to a battle-weary shell.

"Sarah..."

"I can't," she said, staring at the ground. "You don't understand."

"You're right. But I'd like to. I want to get inside your sister's head."

Sarah shook her head. "No, you really don't. It's not a nice place to be."

"I don't know what power she has over you but is this really what you want? Do you want to teach your daughter to run?"

Sarah met her gaze, her eyes blazing at the mention of her child.

"She doesn't even have friends, does she? You don't stay anywhere long enough for her to bond. How old is she... six... seven?"

"Six."

"She needs to settle, so why can't you stay?"

"Because she found us."

"Sarah, I want to help you but you've got to give me something."

Sarah smiled. "No one can help me. I've never spoken to anyone who..."

"You've never spoken to me," Kim said, stepping away from the door. "I have suspicions about her behaviour and if I'm right I won't rest until she's caught."

Sarah eyed her with interest. "What's going on with the two of you?"

Kim smiled. "Hey, I asked first."

Sarah considered for a long moment. She took a deep breath and closed the door.

"If I show you something, will you leave me in peace?"

Kim nodded and followed her back to the kitchen. Sarah nodded for Kim to sit back down.

Sarah reached into the cutlery drawer and retrieved an envelope. "This is why."

She handed the letter to Kim. "Read it."

Kim unfolded the single sheet of paper, read it, and then read it again, before shrugging her shoulders. If this was the best she could get on Alexandra Thorne she was well and truly stuffed.

"It seems like a perfectly natural letter from an older sister."

"I've lived here with my husband and daughter for nine months. That's how long it took her to find me this time."

"This time?"

"I've moved my family five times in seven years to hide my child from this woman and every time she finds me. Read the letter again. Note how she mentions exactly where the house is, the location of Maddie's school, and even my daughter's new haircut. She's taunting me. Playing on my fears—because she knows exactly what I'll do next."

Kim read the letter for a third time, putting the Alex she suspected behind the words. There was menace in every sentence.

"But why do you run?" Kim asked.

"You don't know her as well as I'd hoped."

Sarah took back the letter and sighed heavily.

"My sister is a sociopath. You already know that she is a very attractive, enigmatic person. She's intelligent and charming. She is also ruthless and completely without conscience. She is a dangerous person, who will stop at nothing to get what she wants."

Sarah folded the letter and then stared at it. "Quite simply, she has no ability to feel any connection with another living thing."

"What makes you think your sister is a sociopath?"

"Because she has never had an emotional attachment to anything or anyone in her life."

"What about her husband and two boys?" Kim asked.

Sarah frowned. "She's never been married and certainly has no children. Sociopaths do marry and have children as trophies and a cover but there's no emotional connection."

Kim raised an eyebrow.

Sarah smiled. "You see? You can't believe that someone might treat children as a status symbol like a new car or a bigger house, and that is what the sociopath relies on. People like us can't understand their motives and so make excuses for them. It's how they stay hidden."

Sarah shook her head sadly. "And that is why she will never be stopped."

"She told me you were dead," Kim offered.

Sarah showed no surprise. "I wish to her I was. Perhaps then she would leave me alone."

The woman offered Kim a look that was filled with sad resignation. This was her life and no one could change it. She'd spent years trying to outrun her sister and that was the way it would stay.

Sarah glanced towards the front door. She had shared the letters and now it was time for Kim to leave.

"Sarah, I think she's using her patients for experimental purposes," Kim blurted out. "And I'd like to stop her. I'd like to put your sister behind bars."

Sarah tipped her head to the side and Kim detected a glimmer of interest.

"Come on, Sarah," Kim pleaded. "Help me give you back your life."

Kim watched her struggle with the indecision of actually placing that trust with someone she didn't even know.

She hoped she had said enough.

Sarah offered her a watery smile. "Detective Inspector, I think we need coffee."

FORTY-FOUR

Two cups of steaming coffee sat on the table between them.

"You have to understand this isn't easy for me," Sarah said, resting her elbows on the table. "I've known my whole life that there's something missing from my sister but no one ever believed me." She shrugged. "It's why I run."

Kim got it. Her own suspicions were being disregarded by her colleagues and boss.

"You're the first person that doesn't think I'm completely insane," Kim observed.

"Ditto," Sarah added, wryly.

"So, do you think it's possible...what I said?"

"No, I think it's probable." Sarah cupped her hands around the coffee mug and shuddered. "I remember when I had just turned five and I noticed Alex was spending a lot of time in her bedroom, only leaving for meals and school. One night, Alex woke me excitedly clapping her hands. She dragged me from my bed to her room, sat me on the edge of her bed, and removed a tall encyclopaedia from in front of the hamster cage.

"The hamster was trapped between the vertical bars of the cage, dead. Beside the cage, outside the animal's reach but within its view, was food and water. It had died a painful death in an effort to stop itself from starving."

"Jesus," Kim said, horrified.

"I didn't really understand at first. I thought she was playing some kind of game but then she started explaining the hamster's progress, once she had prized the bars slightly wider. She'd done charts and everything."

Kim said nothing.

"She'd watched it for days, growing weaker and hungrier before spotting the widened gap."

"But why?" Kim asked.

"To see how far it would go to get what it wants," Sarah answered, closing her eyes. "I cried so hard. The desperate, tortured face of the hamster gave me nightmares for months."

Kim was disgusted by the memory that Sarah had shared but there was something else she now wanted to know.

"Was she close to either of your parents?"

Sarah shook her head. "My mother didn't touch Alex very much. There was a politeness, a cordiality that existed between them, as though their relationship was two steps removed from mother and daughter. I've since thought my mother knew before anyone else exactly what kind of person Alex would become.

"I remember once when Mum was tickling me and blowing raspberries on my stomach. We were laughing so hard we were crying and then I saw Alex standing in the doorway. I swear I saw tears in her eyes but she turned and left the room before my mum even saw her. She couldn't have been older than six or seven but I never saw that look again."

"But what does she want from you?" Kim asked.

"To torment me. She understands my fear of her and it offers her amusement to toy with me. All I know is that so far she's been satisfied by pulling on my fear like a puppet. Her warning notes have always been enough."

"Do you think she would go further?"

"I don't know but I don't want to put it to the test. She hates me and enjoys chasing me around the country and that's fine because while we're moving around, we're safe."

Sarah met her gaze. A joyless smile shaped her mouth. "Pathetic, eh?"

Kim shook her head. "I think you're stronger than you realise. You do everything you can to keep your family safe. In spite of your sister you have a lovely home, a husband and a child. She may be winning small battles but you are winning the war."

The first genuine smile she'd seen lifted Sarah's lips properly. "Thank you. I appreciate it."

"Just one last question. Sarah, why does she hate you so much?" Kim asked, drinking the last of her coffee.

"Because she wanted me on board. She wanted me to be like her. Quite simply, I think she wanted a friend."

FORTY-FIVE

"Okay people, quick recap on the Dunn case before we all get back to it."

She turned to Dawson. "Anything from the neighbours?"

He shook his head, "Not a thing. The whole bloody street is suffocating under net curtains and I'm sick of drinking tea."

He sounded like a six-year-old who'd been told to tidy away his Lego, but for once she had to agree. There were few jobs where one could get paid to drink tea for hours but there weren't many detectives that would sign up for it.

"The Dunn property. Did we discover anything other than the fibre and the fluid?"

"Yeah, I found out that Kev's still an arsehole."

No one in the room spoke.

Dawson looked at both her and Bryant. "Oh come on, one of you could disagree."

Kim stifled her smile. She wondered if the two of them had any idea what a good team they actually made.

"Still nothing from the lab, Guv," Stacey offered.

Kim wasn't surprised. She'd give anything for whatever technology they used on the television where hairs, fibres, and fluid could be matched in hours, even minutes for the convenience of a forty-four minute show.

"What do we know about this book club, Stace?"

"It's run by a shop owner in Rowley Regis; Charles Cook. They meet first Tuesday of every month at Druckers in Merry Hill. There's a sad attempt at a Facebook page that has three likes, two posts to the page but nothing in the last four months. I've messaged the two that posted."

"Any reply?"

Stacey nodded. "One guy went to one meeting but then changed job so couldn't goo again. The other one was a bit more interesting. Said there was something not right about this Cook bloke. Didn't like it so stopped gooin after three meetings."

Kim opened her mouth but Stacey continued. "I've already messaged him again to dig a bit deeper. He read me message two hours ago but nothing back since.

"Spoke to Cook and found out the group has less than a dozen members. And I cor join 'cos I'm a woman."

"Aww, Stace," Dawson offered. "You shoulda told him it's not really noticeable."

Stacey glowered in his direction as he smirked at his own joke.

"And if the talking scrotum would shut it, I'd just add that their book of choice this month is *The Longest Road*."

Kim frowned. The title was familiar to her but she couldn't place why.

"Popular book, Stace?" she asked.

"Yep, been in the Amazon top ten for seven months."

That was it, then. She'd probably seen it on a billboard or something.

"Jenks and Whiley didn't give us a lot. We know the teacher took the girls home the day of the domestic and that Wendy's brother picked the girls up often from school."

Dawson raised an eyebrow. Every male the girls had come into contact with was a potential suspect.

"Get his home and work address," she said to Stacey.

"Dawson, go through the old files again. Look for anything at all that we might have missed. And Bryant..." Kim hesitated. What to do with Bryant, when he was normally with her? But not this time. "Help Dawson. I've got a dentist appointment."

She headed to The Bowl for her jacket before her face could give her away.

This particular meeting Kim would be doing on her own.

FORTY-SIX

At 9:30 a.m. Kim pulled into a space around the corner from Alexandra Thorne's premises, feeling a little like a schoolgirl truanting for the first time. Telling Bryant that she had a dentist appointment was the first time she'd ever lied to him and she hoped it would be the last, but with this particular case, she was flying solo.

The door was promptly answered.

As the meeting was at her request, Kim guessed it was appropriate to show some manners.

"Thank you for seeing me, Doctor Thorne."

"Of course, Detective Inspector Stone." Alex smiled widely. "However, as you wish this visit to be a non-professional one, I insist that you call me Alex."

Kim nodded her agreement and followed Alex into the office. The doctor looked impeccable in tailored cream trousers and an aqua silk shirt. She wore no jewellery and her hair was perfectly styled.

"Please, sit anywhere you like."

"No patients this morning?" Kim asked, realising her words sounded like an interrogation question. In her head she had meant to say, "I hope I'm not keeping you," but it looked like her reservoir of good manners was all dried up.

"No, this is a free period that I normally use to take care of billing." A faint look of distaste crossed her face. "Not my favourite part of the job, but we all have to live."

And nicely too, Kim thought, knowing the doctor leased the whole building. She guessed that it didn't come cheap.

Kim knew she had to say something about their last meeting when she had been less than graceful about Alex's success in keeping Barry Grant on the ledge.

"Listen, about the other night…"

Alex held up her hand and laughed. "Please don't say anything. I'm not at all sure I could accept any kind of compliment from you."

Kim marvelled at Alex's assumption that she was about to offer a compliment. Of course, whatever else could Kim have been about to say?

This was a different Alex to the ones she'd seen previously. The first visit she had been professional and severe, with a hint of coyness for Bryant's benefit. At the cemetery she had been introspective and vulnerable. With Barry, Alex had been proactive and driven. Right now she seemed almost playful and flirtatious.

"I need to be sure this conversation goes no further," Kim stated.

To appeal to the doctor's curiosity, Kim had told Alex that there were issues she'd like to discuss but she couldn't have a registered visit on her record. Any other psychiatrist would have told her to get stuffed, but she had not been surprised at Alex's generous donation of her time. Alex wanted something from her but she still wasn't sure what.

"Of course, Kim. As far as I'm concerned this is no more than two acquaintances having a chat over coffee, talking of which, I'm guessing white, no sugar?"

Kim nodded. It occurred to her that Alex had stripped her of her title without even asking for permission. Few people called her Kim. It made her a little uncomfortable but under the pretext of the visit she couldn't complain.

As Alex placed the coffee on the table between them, Kim realised that when Alex had told her to sit, she had been standing in front of the only other available chair, forcing Kim to sit in the patient chair. Kim knew she was going to have to be careful.

"So, what can I help you with?"

Kim chose her words carefully. "When we were talking at the cemetery, you said some things that got me thinking."

Kim raised her eyes. Someone less astute might have missed the triumph that emerged momentarily in Alex's expression, quickly replaced by an apologetic shake of the head. But Kim noted it all.

"I'm so sorry. I should never have spoken the way I did. I didn't mean to make you uncomfortable. I have few friends and I suppose a place like that amplifies your vulnerabilities." Alex smiled and tipped her head back. "Additionally I think you are a very easy person to talk to."

Again with the flattery, Kim thought. Fortunately she was impervious to it, especially when she herself knew she possessed the warmth and charm of a Middle Eastern dictator.

Kim just nodded and remained silent, forcing Alex to continue.

"None of us are perfect. We all have insecurities, but usually we hide our weaknesses from those around us for fear it might diminish their respect. Take yourself, for example; whatever you wish to discuss is something you probably wouldn't share with your work colleagues."

Alex was right. She had arranged this meeting under the pretext of discussing sleep disorders and although it was nothing more than a ruse it was a problem that she didn't share with anyone.

Kim sipped her coffee, again forcing Alex to keep talking.

"A woman in your position, with authority over a team formed predominantly of males, can't afford to show vulnerabilities. You probably think your team would respect you less and so you work harder to hide any weaknesses. Their opinion of you may not affect your ability to do your job but their validation and respect is imperative to you for more reasons than you care to admit."

Kim decided it was probably a good idea to stop the doctor talking right about now. Her theory was a little too close for comfort.

"You talked about sleep disorders. I could use some advice on that."

"Oh, Kim, I'm sorry. I've made you feel uncomfortable. I apologise. Occupational hazard, I'm afraid."

Kim detected more amusement than sincerity in the words and recognised the prod as a mild rebuke: *Do you see what happens if you keep me talking?*

"Not at all," Kim said, smiling. The forced expression felt alien on her face so she removed it.

"Have you ever sought help for the problem?"

Kim shook her head. She wasn't seeking a cure. She'd given up on that many years ago. No, she was here for one reason; to establish Alex Thorne's guilt or any involvement in a crime.

Alex settled back into her chair, crossed her legs, and smiled. "Well, the good news is that people who suffer with insomnia have a higher metabolic rate and tend to live longer than people who sleep for seven to eight hours per night. Severe insomnia is classed as less than three and a half hours per night."

"That's me."

"Have you tried any of the remedies, like dark therapy or cognitive behaviour therapy? Have you carried out sleep hygiene?"

Kim shook her head. All things she'd read about but never bothered to try. Getting help for her sleep disorder was not her reason for coming.

"You see, there are different types of insomnia. Difficulty in falling asleep often comes from anxiety. Some people go to sleep okay but keep waking during the night and others rise very early regardless of the time they go to sleep."

"I can't go to sleep," Kim said, honestly. It didn't hurt to offer a small amount of information.

"That can be a symptom of Post-Traumatic Stress Disorder. There can exist a paradoxical intention to try and stay awake."

"Trust me, I want to sleep."

Alex looked thoughtful. "How long ago did the problem start?"

"Years ago," she answered, vaguely. The truth without the time line.

"Have you heard the term somniphobia?"

Kim shook her head and tried to keep her breathing even. Perhaps this had not been such a good idea after all.

"It's an abnormal fear of sleep, often established in childhood, following a trauma."

Kim could swear that the doctor's voice lowered slightly, gently. Or she could just be completely paranoid. The words "childhood" and "trauma" were spoken more like a whisper.

"No, it was in college, I think."

The doctor said nothing.

Kim spoke with a half-smile. "My childhood was pretty normal; loved sweets, hated cabbage, normal arguments with parents about staying out too late."

Alex smiled at her and nodded.

"I think it might have been the stress of exams."

Just in time, Kim realised the doctor had used her own technique of remaining silent against her. Luckily she'd realised before she'd revealed any truth of her childhood at all.

"You know, Kim, it's surprising how many times you used the word 'normal.' Most people say that about their childhood and yet there is no such thing unless you live in a television commercial. What did your parents do?"

Kim thought quickly and chose the sixth set of foster parents. "My mum worked part-time at Sainsbury's and my dad was a bus driver."

"Any siblings?"

Kim's mouth dried and she only trusted herself to shake her head.

"No major losses or traumatic events before the age of ten?"

Again, Kim shook her head.

Alex laughed. "Then you truly did have a charmed childhood."

"How soon after the loss of your family did your sleeping problems start?" Kim asked, diverting the conversation from herself. Perhaps she would learn something if the doctor started talking about herself.

Alex appeared momentarily surprised, but she recovered well. Her eyes glanced back to the photo on the desk and her voice was barely audible. Kim watched with renewed interest, now knowing the family never existed.

"Losing Robert and the boys almost destroyed me. Robert was my soulmate. Unlike yourself we'd both had troubled childhoods and were drawn to each other. We tried for two years before Mitchell was born. He was quiet and sensitive. Nineteen months later came Harry, who was the complete opposite of his brother." Alex looked at her, tears reddening her eyes. "My family was complete and then one day wiped out by a tired lorry driver who walked away with a broken wrist."

Despite herself, Kim was entranced by Alex and couldn't help doubting everything that had driven her to arrange this meeting. Her performance outshone Paltrow, Berry, and Streep combined. And still there was something missing. And Kim was now surer than ever.

"Didn't you have any family to support you?"

Alex shook her head and collected herself. "My parents had passed away and I think I already mentioned that my sister died when I was nine years o.d."

If she hadn't been aware of the facts, Kim would have believed every word. But she knew the truth—and that made Alex's performance all the more horrific.

"That's awful, I'm so sorry. Were you close to..."

"Sarah. Her name was Sarah. She was younger and followed me everywhere. One day I told her to get lost. She went to the pond and fell in. My mother was, umm let's say, *forgetful* and wasn't watching her. It's quite profound losing a sibling at a young age, especially when there is a part of you that feels that you should have been able to save them."

Kim clenched her jaw and tried to ignore the light-headedness that threatened her. She had to get out of this room before she lost the ability to breathe.

"But you wouldn't understand that, with your normal child-hood."

Kim was saved by the sound of the buzzer. Annoyance flashed across Alex's face as Kim propelled herself to a standing position.

"I really must..."

"I'm sorry, Kim. My ten thirty must be early."

"Thank you for your time, Doctor. I guess I'll look up some of those techniques you mentioned."

"Please feel free to come and see me again. I've quite enjoyed our little chat."

Kim nodded her thanks and followed the doctor to the door. She glanced briefly at the woman as they passed but her focus was on reaching the safety of her Golf before she collapsed.

Kim managed to get herself into the vehicle successfully but putting the key into the ignition proved one challenge too far and the keys fell into the foot well.

There was no question that although Kim might have requested the meeting, it was most definitely Alex's agenda they had followed.

Kim banged her hand on the steering wheel. Damn it, that was not the meeting she'd planned.

The doctor had lied again about the family that didn't exist and fabricated a whole history about a dead sibling. Kim felt sick to her stomach.

Kim had known that Alex would be a formidable adversary. Her intelligence and lack of emotional response already afforded her the edge. Even so, Kim had been prepared to enter into battle with the tools they held here and now. A fair fight would be fought in the present.

If Kim was even half right about Alex's manipulations, the knowledge she had gained of her past presented a whole different ball game.

Alex had clearly found her history for a reason. She had to wonder what it might cost her to discover why.

FORTY-SEVEN

Alex asked her next appointment to wait for a few minutes in the small foyer while she collected herself. She was both irritated and jubilant. Jessica Ross could not have timed her early arrival any worse if she'd tried.

The call from Kim yesterday had been a surprise and had come just as she'd been wondering how to engineer their next meeting. Alex had arisen extra early to prepare, with nervous excitement akin to first-date nerves. The fact that Kim had made contact with her without any kind of intervention had further convinced Alex of the affinity that existed between them.

She had known that each meeting with Kim would give her more ammunition and today she had learned a lot. An idea was beginning to form of just how the detective inspector might fit into her plans.

Alex was thrilled at Kim's denial of her horrific childhood and the clarity of the pain those events had caused. It was clear that she had not sought help for the demons that haunted her, and however well Kim thought she hid her emotions behind the rigid exterior, she could not hide from someone who had spent their life studying people and their emotions.

Because Kim had not dealt with the pain of her childhood, the detective's grip on sanity was tenuous at best. If dealt with, the memories would still bring feelings of pain and loss but not the threat of being engulfed. Alex couldn't help but wonder how far she could push Kim until she fell into the abyss of her fragile psyche. The only thing keeping her safe was the distance she had tried to put between herself and those hurtful memories.

Ultimately, Alex knew her dealings with the detective were going to be fruitful and educational at best, but at the very worst, entertaining.

Her boredom threshold craved more challenge. Someone like Kim challenged her. There was so much conflict there that it emanated like a beacon. Kim had issues that even she wasn't aware of, and that excited Alex. Kim was a new toy that she could play with for a very long time.

She forced her thoughts away from Kim, took a deep breath, and affixed her glasses. Irritation was not a good trait to show to her patients. Not for what she charged an hour.

"Mrs. Ross, if you'd like to come in," she said, warmly, opening the connecting door. The female shuffled in without really looking at her.

Some of her court-ordered patients started off this way. Not particularly happy to be seeing a psychiatrist but with little choice in the matter.

She quickly appraised the female. She still had a slight bulge where the baby had once rested and although her child was now seven months old, Jessica Ross had not yet bothered to shift the surplus weight. Her hair was unstyled and straggled down past her shoulders. She moved with the gait of a homeless person, devoid of hope. She wore no make-up and her haggard complexion aged her twenty-five-year-old looks by ten years.

This wasn't a case that held any significant interest for Alex. It would pay for the new laptop computer she wanted and possibly a service on her car if she could stretch it out a bit.

She immediately sat. This patient didn't warrant a coffee. Colombia Gold was expensive.

"So, Jessica, you've been court-ordered into therapy following a violent incident that happened with your baby?"

Although Alex's voice was soft, her words bit and the woman visibly winced. Alex was satisfied she'd caused a little pain. *Thanks for interrupting my meeting, bitch.*

Alex placed the notepad on the table and sat back. It wouldn't hurt to start stretching this case from the very beginning.

"I can see that you're feeling quite stressed and uncomfortable, so let's not rush it. Why don't you tell me a little about yourself?"

Jessica's shoulders relaxed slightly with the relief of not having to get into it straight away.

Alex prompted. "Just tell me about growing up, family, that kind of thing."

Jessica nodded, already grateful.

God, people were pathetic, Alex thought, tuning out. Transparency was so lacking in stimulation.

"...holidays were normally in Blackpool. I remember one time at the beach..."

Alex tuned out as a slow smile spread across Jessica's face. Jesus, she was reliving a fond memory. Alex nodded occasionally, urging her to continue whilst thinking about the disappointments she had suffered so far.

Ruth was by far the biggest disappointment to her—not least because of the time that had been invested. She had not been an opportune candidate like Barry, who also had not performed as Alex would have liked, although at least he had been useful in arranging an unexpected meeting between herself and Kim.

Shane had been a promising candidate initially, but his instability had been further evidenced in her home. She shuddered at the memory. Not the fear she had initially felt when he'd startled her, but that she hadn't seen it coming. Shane would serve as a reminder that loose ends needed to be tied up.

Alex had already decided that Hardwick House was no longer a part of her life. The demand on her time did not equate with the benefits. She had hoped the place would provide a steady stream of subjects from which she could pick and choose, but she had underestimated both the quality and quantity of the fare on offer. For a while the challenge of seducing David Hardwick had been tantalising and had made her visits to the house of misfits at least tolerable. However, even that challenge was failing to keep her entertained. His game of playing hard to get had become tiresome.

She would, at some stage, send a letter to David explaining that recent events had affected her emotionally and that she no longer felt able to be of service to the facility. In the meantime she made a note on her pad to block the calls on her phone.

"…dropped out of college because of the anxiety and panic attacks…"

Still no response was needed from her and it took all Alex's energy not to roll her eyes. This woman had weak, poor victim plastered all over her face. Alex felt that the only challenge she would face with this particular patient was not throwing her out.

It suddenly occurred to Alex why she found this woman so irritating. There was a quality in her that reminded Alex of Sarah. Alex made another note on her pad. She hadn't checked the online estate agents for a couple of days. She felt sure there would be a new listing for Llangollen by now. Yes, a bijou two-bed terraced cottage that was probably being advertised as an "exceptional bargain" for a quick sale.

It only normally took a couple of letters to galvanise her sister into action. If not, Alex had a few more tricks up her sleeve to prompt Sarah into getting out her running shoes. On your marks, get ready, now run, Sis.

Although her sister was quite predictable by now, Alex continued the game just because she could and it gave her some measure of entertainment to have an involvement in Sarah's life. The fact that the pathetic fool allowed herself to be uprooted every few years was entertainment in itself.

"...it started a couple of weeks after the birth..."

Yada, yada, yada. Alex wondered if her boredom would be relieved if she started plucking the fine, light hairs out of her arms one by one. It would probably be less painful.

Oh Lord, spare me from this tedium. In Alex's opinion postnatal depression was turning into the most fashionable accessory for most first-time mothers and was being diagnosed indiscriminately. There were no baby blues or periods of adjustment anymore.

"...I just felt worthless and I wanted to understand what had caused these feelings..."

Probably your own subconscious being honest with you, Alex thought as she nodded at the woman's distress.

"...felt guilty for all the negative thoughts. I felt like I was letting my husband down. He was so excited and was enjoying the baby and I couldn't tell him the truth." She shook her head, fighting back tears. "I thought I was going crazy..."

All very textbook, Alex thought, although Jessica had arrived at this stage quicker than she'd thought. Alex would now be forced to endure the monotony of asking some questions.

"Did you experience any suicidal thoughts?"

Jessica hesitated then nodded, wiping her eyes. "Which just gave me something else to feel guilty about: contemplating leaving them."

"What happened that day?" Alex asked. She now wanted this useless woman gone. If she had to guess, she'd say the child just wouldn't stop crying and she'd gripped it by the arms too tightly or some other banal reason.

"Which one?" Jessica asked.

The question surprised Alex. She had assumed there had been only one episode of violence towards the child and that social services had been involved from the beginning.

"The first one," Alex responded, offering her full attention. This was now getting interesting.

"It was one of my worst days. The day before I'd felt on top of the world, really good, almost too good. I'd been full of energy and excitement. Then bump, the next day was darker than all the rest. I was terrified of everything. Even the kettle switching off was enough to set my teeth chattering. I remember that I couldn't recall where I kept the washing powder. It was really strange. I found myself looking for it in the garden shed.

"Jamie started to cry and at first I couldn't find his bedroom. It was so weird. We've lived in that house for three years and I couldn't find the second bedroom."

Alex put down her notepad and sat forward. "Go on," she instructed, giving this new patient her full attention.

"I stood above his crib and he stopped crying. I looked down at him and suddenly I heard these voices, very low at first, telling me to pinch him. It was garbled but as soon as I heard it, I knew that everything would feel better if I got his skin between my fingers and squeezed."

Alex was alert to every word now. "And is that what you did?"

Jessica coloured, tears gathering in her eyes as she nodded.

Alex wanted to clap her hands together. Overworked social services had sent her a gift. This woman had been diagnosed as suffering from postnatal depression and exhibited all the signs. But on top of the obvious, Jessica had experienced euphoria, confusion, and verbal hallucinations. Jessica Ross was suffering with postnatal psychosis, a very different kind of animal and one that made her suddenly very interesting indeed.

"Oh dear me, I've just realised," Alex said, warmly, as she rose from the chair. "I haven't even made us a coffee. Bear with me while I fire up the coffee machine."

She smiled reassuringly at case study number four.

FORTY-EIGHT

Bryant parked the car behind Tesco in the centre of Blackheath.

"You know, you might have fooled them, but I'm not as stupid as I look."

"You couldn't be," she quipped.

"I know you weren't at the dentist," he said, staring forward.

"I do have teeth, you know," Kim clarified, tapping her top lip.

"Yeah, I've seen them rip grown men to pieces, but that's not what I meant. In three years you've never made a medical appointment in work time. Not even once."

It was on the tip of her tongue to argue but she changed her mind. Bryant knew she had lied and Kim knew he knew she had lied. She had no wish to make things any worse.

"I just need to be sure you know what you're doing," he said, without turning her way.

Kim was tempted to lay one hand on his arm, to reassure him, but she didn't and the moment passed.

"Come on my little worrywart, we have a shadow to find."

The shoe shop was located in the high street, nestled between a butchers and the entrance to the indoor market.

A bell sounded as Kim held the door open for Bryant.

Where the smell of car parts had been inviting to her, this small space was anything but. There was a musty air, as though the stock had lain stagnant and still for a very long time; not so much displayed as preserved.

Handmade price signs peeled from walls filled with dated handbags. A central island held an array of purses and wallets. It was a store with multiple personality disorder. Or a shop just trying to survive.

A male appeared from the back office and slid behind the counter. Kim guessed him to be late forties. His grey jeans were creased with a waistband that had been swallowed by his stomach. A black T-shirt showed sweat marks at the armpits. She couldn't help wondering if his clothes were changed with the same frequency as the stock. But the picture was becoming clearer as to the shop's popularity. Inviting, it was not.

Bryant stepped forward. Kim stood back and observed the male carefully.

"We'd like to talk to you about Leonard Dunn. He's a member of a book club you run."

Kim saw a smudge of red skin appear above the neckline of the man's T-shirt.

"You know, of course, he's been arrested for abusing his two daughters?"

Although Bryant spoke gently, the starkness of the question remained.

Charlie Cook shook his head vigorously. "I doe know nothing about any of that. We just meet now and again to talk about books."

His eyes darted between them.

Bryant nodded his understanding.

"Yeah, I'm in a book club, myself. Great to meet up with the boys now and again."

Kim showed no surprise at his lie.

Bryant moved forward and leaned on the counter. "Missus thinks it's a cover-up for something else."

The redness travelled north.

"It's no cover-up...I swear...we read books...and then discuss 'em. It's all we do...honest to God..."

"Yeah, my missus thinks we just go out on the piss."

Charlie visibly relaxed. He smiled and the redness dropped a notch.

"But see, the thing is, we know someone else is involved in what Leonard Dunn was doing."

The redness rose up like a blanket.

Charlie shook his head vigorously. "Nah, mate...no way. Not one of us. No chance. Sick, mate. Nah, not little girls...makes me ill. All we do is talk about books. Just the thought..."

"Okay, Charlie," Bryant said, holding up a hand. "But we gotta ask."

"Oh yeah...yeah...course. I get it."

"Well, if you think of anything that might help, give us a shout."

Charlie's skin began to return to its normal colour at the prospect of them leaving.

He offered a trembling hand across the counter and Bryant was brave enough to take it.

Kim headed towards the door. Bryant followed for a few steps and turned.

"Oh, my club read *The Longest Road*, last month," Bryant offered, naming the book Stacey had mentioned.

"Yeah, yeah. Good book."

Bryant shrugged. "Just disappointed that Amy Blake died in the end. I liked that character."

Charlie nodded vigorously. "Yeah...yeah...a real shame."

Kim shook her head and continued to the door.

Bryant materialised beside her as they dodged a group of school kids.

She gave him a sidelong glance. "You know, Bryant, there's a compliment in my throat but it's stuck, right there," she said, pointing to her neck.

"Cheers, Guv, in which case you're gonna love this. Book club, my arse. I read up on that book while you were at the dentist. And there's no such character as Amy Blake."

FORTY-NINE

"Should have bloody said no to this," Dawson moaned, sliding against the car door.

Stacey laughed. "Yeah, let me know when you're gonna say no to the boss. I'll book a venue, sell tickets, the lot."

"Yeah, I suppose this is a night out for you," he said.

Kim had asked them to keep an eye on Charlie Cook. See what he got up to. After interviewing him earlier that day, there was a suspicion that something wasn't right.

He had entered his one-bedroom council flat half an hour ago and they'd been keeping watch ever since.

"For your information, Kev. I might be going out soon."

He turned to look at her in the car.

"No way. You've actually got a date, like a proper one?"

"Maybe."

"Come on, Stace, spill. Male or female?"

Her bisexuality was known to her colleagues, although it wasn't something she advertised. Her parents were old-fashioned and clung to certain beliefs. Anything other than heterosexuality was a choice that should not be made.

But she wasn't from Africa. Her parents were. England was the only home she'd ever known.

"Female," Stacey answered.

Realisation dawned in his eyes. Which grew into a sardonic smile.

"I know who it is."

"Don't be pissed, just 'cos she liked me better than you."

He shook his head. "Nah, fair play, Stace. Trish is a great girl."

Stacey hadn't yet properly decided, but she was erring on the side of yes.

"Hey, Cook's on the move."

Stacey put her hand on the ignition key.

"Hang on," Kev said. "It looks like he's walking."

"Shiiit," she said, as they both exited the car.

The street was in the centre of a housing estate. With alleys and gullies all around. Stacey's best friend as a teenager had lived two hundred metres from where they now stood. The two of them had spent many hours aimlessly walking these streets.

They stood behind a privet hedge. Stacey poked her head around. "He's heading for an alley that leads under a railway bridge."

"Can we get behind him?" Dawson asked.

Stacey shook her head. "It's not long enough. If he turns, he'll see us."

As soon as he was out of view, they charged across the road. Stacey took a quick look. There wasn't enough space between them.

"Where does it lead?" Dawson asked.

"Sutherland Road. If he goes left he's going through a trading estate. Right is a row of terraced houses and opposite is a field and a park."

She took another look. He had exited the top of the gulley.

"Run," Stacey said. They had to catch his direction of travel.

They sprinted to the top of the alley. Stacey looked around. If he'd turned left or right he'd still be in view.

She started to cross the road. "He's gone across the field. If we stay too far behind we'll lose sight of 'im and there's three exits off the park."

"Shit," Dawson said.

Stacey understood what he meant. They couldn't maintain such a safe distance. Without the aid of any street lamps their target would soon disappear from view.

They hurried across the field until he was in view. They were no more than twenty feet behind when they slowed their pace to match Charlie Cook.

Dawson reached out and touched her arm.

"Kev...what the?"

"Stacey, hold my hand?"

Must she? she thought. Truthfully, she didn't know where he'd been.

She took it and squeezed, hard, feeling the bones of his fingers grind together. To his credit he made no sound.

"Where does that lead?" he asked, as Cook headed towards the first exit from the field.

"Houses and a school. Library is at the bottom of the road and a few shops on the other side."

His figure walked into the glow of the street lamps. They immediately altered their speed. The view ahead was clear. There was only one right turn in the road.

They paused in the darkness of the field as he walked to the end of the road and turned right.

Again they ran the distance he'd covered.

This time Dawson looked around the corner.

"He's crossed over," he said, looking for guidance.

Stacey searched her memory. "There's a pub, The Waggon and Horses, I think, an electrical shop and...oh, hang on..."

"What?" Dawson hissed.

"The old school, Reddal Hill, it's now a community centre."

"He's moving out of sight," Dawson said.

They walked along the pavement but on the opposite side of the road.

Another fifty feet and Stacey could see the entrance to the old school. Cook was no more than ten feet away and he turned.

Stacey stopped moving. "Well, at least now we know."

Dawson continued forward. "What you stopping for?"

"'Cos we know where he's gone."

He gave her his knowing smile. "Yeah, but we don't know what for."

Stacey got moving and caught up.

A minute later they turned into the grounds of the old school. A noticeboard was mounted just inside.

There were A4 sheets of varying colour with an assortment of fonts and sizes.

"Bloody hell, it reads like a holiday camp itinerary," Dawson observed.

Stacey read some of the adverts aloud. "Boxing, Karate, Model Railway, Video Club, Gentle Exercise. Oh and for you, Kev, they have some bingo…"

"Look at the activity for tonight, Stace."

Her eyes found his finger on the board.

The sign said, Youth Club.

FIFTY

Kim parked outside the friends and family centre at Eastwood Park Prison, an hour after she had called. A six-car pile-up near Bristol had forced her off the motorway and onto the scenic route through the Malvern Hills.

Before Kim switched off the engine she lowered the window in the driver's door a couple of inches to make sure Barney had enough air while she was inside. He seemed to know he wasn't exiting the car and turned two full circles before settling on the back seat.

The facility had previously been a male juvenile detention centre and a young offender institution before settling as a closed female prison with around 360 inmates. Yet no matter how much effort had been put into blending the facility into its surroundings, the presence of barbed wire signalled that there was something to be afraid of.

To Kim's mind, prison wasn't supposed to look pretty. There was no place for flowers and shrubs to soften the edges. Build them high and build them solid, was her opinion. Prisons were meant to house people who had committed crimes and deter others from doing the same. Efforts to make it look like a community housing project were misguided and a serious case of false advertising.

She recalled a Ross Kemp programme she'd seen about a prison in South America stuffed full of the worst criminals imaginable.

The government sent in food and provisions weekly and then guarded it from the outside, ensuring no one escaped. Far less expensive to run than the English process, yet Kim somehow felt that system wouldn't fly in a more "civilised" country.

Luckily, visiting orders were not required for remand prisons and her phone call to the governor ensured the twenty-four-hour notice period had been waived. Kim showed her ID at the gate and once she confirmed that she had nothing more than small change in her pocket was given a cursory pat-down. She dutifully stood still while the passive dogs did a quick "walk by" and, declared contraband-free, she was led into the visiting room.

The first thing that hit her was the "chatter." Although some pockets of people seemed to speak in hushed tones, a general throng of false animation assaulted her. It was a prison and yet still managed to exude the vibe of a market town coffee shop on a Saturday morning.

It seemed everyone was being cheerful for the sake of someone else. The inmates spoke with exaggerated cheer because they didn't want friends and relatives to worry about their well-being, and visitors acted as though they were meeting for a picnic on the riverbank, like there was nowhere else they'd rather be at the weekend. Kim wondered how many Kleenex would be needed on both sides of the wall later.

She located Ruth sitting at a table halfway down on the left. Kim almost didn't recognise the woman as she nodded at a passing officer.

A quick appraisal confirmed that Ruth had gained a little weight, removing the gaunt appearance from the last time Kim had seen her. Her hair was washed and, though not particularly well styled, hung loose and healthy just past her shoulders. Incarceration seemed to suit Ruth. She looked as though she'd returned from a weekend at a spa.

"Detective Inspector," Ruth said, offering her hand.

Kim fixed a smile on her face, an expression that never felt comfortable, but she wanted to put the prisoner at ease.

"No other visitors today?"

Ruth shook her head. "Mum and Dad came yesterday," she said, as though there was no one else.

"How are they?"

Ruth shrugged. "Having a harder time of all this than I am." She looked around. "I can understand why some people ask their families to stay away. The look on my mum's face says it all. Prison is for other people's children. Visits are the hardest part of the week."

"Most people seem to be enjoying it."

"So you'd think. It's for the visitors' benefit but later it hurts like hell that you've done something to force the people you love to come here and spend their weekends doing this."

"Do you want a coffee?"

Ruth nodded. "Milk and two sugars, please."

Kim headed away from the table, feeling that the situation was slightly surreal. Conversation was polite and sociable despite the fact that Kim had been the arresting officer in Ruth's case. A smidge of animosity might have been appropriate, but Kim sensed none. In fact, her senses picked up nothing but acceptance.

As she waited for the drinks to brew inside the machine, Kim felt eyes upon her. She turned and saw an overweight woman currently being climbed over by three young children giving her the hard stare. She didn't recognise the female but some seasoned criminals could pick out a copper from fifty metres.

Kim returned to the table and placed the drinks down.

"So, how are you coping?"

Ruth shrugged. "Okay. It doesn't take long to adapt to prison life. Everything is controlled: getting up, taking exercise, when to shower, when to eat, when to go to bed. Very little changes each day. You get used to the staff, the other inmates, and the corner of the room that belongs to you. There's very little to worry about, no decisions to make."

Kim detected a note of relief in that last sentence.

Ruth looked around. "It could be worse. I've joined the early morning walking club, I've signed up for a couple of courses, and there's an occasional social evening."

"You seem to have adapted very well," Kim said, thinking that she was getting the "tourist" version of the facility. Despite the things Ruth had mentioned as well as a decent mother and baby unit, the prison had the fourth highest suicide rate in the country.

Ruth smiled. "I'm going to be here for a very long time. My choices are limited. And if that's why you're here, I can confirm that I'll be pleading guilty. To what charge is for the lawyers to sort out, but I won't be fighting the punishment."

The words were delivered as though she was discussing losing a game of chess, not years of her life.

Ruth laughed softly. "I'm sorry but I appear to have rendered you speechless."

This was not the woman she had arrested. The person sat before her now appeared stable, resigned, almost content.

"But you're entitled to a trial." It was a justice system Kim trusted.

Ruth shook her head. "There won't be a trial. I will not put my family and his mother through that. Don't look so shocked. I'm not psychologically impaired. I did it and I'm prepared for the consequences of my actions. Taking a life is not something that can go unpunished. I have to pay the debt that society dictates and then start again."

Kim had waited a long time to meet someone who echoed her own sentiments but she hadn't expected it to be someone she'd arrested, and she certainly hadn't anticipated the vague measure of discomfort it gave her. This woman was accepting her punishment a little too easily and Kim couldn't help but feel she wasn't the only person to blame.

"I hope I've answered your question," Ruth said, moving her legs to stand.

Kim shook her head. "Please sit, that's not why I'm here."

The measured calmness appeared to falter for just a second as a frown cut across her forehead.

"Can we talk about Doctor Thorne?"

Ruth's eyes narrowed. "I'm sorry, I don't understand."

Kim knew she had to tread carefully. "It would be helpful if you could tell me a little about your sessions together."

"For what reason?"

Kim noted the sudden curtness in her tone.

"It would help the CPS understand better."

Ruth didn't appear convinced and her arms crossed in front of her. "Well, we just talked, as you might expect. We discussed many things during our time together."

"Can you tell me about your last session? It would be really helpful."

"We talked for a while and she took me through a symbolic visualisation exercise."

Ruth looked uncomfortable and Kim could feel her retreating. Not now, she silently begged. She needed to know what the hell a symbolic visualisation exercise was. Her gut told her in this case it was not anything good. Subtlety aside, Kim knew she had to just go for it if she was to learn anything.

"Ruth, was there anything in that last session that could have inspired you to do what you did?"

"It was all my own doing. I took the knife, I waited for him, I followed him, and I stabbed him."

Kim could see the emotion building in the woman opposite. A flush was spreading across her chest and the muscles in her face were tight.

"But don't you think it's possible that you were being manipulated, used by Doctor Thorne? I mean, by getting you to imagine killing Allan Harris, by using a knife in the symbolic exercise, is it possible that the doctor was intentionally...?"

"Don't be ridiculous. How could she have known that I would use her efforts to help me as...?"

Ruth's words trailed away as she realised she'd just confirmed what had been a lucky guess on Kim's part. The crime mirrored the session.

"Ruth, please talk to me."

Ruth shook her head vehemently. "Detective Inspector, I will not say one word against Doctor Thorne. She is a skilled, intuitive psychiatrist who has helped me through the worst time in my life. I don't know what you think she's done, but I can tell you that she has been my saviour. I think you should leave and take your disgusting accusations with you."

"Ruth..."

"Please leave and don't come back."

Ruth glared at her before leaving the table.

Kim cursed under her breath. The bloody woman was so wrapped up in her own flagellation she wasn't even open to the suggestion that perhaps there were more people to blame for the crime. She had committed herself to attrition and there would be no budging her.

Kim returned to the car, now knowing what she had previously only suspected: that Alex had been instrumental in manipulating Ruth. What she didn't know was why.

Kim wondered if the doctor was playing some kind of sick game of power, seeing how far she could push people, but she didn't think that was it. She remembered the first time she'd met Alex after Allan's death and she'd asked if she could visit Ruth. Had that been to cover her tracks or something more? If the aim had simply been to manipulate Ruth, then knowing what Ruth had done would have been triumph enough, but it wasn't. She had wanted to gauge Ruth after the fact.

No, it wasn't as straightforward as mind-fucking. Alex wanted to learn something and Kim had to try and figure out exactly what that was. It was going to take a trip into her past to find out.

Kim could not ignore the power that Alex now held in her hands. Having access to the horrors of her past definitely made it an unfair fight. Alex could examine these events openly and not lose her mind. Kim didn't have that luxury.

Alex could use every fact to drag her closer to the darkness and Kim wasn't even sure how to fight back. What she needed was a better understanding of exactly what she was up against.

She suspected there was only one man who could help her now.

FIFTY-ONE

Bardsley House, four miles east of Chester town centre, was used to house the criminally insane. Open since the late 1800s, it had never offered day trips to the wealthy, a guided tour through the stages of insanity like Bedlam in London. Bardsley House kept its patients private, behind closed doors and away from curious eyes. Externally, it bore no sign of the madness within.

The half-mile gravel drive wound its way through rich, undulating lawns and a 700-acre deer park before ending at an imposing structure that had retained its 17th-century appearance.

As she approached the entrance, Alex decided there were far worse places to be crazy.

The reception area was unlike a normal hospital foyer. Comfortable wing-backed chairs littered the area, with occasional tables scattered throughout. Watercolours of local landscapes dotted the walls and pan pipes sounded gently from a speaker that rested above a CCTV camera.

Alex's finger was poised above a bell when the door opened and she was met by an overweight woman in her late fifties. A quick assessment told her that the woman had been at the facility for some time. She was dressed in black trousers formed of a cheap polyester mix, with a white T-shirt covered by a plain blue pinafore. Her nails were multicoloured, and bright yellow costume jewellery adorned her wrist and throat. Her short hair was dyed a vivid purple. A simple name badge stated, "Helen." No title or position, just Helen.

Alex held out her hand. "Hello, my name is…"

"Doctor Thorne," Helen completed with a wide, open smile. The woman was clearly accessible and trusting. Just the kind of person Alex loved.

"Doctor Price told us you were coming. He asked that we assist you in any way we can."

Of course he did, Alex thought. Doctor Nathaniel Price was the registrar of the hospital and their "friendship" went back to medical school when Alex had sussed out he was having a homosexual relationship with one of the tutors. His secret had been of little use to her at the time and she wasn't prone to frivolous malice. There had to be a benefit to her; at the very least, her own entertainment. Back then his secret would have been low impact; news for a week or two, quickly swallowed into the whirlpool of university shallowness. But now it meant more, especially to his wife and three daughters.

Fortunately, Alex hadn't needed to use the threat. It had been there, travelling along the phone lines. It was enough for him that she knew, and if he was as intuitive as she suspected, he also knew that she'd use it. He was probably still at it secretly. She made a quick mental note to find out. A little extra insurance never hurt.

"That's very kind of you, Helen," she said, smiling and shaking her hand warmly. Fat, ugly folks always liked attention from the beautiful people.

Helen led her from the foyer along a short corridor and took a left turn into a small orderly office.

"Please, sit."

Alex did so. The space was functional and small, with a window overlooking an ornate fountain on the east side of the grounds.

The mouth of the dolphin looked as though it hadn't spouted water in fifty years.

"I've been Care Manager here for twenty-two years, so if there's anything I can help you with, feel free to ask."

Alex sat back. "I don't know how much Doctor Price told you."

"Just that you had a similar case at the moment and that any insight would be helpful."

Alex nodded regretfully. "Obviously I can't go into detail, but if you could discuss Patricia Stone with me and if I could meet her briefly, I think it would help me treat my patient more effectively."

Helen seemed happy to share. "Okay, I'll just talk and if you have any questions feel free to jump in."

Alex took out a notebook. Helen swigged from a can of Diet Coke; amusing, considering the woman's girth.

"I assume you know the bare details of Patty's earlier life. She was placed here in 1987, following the tragedy.

"She had been diagnosed with schizophrenia years earlier but was responding to drugs and was released during the era of de-institutionalisation.

"When she was brought into our care she exhibited many of the characteristics of schizophrenia. She suffered delusions, hallucinations, disorganised speech and catatonic behaviour. She had been socially dysfunctional and the signs had lasted for more than six months. The exclusion of known organic causes had been confirmed."

"Can you be more specific on the nature of the delusions and hallucinations?" Alex asked. This first-year medical lesson was wearing thin.

"Well, initially she heard voices arguing in her head, completely independent of herself. She was the referee, if you like, the peace-maker. The voices always wanted her to side with one of them. She also suffered with delusional perception. There is a record, before my time, that when a fellow patient pushed the water jug towards her during lunch-time it meant the nursing staff were trying to kill her and she could only protect herself by urinating in the middle of the dining room.

"Not long after I came here, Patty developed a phobia of windows, fearing that if the window was open her thoughts were being sucked out of her mind."

"Has she suffered any violent episodes?"

Helen nodded sadly. It was clear that this woman was extremely fond of Patricia Stone. How very unprofessional to develop such feelings for a patient, Alex mused.

"Unfortunately, yes. She is not violent by nature but there are times when it is difficult to control her."

"Can you tell me about those incidents?"

Helen reached for the file so she could offer detail.

"In '92, she attacked a fellow patient, claiming that the elderly woman was flashing thoughts into her mind and she had to make it stop. In June of 1997, she attacked another patient, claiming that he was projecting feelings into her. A few months later she insisted this same patient was reading her thoughts aloud. Six years ago, she attacked a visitor, claiming that he had gained mental control of her and had made her scratch her knee until it bled. And most recently she floored a young nurse for projecting impulses into her mind."

Alex was intrigued. Patty Stone had almost covered the entire scope of Schneider's first-rank symptoms. Any one of which would indicate schizophrenia.

Helen closed the file. "Please don't misunderstand. These episodes are few and far between. Otherwise she is a model patient; co-operative and reasonably pleasant. Such an episode prompts us to re-evaluate her medication. Initially she was on chlorpromazine but now she's on clozapine."

Clozapine was often given to schizophrenic patients who had been difficult to treat. The drug produced fewer side effects.

"Is there any link in her behaviour or episodes with visits from her family?"

"Patty hasn't had a visitor in all these years."

Alex feigned surprise. "Oh, I thought her daughter..."

"Sadly not. She calls each month and has done since she turned eighteen, but she never visits."

"That must be hard for Patty."

Helen opened her hands. "It's not our place to interfere in family dynamics. We simply do the best for the patients in our care."

"Is there any hope for Patty's release at any stage?"

Helen was thoughtful. "That's a difficult question, Doctor Thorne. There are times when Patty is very stable and it is not difficult to imagine her leading a life outside this facility, but her periodic outbursts of violence render that possibility unlikely. Bear in mind she has been institutionalised for more than a quarter of a century. There is a safety, a familiarity to her life here. We are not a fast-food type of facility. Our aim is not a quick turnaround. We give care to patients that need it and we accept that for some that may be a very long time, and in some cases for the rest of their lives."

Alex nodded earnestly, thinking that if this woman was not responsible for writing the PR brochure, she should be.

"It's expensive care, though. I mean, this facility is unlike many I've visited."

"We have a mixture of private patients who fund their stay here; others are funded by the social care system."

Of course they were, Alex thought, especially patients failed by that care system who had gone on to cause neglect and death.

"Thank you, Helen. You've been very helpful. It's clear that you are an integral part of the quality of care offered here."

Helen looked suitably flattered. "I understand that you would like to meet Patty?"

That had been easier than she'd thought. "If at all possible."

"I told Doctor Price that I wouldn't force her to meet with you. As I said, she has received no visitors and if she feels uncomfortable or doesn't want to meet you then that will be the end of it."

Alex nodded her grateful acquiescence. Beneath all that blubber the woman had a backbone.

"And I will stay with you at all times. Is that understood?"

Alex nodded, liking this woman less and less.

Helen stood and indicated that Alex should follow. Once again she was back in the corridor with the pan pipes. Eerily, there was no other sound. Helen carried no keys and each door was opened by an access code, keyed in quickly through habit.

Helen came to a halt outside a heavy oak door. "I'd rather you didn't enter the general population area. Our patients understand routine. They know when visitors are due and I don't want them unsettled."

Alex was guided into a vast room, seemingly untouched by the facility or its inmates.

"Please take a seat. I'll go and speak with Patty."

Alex thanked her but didn't sit immediately. She wandered the room lined on two walls with books that stretched from floor to ceiling. The third wall was filled with art that she recognised as Gainsborough, van Dyck, and Sir Peter Lely.

Alex chose a seat carefully. She faced the window so that Patty would hopefully sit opposite her and not be distracted by any outside interest. Despite Helen's words, Alex felt confident that Patty would meet with her. Her journey had already been worth her time. The fact that Kim had never visited her mother yet continued to call every month fascinated her.

Alex was unsure what further insight she might gain, but she was eager to meet the woman that had produced Kim and had been instrumental in forming every complex personality trait the detective possessed. Meeting Kim's family cemented their relationship even further. Alex guessed that none of the people in Kim's life had ever met her only living relative, and so this would be their bond alone.

The door opened and Alex hid her surprise at Patty Stone's appearance. The woman was slight but not frail. Her hair was completely grey and cut short. She wore loose jeans and a floral jumper. Her feet were encased in light blue slip-on pumps. She'd been taken from a cottage garden, minus the sunhat and flower basket.

Alex smiled as the woman approached, noting the stiffness and slowness in her movements.

"Hello, Patty. How are you today?"

Patty allowed her hand to be taken. It was warm but limp. On the face of it, this delicate middle-aged lady looked older than her fifty-eight years and hardly capable of violent outbursts, but Alex knew that looks could be deceiving.

She sat and fixed Alex with an unnerving gaze. Alex looked into the unnaturally dark irises that Patty had gifted her daughter. Suddenly, without blinking or moving any other muscle, Patty slapped her own thigh.

Alex ignored the movement. "So, Patty, is it okay if we talk for a little while?"

Patty appeared to be listening, but not to her. After six or seven seconds, Patty nodded.

"I'd like to talk about your daughter, Kimberly, if possible."

"You know Kimmy?" No hesitation but a slap of the thigh.

Alex glanced sideways to where Helen sat reading a magazine. Far enough away not to intrude, but close enough to listen to everything that was being said. And to measure Patty's reaction. Alex had to make sure she phrased her questions carefully.

Alex nodded and met the woman's stare, shocked by the intensity she saw there, just for a second, before it was blinked back into docility.

"I met Kim recently. I believe you haven't seen her for some time."

Patty looked up to her left, frowning.

"My apologies, Patty. You haven't seen *Kimmy* for some time?"

A single tear ran down her cheek as her hands started moving, as though knitting.

"Kimmy safe?"

"Yes Patty, Kimmy is safe. She has a very important job as a police officer."

"Kimmy safe."

Alex nodded despite the fact Patty's gaze was fixed above her head.

"Kimmy calls, I'm safe."

Alex continued to nod. It was often pointless to try to fathom the disorganised speech of a schizophrenic. Alex noted that Helen had not turned one page of the magazine she was holding.

"Can you tell me anything about Kimmy's childhood?" Alex pushed. She didn't think she would get anything useful.

The hands began to knit faster. "Mikey safe, Kimmy safe. Devil comes, devil takes."

Patty stopped dead and turned her head to the side, listening, although there was no other sound in the room. Oh for goodness' sake, woman, just get on with it, Alex thought.

She started shaking her head. "No, Kimmy's friend. Kimmy safe." She paused to listen to a response that was only in her head.

Patty stopped knitting long enough to slap her thigh and then resumed knitting, more quickly.

"No, Kimmy's friend. Friend Kimmy. Kimmy safe?"

She fixed Alex with a stare that she felt had the vision of an X-ray. "Isn't she?"

The dark, brooding eyes seemed to look straight into her soul. Alex nodded.

With the swiftness of a gazelle, Patty was upon her. It took a second for Alex to catch up. Patty's hands were in her hair, her nails scraping at the flesh. Alex instinctively raised her arms to push Patty off. She was vaguely aware of Helen shouting for Patty to stop.

Patty's hands were everywhere, clawing at her scalp. A guttural sound came from her mouth. Spittle landed on Alex's cheek. She almost vomited as the saliva travelled towards her lips. She lowered her head to protect her face but she could already feel her cheeks and temple smarting.

Alex tried again to push her off, but the advantage was with the slight woman that towered over her.

Alex saw the arms of Helen encircle Patty's waist from behind to prize her off. Patty's right hand was fisted around a clump of hair. As Helen pulled Patty backwards, Alex cried out as the roots were ripped from the scalp. Patty's other hand was desperately grabbing more hair.

"You reach up and grab her other hand and I'll pull," Helen called.

Alex reached out and found Patty's left hand. The grip around her hair was strong. Alex's eyes watered as Patty pulled. She loosened the fingers one by one.

"Pull," she shouted to Helen.

Patty's arms continued to flail towards Alex even as she was being pulled backwards by Helen.

Alex watched as Patty was carried out of the room. Her eyes wildly stared Alex down. Gone was the diminutive figure taken from a country garden and in its place was a spitting, feral animal.

"Wait here and I'll get someone to check you over," Helen said, bundling Patty out of the door.

When the door closed, Alex smoothed down her hair and headed out the door. She had no intention of waiting around any longer. She'd had enough. She wasn't going to get anything else from the psychotic lunatic.

Once back in her car she surveyed the damage. One long scratch travelled from her temple to her jaw. The thin line was red but not bleeding. Red blotches from Patty's nails dotted the rest of her face. Most of the damage was beneath her hair.

Her whole head felt as though it was on fire.

The visit had given her much more than she'd bargained for and she had to wonder if it had been worth it.

There was something about Patty that was not quite making sense to Alex. She took out her notebook.

The movement disorders were quite pronounced, despite the medication. Patty's methodical journey through the majority of Schneider's first-rank symptoms of the disease was something Alex had rarely witnessed. The periodic violent episodes that occurred with a precise regularity were intriguing, as were the garbled, apparently nonsensical, words she spoke.

Alex tapped her fingernails on the steering wheel. "Of course," she said to herself as the pieces came together. Alex couldn't help but smile at the cunning of the wily old woman as the pieces finally fell into place.

Despite the injuries, Alex couldn't help enjoying the irony that the most insightful person she'd met in years happened to be a paranoid schizophrenic.

As she put the car into reverse, Alex smiled to herself that the journey had been well worth her while after all.

FIFTY-TWO

The two-storey building in Brockmoor had changed little since Kim's last visit. The front door needed a lick of paint and the brass doorknob was dull and blackened in places. She didn't know for certain that he still lived and worked at this address but she had to try.

She hesitated before pressing the button, unsure how her visit would be received, or if he would remember her at all.

She tentatively rang the bell and held her breath. Heavy footsteps and a low grumbling tugged at her mouth.

The door was opened by a man smaller and wider than she remembered. His wiry grey hair stuck out at all angles, like Einstein. His glasses hung around his neck. He had hardly changed at all.

"I'm sorry, Miss, but I'm not buying..." His words trailed off as his gaze found her eyes. He placed his glasses on the end of his nose. "Kim?"

She nodded, awaiting his response. She had stopped coming to see him for one simple reason: he was too good at his job and had started getting a little too close. She had offered no thanks, no explanation, and no goodbye.

"Come in, come in," he said, standing back. There was no anger or disappointment in his tone. Yes, she should have known.

She followed him through to the consulting room and was immediately struck by the contrast to Alex's treatment room.

Doctor Thorne offered the illusion of comfort. Well-placed expensive chairs, an oriental rug, plastic plants, candles, velvet drapes at sash windows. But this room housed old chairs made comfortable by use, a little worn in places but clean and welcoming. Scattered around the room were bonsai trees at varying stages of sculpture. No certificates shouted his credentials from the wall. They didn't need to.

"How are you, my dear?" he asked. From anyone else it was a banal question meant as a polite formality. From him it was loaded with knowledge and understanding.

"I get by, Ted."

"I will allow my curiosity to steep long enough to make you a cup of coffee."

She followed him to the kitchen at the rear of the house. The room was dated with old oak cupboards and units, darkening the small room. Mismatched crockery drained on the sink unit.

"No second wife?"

"No, my dear, it wouldn't have been fair. No woman would have held a candle to Eleanor and it would have been wrong. I could never have lowered my expectations. There have been dalliances over the years but my refusal to take it to the next level has always been a sticking point."

Kim said nothing as he poured boiling water into a West Bromwich Albion mug and an Aston Villa mug. He handed her the Villa mug. "They lost at the weekend so that mug is out of favour."

She took the drink and headed back to the comfy room.

"So, what's happened with you since you stood me up twenty years ago?"

Jeez, his memory was keen. An apology at this stage was pointless. She sat in the chair that was familiar to her. It felt exactly as it had back then.

"I went to college, then entered the police force. I like the job I do."

"What rank are you?"

"Detective Inspector."

"Hmm...well done, but why have you settled for that point on the food chain?"

Christ, this man was challenging to be around. Not one seemingly innocuous fact went unnoticed. It was one of the things that made him an excellent psychologist.

"Who said I have?"

"Because if you wanted to be higher you would be."

It was a simple statement and totally true. She'd been in his company for less than ten minutes and already he could read her like a book.

"How about you? Have you finally retired—or are you still poking your nose into other people's business?"

He smiled. "Ooh, nicely done, my dear. Misdirection and an attempt at humour all in one sentence. You have come a long way, but I'll let it pass, seeing as you came to see me and your reasons will become clear eventually." He took a sip of coffee. "I suppose I'm semi-retired. I see two or three patients at any one time and sometimes more if needed."

Kim guessed that the "if needed" occurred when social services asked him. Ted had always worked for the state, primarily on child abuse and neglect cases. Kim could only imagine the tales of horror that he'd heard, the disturbing pictures he'd had to endure.

"How do you do it, Ted?"

He thought for a moment. "Because I like to think I've made a difference. Because then I can sleep at night."

It certainly wasn't for the financial rewards, Kim thought. He lived in the two rooms on the upper floor. He really was one of the good guys.

He chuckled. "You know, I remember once, I had this little girl who was so angry, so defensive, that for three whole sessions she refused to say a word. I think she was six at the time. Nothing worked. I tried lollipops, toys, a walk into the garden, but she simply refused to speak."

Kim stiffened. This was a place she did not wish to go.

"The next time I saw her she was nine and in between foster homes, unable to settle or adapt. When I offered her a Wagon Wheel, the first words I ever heard her utter were, 'What's up, Doc, run out of lollipops?' And then I saw her again aged fifteen when she categorically refused to discuss what had happened in that last foster home even though..."

"Ted, I need your help," she interrupted. She trusted this man's abilities without question, but she could not allow him anywhere near those fenced-off areas. He was too good at what he did.

He caught her gaze and held it. "I only wish you would let me help. Your life could be..."

"Doc, please."

He took a pipe from the side table and held a match to the tobacco. The smell of sulphur filled the room. "You can ask me anything, Kim."

Kim felt herself relax. He had never pushed her too hard and for that she was grateful.

"I've been working on a murder case. You may have seen it on the news or read about it."

"The rape victim?"

Kim nodded. "This may seem completely ridiculous, but the female was under the care of a psychiatrist, a very accomplished and intelligent woman. During our first meeting something pricked at the hairs on my neck but I couldn't put my finger on it. I think the psychiatrist was somehow involved."

Kim saw the doubtful look on Ted's face.

"I know, I know it seems doubtful. But after that initial meeting, I met her at the cemetery. It all seemed accidental but was like she'd set it up. We've met a couple of times since and after each meeting I felt that she knew everything about me, that she'd taken the time to research me."

"You may have simply overreacted to someone who might be insightful and intuitive. Do you not wonder if you have an aversion to people like her? You've been scrutinized all your life by people wishing to analyse you."

Kim shrugged. "Her sister thinks Alex is a sociopath, and there's a part of me that thinks she's right, but at this point I have no idea what I'm dealing with."

Ted let out a long whistle. "And if she is, how exactly can I help you?"

"I need to get in the mind of a sociopath so I can try and play her game."

"That would be a foolhardy expedition for anyone, but for you it is positively suicidal. You're not equipped to deal with this woman, Kim, and I cannot condone your plan."

Kim's eyes blazed at his lack of faith. "So, you're refusing to help me?"

Ted thought for a moment. "If you're right that she knows of your past, then her only motivation can be to use that information against you somehow. And this would be dangerous enough if it were a past you had dealt with. So, to answer your question, the advice I'd give to anyone else would be to run and don't stop. To you I'd say, *run faster*."

She stared him down. "I ask again, are you refusing to help me?"

He held her gaze. "Yes, my dear, I am."

Kim grabbed her jacket and stormed out of the door.

FIFTY-THREE

Kim counted the fish as they circled the pond looking for food.

"Moby died," Ted said, offering her a fresh coffee. "Do you remember?"

Kim took the drink and nodded, recalling another time she'd stormed out and headed for the garden.

"You asked me what their names were and I told you they didn't have names. Oh, you weren't happy with that and insisted that everything should have a name." He chuckled. "If I recall it was Moby, Willy, and…"

"Jaws."

"Of course. And then the collar doves came and you wanted to name every…"

"Ted, I'm gonna do it anyway, with or without your help."

"I know."

She turned to face him. "So, will you help me…please?"

"Let's sit down."

He guided her to the companion set beneath a parasol that was never lowered, keeping the wooden chairs dry, whatever the weather.

"Let's play two for one."

Jeez, this man forgot nothing. One of his techniques was to let the patient ask so many questions before he could ask any. The number was the ratio of questions.

"Three for one," she stated.

During their brief time together she had learned more about him than he ever had about her, or so she'd thought at the time.

She knew the love of his life had lost her fight with cancer at the premature age of thirty-seven. She knew that he was a keen gardener and took the odd cutting from overpriced garden centres. She knew he hid his collection of Terry Pratchett novels in his bedroom so as not to unsettle his patients, and that he stayed up until all hours watching late-night poker. She also knew he was the closest she'd ever come to sharing her past with another human being in her entire life.

He nodded his acceptance. "One pass."

"Three passes." There were certain things she would not discuss anywhere.

"I accept the rules of the game. Let us commence."

"Okay, first question, what exactly is a sociopath?"

"It's a person without a conscience. It is simply missing from their genetic make-up. They are unable to feel concern or love for any other living thing and it is surprisingly present, in about four per cent of the population.

"These people are often charismatic, sexy, entertaining, and have a superficial charm that allows them to seduce people."

Kim recalled how initially Bryant had been bowled over by the charisma Alex had radiated and she herself had to admit that she'd become intrigued by the woman.

"It's all a front. Sociopaths have no interest in bonding emotionally despite their ability to draw people in."

"Do they understand the difference between right and wrong?"

Ted nodded. "Intellectually, of course, but they have no inner guide advising them to adhere to it. Conscience is not a behaviour. It is something we feel. You have police officers that report to you?"

"Of course."

"And after a day working longer hours than normal, what do you do?"

"Tell them they should have worked quicker."

Ted smiled. "Amusing, my dear, but answer the question."

"Buy them supper and tell them to come in later the next day."

"Why would you do that? It's their job."

"Just because."

"Do you do it to become popular with the team?"

"Oh yeah, 'cos that keeps me up at night."

"Precisely. It's a decision made in your conscience. It's the right thing to do. It's born from an emotional attachment." He held up his hands. "Oh, I know you're going to dispute that point, but you're not a sociopath."

"Thanks for confirming I'm not insane, Doc."

"Ah, but neither is the sociopath. Their behaviour is the result of choice. They understand the difference between right and wrong but choose not to adhere to it. Just as some people learn to live without a limb, a sociopath must learn to live without a conscience."

"But how do they become one in the first place?"

"Well, evil doesn't attach itself to any racial group, physical type, gender, or societal role. And I think you'll find I've answered three questions."

Kim rolled her eyes. "Shoot."

"What happened in foster home number two?"

"Pass. So is it born or does it develop?"

Ted smiled. He'd expected that. "Studies show probably both. A predisposition for the condition may be genetic but the environment dictates how it is expressed."

Kim remained silent, knowing he would elaborate without her spending another question.

"There is a theory that maternal rejection can contribute to a sociopathic disposition. Attachment Theory is relatively new, but to summarise: disturbances within the parent and child bond in the early years may have a huge effect when the child becomes an adult. That is beyond my area of expertise, however there is evidence to suggest that the wider environment plays a bigger part."

Kim tipped her head.

"Western philosophy rewards the pursuit of all things material."

"Are you saying there are less sociopaths in Eastern society?"

"Interesting question. There is far less sociopathic behaviour in, let's say, Japan."

Kim was confused.

Ted continued. "Okay, let's say you're a budding sociopath and for entertainment you'd like to insert a firework into a kitten's mouth just to see how the blood spatter would look on the wall."

Kim shuddered.

"Yes, quite. But would you be quite so eager to carry out the experiment if every single person around you believed it was a bad thing to do? Sociopathy is as much about the behaviour. Now, as a young sociopath, the urge to blow up kitty would be the same but your choice to act on it might be different based on the overriding culture."

Kim thought about the next question in relation to herself. She was almost afraid to ask. "What do they want?"

"Oh, Kim. Why won't you let me help you forgive your mother?"

"I still have a question left but that one is gonna be a Pass. What do they want?"

Ted shook his head. "My dear, Indira Gandhi said forgiveness is a virtue of the brave."

"And William Blake said it is easier to forgive an enemy than to forgive a friend. And if it's your mother, it's damn near impossible. That last bit was me."

"But if you would…"

"I passed, Ted. What does a sociopath want?"

Ted opened his hands expressively. "They want what they want. Sociopaths are not identical robots. They all have varying characteristics. Some will have a low IQ and may try to control a small group of people. Some will have a high IQ and would aspire to great power."

"What about murder?"

"Very few sociopaths are murderers and few murderers are sociopaths. Murder would only be possible if the person has violent tendencies to begin with. Their only aim is to get what they want; in effect, to win."

Kim thought about Ruth. "Can they control minds, like hypnotism?"

"Hypnotism isn't mind control. Hypnotism will not persuade anyone to go against their core beliefs.

"Manipulation on the other hand is a very different thing. Total mind control is for the movies, but exploitation of a thought, however far in the subconscious, is a very skilful trait."

"Go on," she urged. That wouldn't count as a question.

"To persuade someone to do something completely alien is a pretty difficult thing to do. Let's say one day after a dressing-down from your boss, you briefly picture yourself emptying a scalding cup of coffee into his lap. The moment is gone and you don't think of it again. In the right hands, two weeks later, you may well walk into his office and do it."

Kim could count too. "I have my next question ready, but we both know it's your turn."

"Where is your happy place?"

It was on the tip of her tongue to offer another pass, but although the memories were painful they were not life-threatening.

"Foster home number four. Keith and Erica."

"Why?"

Kim laughed. "I think you'll find that's another question, but I will answer you. Because they didn't try and repair me. For three years they allowed me to be myself without reproach or expectation. They allowed me to just be."

Ted nodded his understanding. "Thank you, Kim. Next question."

Kim pulled herself back to the present. "What did you mean by the right hands?"

"Okay, if I wanted to, I could get you to relive the humiliation of being berated by your boss. I'd prod you to make that feel even worse, then I'd get you to visualise the punishment so you could enjoy the revenge, and then I'd give you reasons to justify doing it, and by doing all of that I'd be pretty much giving you permission to walk in there and do it."

"But how is that not total mind control?"

"Because you'd already had the thought in the first place and your actions are being carried out consciously. You won't even know that the manipulation has taken place."

Kim thought about Ruth and things began to make a bit more sense. Of course Ruth had fantasised about driving a knife into her attacker. The thought had existed somewhere in her mind and Alex knew that. There was no link between Alex and Allan Harris that she knew of, so what had Alex been trying to achieve?

"Do these people have no emotions at all?"

"They have what we call the primitive emotions: immediate pain or pleasure, short-term frustrations and successes. The higher emotions like love and empathy are not present in the sociopath.

The lack of experience of love reduces life to an endless game of attempted domination over other people."

"Is that how they fill their time?"

"Oh Kim, we both know it's my turn. Will you ever let go of the guilt you feel for Mikey?"

Kim shook her head. "No."

"But don't you wish…"

"I answered the question, Doc."

"Okay, to answer your question, the boredom is almost painful, like a child that needs constant stimulation. It's the same for the sociopath. The games eventually get boring, the entertainment wanes, and so the games must get bigger and better, more elaborate."

Kim thought about Sarah constantly running from her sister. How much entertainment had Alex gleaned from that little power play over the years?

Kim felt her frustration growing. "But there has to be a way of exposing them."

"So, this psychiatrist you're interested in. You think she may have been instrumental in a murder. What's your next step?"

It wasn't his turn but she answered it anyway. "To get a warrant?"

Ted laughed out loud. "On what grounds? She is well respected in her field, I'm sure. I'll bet you there have been no professional complaints about her conduct. The woman in prison is unlikely to speak against her unless you can convince her just how deeply she's been manipulated. So, how exactly will you get a warrant? Your superiors will think you have lost the plot and now your credibility is completely gone."

"Thanks, Doc."

"I'm just being honest. Sociopaths can fall, but it needs enough people to stand up and point them out. I think it was Einstein who said, 'The world is a dangerous place to live, not because of the people who are evil, but because of the people who don't do anything about it.'"

"Can they be cured?"

"Why would they want to? Responsibility is a burden that other people accept but they can't understand why. Sociopathy as a disease causes no discomfort whatsoever to the sufferer."

"But counselling..."

"You're missing the point, Kim," Ted said, exasperated. "They are completely satisfied with themselves. They have no wish to change."

"But don't they get lonely?"

"There is no frame of reference. It would be like asking a person who has been blind all their life to describe the colour blue. They have no reference of what blue is."

Kim thought her head might explode at any moment with everything Ted had told her.

He opened his mouth to speak but she held up her hands to stop him. "I know it's your turn but I've got one pass left which I'm definitely gonna use, so I wouldn't bother wasting your breath." She smiled to soften her words. If she had ever chosen to share her past with anybody, it would have been him.

"You always were very good at this game, Kim."

"So, any advice on how to deal with this woman?"

"I repeat my earlier instruction. Stay away from her, Kim. You are not equipped to come out of this intact."

Kim felt the conversation turning back to her. She drained her coffee and stood. "Well, Doc, thanks for your time."

He remained seated. "Won't you even consider coming back to see me?"

Kim shook her head and aimed for the side gate.

"You know, of all the children I saw over the years, I always viewed you as my most abject failure."

She spoke quietly, without turning. "Why, Doc—'cos I was just too broken to mend?"

"No, simply because I wanted to help you so much it hurt."

Kim swallowed the emotion that had gathered in her throat. She had the urge to give him something.

"I have a dog."

"That's good news, Kim. I'm pleased that you got yourself a dog, now you just have to work out why."

FIFTY-FOUR

Kim parked the car and turned to Bryant. "I'll lead this one. We need to tread carefully."

His guffaw was covered by a cough.

She appraised the property before her. A row of four three-storey town houses had been built in the space previously occupied by two bungalows. The new, orange brick stood out against the rest of an estate that had sprung up in the late fifties. The driveway held a shiny silver Audi with a Corsa parked in front on the road.

"Bloody Nora," Bryant said, turning sideways and inching crab-like between the Audi and the wall to the next property.

The door was answered by a male dressed in a navy suit. The burgundy tie had been loosened at the collar. The strong chin showed just a light stubble that had probably crept up during the course of the day.

"Can I help you?"

"Detective Inspector Kim Stone, Detective Sergeant Bryant. May we speak with you for a...?"

"Step away from my property, Detective Inspector. I will not allow you to torture my sister further."

His face had changed season. The tolerant smile reserved for unexpected visitors was replaced with pure disgust.

Kim could understand it. She had been less than pleasant to his sibling on their last meeting.

"Mr. Parks, if I could just have a minute..."

"What the hell could *you* possibly want?" Wendy asked, appearing beside her brother. Although Bryant was beside her, the disgust was obviously reserved for Kim alone.

A small look of triumph passed across Robin's features as he folded his arms across his chest.

Kim could see instantly that Wendy had lost weight. Already slight, and with her black hair pulled back from her face, Kim was reminded of Olive Oyl.

Pure hatred shone from her eyes.

Kim realised quickly that she had to rethink her interview strategy. Robin Parks was definitely a hostile subject and would not answer any questions directly and it looked like Wendy could cheerfully gut her like a fish. But she had to get in the house.

"Wendy, I've seen the girls," she offered.

The hatred dulled, replaced by shock and then concern.

"Move aside, Robin," Wendy said.

He didn't move but regarded his sister incredulously.

"Are you mad? I'm not letting these people into my..."

Wendy took hold of the door and opened it.

Robin stepped aside.

Kim followed Wendy through to a tastefully decorated lounge dominated by a wall-mounted television. A one-piece leather sofa curled around the room with a recliner seat at the end.

Wendy took a seat at the furthest point, but not before Kim saw the extent of her weight loss.

Wendy folded her hands tightly into her lap. "You've seen my girls?"

Kim moved along so that both she and Bryant could sit even though the invitation had not been made.

Kim knew this woman itched to launch across the room and beat the life out of her but greater was her need to know about her children.

Kim nodded. "They are okay," Kim said and felt the need to add more. "Daisy was wearing a dalmation onesie and Louisa was dressed as an owl."

Wendy tried valiantly to keep the tears back but they broke free and exploded down her cheeks.

"Their favourites. I made sure I sent their favourites."

The room fell silent. Kim opened her mouth but Wendy beat her to it.

"I no longer care if you believe me. But the truth is, I *didn't* know. Either he was very clever or I was very stupid but if I had known that bastard would not be taking up any space on this earth anymore."

A couple of spots of spittle launched from her mouth as she spoke.

"You may not understand this but I am filled with a rage so hot I can actually feel it burning. I have never been violent in my life but I dream of putting my hands around his throat and squeezing every last breath out of him. It's all I can think about."

Robin entered the room and sat beside his sister.

This hadn't been the initial plan in her mind, but Kim knew how to improvise. Attempting to question Robin Parks directly would lead to a speedy ejection from the premises, whereby they would learn nothing.

"I would give my life to go back and stop it from happening. I would give anything to undo their hurt and believe me I will spend the rest of my life trying."

Robin took Wendy's hand and began to stroke it.

Kim believed her. And she knew she'd been wrong. This woman had not known.

"Wendy, there was someone else in the room."

Kim kept the words as gentle as she could but each one of them travelled like bullets across the room.

A cry escaped from Wendy's lips and a whole new horror entered her eyes. Kim would have liked to confirm that it was a voyeur only, but she wouldn't give false reassurances.

Although she was speaking directly to Wendy, it was the reaction of her brother that Kim watched. She knew that Bryant was watching him too. She had no doubt that her partner had understood the change in direction of the meeting.

Robin stopped stroking Wendy's hand. "I think you should…"

"Are you absolutely sure?" Wendy asked imploringly.

Kim simply nodded her head.

"That's ridiculous," Robin said, placing a protective arm around Wendy's shoulders.

Kim ignored him. The minute she addressed him directly she would certainly be made to leave.

"Is there anyone you can think of that your husband knew…"

"I can't believe it…I can't even think…I just…"

"Why would my sister know who this fictional person is? She's told you…"

"The person is not fictional, Mr. Parks. It has been confirmed."

Still no direct question.

Despite her distress, Wendy's motherly instinct was still intact. Her lip trembled. "Daisy confirmed it. That's why you've seen her?"

Kim nodded and took a deep breath.

"Wendy, it was someone she knew."

Robin exploded to his feet. "No…no…no…I will tolerate this no more. She doesn't know anything, don't you understand?"

He moved across the room, heading straight for her.

Bryant was already on his feet. "I wouldn't do that, Mr. Parks."

Kim stood and looked around them both. "Wendy, I'm doing this for your daughters."

Robin attempted to reach around Bryant and grab her forearm.

She snatched it away and took a step towards him. "Do you want to try that one again?"

"It's time for you to leave," he said, stepping back.

Kim ignored him and addressed Wendy. "Don't you want me to catch the bastard who was in there?"

"Robin, stop it," Wendy cried, rising. She stood and slowly traversed the room.

"If I think of anything, I'll let you know. It really is time for you to leave and I hope never to see you again."

Kim looked at Robin, poised to physically remove her from the house, and at Bryant, who was just waiting for him to try.

It was costing Wendy every ounce of strength to remain upright.

Yes, she had definitely outstayed her welcome.

"Well done on treading carefully in there, Guv," Bryant offered, walking to the car.

She said nothing. Ultimately, Kim had got what she'd come for.

FIFTY-FIVE

It felt like weeks since she'd last had a briefing, when in fact it had been a couple of days.

"Okay, Stace, any update on Charlie Cook?"

"Not much, Guv. I've been in touch with the community centre but they only keep records for certain events. Most of the activities am run by third parties and the centre just provides a venue. Still working through 'em to see if I can find out where Charlie Cook went."

"Do we still think it's the youth club?" Bryant asked.

Kim shrugged. "I don't like it," Kim said, honestly. "Anyone involved in youth clubs has to be DBS'd, but we all know the problems with that."

The Disclosure and Barring Service had taken the place of the Criminal Records Bureau check and was required for anyone working with children. The name change hadn't sewn up the hole in the net.

"Anything back on the fluid and hair?"

Stacey shook her head. "Sent 'em a reminder this morning."

Kim wondered what part of "ASAP" the lab didn't understand.

"What about the bloke at the car parts, Guv?"

Kim shook her head. There had been something a bit loose, but her only issue was his lack of emotional response. And as Bryant had pointed out more than once, she wasn't the best judge of that.

Kim could feel the despondency weaving through her team. They all preferred a case that was logical and methodical, where one clue led to another. But not all cases were that obliging. Some were messy, like trudging through quicksand in wellington boots. Even worse was reworking a case that had already been solved. The same people were being interviewed and questioned and nothing was breaking free. It killed morale quicker than a pay freeze.

"Listen, guys, I know how hard you've been working for very little reward. I feel your frustration. But we'll get there. This team doesn't quit."

They all nodded in her direction.

"But this team also needs a bit of downtime. Get out of here and don't come back until Monday. And then we'll start bringing them in."

"Go on, get out," Kim growled.

Dawson was first out of the door, closely followed by Stacey. Kim glanced behind her. "That means you too, Bryant."

"You gonna do the same, Guv?" he asked, reaching for his jacket.

"Of course I am," she said, looking away.

It was time to start rattling some cages. Someone knew more than they were letting on. It was time to shake something loose.

FIFTY-SIX

Alex's eyes went to the door each time it opened, awaiting the arrival of her new best friend. Their relationship had changed during the last meeting. Now they were on first-name terms and the project was progressing nicely.

When Kim had called her earlier that morning and asked to meet for coffee, she had been thinking the exact same thing. Further proof of their mutual curiosity. Kim had suggested the cosy coffee shop fifty feet from Alex's office and she'd been more than happy to agree.

The door opened and Alex watched as Kim approached in her trademark black. Alex wondered if the woman had any idea of the attention she commanded. Her walk was purposeful and decisive. Her eyes set a path that her feet dared not deviate.

"Doctor," Kim said sitting down.

Alex noted that Kim had reverted to titles. During their last meeting they had graduated to first names and Alex wasn't one to move backwards.

If Kim noticed the faint scratch marks below the concealer she chose not to mention it.

"It's good to see you, Kim. I took the liberty of getting you a latte."

Kim folded her legs beneath the table. "Thank you, Doctor, but it's Detective Inspector and I have a few questions for you."

There was no effort to soften the rebuke with a smile and Alex felt oddly disappointed. Whether Kim's impromptu visit to her office had been genuine or not, it would have been more satisfying to play with the woman by simulating friendship. But no matter, she'd work with what she had.

"I take it we're not discussing sleep disorders this time?"

"Well, we can if you'd like. Didn't yours start after the death of your family?"

Alex tipped her head and said nothing. That sounded like a rhetorical question.

"Oh, I'm sorry, I forgot; they're not your family and they didn't die."

Alex contained her surprise. She briefly considered allowing her eyes to fill and talk beseechingly about loneliness, her career, and all the sacrifices of a personal life, but they had passed that point. Kim wasn't going to fall for it, so Alex wouldn't waste her energy on that game play. Ultimately, she was flattered that Kim had gone to the trouble of finding out.

"It's a lie, isn't it?"

Alex shrugged. "A harmless one. My patients are reassured by both my extensive education and my life experience."

"But it's not an accurate reflection of you, is it, Doctor?"

"Very few of us are ever completely ourselves; I would imagine you know that as well as anyone. The photograph on my desk is there for people to make assumptions and they do. We all present a façade to the world. And it suited me to present a family. Even to you, Kim."

Kim's eyes flamed at the use of her first name, but she held herself in check.

"So, it's a manipulation?"

"Yes, I suppose, but as I said, a harmless one."

"Are all your manipulations harmless?" Kim asked, tipping her head.

"I have no idea what you mean."

"Do you manipulate your patients in other ways?"

Alex allowed the corner of her lips to turn up slightly, aiming at bemused. "What exactly are you accusing me of?"

"It was a question, not an accusation."

So, the detective was analysing every word she said. Good. Take this, Alex thought.

"Kim, I have many patients. I deal with conditions along the whole spectrum of mental health, from a bout of stress to paranoid schizophrenia. I treat people who will never recover from childhood trauma. I treat people with all types of guilt, survivor and otherwise."

Alex wasn't sure how many points she'd scored, but a slight stiffening of the back confirmed that one or two poison darts had found the target.

"So, if you'd care to be more specific, I'll help you in any way I can."

"Ruth Willis."

Alex was intrigued by what Kim thought she knew.

"Sometimes people cannot be fixed, Kim. I would imagine that you have unsolved cases in your past; incidents that, despite your best efforts, you were unable to bring to a successful conclusion. Ideally I would have liked to move Ruth to the next stage of her life, but she is a very troubled young lady. You see, sometimes there is safety in the anger, and often vengeance is the glue that holds them together." Alex lowered her eyes. "Ruth will never recover from what she's done."

"She's doing quite well, actually," Kim shot back at her.

As expected, Alex had learned what she wanted to know. The detective had been to see Ruth. But it was of no concern. No one would ever believe Ruth if she dared speak out.

"It was an interesting visualisation exercise you used during your last session."

Alex shrugged. "It is a technique used widely for many reasons: stress relief, goal achievement, and it works well for letting go of negative emotions. It is symbolic."

"Or a blueprint for an unstable mind?"

Alex laughed. She hadn't enjoyed herself this much since she'd convinced a chat room full of bulimia sufferers that they'd been getting the best of both worlds.

"Oh, please, visualisation techniques can include all manner of things but people don't actually go out and do them. It's a technique, not an instruction."

"And you couldn't have known that Ruth was too unstable to act out the symbolic role-play?"

Alex thought for a moment. "You believe wholeheartedly in the integrity of your profession and the individuals within the police force that uphold the law?"

"You're answering a question with a question, but yes I do."

"It is a system in which you believe, regardless of any imperfections?"

"Of course."

"Although it was before your time in the force, I'm sure you will have heard of the Carl Bridgewater case. A thirteen-year-old paper boy was shot dead at a farm not far from here. The Midlands Serious Crime Squad fixated on a group of four males and eventually secured convictions for all four on what was painfully scarce evidence.

"Following investigations into their methods the Serious Crime Squad was disbanded for, amongst other things, fabricating evidence, and many of their convictions were overturned. Years later, the three living males convicted of murdering Carl Bridgewater were released from prison on appeal."

Alex tipped her head to the right. "So, please, tell me what part of that particular process you are most proud of?"

"One of the males made a full confession," Kim defended.

"After severely questionable methods of interrogation. What I'm trying to demonstrate with that particular example is that, at worst, those police officers were aware that they were framing innocent men, in which case the system failed. Or perhaps they were overzealous in their methods but got the right men, who were then released on appeal; again, the system failed.

"Every single profession is fraught with inconsistencies. It is the exception that often proves the rule. I believe passionately in what I do, but do I accept that not everyone will behave the way I'd like them to? Of course I do, because that is human nature."

Kim's brow furrowed. "So, to use your example, those police officers either deliberately manipulated the evidence or they were grossly incompetent. Which one of those options is responsible for your failure with Ruth, Doctor?"

Alex chuckled. She really did like a challenging conversation. "The failure was all Ruth's, I can assure you."

Kim fixed her with that disarming stare. "But that's what I don't understand. Either you deliberately chose a form of treatment that you knew would inspire her to take the action she did, or you made a mistake in carrying out that exercise. Either way, you are partially responsible for the subsequent events. Do you not agree, Doctor?"

Alex sighed deeply. "Have suspects committed suicide in police holding cells?"

Kim nodded.

"Why? How has that been possible?"

Kim said nothing.

"Putting a suspect in custody is part of your judicial process and so you do it. You cannot know that an individual will take that opportunity to end his life. If you did, you would not do it."

"Perhaps you would if you wanted to see the reaction."

"A person who has dedicated their life to the mental health profession would have no interest in patients as subject matter."

For the first time, Kim smiled. "Noticeably delivered in the third person."

Disappointingly, Alex felt the first stages of boredom setting in.

"Okay, Kim. *I* would not use my knowledge and expertise in such a way."

Kim paused and tipped her head. "Hmm... your dead sister would tend to disagree."

Alex was momentarily surprised by the mention of Sarah. Communication between Kim and her sister was not something she had factored in—she preferred to keep her games separate. However, she recovered her composure quickly.

"My sister and I are not close. She is not a credible source on my professional life."

"Really? Your letters to her indicate that you like to keep her abreast of your patients' progress."

Alex felt tension seep into her neck. How dare that spineless little bitch interfere with her life?

"In fact, she feels that you've been torturing and harassing her for years."

Alex tried to smile the tension from her jaws. "Jealousy is a very ugly trait. When you have siblings there is always a competitiveness that emerges. I have been very successful in my career. My IQ is superior and I was favoured as a child, so you see, she has many motives for being bitter."

Kim nodded her understanding. "Yes, she talked in great detail about your childhood together. We talked about your differing views on pet care."

It took all of Alex's energy not to groan out loud. Jesus, had the pathetic little creature still not forgotten that one little incident?

Alex didn't like being wrong-footed. She'd never enjoyed surprises as a child, and when cornered, her defences turned to attack. Alex was about to hit the fast-forward button.

"Oh, Kim, family relationships are such complicated things. If Mikey hadn't died right beside you, you would know these things, but unfortunately for you, your childhood abuse and neglect has left you with much more than survivor guilt. You are…"

"You know nothing about…"

Alex was rewarded by emotion blazing in the woman's eyes.

"Oh, but I do," Alex said, pleasantly. "I know a lot about you. I know that your pain didn't end once you escaped your mother. There are probably things that happened in those foster homes that you have never shared with anyone."

"I see you've done your homework, Doctor. Ten out of ten."

Alex heard the shift in the woman's voice and knew that she'd hit a nerve.

"Oh, but I always like to get top marks, Kim. I know that the only validation you get is through your work. I know that your life is solitary and that you are emotionally cold. When your personal space is violated you feel suffocated and have to free yourself. Your relationships are based on your own terms or not at all."

The colour was fading from the detective's cheeks. But Alex fancied another twist of the knife.

"At any moment you could fall into the blackness that follows you every minute of every day. I know there are days when you are tempted to loosen that grip and allow yourself to be swallowed by your own mind."

Alex stopped herself. She wanted to say more but she'd done enough to make her point. The rest would come later.

She reached for her handbag and stood. "Until the next time, Detective Inspector."

The black eyes bore into her with pure hatred. Alex felt gratified and couldn't resist one last dig.

As she passed the back of Kim's chair, she swooped in and kissed Kim on the cheek.

"Oh, and Kimmy, Mummy said hi."

FIFTY-SEVEN

Kim let herself back into the house, the meeting still ringing in her ears. She had run two red lights and overtaken anything that had stood in her way. The recklessness had not exorcised the rage from her body and the urge to hurt something remained.

"Fuck that fucking woman," she shouted, throwing her jacket at the coffee table. A magazine and two spark plugs skidded to the floor.

Barney walked towards her, wagging his tail, seemingly impervious to her mood.

"If you know what's good for you, stay out of my way," she advised.

Barney followed her into the kitchen as though he knew he was in no danger from her. And he was right.

Barney reacted with the same enthusiasm he did every time she came home. A few tail wags and then he sat in front of the second cupboard door: the food cupboard.

Kim switched on the kettle and sat at the dining table. She had considered stepping into the garage but her mind was still ablaze with questions.

Barney sat and leaned against her leg the same way he had when she'd visited his old master. But this time her hand found its way to the top of his head. He remained still beneath the stroking movement of her palm.

She admitted that not all of her anger was aimed at the doctor. Never had she felt so constricted. Two cases were constantly moving out of her grasp.

The private life of Leonard Dunn had been evaluated countless times. They had interviewed hundreds of people during the initial investigation that had led to his arrest and now they were chasing a ghost. Everyone was a potential suspect and, with dread, she knew what she had to do.

She took out her phone and tapped a few names into the list key.

Brett Lovett from Car Spares National.

Charles Cook from Blackheath.

Wendy Dunn.

Robin Parks.

She knew she was on borrowed time with the Dunn investigation. New cases were landing on her desk every day. Each time Woody asked to see her, she braced herself for the instruction to shelve the Dunn case. She dreaded hearing that order from his mouth. Because she knew she couldn't comply.

She would not stop until she found the person who had stood in that room and watched a young girl being abused by her father. At the least, that person had left the house knowing it would happen again and yet had failed to come to the police station. At worst... well, that didn't bear thinking about.

Kim opened her mouth to slacken her jaw. The tension had travelled there and rested.

No, she would never let it rest. Not until she found the bastard.

And then there was the case she was flying solo.

She knew that their next meeting would not be so civilised. In the meantime, she would need to devise some kind of mental armour to keep Alex out. Ted had advised her to steer clear. He had advised her to "run faster."

The woman seemed to know everything about her. The gloves were off between them now and a small part of her was relieved that she had been right about Alex all along. Now she had to find a way to prove it.

Kim fired up Yahoo and again plugged the doctor's name into a search. The first time she'd done this she had only entered the websites with official articles either about Alex or written by her, but as she scrolled through the results she hit websites where the doctor had been named.

She entered website after blog after chat room, ferreting out the references to the doctor. Forty minutes later, Kim was considering nominating Alex for a Nobel Peace Prize. The statements were gushing, and in some cases reverent.

Kim refilled her coffee mug thinking, Jesus, I'm trying to nail Mother Theresa. She got back to it and eventually found a post that grabbed her attention.

It was almost hidden in a chat room hyperlinked from an agoraphobia website and simply asked if anyone had ever been treated by Doctor Thorne. Kim counted seventeen responses, all positive, but she saw no return post from the person who had started the thread.

Kim accepted this was no smoking gun, but the poster, DaiHard137, had asked the question for a reason. The fact there was no further post indicated that the poster hadn't received the response they'd been hoping for. If DaiHard137 wished to compliment the doctor, why no second post agreeing with all the plaudits that had followed?

A knot of excitement grumbled in her stomach and then died. There was no way in hell of finding out who DaiHard137 was. Of course, there were people in the Tech department at the station who could probably track the user in minutes but her request for the search would create an audit trail straight back to Woody's office.

She took out a fresh notepad and began writing notes on every contact she'd had with the doctor, trying her best to recall where each conversation had taken place. Kim's pen hovered above the page as she recalled their meeting at Alex's practice. The female patient she had passed on the way out; the one who had disturbed their meeting. There was something familiar about her. Kim tried to recall more detail from her memory but she'd been distracted. She could visualise the face: nervous, anxious, but she just couldn't place it.

Kim left the desk and walked around the room, ticking off the possibilities. She wasn't a witness, Kim knew they had not spoken, so that ruled out any of the cases she'd worked on. She considered that the female was familiar to her from around town but she dismissed this.

Court. The word bounded into her mind. It wasn't one of her cases but it suddenly clicked into place.

She dialled Bryant's number. He answered on the second ring.

"Bryant, cast your mind back to that fraud case a couple of weeks ago. What other cases were being tried?"

Bryant would know. He'd been talking to one of the victim-support officers. Bryant talked to everyone.

"Err... an aggravated burglary and a child abuse case."

That was it. The female she'd seen coming out of Alex's office had most likely been court-ordered to attend therapy.

"Thanks, Bryant."

She hung up before he could ask any questions.

As her excitement began to grow, so did the fear. She was treating a woman who had already caused or allowed harm to her child. And that was before Alex got started on her. She dreaded to think what Jessica could do under the care of Alex.

Kim's head fell into her hands. No one was going to believe her. What was she supposed to do? How could she track down this woman and if she did, what the hell would she say?

She rubbed her eyes and glanced back at the computer screen. Her mouth fell open. "Are you kidding me?" she said aloud.

Barney obviously thought she was talking to him. He jumped from the sofa and sat beside her. Her left arm fell to her side and absently started stroking his head.

"No way," she breathed, looking again at the name of the poster on that thread. She'd thought DaiHard137 was a pretty clever name and it was, especially if your name was David Hardwick of Hardwick House.

FIFTY-EIGHT

The face of the man that opened the door was immediately confused. "Detective Inspector?"

Kim had considered a call to Woody to alert him to her fears but still she had no proof to offer. She was hoping she could find something here.

"You remember me?" She asked.

"Of course. It was a memorable evening for us all. Is there a problem?"

With the people housed within these walls, Kim supposed that police knocking on the door was a constant threat.

She shook her head. "May I come in?"

"Of course."

He held the door open for her and she walked past. The clean odour of pine emanated from his skin.

"Come through to the kitchen."

She followed him and sat down. He placed himself on the other side of the worn wooden table. A tall man appeared in the doorway. He wore light-coloured jeans and a sweatshirt bearing the name of a university. His eyes looked up and to the left and he tapped his two index fingers together.

"Dougie, this is ... I'm sorry, I don't know ..."

"Detective Inspector Stone."

"Dougie, this lady is a police officer who is here to ... actually I'm not sure why she's here, but there isn't anything wrong, okay?"

He nodded and wandered away.

"Dougie gets uncomfortable with new people."

Kim was confused. "Isn't this a kind of halfway house for ex-criminals?"

"Well researched, Detective Inspector."

"What did Dougie do?"

"Hmm...Dougie isn't an official resident. He isn't actually halfway to anywhere."

Kim frowned. That seemed unkind.

"My apologies, that sounded worse than it was meant. I mean that Dougie will be with us for as long as he chooses. He does not appear on our books, as he doesn't fit the criteria for placement at Hardwick House, but you'll have noticed that he is severely autistic and so appears as a sundry expense on our accounts."

"What is the criteria for a placement here?" Kim asked. She would get to the post in a little while. First she wanted to understand what had drawn Alex to this particular facility.

"First-time offence and genuine remorse for the crime. Look, do you mind if we talk outside? I'm working on something."

Kim followed out of the back door. A Jawa 500 speedway bike lay injured on the ground.

"You ride speedway?"

His face tensed. "Used to, but a bit too much broadsiding into bends shot my knee to bits."

A mixture of emotions emanated from him: sadness, regret, longing. The sport had obviously been important to him.

He sat on the tarpaulin that covered the ground and protected the bike from the wet grass. Kim took a white plastic patio chair.

"Nice bike," she offered.

He offered her a "what do you know" kind of smile.

"So, what exactly does this place offer?" she asked.

"Reintegration into modern society, primarily. I challenge you to name me one thing that has remained unchanged in the last ten years."

Kim thought for a moment. "Corned beef."

David turned with a bemused look on his face. "What?"

"Well, with all the advances in technology, why is there still that godforsaken key attached to the bottom of the tin that invariably snaps when you wind it around?"

David laughed out loud.

"Seriously, why has no one ever addressed the problem?"

David sat back down, his face relaxed. "You know, I can see your point." He paused and met her gaze. Kim saw a spark of attraction in his eyes and was tempted to look away, but she held her ground.

"What's your story, Detective Inspector? How did you get to be a police officer?"

No way was that happening. However much at ease she was. "I like putting bad people away."

"Okay, that's the end of that conversation. Now would you like to tell me why you're here?"

Kim looked around to see Dougie walk out of the back door and in again. David ignored it.

"Have you been to see Barry?"

David looked pained. "Yeah. He's still on life support."

"Did you have any idea that he was going to see his ex-wife?"

David shook his head. "No, and if I had I would have discouraged it immediately. I just don't get the sudden change in him. He seemed eager to move forward and make a new life for himself."

That didn't sound like a man ready to kill his family, Kim thought to herself.

"I have to say, Doctor Thorne was pretty spectacular in keeping him talking for as long as she did, don't you think?"

David nodded and lowered his eyes. He still had not touched anything on the bike, just looked at it a lot.

"You must be pleased to have such a well-respected psychiatrist on your staff here?"

"She's not here in any official capacity," he clarified.

"Oh, I don't understand." Kim had guessed as much but she wanted to hear the story.

"Alex came to us about eighteen months ago, after the death of her husband and two sons. They'd been killed by a drink-driver, a first-time offender who received a prison sentence of five years for taking three lives. She knew all about our philosophy of helping first-time offenders and she said it would be cathartic if she could actually help people like the man that had killed her family."

Clearly this lie was one of her favourites. "And you were happy with that?"

"Have you heard of looking a gift horse in the mouth?"

Kim wasn't sure that was a direct answer.

Dougie wandered out and back into the kitchen, twice.

"He's heard Alex's name. He has remarkable hearing. He worships her. When she's here he follows her constantly."

That Alex hadn't found some way to exploit that yet was a mystery to Kim.

"You obviously hold a great deal of respect for her."

"She is a very accomplished and renowned psychiatrist."

Still no actual agreement, just a statement of fact. This conversation was turning into a dance and Kim wasn't sure who was leading whom.

"Hmm… I think it says something special about her if she's willing to dedicate her time to the cause for no payment, don't you?"

"I think anyone that dedicates their time to…"

"Jesus, will you just give me a straight answer?"

Kim had decided she would lead.

"Your answers to my questions are so well phrased so as not to commit yourself to an opinion that you're going to need a doctor to get the splinters out your ass."

"I didn't realise this was an interrogation."

"It's a conversation, David."

"Do I need a lawyer?"

His eyes were light green and intense.

"Only for crimes against directness."

He smiled. "What exactly do you want to know?"

"Why you have doubts about either the capability or practice of Doctor Alexandra Thorne."

"Who said that I do?"

"One single post in an obscure chat room Mr. DaiHard137."

David sat back in his chair. "It was a while ago."

"Didn't get the response you were expecting, eh?"

"I wasn't anticipating any particular response. It was a simple question."

"But why?"

"Why is it important to you?"

This man was infuriating. There was something here in this place and Kim just needed to find it.

"Would it surprise you to know that her family didn't die in a car accident, because they never existed?"

David frowned. "How do you know that? Why would she make it up?"

"I know because I've confronted her about it and she's admitted that she was never married. Why is a totally different question, but there is evidence to suggest she's been manipulating her patients into carrying out actions that they would not normally do."

Dougie came into the garden and stared at her for a few seconds before leaving again.

"You need to keep your voice down. He's getting agitated."

Kim nodded her understanding and lowered her voice. "I have no direct proof of anything I'm saying to you, but I think you feel that something isn't quite right either. Am I right?"

David was thoughtful. "I don't think I have anything useful to offer. I'm struggling to believe what you're saying and yet I've never been completely comfortable around her. There is something almost remote in Alex; she deals in emotion but doesn't seem to fully understand it. But if you saw my question in the chatroom, then you saw the response from people she has treated."

Kim nodded, feeling deflated. There was nothing here after all. David just had a gut feeling that something wasn't right with the doctor but he had no actual proof of her efforts to manipulate vulnerable people.

"If what you say is right, what do you think she's capable of?"

"From what I've learned, she's capable of anything she puts her mind to. My only problem is that I have no idea how to stop her."

Disappointment flowed through her. She would never be able to prove this woman's involvement in the death of Allan Harris, never mind expose any other crimes she may have been a party to.

It was time for her to leave, but she had one question left to ask. "David, I can't help wondering why you've been sitting beside that bike for fifteen minutes now and you haven't touched a thing. Anything I can do?"

He shook his head dismissively. "Umm...no offence but the mechanical characteristics of a speedway motorbike are a little out of..."

"Oh, is that because they have only one gear and no brakes?"

His tone grated on her nerves. Uncharacteristically, she'd been trying to be helpful. Now she had his attention.

"Or is it because the use of methanol as a fuel allows for increased compression ratio to the engine, producing more power than other fuels, giving higher speeds when cornering? Or..."

"Will you marry me?" David asked.

"Now do you want to tell me what the problem is?"

"She's just not starting. I normally turn her over every couple of months but this time she's not having any of it."

Kim thought for a moment. "Could be the starter motor shorting out. Before spending money on new parts, try running an earthing strip from the starter motor casing to the frame."

"You have no idea just how aroused I am right now."

Kim laughed out loud but was prevented from replying by the presence of Dougie standing beside her. Very gently, he reached down and touched her left hand.

"Dougie…" David warned, meeting her questioning eyes. "He never touches people."

Him and me both, Kim thought.

"It's okay," she said. His skin was cool and soft. He slipped his large hand inside her much smaller one and still didn't look at her.

A single tear had rolled down his cheek. Kim looked to David for guidance. He shrugged, clearly unsure of this changed behaviour.

Dougie's grip was firm as he tugged at her hand. Kim detected no malice or danger, just a gentle sadness.

She spoke quietly. "Do you want me to come with you, Dougie?"

He nodded while still looking up and to the left.

Kim stood and let him guide her through the kitchen and hallway. His grip on her hand was firm but not threatening. David frowned but followed.

"Dougie, what are you doing?" David asked, as the three of them mounted the stairs to the first floor.

He didn't answer but continued to move forward purposefully. He turned the door handle to his room and pushed the door open.

"Dougie, you know that ladies aren't allowed into the rooms."

Dougie loosed her hand as she stepped inside. His room was similar to that of a twelve-year-old. Posters of fast cars were pinned to the wall at the exact same height around the room. His bed was a three-quarter, covered with a racing car quilt. One shelf was full of *Top Gear* DVDs. A framed photo of one of the presenters sat on his bedside cabinet. Kim turned to David, who shrugged.

"He loves Jeremy Clarkson, what can I say?"

The shelf beneath the DVDs housed a collection of exercise books. Some were inexpensive flimsy books found in stationery stores and others were ring binders with colourful patterns on the front.

"He loves writing books. The cheap ones are from me and the others are presents. He doesn't use them, he just likes having them."

Dougie stamped his foot twice at David's words, obviously displeased. Kim saw a pencil tucked behind the photo frame.

"Are you sure he doesn't use them?"

David looked as puzzled as she felt. She turned to the gangly male beside her. "Dougie, is there something you'd like to show me?"

Dougie counted along the exercise books and took out the third from the left. He didn't look at the pages but counted to the seventh page and opened it, then passed it to her.

The writing inside was painfully small. Her eyesight was 20/20 but she had to squint to make out some of the words. It was written in script form with a name and then speech marks.

She looked to the book and back up at Dougie. Goosebumps rose from her skin.

"Dougie, do you have eidetic memory?"

Dougie offered no response.

David was as confused as she. "What the…"

She took another look.

"David, you thought Dougie was lovesick. You thought he was following Alex around because he liked her, but he was recording her every word." She tapped her head. "In here."

She leafed through the book. The pages were filled with writing.

She looked back to him, open-mouthed. "This incredible, gifted young man knew what she was before anyone else."

Kim stepped forward and touched his cheek, gently. He did not pull away

Relief and gratitude flooded her body. "Thank you for showing me your work."

Kim read a paragraph in the book, feeling her anger rise as she did.

IT'S BECAUSE YOU ARE A WASTE OF MY TIME. YOU ARE SO DAMAGED THAT YOU WILL NEVER LEAD A REMOTELY NORMAL LIFE. THERE IS NO HOPE FOR YOU. THE NIGHT- MARES WILL NEVER GO AWAY AND EVERY BALDING MIDDLE AGED MALE WILL BE YOUR UNCLE. YOU WILL NEVER BE FREE FROM HIM OR WHAT HE DID TO YOU. NO ONE WILL EVER LOVE YOU BECAUSE YOU ARE CONTAMINATED AND THE TORMENT YOU GO THROUGH WILL BE WITH YOU FOREVER

She lifted her eyes from the page. "David, who the hell is Shane?"

FIFTY-NINE

The property was two large houses converted to four one-bedroom flats. Nameplates and a bell were mounted in the doorway.

"Come on, Charlie," Dawson moaned. "It's bloody cold out here."

"Keep yer knickers on, Kev," Stacey said.

She pressed one of the other buttons. "Hello, is that Mrs. Preece? Could you buzz to open the door? It's the police and we're here..."

Stacey stopped talking when the line cut off. She waited for the buzz of the lock being released. It didn't sound.

Dawson nudged her out of the way.

He pressed another button. "Mr. Hawkins, I have a delivery from Amazon."

The buzzer sounded.

Stacey followed him in. "How the hell..."

"Everybody orders stuff from Amazon."

He turned left and knocked on the door. No answer. Dawson knocked again.

"This guy is starting to seriously piss me off now. He won't like the interview if he makes me angry."

"What yer gonna do, waterboard him?"

Dawson chuckled. "Stace, that was almost funny."

"I don't like this, Kev," she said, leaning down. She looked through the letter box. The jacket and shoes Cook had been wearing a couple of nights before were within her view in the hallway.

"He's in there but it's silent. It don't feel right."

They knocked together and shouted.

"For once, Stace, I agree with you. I think we need to get in."

"Should we call the fire service?" Stacey asked.

"No, we'll use the equipment instead."

Dawson raised the extinguisher and aimed it towards the lock.

"Have you got my package?" said an elderly voice from the stairs.

"Postman said he'd got the wrong address," Dawson shouted back.

He hit the door hard with the extinguisher. It burst open on impact. Stacey couldn't help but be impressed.

"Hey, what are you doing down there?"

"We're the police," Stacey shouted back as Dawson called for Charlie.

"Do you have my package?"

"No, we're the police," Stacey repeated but louder, following Dawson inside.

"Awww...shit," Dawson said, standing in the doorway.

Stacey came to rest beside him. Her mind echoed his words verbatim.

The grossly overweight man lay sprawled on the bed, face down. He wore light blue boxers and a covering of hair. His right leg dangled off the side of the bed. Aspirin packets sat next to a glass of water.

Stacey sprang into action. She touched the side of his neck. She didn't remove her fingers until she was sure.

"Call an ambulance, Kev. He's still alive. Tell them unconscious but breathing."

Dawson took out his phone and began to call it through. Stacey grabbed the boxes and started to count.

Dawson was reciting the address and the state of the patient.

"I make it about twenty-five tablets," she said.

Dawson repeated the dose to the dispatcher before ending the call.

They stood and looked at each other.

"Shouldn't we be doing something?" Stacey asked.

Dawson looked around. "You could make him a cuppa but I don't think he'll drink it."

Stacey offered him a filthy look.

He opened his arms. "What do you want me to say? Can't give him CPR, thank God. He's still breathing."

"Jesus, Kev, knock it off. Errr...insensitive."

She moved towards the bed and leaned in close to his ear. "Charlie, I'm Detective Constable Wood and..."

"Bloody hell, Stace, great thing to tell a man already close to death."

Stacey turned and glared at him as Dawson stepped past her to squeeze the man's bare shoulder. "Alright, Charlie. It's Kev. Everything's gonna be okay. Help is on the way. They'll be here any minute but we're not going to leave until they're here."

Yeah, that was better, Stacey admitted, but only to herself.

"A cry for help?" she asked Dawson.

Dawson shook his head and stepped away, lowering his voice.

"Nah, it's a serious attempt. He meant to die. No bloke wants to be found like that and then live to tell the tale."

And at this moment, they didn't know if he would.

What exactly was Charlie Cook running from?

SIXTY

As she poured the aromatic Colombian Gold, Alex acknowledged that she had planned this session very carefully. Ideally she would have preferred longer to work with Jessica but she was growing impatient for a result. She desperately hoped that Jessica would not be a disappointment to her, like the others.

This was the biggest play of them all. If she could pull this off it would erase the failures of her other subjects. Kim was still a work in progress but Jessica was in a whole different league.

If Alex was interested in helping this woman properly she would be endeavouring to explore Jessica's past, but that was not her priority. She had limited time. Most women with postnatal psychosis had already experienced an episode of serious mental illness.

Alex was still surprised that the social workers had dismissed it as postnatal depression instead of psychosis even though it only occurred once in every five hundred women. In Jessica, they had found the normal symptoms of depression but hadn't seen the additional pointers that elevated it into Psychosis.

Jessica had also been prone to severe disturbance of mood, mania, muddled thoughts, false ideas, and hearing voices. The onset of the symptoms had occurred quickly after the birth of the child, all indicating post-natal psychosis, a condition that required round-the-clock supervision by competent adults.

Such psychosis often resulted in maternal filicide and Alex needed to establish which major motive was responsible for Jessica wanting to harm her child. She had researched well-known cases for each of the possibilities and they were all fixed in her mind, ready.

She placed the coffee on the table. She really needed to get started.

"I understand that you told the authorities that you rolled over onto Jamie while taking a nap with him beside you. We both know that's not true but here I want you to talk openly."

Jessica looked doubtful.

"Whatever you say here is confidential. I am here to help you and I can only do that with total honesty. The sooner you tell me everything the quicker I can give you the help that you need."

Jessica shook her head and stared into the depths of her lap.

Alex had guessed it would be difficult to persuade the woman to divulge her deepest secrets. No mother would wish for Jessica's thoughts, never mind the burden of saying them out loud. But Alex needed that honesty. She needed those words.

"Was it anything to do with your husband? Were you angry with him?" Alex spoke gently and evenly. "Spousal revenge is far more common than people think." She paused to search for a memory that was stored at the front of her mind.

"A few years ago a man named Arthur Philip Freeman threw his four-year-old daughter Darcy from the West Gate Bridge in Melbourne during a bitter custody battle. It's believed he did this purely to make his spouse suffer."

Alex thought this motive was unlikely for Jessica, as she had said nothing to demonstrate any hostility between herself and her husband. But there was a method to her madness.

"Were you so angry with your husband that you decided to hurt him by hurting Jamie?"

Jessica slowly shook her head. Good. There was no defence that the incident was accidental. Her head was still cast downwards but the eyes were no longer staring beyond her lap, instead staring at it.

She was listening and that was exactly what Alex wanted. Jessica was not yet ready to admit she was wrong. The judgement of society and her family was responsible for the submission that was weighing her down. What Jessica wanted was understanding, acceptance. Permission. And the knowledge that she was not alone.

"May I ask if Jamie was planned?"

"Oh yes," Jessica answered immediately. Good, she was alert and connected. And finally she had spoken.

Alex hadn't seriously thought it was a case of unwanted child filicide but that made no difference to her next move.

She sat back in her chair and just talked.

"You might not remember but it was all over the news in the mid-nineties. A woman in South Carolina, Susan Smith I think her name was, reported to the police that she'd been carjacked by a black man who had driven away with her two small sons still in the car.

"Nine days of tearful pleas played out on television for the safe return of her children ended when she confessed to letting her car roll into a nearby lake, drowning her children inside. All to keep her wealthy lover."

There was no horrified shudder that ran through the body of her patient. Only a slight tip of the head that signalled her attention.

Good. She had achieved the first of the three stages. Understanding. Jessica needed to feel that she was not alone.

"Honestly, Jessica, the problem is a lot more widespread than people think. You're not the first person I've treated for this condition and you certainly won't be the last. Your feelings are nothing to be ashamed of. They are part of you and I promise you'll receive no judgement in this room from me."

Finally, Jessica raised her head and they made eye contact. Alex smiled sympathetically and continued.

"I promise I can help you but you have to tell me the truth."

There was a slight movement of the head. Excellent, they were moving towards acceptance and Alex was left with two possible motives, altruism or delirium, either of which she could work with. From their earlier conversation, she had no reason to suspect Jessica had been delirious. So that left altruism. And in reaching this conclusion Alex had guided Jessica on a journey through successful acts of matricide and now the woman was listening.

Alex sat forward, resting her elbows on her knees.

"I think you wanted to protect your child, Jessica."

A single tear appeared and travelled over her cheek.

Oh you fools, Alex thought of the social workers. If they had known the true extent of her illness the child would more than likely have been removed from her care. But that would not have suited Alex one little bit. Social Services could not have sent her a better gift if the woman had appeared wearing a big, red bow.

"You love Jamie so much you can't bear the thought of him being hurt. You want to shield him from every bad thing in the world. Am I right?" Alex asked, softly.

Jessica slowly began to nod her head.

"He's so beautiful and perfect and innocent; you can't bear the thought of him experiencing any pain at all."

Jessica nodded, more definite.

Alex just needed one last vital piece of information before she could move on to the third part of the process. Permission.

"Can you remember when the thoughts began?"

The tears dried as she gave the question some thought.

"It was the news," Jessica offered, mechanically. She'd been prescribed medication which had a dulling effect but, of course, it wasn't the right medication for her condition. Lithium or electro-shock treatment were the most effective but this was further information that it didn't suit Alex to share with the authorities.

"Go on."

"Not long after I got back from hospital, there was a news report about a bombing in Pakistan. I looked at the pictures and felt frightened of the world I'd brought Jamie into. At first I just tuned into the news programmes now and again, but then I had the twenty-four-hour channels on all day every day. Eventually, I'd be holding Jamie with one hand and checking the news on my phone at the same time. It was like an addiction."

"What were you looking for?"

"Hope. But the whole world was filled with death and destruction and hatred. I couldn't understand why I hadn't seen all this before I became pregnant. How could I have brought him into such a terrible world?"

Alex nodded her understanding. Jessica's motive was the most common: altruistic. She genuinely believed her child would be better off dead, for any number of reasons. The condition often manifested because the mother felt that she could not protect the child adequately from threats, whether real or imagined.

"Can you tell me some of the things that frightened you?"

"One day I was reading about bombs exploding, whole families being tortured and killed in third world countries. There was hunger, starvation, drought, civil war. I tried to tell myself that all these things happened in someone else's country but then I saw articles on car accidents, children being stabbed by other children, a man beaten to death for a bottle of wine, and I realised that it was all getting closer. Too close."

Jessica stared into the distance without blinking as she recounted all of her fears. And there were quite a few to work through. Alex was pleased that she didn't have to bother.

"So, what did you do?"

"I had Jamie on the sofa beside me and suddenly I felt this overwhelming urge to save him; protect him from the evils surrounding him. I visualised him just falling asleep and being safe. I just lay against him and closed my eyes. For a while I felt calm, as though I was finally taking proper care of my child."

"What happened next?"

"Mitch came back from work early to check on me. I didn't hear him come in. He pushed me aside, grabbed Jamie, and rushed him to the hospital."

"How did you feel? And please, for the sake of your recovery, be honest."

Jessica closed her eyes and hesitated for so long Alex wondered if she'd fallen asleep.

Alex prompted. "Jessica, please. I really would like to help you but I can't unless you tell me the whole truth."

Jessica sighed deeply but didn't open her eyes. "I felt disappointed. Jamie wasn't even struggling. It was like he knew what I was trying to do and understood it. He was just going to go to sleep. It felt so right."

Alex marvelled at just how simple this was going to be.

"Did Mitchell understand once you explained it to him?"

Jessica shook her head. "I didn't tell him. He'd already assumed I had just fallen asleep and rolled onto the baby. That was what he told the hospital staff but social services got involved and prosecuted me for child neglect."

Alex heard the disbelief in Jessica's voice. In her own delusional haze Jessica couldn't comprehend that anyone would even think that about her. The fact that she'd lied to her husband signalled that the belief in her own motivation was still within her.

"The judge ordered me to get counselling and that was it. I've kept up the charade because it seems to be what everyone wants to hear. You're the first person I've been honest with."

"And how does that feel?" Alex asked, kindly. Trust was important.

"Better. Everyone around me has the same expression. Even my own mother looks terrified if I go within ten feet of my baby."

"Are they right to watch you closely?"

Jessica hesitated. "I would never do anything that was not in the best interest of my child. Never."

Alex noted the play on words. Yes, the motivation was definitely still there. Alex forced herself to go slowly.

Still, Jessica was seeking permission to do what she felt was right. Alex forced the smile out of her face.

"Strangely, it is a Western belief that your motives are wrong. There is a Buddhist belief in transmigration that dictates that a child who is killed will be reborn in better circumstances."

Alex nodded with a look of "go figure" on her face. She didn't explain that this was believed by people who were too poor to feed their children and so felt that the child would be reborn in circumstances whereby it wouldn't starve to death.

Jessica was nodding intently.

Alex really should be alerting social services that this woman was still a danger to her child. She should be informing them that she was not suffering from postnatal depression. She should be telling them that the medication she was taking was not correct for her condition.

However, none of these actions suited her purpose.

Alex removed her glasses and looked up to the left, searching for a memory that was rehearsed, ready and waiting. Jessica's eyes never strayed from her face. Alex wanted to laugh out loud. She could not have scripted this session any better and real excitement began to form in her stomach. Jessica could be the one.

She lowered her eyes to meet the expectant gaze of Jessica. "Actually, come to think of it, your situation reminds me of an

American woman called Andrea Yates. She had similar fears to you, only she saw the devil everywhere. She was devoutly religious and loved her children very much.

"Every day she was terrified that the devil would claim them and that as they grew older she would not be able to keep them safe.

"The authorities felt that Andrea should never be left alone with her five children, so the family set up a rota system so that someone was always in the house with her. Like you, she was monitored every single day. But one day her husband, also a religious man, decided that the authorities were wrong and placed his trust in God to take care of his family. He left for work before the next caretaker arrived and Andrea seized her opportunity. She drowned her children one by one in the bathtub."

Alex looked for shock in Jessica's features but saw only undivided attention.

"Throughout her trial Andrea maintained that she'd done it out of love for her children, to protect them. Society judged her to be wrong but I'd like you to give some thought to how you feel about that case before our next session."

Right on cue, the alarm on her watch sounded. "Okay, Jessica, that's all for today." She sighed heavily. "My next session is a five-year-old girl whose face was ravaged after a dog attack." Alex shook her head. "Poor child was just playing in the park."

Alex would have loved to take a photo of the terror on Jessica's face. She guided her patient to the door and opened it. "I'll see you next week, take care."

Jessica nodded and passed through the open door.

Alex closed the door. She hoped there would be no session next week. The next time she wanted to see Jessica's face was on the evening news.

SIXTY-ONE

Jessica Ross stumbled out of the premises. She had to get home. Jamie needed her. The neighbours had a dog they often left out in the garden. It could jump the fence and get into the house.

She put the car into gear, silently thanking God for bringing her to Alex, the one single person that understood what she was going through. Being able to open up and be completely honest with Alex had cleansed her of the crippling self-doubt she harboured for her feelings. The story Doctor Thorne had told her of the American woman, Andrea something, was playing over in her mind. She was running out of time.

...*As they grew older she would not be able to keep them safe.*

Danger was everywhere. The traffic lights at which she now waited could easily malfunction, meaning the cars hurtling down the hill could crash into the side of her Citroen. It had happened in Gornal two years ago and a little girl had been trapped in the wreckage for over an hour.

A car horn sounded behind her. The lights were green. Jessica turned and headed past the garden centre on her left. Two little girls were laughing and running around the car park. They could easily run into the road and be killed. Only last month this stretch of road had claimed a teenage cyclist.

She passed the national speed limit sign but kept to thirty miles an hour between fields on either side. If something were to run out in front of her she would have time to stop.

The vehicle behind rushed up in her rear-view mirror. She saw the crude hand signals he offered as his front bumper played kiss chase with her tailgate. She focussed on the road ahead.

She carefully eased the car to the middle of the road to turn right into the family estate. The car behind honked and sped past on her left, causing a gust of wind to rock the car slightly. She looked to the dashboard. Damn, she'd forgotten to indicate.

She passed a woman pushing a buggy. To her right was a lead that secured a brown Labrador to the handle. On her left was a toddler holding onto the other handle. The dog was on the inside, nearest the houses, and the child was closest to the road. At any second the dog could see a cat and react, taking the whole family with it. Why could people not see these things? Even a simple trip to the park was fraught with danger.

Five-year-old girl… face ravaged… dog attack.

Jessica parked the car in front of her sister's Ford Ka and let out a breath. The little girl with half a face had chased her all the way home.

She looked towards her home and she knew what she had to do. The meeting with Alex had only clarified what she already knew.

"Hi, sis, I'm back," she called from the front door. The sound of Jamie crying met her ears.

Jessica fought the urge to tear into the lounge, grab her child, and protect him. She had to do this right. It was her only chance.

Emma was circling the lounge, rocking Jamie back and forth in her arms. "He's been like this the whole time. I can't settle him."

Jessica offered her sister what she hoped was a bright smile and held out her arms. "Here, let me take him."

Jessica took her child into her arms and rocked him gently. She felt his body relax into her own. Content. He knew.

Jessica caught the brief expression of relief that passed over her sister's face. She resented the fact that everyone thought she had the ability to hurt her child when all she wanted to do was protect him. Any sign of affection to her baby was met with secret little nods and whispers in corners.

"Good visit?" Emma asked, sitting on the sofa.

Jessica nodded. "Talking with Alex is really helpful. I feel so much better already." She stroked her son's hair. "Don't I, little munchkin?"

She continued to walk around, rocking his little body against her own. "I'd never hurt him, Emma," she said, fixing her sister with what she hoped was a clear gaze.

Emma swallowed. "I know, Jess."

She softened her gaze. "Look, he knows I'd never harm him, don't you, angel?"

He gurgled back at her. Emma laughed.

Jamie's eyes started to droop with all the rocking. Jessica kissed his head and placed him into the Moses basket.

...Before the next caretaker arrived...seized her opportunity.

She turned to her sister. It was time for her to leave. "Well, I'm going to have a nice, long bath while Jamie takes a nap. You're welcome to sit and wait if you want to."

She caught Emma's quick glance at the clock above the fireplace. She had three children of her own and many things to do.

"Mum's going to be here in twenty minutes, Em. I'll be fine."

Emma looked doubtful.

Jessica smiled reassuringly. "Emma, I'm really okay, I promise. I feel so much better."

Emma looked away. "It's okay. I'll just wait for a little bit, make sure he's settled off to sleep."

Jessica shrugged and headed up the stairs, wishing her sister would just leave. Time was running out. She was halfway up when she heard her name.

"What is it, Em?"

She turned to find Emma at the bottom of the stairs, reaching for her coat. "You're right. I know it's okay. I trust you."

Jessica returned to the hallway and hugged her sister. Finally she was going. "I really am fine, Em. Don't worry."

She opened the front door to let her sister out of the house. Emma turned. "You're sure?"

Jessica gave her one last hug and nodded. "We'll be fine. I only want what's best for him."

Emma walked slowly to her car, probably questioning her decision, but Jessica offered a bright smile as reassurance. If Emma tried to call their mother she would already be on her way and wouldn't answer her mobile while driving. If she called Mitch it would take him at least twenty minutes to get home.

As her sister pulled away, Jessica offered one last wave and closed the door behind her.

The second she entered the lounge a calmness settled around her that she welcomed. The sound of the television faded into the background.

After her session with Alex she had no doubt that she had been right all along. Initially, Jessica had questioned herself due to the reactions of everyone around her and so she had pretended, she had appeased, and all along she'd been the one in the right.

Her session with Alex had not only given her the confidence in her own convictions, it had vindicated her. She no longer felt guilty for her thoughts. She felt righteous and empowered.

"Come to Mummy, sweetheart," she cooed, reaching into the Moses basket.

His sleepy little body squirmed once and then burrowed into her; his safe place.

She selected a knife from the kitchen drawer and mounted the stairs. She placed Jamie gently in the middle of the bed she shared with Mitch.

In the en-suite bathroom, she placed the knife on the edge of the tub and ran both the hot and cold water to fill the bath quickly. Her son would not be without her for long.

She went to Jamie's room and took a moment to select his outfit, settling on a white romper suit covered with blue baby dinosaurs. It was her favourite.

Back in the bathroom she turned off the taps and undressed quickly, slipping into a white towelling robe.

As she entered the bedroom, she took a moment to observe her son, awake now, intrigued by these new surroundings. His small hands grabbed at the quilt cover. Jessica felt a rush of pride.

She stood for a moment at the bedroom window, observing a world that allowed the danger to creep closer every day. Satisfied, she closed the blinds and blocked out the terror. The crawling, invisible evil would never get the opportunity to harm her child.

The darkened room became intimate and safe.

Jessica smiled down at her child as she removed his white babygro. His legs flailed as she changed his nappy and redressed him in the romper suit.

Jamie was safe, right here. Nothing had yet hurt him and at this moment nothing could. As a mother it was up to Jessica to protect him. And she would.

A child who is killed will be reborn in better circumstances.

In another time the world would not be filled with cruelty and violence. Children would have the freedom to grow up without fear and intimidation. In another life, her son would be safe.

Jessica stared down into the eyes of her child as she reached for the pillow.

Jamie gurgled up at her, his limbs shooting out in all directions; happy, excited.

"I love you so much it hurts, my darling. I know you understand that I have to protect you from this world. I cannot allow you to be hurt or damaged by anything. There is danger everywhere and I have to keep you safe. I know you feel it too, don't you, sweetheart?"

He squealed with delight and Jessica knew, beyond a shadow of a doubt, that she was doing the best thing, the only thing possible to protect her child.

She leaned over him and placed kisses on his chubby cheeks, his forehead, and the tip of his nose.

"We will be together soon, my darling, sweetest angel."

Jessica lowered the pillow and covered the face of her son.

SIXTY-TWO

Shit, Kim thought, as she watched Jessica Ross close the blinds. There was something not right with this picture.

She had arrived at Alex's practice to confront the doctor about the conversations recorded by Dougie, when Jessica had exited the building. Kim knew nothing of such sessions but she knew a patient was not supposed to leave the premises of their psychiatrist looking like they were being chased by the Devil himself.

The erratic driving and the expression on Jessica's face while hugging the other woman goodbye had not quelled the anxiety building in Kim's stomach. Jessica's serene expression while looking out of the window in her baby son's room chilled the blood in her veins.

Kim detected no other movement in the property and was guessing the woman was now in the house alone.

She swallowed, feeling her own heartbeat quicken. She did not know what she was witnessing but she did know that some kind of conclusion had been reached since Jessica had left Alex's office.

Jesus, who should she call... Bryant? And say what? *A woman is standing in her bedroom window, looking rather contented.* Bryant already had enough evidence on which to get Kim committed, so she certainly wasn't going to offer him any more.

Could she call social services? They knew Jessica's history but they hardly operated a blue-light response. If Kim called as a concerned citizen she would probably be advised to call the police;

the irony in that scenario was not lost on her. But she couldn't just sit here. Something was definitely not right.

"Fuck," she said, knowing she was on her own. She opened the driver's door and sprinted across the road to the Ross house, then pressed the bell and banged on the door simultaneously. If Jessica answered wondering what the hell was going on, Kim would beg for help from the machete-wielding maniac that just happened to have disappeared into thin air.

She opened the letter box to see if Jessica was approaching the door but the house echoed with a stillness that chilled her to the core. No sound from the child or the parent. Damn it, she knew they were both in there. Why the hell wasn't she answering the door?

Kim tried the gate to the side of the house. It was locked. She looked around and spotted a wheel barrow half full of dandelion weeds. She pushed it in front of the gate and used it to help her climb over. The side of the house showed no open windows and no one inside.

She rushed to the rear and tried the handle of the French door. It was locked. Kim had the sense that she was running out of time. She looked around the garden and reached for a shovel. She swung it backwards for momentum and smashed it against the glass panel. On the second attempt, it shattered. Shards flew all around her, a couple embedding themselves into her right hand. She ignored the pain and pulled the sleeve of her jumper over her fist to punch an opening big enough for her to enter.

If Jessica was doing nothing more ominous than taking a shower, Kim was in a whole world of trouble. For once, she hoped that she was.

She ran through the kitchen to the front of the house, almost tripping over a play mat littered with toys. She took the stairs two at a time, the blood surging through her ears. At the top of the stairs she was met with a closed door.

She burst through it and stopped dead, her mind taking a second to register the sight before her.

Jessica was dressed only in a towelling robe and stood looking down at the bed, a cushion dangling from her fingers.

The small, still form dressed in a dinosaur romper suit stared, unseeing, at the ceiling.

Jessica nodded and smiled at her calmly. "He's safe now."

Kim remembered another set of innocent eyes that had stared up to the ceiling, beautiful but lifeless, like a perfect doll. Back then she hadn't known what to do when the last breath left her brother's body. She could only sit and shake him, beg him to come back to her. She had tried everything, but it had done no good. As she'd felt the decreasing warmth of his body against her own, she had eventually closed his eyes and sent Mikey off to heaven.

Kim snapped herself back to life. She needed an ambulance but she didn't have time to make the call and give the details.

She ran to the window, opened it, and screamed as loudly as her lungs would allow. There were three people in the road who all turned and looked.

"Call an ambulance, dead child." She quickly turned from the window and pushed Jessica forcefully out of the way. The woman stumbled backwards, as though in a trance.

Kim lost awareness of her surroundings as she stilled her trembling hands. She wiped the blood from her cut hand onto her jacket before placing two fingers on the baby's neck to confirm what she already knew to be true. He was dead. But she couldn't give up. She wouldn't give up.

Kneeling beside the bed, she filled her cheeks with air, then covered the baby's mouth and nose with her mouth and blew gently into his lungs. She watched as his chest rose artificially and waited until it fell before repeating the process four more times. She placed two fingers in the centre of his chest and pressed down sharply to around a third of the depth of his chest. She did this thirty times and placed her ear to his mouth. Nothing.

She stopped to give two rescue breaths, fighting the frustration of the pace. With an adult, she could have been more forceful.

"Come on," she whispered on the second set of compressions.

Kim had no idea how long she'd been working, but a mixture of sirens squealed in the distance.

"Come on, sweetheart, you can do it."

Kim gave two more breaths and paused as her gaze rested on the tiny chest that was unmistakably rising and falling on its own. The life returned to his eyes and a small wail escaped his tiny lips. It was the sweetest sound Kim had ever heard.

The cry seemed to galvanise Jessica, who snapped from her trancelike state and moved towards the bed.

"Get the fuck away from him," Kim growled as she formed a protective circle around his small body with her arms. The blood from her right hand transferred onto the bedcovers.

Jessica stopped dead and stared across at her child. Her face was filled with confusion. Kim didn't know if this was due to her own actions of trying to kill her child or wondering how the baby was still alive.

Kim heard the crash of the front door being broken down, followed by the thunder of footsteps on the stairs. Relief flooded through her. She couldn't bear to be in the same room as this woman for much longer.

A male paramedic and a police officer she didn't recognise entered the room. The paramedic stepped around her and bent down to assess the child, who was still breathing.

"The blood is from me," Kim said, moving out of his way.

The constable glanced towards Jessica, who clutched the pillow tightly to her chest. He then looked to Kim for confirmation of his worst fears. Kim nodded.

"Detective Inspector?"

She waved away his questions. "I'll do a full statement later, but for now you need to know that the mother is very sick and was holding the pillow above the child when I entered the room."

"We'll get social services to meet us at the hospital. But why are you..."

"Later, Constable," Kim said, as the fatigue hit her body and the adrenaline in her system reverted to normal levels.

The paramedic's eyes met hers. "He's weak but steady." His eyes went to the blood dripping from her hand. "Let me take a look..."

"It's fine," Kim snapped, thrusting the hand into her jacket pocket.

With one last glance towards the bed, Kim turned and left the house.

Finally, there was no doubt in her mind that Alex had manipulated Jessica into committing such an atrocious act just as she had with Ruth, Barry, and even Shane.

Now she'd had enough. Alex had to be stopped. Whatever the cost.

SIXTY-THREE

"Sir, will you just hear me out?" Kim begged.

Woody banged his fist on the table. Kim would have liked the same outlet for her frustration but the fresh bandage prevented it.

"No, Stone, I will not. This woman has taken enough of your time and you have not one ounce of proof that she's even done anything wrong."

"I have the books. Dougie has recited every…"

"And he'll testify to that on the stand, will he?" he stormed, glaring at her.

Kim's phone sounded in her pocket. She ignored it and so did Woody.

"Believe me, she is hurting people. Not directly, but she is manipulating people into doing things. Ruth Willis…"

"Murdered Allan Harris out of revenge."

"But Jessica has been manipulated…"

"You're being ridiculous. Jessica Ross is severely ill. You can't know this has anything to do with the psychiatrist."

Kim wondered if he was ever going to let her finish a sentence.

Her phone dinged with the receipt of a voicemail.

Woody's irritation moved up a gear.

"I know that she is using her patients for some sick kind of research…"

"That sounds ridiculous here in my office and would sound even more preposterous in a courtroom."

Her phone dinged a text message and Woody's face turned thunderous.

"Stone, I've already sent your team home and I suggest you do the same. I will not discuss this matter with you any further."

She stood as her phone began to ring again.

"And for goodness' sake, answer your damn phone."

Any type of curse from her boss signalled he was only a few degrees short of boiling. The next sentence would signal the end of her career. She had to leave it. For now.

The call had cut off by the time she closed Woody's office door behind her.

The two missed calls were from David Hardwick.

She went straight to the text message.

The first sentence her eyes skimmed over.

SORRY TO BOTHER YOU IF U R BUSY

But the second sentence jumped out at her.

BUT DOUGIE'S NOT BACK FROM HIS WALK

Kim hit the call button and headed down the stairs. David answered on the second ring.

"Thanks for calling…"

"How late is he?" she asked, using her shoulder to push through the front door.

"Twenty minutes, but he's never late…"

"You don't think it's Alex?" she asked, swallowing the unease building in her chest.

"After what we read? I just don't know," he answered honestly.

"But she doesn't know about the books," Kim said. She hadn't had the chance to confront her. She'd been too busy chasing Jessica Ross.

"She might know," David admitted.

Kim's head began to swim. Oh no.

"After you left, I caught Malcolm listening behind the door."

"Oh shit," she said and ended the call.

SIXTY-FOUR

Kim fired up the bike and wrapped her hand around the accelerator. The pain shot through all five fingers and as far as her shoulder. She ignored it and adjusted the position of her palm so the safety pin didn't dig into the area of the wound.

Once she'd collected her jacket and keys, a quick call to David had informed her that Dougie normally walked the canal from Netherton to Brierley Hill where he exited and walked home, passing a fish bar in Quarry Bank that gifted him a cone of chips.

They had agreed that David would start at Netherton, she would start at Brierley Hill, and they would meet somewhere in the middle.

David's words had said there was probably nothing to worry about. His tone said different.

They both knew if Alex had Dougie, there was something to worry about for sure. The doctor didn't like loose ends, and Dougie was very loose indeed.

Kim pulled up at the lights at the top of Thorns Road and wiped moisture from her visor.

The winter had not seen the snowfall of the previous year but the early March rain held just a lacklustre effort at sleet.

She rode past the bright lights of the Merry Hill shopping centre. The bridge David had described sat at the front of a sprawling estate and the seven tower blocks that rose up from its belly.

She parked the bike on a patch of dirt. Her gloves were shoved inside her helmet, which was then secured to the seat.

She stepped around the bike to traverse the slope down onto the canal towpath. Discarded nappy bags and takeaway wrappers littered the route.

Each step took her further away from the illumination of the single street lamp. A deflated football caught her left foot unawares. She stumbled and reached out to steady herself, and a stinger bit at her skin.

Kim swore softly as she continued down into the darkness. The road noise was travelling eerily into the distance.

At most, she could make out twenty feet ahead before she entered total darkness. She had no idea how long that darkness lasted. She continued walking forward into the gaping black mass. It wouldn't be long until she could no longer distinguish the path from the canal.

She moved slowly, occasionally startled by a movement from the water. Kim guessed it was probably rats.

She took out her mobile phone and pointed it to the ground. It could have been no darker around her if she'd chosen to close her eyes. The light from the Torch function enabled her to place one foot in front of the other.

Kim continued to move forward and felt the ground beneath her change. Putting out her left hand, she felt the dripping slime on brick. She'd made it to a tunnel. The smell of urine almost overpowered her, but there was a darker, fouler stench.

A single street lamp from the bridge illuminated the exit from the tunnel and there a white pedal-bin liner lay open, displaying rotten meat. Something small scurried away from her probing light. She covered her nose and moved quickly past it.

Once more she entered the darkness.

Alex had got her playing cat and mouse and right now, Kim felt like the mouse.

"Come on, Dougie, where are you?"

SIXTY-FIVE

Dawson sighed deeply and rested his head against the wall.

Stacey carried on pacing. She'd read every poster on the notice-board a dozen times and was now well versed on the symptoms of at least fifteen diseases.

The door opened to the side ward. Stacey halted and Dawson raised his head with hopeful expectation. They'd been waiting over four hours.

The nurse nodded. "You can see him now. He's weak and fragile but alive. I can't let you stay for very long."

Stacey nodded her agreement as Dawson lifted himself from the chair.

"Bloody hell, Charlie, you had us for a minute there," Dawson said as they entered the room.

Stacey was surprised by his appearance. Although grossly overweight, that was what had probably saved him. Death by aspirin was normally dictated by an ingredient to body weight ratio. And he carried a lot of weight.

His complexion bore no correlation to his heartbeat. Not a smudge of colour graced his face. But he was younger than Stacey had thought initially. Now, she put his age at mid- to late thirties.

"What's going on, Charlie?" Dawson asked, taking the seat beside the bed. Stacey perched herself on the windowsill.

"I've just had enough."

"Is there something you want to tell us, mate?" Kev asked.

"I don't know what you mean."

"Come on, Charlie. There's something going on here. There's a reason you wanted to die. Just tell us and we can help you. It'll feel better once you let it out."

Stacey watched as he swallowed and shook his head.

"Charlie, we know it was you, mate. You were in the basement with those girls, weren't you? You watched while their father..."

"No," he said, closing his eyes. "It wasn't me. I swear it."

Dawson moved closer and lowered his voice. "Oh Charlie, stop lying, eh? We know the book club's a cover. You don't even read the books."

Finally a smudge of colour infused the bleached skin. "I don't always have time..."

"You're hardly run off your feet at the shop. Charlie, trust me, you'll feel better if you just admit it. We know you went to the youth club at the community centre the other night. It was the only event taking place. Why would you be with a group of twelve-year-old girls if you..."

"I wasn't at the youth club," he said, closing his eyes.

"Charlie, we checked. There was nothing else..."

"There are some events that don't get advertised."

Stacey got there first.

"Alcoholics Anonymous," she said to herself.

Dawson turned back to Charlie. "You're an alcoholic?"

There was the longest pause as a tear fell from the corner of his eye. He gently shook his head.

Dawson looked to her and she shrugged.

"I tell them I am," he admitted.

Stacey moved closer. "Because they never turn anyone away."

"You go to AA meetings for company?" Dawson asked incredulously.

Charlie offered a slight nod, filled with shame.

"And the book club? The same? You just get to meet a few guys once a week for a chat?"

"They come from all over the place, every profession. They've all got something to say. I just listen, mostly."

Dawson deflated back into the chair. He'd really hoped they had him, but what they really had was a desperately shy and lonely man who had grabbed at any opportunity to make friends.

"Why this, why now?" Stacey found herself asking.

He shrugged. "The book club was bound to break up once you started asking them questions. It ain't much but it's a bit of company now and again."

"You need to get yourself a woman, mate," Dawson said, getting to his feet.

Charlie smiled, but it looked despairing. "Looking like this, eh?"

Stacey had reached the door. Their work here was done. Charlie Cook was not their man.

Dawson lagged behind. "Do you know Fitness Gym in Dudley?"

Charlie shook his head.

"Just up the road from the indoor market. I'm there most Monday and Wednesday nights. Pop in and we'll get something sorted."

Stacey stepped outside and Dawson followed.

She turned to look at him and shook her head.

"Why are you smiling at me, Stace?"

"No reason, Kev. No reason at all."

He shrugged and reached into his pocket. "Have you checked your phone?"

Stacey took it out and checked it, then frowned.

"Anything from the boss?"

She shook her head.

Their eyes met and a message passed between them. It had been hours since they'd heard from the Guv. And that never, ever happened.

Without speaking, they turned and headed for the station.

SIXTY-SIX

Alex smiled cheerfully at Dougie. He had not been difficult to find. David had told her about the simpleton's walks many times. A creature of habit, he never varied his route.

The Delph Locks were a flight of eight locks linking the Dudley and Stourbridge canal route. Each lock was seventy feet long and eighty-five feet deep. Such a fitting place for Dougie to die, with the hours that he had spent here.

At first the phone call had stunned her, not least because she had no idea that Malcolm had her number. But now she was glad that he had. She'd had seven missed calls during her session with Jessica and out of curiosity had called the number back.

Initially she had not believed him. No way could such a bumbling oaf like Dougie be so clever, but as Malcolm had talked, she had listened.

The initial burst of anger had been at herself. She had foolishly written Dougie off, assuming his attention was because he had liked her. The rage had dulled to a mild irritation once she'd realised Dougie was a problem that was easily solved.

His initial surprise at seeing her had been quelled by her assurances that Kim wanted to talk to him. It was what kept him standing here now.

Alex was pleased to see him look furtively to the right and then to the left.

"Oh, Dougie, did you believe me?"

She shone the torch in his face. A couple of spots of sleet dropped between them. He blinked and put his hand in front of his eyes.

She smiled. "You ridiculous, stupid man. Your life is about to change. There's no need to be frightened. For the first time ever, you get the opportunity to be useful. You are pointless and worthless, but you are my way of sending a message to your precious Kim."

She spat the name at him and shook her head.

"And here was me thinking you were totally gormless, and you go and surprise me, Dougie. I don't like surprises."

She moved a step closer. Shining the torch between them. As the torch beam lowered down his body, she laughed out loud.

She held the shot of light on his groin. "Oh, Dougie, you've wet yourself. How humiliating is that?"

She delighted in his discomfort and revelled in his fear.

"It would have been so much better if you'd been illiterate as well as retarded."

She shone the light into his face again. His head was slightly tipped and his eyes reached up and to the left. His mouth moved as though trying to form a word but, to Alex's knowledge, he'd never spoken.

His hands moved furtively as though he were trying to wring them out.

She took Dougie by the arm to move him closer to the edge.

He offered little resistance as she felt the trembling vibrate from his body to her hand.

Physically, he could overpower her any second he chose to, but just like a German Shepherd, he didn't know he was bigger and stronger. In Dougie's mind she was tougher and so he didn't bother to put up a fight.

His feet scraped across the gravel as he tried to plant them where he stood. It was no more taxing to Alex than handling a bin bag.

"Oh, come on Dougie, don't be difficult," she said, lurching him forward to the lock-side edge.

She shone the torch light down into the abyss. A small cry escaped from his lips. Alex estimated the drop to be thirty feet before the water lapped at the walls.

Smiling, she placed her hand between his shoulder blades.

It took just a nudge from her for Dougie to start tumbling forwards.

SIXTY-SEVEN

Kim heard the splash in the distance. The water had made many sounds beside her but nothing as forceful as that.

She stopped dead and listened keenly but the only sound she could make out now was the blood thundering around her body.

She moved forward quickly. There were still a couple of miles of canal before she reached the meeting point she'd agreed with David, which meant she was clearly on her own.

There was no time to consider her options. She needed to find whatever, or whoever, had made that splash.

As she turned a slight bend in the towpath her eyes fell upon a figure bent over, shining a torch into the lock.

If she hadn't known before what Alex was capable of, she had no doubt in her mind now. The psycho had pushed Dougie in.

Kim could hear the splash of arms flailing about in the water.

If she tried to save Dougie, Alex would have plenty of time to get away and Kim was dealing with no ordinary criminal.

She would never find Alex again.

Kim leaned around the corner and quickly judged the distance between them. Fifty feet.

Once she moved she would have to be quick, making use of the element of surprise, but she knew what she had to do.

Hastily, she removed her jacket and threw it to the ground. The boots would have to stay. She didn't have time. The splashing was becoming quieter.

She took a deep breath, counted to three, and launched herself across the distance.

Kim kept her eyes on Alex the whole time. Although she couldn't see her face, she could guess at the shocked expression. Good, that was all the distraction she needed.

Ten feet, five feet, and bang—she sent Alex hurtling into the water.

Kim took a deep breath and dived right in after her.

SIXTY-EIGHT

Bryant faced Robin Parks across the table.

He wasn't one for making snap judgements or even going with his gut. He left that to the boss. If Bryant didn't like someone initially, he tried to give them the benefit of the doubt.

The man sat back in the chair, lifting the two front legs. His right foot rested on his left knee. He wore dark jeans and a V-neck sweater.

"Mr. Parks, thank you for agreeing to speak to me this evening."

He opened his arms magnanimously. "Anything I can do to help."

Bryant heard an underlying sneer but forced himself not to react.

"Detective Inspector Stone and I recently spoke to you..."

"Detective Inspector? Don't you mean bulldog? She shouldn't be allowed out without a muzzle."

Bryant kicked his own ankle beneath the table. Oh, this was not going well.

"We informed you that we had discovered that there was someone else in the room with your brother-in-law on at least one occasion."

"You might have mentioned it whilst terrorising my sister."

He rocked to and fro on the chair.

"Do you have any idea who that person could be, Mr. Parks?"

"Truthfully, I don't think he exists. I think it's a story your bulldog invented so she can continue to make Wendy's life hell."

"And why would she do that, Mr. Parks?"

Damn it, he'd bitten.

Robin Parks leaned forward. "Because she is a bitter, lonely woman that clearly wishes she'd been born a man and she's taking out her every frustration on innocent people. That's why."

He returned to rocking back and forth, utterly pleased with himself.

"That may be your opinion, Mr. Parks," Bryant said, trying to keep his voice even.

"Surely you have to agree. She is rude, obnoxious…"

"And clearly memorable, as you haven't stopped talking about her since I sat down."

The rocking stopped but Bryant forged ahead.

"Mr. Parks, we have forensic evidence and a hair. And neither belong to Leonard."

The front legs of the chair came in to land. "Really?"

Bryant nodded and then spoke for the tape. "Yes. As you know, Daisy has confirmed that she knew whoever was there. Is there anything you can offer to help?"

The mood in the room had changed.

"I've been in that basement…"

"If you'd like to offer us a sample, I can…"

"Not a fucking chance. I've seen how you lot work. Your boss would have fitted my sister up if she'd been given half the chance."

Robin Parks pushed back his chair and stood.

"I believe I am here of my own volition?"

Bryant nodded his head. He didn't bother to confirm it.

"I see how this is going, so I shall take my leave now."

Bryant stood.

"Mr. Parks, please. It's your nieces we're talking about here. I know how much you love your sister but please remember she's not the victim. Don't let your anger at my boss get in the way of our investigation."

Bryant was shocked to see the man's eyes were filled with rage. "Don't you get it? I have to be angry at someone. This is my family and I love those girls like they were my own. I would give my life to protect either one of them. I have struggled to believe that I didn't spot what my bastard brother-in-law was up to but I categorically refuse to believe there was someone else. I would have known."

"Mr. Parks, I understand…"

"The hell you do," he spat, before storming out of the room.

Bryant fell back into the chair. Was Parks really letting his ego get in the way of the investigation? He couldn't accept that he had not seen the abuse of his own nieces but was no longer able to argue in the face of the evidence. But to have missed the involvement of someone else? Or was his refusal to acknowledge the possibility due to a more sinister reason entirely.

It was time to speak to the boss.

SIXTY-NINE

The water hit Kim's face like an ice sheet.

She felt her left hand collide with a limb on the way in, but she wasn't sure whose it was.

To the left she could hear spluttering and movement. To the right she could feel much slower, less frenzied activity but she couldn't see a thing.

Kim took a chance, kicked out to the left and swam to the right. She was rewarded with a shriek of pain from Alex. She'd suspected the weaker movement somewhere on her right was coming from Dougie, already fatigued.

The canal water moved in all directions around her. Kim took a second to get her bearings and worked from where the torch had been dropped. She swam across the space widthways.

Come on Dougie, where are you?

Her foot became entangled in metal and helplessly she tried to kick it free. It felt like a spider's web around her ankle. She reached into the water and dislodged her leg from the spokes of a bicycle wheel.

On her third trip, she swam into the form of Dougie, barely afloat. His arms still patted the water in a doggy-style movement but his head was bobbing underneath. He made no sound at all.

She reached and grabbed Dougie at the neck, hoisting his body up so that his face was out of the water and he coughed and spluttered the water from his mouth. But instead of relaxing into her, Kim's touch seemed to galvanise him into action, giving him an extra bit of fight. And he was fighting her for his life. Great, he thought she was Alex.

"Dougie, it's me, Kim," she said.

She raised her left hand from the water and laid it gently on his cheek while her legs worked furiously to keep her afloat. She had to let him know he was safe.

She could feel the exhaustion taking over his body.

"It's okay, Dougie, just go limp. Don't fight me."

On cue, he relaxed his body completely and Kim silently thanked him for his trust.

She placed her right hand under his chin and turned on her back. Her legs worked like a steamer beneath the water. Her only source of energy to get them both to safety.

The top of her head banged against the side wall of the canal.

She manoeuvred their position so they were moving alongside the wall. She dragged Dougie with her right hand and guided with her left.

She knew these locks had ladders, but God only knew where they were.

A couple more strokes and her hand hit a metal stanchion. Finally. She grabbed on but before she could pull Dougie in, she felt something against her cheek. Too slowly, she realised it was leather and then she felt the full force of the heel stamp down on her head. The pain blurred her vision for a split second before she realised what it meant. Shit, Alex was above her. She was climbing the ladder out.

Kim could not allow the woman to get away.

"Dougie, paddle," she screamed, momentarily letting him go.

She twisted her body and reached upwards. Her left hand clamped around a stockinged ankle trying to make its escape.

Kim closed her fingers around it and yanked it down.

She heard Alex gasp and although she hadn't dislodged her from the ladder completely, she was down a few rungs.

The metal edge of the ladder pressed against Kim's cheek.

She reached out for Dougie and, managing to capture his hood, held onto the stanchion and pulled him towards her. Every muscle in her body burned.

"Climb the ladder once I'm gone but don't get out, understand?"

She felt him nod against her arm.

Once she was sure he was holding onto the metal, she forced herself onto the ladder. As her body rose above the surface, gallons of water drained from her clothes, almost drawing her back into the lock.

She held on tight to the railings and forced one foot to rise in front of the other. Hers was the only movement on the ladder. Shit, Alex was already out. The climb seemed to go on forever, her muscles screamed louder with every rung.

As she neared the top the torch offered some illumination but there was still no sign of Alex.

She pulled herself free of the ladder. Her legs were weakened and the water in her clothes added the weight of a person on her back.

She stumbled forward but righted herself. Now she could see that Alex was only ten, fifteen feet in front.

Kim willed her legs to move quicker. She flew over the gravel path, gaining every second.

She gave one last kick and lurched forward, slamming Alex right into the ground.

SEVENTY

Kim realised she had miscalculated when her arms encircled the fabric of Alex's sodden trousers instead of her waist. But she had hold of something and she was not letting go.

Alex gasped and fell forward. Kim hung on tightly, gathering Alex's limbs to her body tightly like a hard-won rugby ball.

Alex was now writhing on the ground, trying to pull herself forward and out of Kim's grasp.

Kim felt the fabric of the trousers slipping through her arms as the stockinged feet pounded her chest. Kim was grateful the shoes had been lost.

Grabbing hold of Alex's left ankle, Kim twisted it sharply to the right.

Alex shrieked out in pain but continued moving forward. It was useless, Kim needed something else.

"Alex…I…have the answer…that you want." Kim forced the words out on the short, sharp breaths she had available.

Alex stopped fighting for a second. And that was all it took.

Kim turned Alex onto her back and scrabbled up her body. She locked her knees against Alex's ribs.

They were on the edge of a pool of light cast by the street lamp on the bridge.

Kim could feel the movement of Alex's chest as her lungs expanded, fighting to fill them with air. Her proximity to this woman left a worse taste in her mouth than the water.

"Get...the hell...off me." Alex raged.

Kim shook her head. "Not a chance...you damn psycho."

Kim ached to punch and kick the life out of this woman beneath her, but first they needed to talk.

Kim felt as though they had been staring at each other across the dance floor for weeks. She wiped a strand of wet hair from her eye.

"I have the answer you want."

"What are you...talking about?"

Kim smiled. "I left Jessica's house two hours ago."

"So?"

Kim laughed. "Is that it?"

"You've lost me."

"You manipulated Ruth into murdering Allan Harris. You were behind the actions of Barry Grant. Jessica Ross came to you for help, but she was far more disturbed than the authorities knew. You know what she's done but you couldn't give a shit. It's about how she felt afterwards. Isn't it?"

Kim felt Alex stiffen beneath her.

"Were you as disappointed in Ruth as you were in Shane?"

"I haven't seen Ruth since..."

"You didn't need to. Bryant and I told you what you needed to know. You never asked to see Ruth again."

Alex said nothing.

"Jessica; your latest guinea pig. The woman who left your office this morning and went home to suffocate her child."

"Oh my God, she...?"

"Cut the bullshit, Alex. You wanted me in this game and here I am, so don't insult me. There's nothing I can do about it and that is exactly what you wanted."

Kim felt the body relax beneath her.

"If you say so."

"Do you want to find out what happened?"

Alex remained still. Kim could tell that she desperately wanted to know. The woman was soaked to the skin, lying on her back on a canal towpath and she was offering no resistance. Oh, she really wanted to know.

"Ask me the question and I'll tell you."

Kim could see the tension in her jaw.

"Come on, Alex. Ask the question."

"How does Jessica feel?" she asked, softly.

"Point proven. Don't you even want to know if the baby is dead or alive? I'll answer that, even though you don't give a shit. Jamie is alive, Alex. But you only want to know how Jessica feels."

Alex's stare burned into her.

"Well, let me tell you. She feels as guilty as hell."

Alex bucked against her but Kim was ready. She bore every ounce of her weight down onto Alex's stomach and lay down low, as though riding her bike, altering her own centre of gravity. As the flailing arms attempted to hit her face, she grabbed them and held them tight.

"All your life, you've lived with no conscience... no accountability. You know that a sociopath can never develop a conscience and you wanted to turn that around. You wanted the power to take conscience away. All this to try and turn a vulnerable person into a dangerous sociopath, get them to carry out despicable acts without guilt."

Alex's mouth had formed into a hateful line. All attempts at rebuttal were gone.

Kim continued. "You knew you could manipulate your test subjects into doing what you wanted, but you wanted them to do it without guilt. You were arrogant enough to think you could control human nature."

"Good luck in court. You have no..."

Mid-sentence, Alex bucked her body upwards and dislodged Kim's right knee.

Kim tried to push her back down but she was wriggling every limb she had. Kim reached for Alex's right hand but Alex had got to hers first.

Seizing her bandaged palm, Alex dug her fingers in, hard. The stars in Kim's eyes were immediate as the pain shot as far as her head.

She tried to break her hand free, but Alex squeezed it again.

Kim felt the sickness rise up in her stomach.

Alex squeezed again and Kim fell sideways in agony.

In one swift movement, Alex was astride her and the position of power had been reversed.

"Right, Kimmy, now it's time to talk about you."

SEVENTY-ONE

Bryant stormed into the squad room.

"Tell me one of you has heard from her?"

Dawson and Stacey shook their heads.

Bryant took out his phone.

"Christ, Bryant, we've probably killed her battery with missed calls."

Bryant tried again anyway. As the call rang out, he had an ominous sensation.

A feeling of trepidation rolled around in his stomach that was mirrored by both of his colleagues. He had the inexplicable feeling that he'd let her down.

He had known that Kim was still investigating Doctor Thorne, because she was unable to leave it alone. So many times she had tried to speak to Bryant about her suspicions and he'd blown her off; told her she was imagining things. He knew he'd underestimated her resolve. In Kim's world, no one got away.

And now no one knew where she was.

"Should we go looking?" Stacey asked.

"And start where?" he asked.

The three of them running around the West Midlands looking for their boss was bound to get back to Woody, and that would not be a good thing for Kim.

"Shit, guys, we've just gotta trust her."

Perhaps they were worrying for nothing. She was entitled to turn off her phone. Have some time to herself. It was a lovely thought but not one he could actually believe.

He just knew his friend was in trouble and there was nothing he could do to help.

SEVENTY-TWO

"Don't you fucking dare call me that," Kim screamed at her.

Alex offered a smile in response, finding this position far more comfortable. She preferred to be on top looking down.

Now she was going to have some fun.

"Sorry, that's a term used only by your mother."

Alex was suitably rewarded by the utter hatred she saw reflected in her adversary's eyes. Love, hate, so clearly entwined. She'd take it.

Kim bucked and thrashed against her, but she had the thigh muscles of a horse rider and held Kim firm. All the time Kim had been talking, Alex had known if she could just get on top, the game was hers for the taking.

Violence had never been her forte. And physical combat was not where Kim's weaknesses lay. Alex had no wish to break Kim's bones. Because eventually they would heal and she would remain unaffected by their game. No, the frailties of the woman beneath her were deliciously set in the past. Playing around with the mind was her art and it was time to break the detective in half.

"You intrigue me, Kim. You're highly intelligent but isolated within yourself. You constantly fight against the life that fate had mapped out for you."

"Fabulous insight but can we get to it? I have things to do."

"Sarcasm, Kim, your usual defence of choice. But don't you think about that all the time? Every day you battle against what you should have been."

"And, what should I have been, Freud?"

"An alcoholic, a drug addict. The fact that the only person you've ever truly loved died so horrendously right beside you should have produced a bitter, mean individual full of hate. Your early life experiences at the mercy of your own mother..."

"Is this your idea of a pissing contest, Alex?" Kim asked, turning her body to the side.

Alex readjusted her position. She leaned forward, pinning Kim to the floor by her forearms, forming the woman's body into a cross.

Their faces were much closer now.

Alex paused to enjoy the hatred. She lowered her voice to a whisper. "I've read the book and I understand the way you live. You will never trust another human being for as long as you live, and who could blame you? Your brother..."

"Leave him out of this, you fu—"

"Mikey was the only person you've ever loved and he was taken from you by your mother. She abused and neglected you both until he could bear it no more. And yet you still call your mother once a month, don't you, Kimmy?"

Alex allowed herself to enjoy the triumph that was sweeping through her. This woman was so badly scarred by the past that any trip back could break her forever.

"Your hatred for her is what keeps you together. Every achievement, every victory is two fingers to her. You don't even ask why she did the things she did. You can't afford to. If you did, you might be forced to forgive. So she must be completely evil, right?"

"You don't know anything about..."

"I know your mother has violent episodes right before every parole hearing. Yes, Kimmy, your mother keeps herself locked up for you. It is the only gift she can give her daughter. So, how does that compute with the image you've built?"

No response from the eyes. Not even a flicker or a blink.

Alex was thrilled that the bullets were hitting their target. Every single one of them.

"The bruises and hospital visits are documented in the book. Your mother's delusions persuaded her that Mikey was the devil and she constantly tried to kill him. You had to watch constantly just to keep him alive."

Alex smiled to herself as the eyes so close to her own began to empty of emotion. Kim was travelling back to the past and Alex would happily take her there.

"And yet in the end you could do nothing but watch him slip away. You lay beside him with a few crackers and a bit of Coke. You rationed those supplies; fed Mikey but took little for yourself, but it still wasn't enough, was it? You told him it would be okay, that someone would come, but they didn't, did they? And you lay there holding him as he quietly lost his fight for life.

"How long did you lie beside his dead body before help came, Kim?"

Alex expected her adversary to buck but there was no movement from between her thighs. The gaze stared unseeing right past her. Alex knew that she had broken this woman. She had played on her weaknesses like a violin. Not a flicker of movement or emotion was present. She had taken Kim back to the past and left her there. Alex prayed that she never made it back.

Kim Stone would never be the same again.

SEVENTY-THREE

Kim kept her gaze on the street lamp as her index finger continued to move.

Just ... one ... more ... there it was. The safety pin was dislodged from the bandage.

Kim refocused her eyes and smiled. "Was that really your best shot, Doc?"

She enjoyed the confusion on Alex's face for just a second before she whipped the bandaged hand up from the ground.

Her palm met with Alex's neck. Kim felt the pin enter the skin and she pushed her hand in closer, burrowing the point as far as she could.

Alex screamed out in pain and attempted to fall to the side, but Kim formed a grip around her neck and twisted herself out from beneath.

She raised herself to a standing position, dragging Alex up with her. Alex's hand clawed at her fingers but Kim would not let go.

Her grip held the woman upright as she looked deeply into fearful eyes.

"I expected so much more from you, Alex."

Alex tried again to pry Kim's hand away.

"But I wanted you standing for this."

Kim drew back her left hand and, using every ounce of strength she possessed, she launched it forward into Alex's face.

The force of the punch pitched Alex backwards, forcing Kim's right hand to jolt free.

Kim staggered forward and towered above her. Ready, just in case she got up.

A movement to her left caught her eye. A figure was running towards her.

"Kim...Kim...what the hell...?"

David stopped short of the inert form lying on the ground.

Kim's legs gave a wobble of fatigue and David reached out to steady her.

Kim shook her head. "Get Dougie, he's on the ladder."

David took one more look at her and then headed in the direction she'd pointed.

Kim knew that Dougie would have done exactly what she'd told him to do. Out of the water he'd have been vulnerable and Kim had needed all of Alex's attention on her.

Dougie would be cold, wet, frightened, and fatigued. But alive.

Kim sank to the floor beside Alex, watched as the blue eyes opened. A trickle of blood ran down her neck and into her hair.

The battle was over.

Kim stared into the darkness, relieved to see two figures emerge.

"You know I'll never let you go," Alex said, quietly.

Kim watched David guide Dougie onto solid ground as she spoke. "And that has been your undoing."

The two figures appeared beside her.

"Alexandra Thorne, I am arresting you on suspicion of the attempted murder of Douglas Parry. You do not have to say anything. But it may harm your defence if you do not mention when questioned something which you later rely on in court. Anything you do say may be given in evidence."

Kim pushed herself to her feet. The longer she stayed on the ground the harder it would be to get up.

Sirens sounded in the distance.

She looked at David. "You?"

He nodded.

Her own phone was somewhere at the bottom of the canal.

She stepped forward and stood before Dougie. Kim placed her left hand against his cheek. He didn't pull away.

"Thank you for trusting that I would save you. I know how difficult that was."

His eyes continued to stare up to the left but his right hand rose up and covered her own.

A surge of emotion flooded into her body. That was good enough for her.

The contact was broken as footsteps sounded from all directions. Beams of torchlight fell upon them. Kim shielded her eyes.

"Marm…"

Kim was delighted to see her old friend Sergeant Jarvis. Their disagreement at the crime scene of a rapist seemed such a very long time ago.

Kim pointed to Alex. "She's to be taken to the station. The charge is attempted murder and she's been read her rights."

He nodded as the two officers reached down and helped Alex to her feet.

"And these two need to be taken home. Any questions can wait until morning."

David stepped forward. "Kim… I don't know…"

Kim held up her hand. "Just get Dougie home and get him dry."

David nodded and then smiled.

"That's a powerful left hook you've got there."

Kim shrugged and held up her hand. The knuckles were swollen and reddened from the blow.

She stared at her hand for a moment and a new sickness began to form.

"Oh… shit," she said to no one in particular as the picture of the Dunn girls came into her mind.

Now she knew who had been in the room.

SEVENTY-FOUR

Kim dismounted the bike and groaned into the darkness. Today was turning into a day without end. She couldn't even recall the last time she'd seen the station but right now it was a welcoming sight. As was the man that stood waiting at the entrance.

Sodden clothes still clung to her body, sending the occasional shiver right down to her bones.

Her body screamed with every forward movement. A pool of blood had surfaced on the fabric now wrapped loosely around her hand.

Kim dreamt of a long hot bath and a rest on the sofa with Barney, but for now it would just have to wait.

"Jesus, Kim..."

She noticed the use of her name.

He looked her up and down with horror and opened his mouth to speak.

She held up her hand. "Really...no."

He nodded his head and the hundred jokes about her appearance died in his mouth.

"Are they here?" she asked as he held the door open.

She had called him with instructions from David's phone.

"Yeah, but I still don't understand what..."

"You will," Kim offered. She was not going to explain herself twice.

Bryant followed her lead as she revisited a room she'd stood in before.

Again, she followed the maze, but unlike the last time, both constables were standing.

Both were dressed in sweatshirts and jeans.

"Almost, boys. You almost had me stumped," she said, leaning against a locker. Her body was glad of the support.

"But not quite."

Jenks's face turned crimson. The trembling in his legs was visible through his jeans. He lowered himself to the bench.

The older one, Whiley, stared past her. A slackness was pulling at his jaw.

"Was that the intention, when you punched him? That his case would never get to court?"

Jenks hesitated for a second. "No ... I just saw red ... I thought about those little girls ..."

"Shut up, Jenks. I wasn't talking to you." She turned to the constable who faced retirement.

"Whiley, I'm talking to you."

Every spot of colour drained from his face.

"It wasn't Jenks that punched him, but you let him take the fall. You hit him and then got your colleague to say he'd done it because of your retirement."

She turned once again to Jenks. "Is that why he asked you to do it? Did he tell you he just couldn't control himself because of those little girls?"

Jenks nodded, his eyebrows drawn together as he looked from her to Whiley.

"You've been had, mate," she said, shaking her head. "It's got nothing to do with his retirement. It's because he was in the room."

Jenks's mouth dropped open and he began to shake his head. Kim did not have the energy to convince him.

There was one thing she needed to know.

She dragged her body to the other side of the room and stood inches away from Whiley.

She stared right into his eyes. And there she saw the truth.

"Did you touch them?"

"I swear . . . it wasn't me . . . I don't know . . ."

"Open your locker, Whiley."

Realisation dawned in his eyes.

She held out her hand. "Either open it yourself or give me the key."

His trembling hand snaked out of his pocket.

Kim took the key and turned it in the lock.

The cramped space held shirts and jumpers hanging from the bar. The floor of the locker was piled high with boots and high-visibility equipment. But it was the top shelf of the locker she reached for.

Her hand landed on a book. She took it out and showed it to Bryant.

"*The Longest Road*," he said, shaking his head.

"You already knew him," Jenks shouted. "He called you by your first name when we attended that call." The disbelief in his voice was clear. "I never clocked it, but you fucking well knew him."

Jenks rose from the bench but Bryant was already beside him.

"You fucking bastard," Jenks screamed, around Bryant.

Kim turned back to Whiley.

"I ask once more. Did you ever touch them?"

Kim thought the emotion inside her was spent. But as her knee raised slowly to his groin, she knew there was always a little bit more.

"Did you touch . . ."

"No...no...no..." he said, wiping the beads of sweat from his chin. "I just wanted to see. I was curious...I swear I didn't..."

Kim stepped away, the nausea too high in her throat. One more word and that would be it.

"Sergeant," she called to the doorway.

Again, Sergeant Travis appeared.

"Busy night, Marm," he said, with a smile behind his eyes.

She offered him a cordial nod. Now they understood each other.

"Please get this disgusting thing out of my sight."

"With pleasure, Marm."

Kim collapsed onto the bench beside Jenks. His hands still trembled with rage.

"You'll get a slap on the arse for your part in it, Jenks. But you will have a career after this."

"Thank you. But how did you know?"

"Yeah, Guv, how did you know?" Bryant repeated.

She took Jenks's right hand and turned it over. "You were holding your head in your hands. No swelling, no marks when I came into the locker room just after it happened. Whiley kept his hands in his pockets."

"Is that all?" Bryant asked, rubbing his chin.

"Not quite. When you mentioned the name of that book, I knew I'd either heard it or seen it somewhere."

Kim didn't mention the reading glasses, or the fact that during the visit for the domestic incident Whiley had been quick to remove Dunn to the kitchen and that he'd taken the liberty of sending the girls to bed. No wonder Wendy Dunn had never clocked it. He was a bloody police officer.

She turned back to Jenks. "Whiley caught me up in the corridor after the assault, just to reinforce what you'd done. He also hinted to me that you knew where the property was. I knew it was someone the girls had already met, and once I realised that you didn't hit him, there was only one person's actions left to question. Whiley has never been violent in his career and Dunn is not the first abuser he's met, so there had to be more to it than that."

"Jeez, Guv, talk about a leap of..."

"I'll leave you to get all the details. You get to interview him."

"It will be my absolute pleasure."

Kim pushed herself to a standing position. "But can you do me a huge favour first?"

"Course."

"Grab your car and just take me home."

SEVENTY-FIVE

Kim stood before Mikey's grave, seeking answers to the questions still rattling around in her head.

Woody had insisted she take a week off. And for once she'd offered no argument.

The first couple of days had been spent sleeping and walking the dog. Eventually Barney had stopped responding to the jangle of the lead and had steadfastly refused to move from the sofa.

Initially, she had been unable to focus on the bike and had spent many hours staring at the manuals and diagrams, unable to decipher even the simplest instruction. Three days ago she had managed to fish the broken nut from the exhaust manifold.

The encounter on the canal side had left her with too many questions. Everything in her past was separated, boxed, and labelled in her mind. It was a corner of her brain she did not visit, yet Alex had stormed in there and decimated the packaging, leaving memories and emotions strewn around.

For a moment there Kim had been tempted. Part of her had wanted to follow Alex into the darkness. To let it all go, to give up the fight. To dissolve into the memories of Mikey and the first six years of her life. But she hadn't because then Alex would have got away.

It had taken a while to fold everything away and reapply the tape. In the days since, Kim had wondered how tenuous her grip on sanity really was. She guessed that the time was coming to make a decision. Either open the compartments of her mind completely and examine the contents, or close them even tighter. She knew the consequences of both actions. To let it all out would consume her. There might be no way back to life as she knew it.

If she nailed the boxes shut she would be safe from the darkness; she would maintain her sanity and be protected, but condemned to a life of loneliness and mistrust.

Her feelings towards Alex were no less complicated. She hated the doctor for her ruthlessness in playing with people's lives and emotions and yet was fascinated by the woman's ability to do it. She hated the doctor for exposing all of her darkest fears, yet admired the woman's skill in almost destroying her.

Kim took a deep breath and folded herself slowly beside the cold stone. Her right hand traced the name of her dead twin. Emotion gathered in her throat as she sent him a silent message.

"Sweetheart, I'm sorry but I'm not ready for you yet. I miss you every single day and when I'm strong enough I promise I'll remember every minute we had together.

A movement to her left caught her eye. A familiar figure walked up the hill towards her.

Her voice was no more than a whisper. "But for now, I'd like to introduce you to my friend."

Bryant reached her and held out a takeaway coffee.

Kim nodded towards the headstone. "This is my twin brother. He died."

Bryant turned his head to the grave.

One of Bryant's best assets was knowing when to ask questions and when to keep quiet.

She stepped away from the grave and sat on the bench.

Bryant sat beside her. "Kim..."

"Tell me where we are," she said, taking a sip of her drink.

"Okay, Whiley has confessed to being in the basement with Dunn. He claimed it was his only time and the recordings supported his words. With his testimony on top of the rest of the evidence Dunn is not going to walk, despite the smack in the face."

"Did you go and see Ruth?"

Bryant nodded. "By the time I'd told her everything she practically begged for the opportunity to testify against the doctor. A plea is being worked out in Ruth's favour. She'll serve time but will still have a whole chunk of life left to live."

About Ruth, Alex had been correct. She would never have committed the crime without intervention.

Kim already knew that Jessica had been re-diagnosed with puerperal psychosis and had been removed from her family and placed into residential care. As a favour to Kim, Ted had agreed to treat her and Kim felt confident she would get the best possible help.

She'd called Sarah Lewis herself. The "For Sale" sign had been removed from the front of the house. The small family could finally put down roots.

"Barry Grant is off life support but still in intensive care. The prognosis is mixed. His memory was impaired and the irony that he'll never walk again is not lost on anyone."

She'd spoken to David, who had visited Shane in prison. Shane had been uncommunicative and had revealed nothing of the events that had sent him back to prison. He had instructed David not to visit him again.

During her conversations with David he had dropped not so subtle hints about his wish to see her restoration project. Although Kim hadn't invited him around yet, the possibility hadn't been completely discounted.

So, most of Alex's victims were doing well, but with regard to herself, Kim wasn't quite so sure. Externally, her façade was back.

She was ready to work cases; she was sleeping badly and drinking more caffeine than was good for her.

"Okay, thanks for the update, now get lost and go back to your family."

"You do know this isn't your property and you can't really tell me when to leave."

"Yeah, but what if I say please?"

"I'd put you into the recovery position and call for a paramedic."

"Almost funny," she groaned.

He stood. "But seeing as you asked like a normal person, I'll leave you in peace."

He took two steps and turned. "Kim, thank you."

"Yeah, whatever, now piss off."

He laughed as he turned and walked away.

She stood and surveyed the view over the heart of the Black Country. It was not a beautiful vista. It was a basin that had more than its fair share of poverty and crime.

A smile tugged at her lips as she remembered that somewhere down there was a baby boy whose heart still beat strongly within his dinosaur pyjamas. Like Kim herself, baby Jamie had fought back from the brink and won.

LETTER FROM ANGELA

First of all, I want to say a huge thank you for choosing to read *Evil Games*. I hope you enjoyed the second instalment of Kim's journey and hope you feel the same way I do. Whilst not always perfect she is someone you would want fighting your corner.

If you did enjoy it, I would be forever grateful if you'd write a review. I'd love to hear what you think, and it can also help other readers discover one of my books for the first time. Or maybe you can recommend it to your friends and family…

A story begins as a seed of an idea that grows from watching and listening to everyone around you. Each individual is unique and we all have a story. I want to capture as many of those tales as I can and I hope you will join both Kim Stone and myself on our travels, wherever they may lead.

If so, I'd love to hear from you—get in touch on my Facebook or Goodreads page, Twitter, or through my website.

And if you'd like to keep up-to-date with all my latest releases, just sign up at the website link below.

Thank you so much for your support; it is hugely appreciated.

Angela Marsons

www.bookouture.com/angela-marsons
www.angelamarsons-books.com
www.facebook.com/angelamarsonsauthor
www.twitter.com/@WriteAngie

ACKNOWLEDGMENTS

I began the process of writing *Evil Games* with the intention of representing the nature of a true sociopath. There were times throughout the book that I almost gave Alexandra Thorne an Achilles' heel or a minor weakness to offer hope of her eventual salvation. Ultimately I remained true to the facts: that however unpalatable and disturbing it may be, there are people amongst us that have no capacity for remorse. But, luckily for us there are also individuals like Kim Stone who will stand in their way.

Two books in particular became invaluable whilst researching *Evil Games*.

The Sociopath Next Door by Martha Stout.

Without Conscience by Robert D. Hare PhD.

As ever, I would like to thank the team at Bookouture for their continued passion for Kim Stone and her stories. Their encouragement, enthusiasm, and belief have turned my long-held dreams into a wonderful reality. Keshini, Oliver, Claire, and Kim: *Thank you* will never say it all.

Together with the amazing Bookouture authors, I am privileged to be a part of this talented and supportive family.

My sincere thanks to my mum, who drives her buggy with a copy of my book attached to the front, and to my dad, who walks with her. Their enthusiasm and support is amazing.

My gratitude goes to all the wonderful bloggers and reviewers who have not only read and reviewed my books but also have taken Kim Stone to their hearts and championed her journey. Their love of books and passionate support is inspirational.

A shout-out goes to the lovely members of my local book club: Pauline Hollis, Merl Roberts, Dee Weston, Jo Thomson, Sylvia Cadby, and Lynette Wells.

Finally, there are no words to describe my thanks to my partner, Julie. Every book is a testament to her unfailing belief. She was my light on the dark days and she would never let me stop. She is truly my world.

ABOUT THE AUTHOR

Angela Marsons is the *USA Today* bestselling author of the Detective Kim Stone series, and her books have sold more than four million copies and have been translated into twenty-seven languages. She lives in the Black Country in the West Midlands of England with her partner and their two golden retrievers. She first discovered her love of writing at junior school when actual lessons came second to watching other people and quietly making up her own stories about them. Her report card invariably read, "Angela would do well if she minded her own business as well as she minds other people's." After writing women's fiction, Angela turned to crime—fictionally speaking, of course—and developed a character that refused to go away.

For more information you can visit:

AngelaMarsons-Books.com
Facebook.com/AngelaMarsonsAuthor
Twitter @WriteAngie